SHADOW
PATRIOTS

James C Edwards

COPYRIGHT

I dedicate this book, "Shadow Patriots," to the sources of my inspiration and strength.

I wanted to thank God, the maker of the universe, for granting me the gift of a creative mind. Your boundless imagination and creativity have illuminated the path of my storytelling journey. With every twist and turn of the narrative, I am reminded of the wondrous tapestry of creation that you have woven through Jesus. While this book is not religious, it was created with that gift in mind.

Finally, I want to thank my wife Amber, your unwavering support and encouragement have been my guiding light throughout this creative endeavor. Your belief in me and my stories has been a constant source of inspiration. You are my greatest ally. Thank you for being the steady hand that guides me through the labyrinth of creativity.

1

THE SKY WAS ABLAZE with unnatural colors, a surreal palette that no brush could hope to capture. As a lone station wagon struggled against the certainty of the encroaching doom, the family inside clung to each other, their sobs lost in the roar of the relentless engine. The father, his hands white-knuckled on the wheel, drove into the horizon of the blue yonder. Still, the monstrous cloud pursued them—a harbinger of the end times, swallowing the life they once knew.

The station wagon, a relic of happier times, hurtled through desolation, the family's desperation palpable in the tight confines of the car. The sky—now a canvas of apocalyptic hues—loomed over them as an ominous backdrop to their escape. They were homeward bound to Idaho, yet home seemed a concept belonging to another lifetime. Unaware of the reason the sky was changing, they could only react to its eerie transformation, a silent alarm to flee. Mile by mile, they pushed away from the cataclysm, each turn of the wheel a prayer for salvation, for a return to normalcy that they feared might never come.

On the other side of the highway, they could see ambulances and firetrucks driving toward the chaos. Unsure what was happening, Neil continued pushing his accelerator, but his engine could move no further. A pop under the hood signified the engine had spun its last RPM. The car slowly came to a stop on the highway, which was eerily abandoned. Neil got out of the car and pulled his kids and wife out.

"Allison, get under the car—now," Neil said, frantically pulling luggage out of the back of the car. Allison cried as she held their two children and slid under the car. Neil shoved suitcases, beach floats, and whatever he could find around the perimeter of the vehicle to attempt a tight seal.

"No matter what you hear, honey. Don't come out from underneath." Neil said as Allison fearfully nodded; her face streaked in hot tears as he shoved the final piece of luggage around them. Neil hoped it would protect them, but he wasn't sure. A wave of heat washed through the air as the unnatural tableau of colors came closer.

Suddenly, Neil screamed in agony as the heated air surrounded him; his skin blistered and peeled off in sheets as he fell backward to the ground.

His final words escaped as a whisper, "I love you, Allison, Luke, and Lily."

The car rocked violently as the hot wind pounded against it; Allison snuggled Luke and Lily close to herself, shielding their ears from the blood-curdling scream she heard from Neil.

There was no indication of time as they huddled together in the darkness underneath the car. The heat from outside was warming the air underneath the car. Allison took a deep breath and pulled her kids closer to herself.

For what seemed like days, Allison and her kids remained huddled underneath the old station wagon; her foot felt water seeping through the end of the car where her feet were. She heard a voice coming from outside.

"Dispatch—dispatch. Dammit!" The voice screamed outside. Cool air suddenly began to filter in underneath the car as some of the bags were removed.

"Are you okay?" The voice said through the opening.

"I—I—I am not sure. Is Neil okay out there?" Allison asked, knowing the answer but wanting to fool herself.

"I am sorry." The voice came back as Allison began to slide out from underneath the car; she motioned for her kids to stay underneath the car for a bit longer. As she slid out, she shielded her eyes from the bright sun that she hadn't seen in what felt like days. The voice came from a young woman in Marine fatigues who reached out her hand.

"My name is Samantha. Are you okay?" Samantha asked, lifting the shaking woman to her feet.

"Oh my God—Neil." As Allison's eyes adjusted, she saw Neil lying on the ground; his clothing and much of his skin had been burned away. Her tears began streaming as she ran to where his body was and kneeled next to it. She leaned over and placed her forehead on what remained of his. Deep-throated sobs began to escape her as she held his body, "thank you for saving us, honey."

"Daddy?" Allison heard the voice of her youngest, Lily. She looked up and saw Luke and Lily standing beside the car. "Daddy?" Luke joined in as Allison stood and ran over to her children. She covered their eyes and knelt beside them, "Daddy is in heaven, sweetie." Her voice was interrupted by even deeper sobbing.

Samantha grabbed a blanket from the back of her Jeep and covered Neil's body. Allison looked up and silently thanked her as she kissed her children.

"What happened, Samantha?" Allison asked while looking at the blanket used to cover Neil's body. Samantha moved to be between the kids and Neil's body, "We aren't really sure. There was some kind of explosion in the Pacific, and the entire coastal border of the United States has been destroyed. We aren't sure if we were attacked or something else." Samantha's look of concern didn't mask her confusion over what had happened. "Allison, I want to get you and your kids to safety. I was heading to my family's ranch in Montana; y'all are welcome to come with me until I can get you home." Samantha said with a concerned smile, "I'll send my brothers to retrieve his remains so you can give him a proper burial." Samantha added as Allison nodded. "Thank you, Samantha. I don't know how much longer we would have been under there had you not come along."

Allison opened the back door to the station wagon and pulled Lily's car seat out; Samantha took it and positioned it in the back of her Jeep. Lily ran back over to Neil's body, covered by the blanket. She was too young to really understand what had happened, but somehow, the young girl was drawn to the body of her father. "I love you daddy." Allison tried to hold back her tears as Lily turned back and grabbed a teddy on the floorboard of the station wagon.

Allison picked her up and fastened her into the car seat while Luke climbed in beside her. Samantha cranked the Jeep up, and Allison slid beside her children in the back seat of the Jeep. "It's a little bit of a drive to Big Sky, but that's my family's ranch. There, you can clean up, get some rest, and eat." Samantha smiled while pulling her iPhone out of her center console.

"Jake, I found some survivors near Alturas, California. Get a few men together to come and retrieve some remains. We are headed to Big Sky." She said as she put the phone on speaker and put it in her cup holder.

"What do you mean 'remains'?" Jake's voice said through the speaker.

"Careful, Jake, I have the family with me. Their car and the remains are where 299 and 395 converge, where the flood waters peaked. We'll talk later." Samantha warned with an uncomfortable smirk on her face.

"Okay, sis, we were fishing at Goose Lake, so we aren't terribly far. Are you okay, Sam?" Jake asked seriously.

"Jake, It is horrific. We still have no idea what happened; hundreds of thousands, millions of lives —gone." Samantha said, looking in her rearview at Allison and the children. She was trying to keep her voice low enough not to disturb them as much as possible. Her phone died as she pulled onto another back road. Sighing out loud as she brushed her brunette hair out of her eyes.

The Jeep rumbled down the lonely road, an island of movement in a sea of stillness. Samantha drove with a steady hand, her eyes occasionally glancing in the rearview mirror at Allison and her children. The landscape outside was a striking contrast to the lively chatter that once filled these highways.

"We'll be safe at Big Sky," Samantha reassured, her voice a mix of determination and sorrow. "My family's ranch has everything we need to get through this."

As the miles passed, Allison gazed out the window, her mind a whirlwind of memories and loss. Luke and Lily, exhausted from the ordeal, eventually succumbed to sleep, their gentle breathing serving as a poignant reminder of the life that persisted amidst the chaos.

Samantha's phone buzzed again. "We're doing our best to gather information," Jake's voice crackled through the speaker. "But communications are down in most areas. It's like the whole world's gone silent. We retrieved the body and are headed towards Big Sky as well. Stay safe, sis."

Miles and hours passed as Allison fell asleep in the back of the Jeep; ahead, Samantha saw a lone gas station. She needed to refuel and maybe get some snacks for the remainder of their drive. She pulled under the bright lights of the gas station, sliding out of her Jeep; she checked on her passengers and then walked inside. Opening the door, a bell rang. The man behind the counter held his shotgun in his hand, his eyes looking suspiciously as Samantha walked in and grabbed a few Slim Jims and candy bars. She smiled at the attendant, "How fresh is the coffee?"

"Made it an hour ago," The man grumbled, still maintaining a watchful eye on Samantha, "now, don't you be coming in here for trouble, miss."

Samantha grabbed everything and headed to the front, spreading it out on the counter; she smiled at the wary man. "Sir, I am just trying to get home. I am not going to cause you trouble." Samantha knew the man was weary; after the tsunami on the West Coast, many were preparing for the worst. A television was playing behind him with the nightly news on. Brian McGee from KKOV 46 in Reno was speaking to Senator Ulysses Mars from North Carolina about the supposed attack on the United States.

After reassuring the wary attendant and purchasing the snacks and coffee, Samantha stepped back into the night to refuel the Jeep. The process was a welcome moment of normalcy; each click of the fuel nozzle was a small, grounding reminder of routine in a world now unfamiliar. She methodically filled the tank, her thoughts momentarily adrift in the uncertainty of their situation.

Back in the Jeep, Samantha distributed the snacks to Allison and her children, their faces reflecting a mix of gratitude and exhaustion. The road to Big Sky Ranch seemed longer under the weight of uncertainty. Still, Samantha's steady driving and the Jeep's headlights cutting through the darkness provided a sense of security.

The Jeep's cabin was filled with the soft sounds of munching snacks and the occasional sip of coffee. The television broadcast from the gas station, featuring Senator Ulysses Mars discussing the national crisis, lingered in Samantha's mind, deepening the significance of their journey. The drive to Big Sky Ranch stretched on, with the distant lights of the ranch growing closer, offering hope and safety in the enveloping darkness. As they approached, a palpable sense of relief mixed with apprehension for what lay ahead. Samantha's steady hand at the wheel and the rhythmic hum of the engine provided a comforting presence as they navigated the uncertain road leading to a new chapter in the lives of Allison and her children.

As they neared the ranch, the first signs of life appeared—distant lights from the ranch house. Samantha's voice broke the silence, "We're almost there," her tone a mix of relief and apprehension as the Jeep's tires crunched on the gravel driveway. The ranch was large; Allison and the kids looked around, amazed at all the cows and other animals roaming the fields. Lily smiled as she pointed at a horse, letting a giggle escape.

"That's Rosco; he is my horse. I have had him since I was a little older than you, Lily." Samantha said as Lily smiled brightly, Rosco running along the fence with Samantha's Jeep.

"Before we get inside, Allison, I need to tell you. My father is the Governor of Montana, so there may be reporters and stuff here." Samantha commented as the Jeep came to a halt in front of the large house in the middle of the ranch.

A shaggy golden retriever ran up beside the vehicle, barking while wagging his tail. Lily pointed and giggled as Allison unbuckled her from the car seat. Luke jumped out and immediately started to play with the dog. Samantha smiled, "This is Billy, he is my dad's dog." She said as a tall man walked onto the porch. The man had a leather trench coat and a cowboy hat on, a revolver hung from his waist, and a cigar lit in his mouth.

"Hi, Dad, I'm home." Samantha smiled as he nodded, "Allison, this is my father, Governor Jeremiah Johnson; he isn't as intimidating as he looks." Her face filled with a genuine smile as Jeremiah removed his hat and nodded.

"Ma'am, welcome to our home. Jake told me you were caught in the heat from the explosion. So sorry to hear about your husband." His voice was genuine as he offered a consoling hand.

"Yes, sir. Do we know any more about what happened?" Allison asked as her eyes drifted to her kids running around with Billy.

"We still don't know much. A group called The Confederation claimed responsibility, but according to the President, we don't know who or what they are." Jeremiah spoke as fog spilled from his lips from a mix of the cold air and cigar smoke, "Samantha, take them to Elkview Cabin. They can get cleaned up and stay there until we can get them home." He continued as he turned back towards the house.

"Okay, Dad," Samantha said while turning back to Allison and her children, "that is our best cabin, so I am jealous. Mom told me she had prepared some food and left it there for y'all."

Allison woke from a fitful sleep; Luke and Lily breathed heavily as they still slept beside her. She slid her arm out from underneath Luke's head, and she stood beside the bed.

I can't believe Neil is gone.

Her thoughts swirled, and her head began to throb as she thought about Neil's sacrifice for her and the kids. She looked at the children and then turned to walk out of the room.

Just in the last week, the world has changed so much, and she couldn't put her finger on what was happening, but the energy was certainly different. She found her way into the kitchen and saw that the clock read 6 am. She yawned and then looked over at the coffee maker. She began opening cabinets and drawers to see if there was any coffee. She found a bag of Appalachian Nights coffee in the roundabout; she opened the bag and smelled it. The rich aroma filled her nostrils and made her smile.

After starting the coffee maker, she went into the bathroom and washed her face; the cool water invigorated her. Examining her features in the mirror, she could tell she had lost weight from how long she and the kids had been under the car.

She poured herself a cup and then stepped out on the covered porch. In the field, she saw a dozen or so elk grazing.

Samantha was right in saying that this cabin is very nice. I can see why they call it Elkview.

She smiled while sitting in a rocking chair and sipping her coffee. The morning was cold and a little foggy. Streaks of orange and yellow started spreading through the sky. An enormous elk bull with a large rack of antlers looked up in her direction and started wailing. They all turned and began to disappear into the woods as the sun climbed higher into the sky.

Allison finished her coffee and walked inside, pouring herself another cup. She sat on the sofa and turned on the television. Montana Morning was on, and the weatherman was pointing at maps and showing a five-day forecast.

She turned the television up as the main anchors popped back up on the screen.

"...unfortunately, we still don't know much about what happened on the West Coast. All we know right now is that the preliminary count of missing and dead is in the millions. This is the worst attack on United States soil ever."

The screen showed drone footage of San Francisco destroyed, with buildings and bridges collapsed and Pacific waters covering the entire city. Other drone footage showed flood waters devouring over a third of the whole coastline. The only city that seemed to survive was Los Angeles.

As the anchors talked over the footage, Allison's eyes teared up at the devastation. President Arthur Hastings popped up on the screen, addressing the nation.

"My fellow Americans, tonight we stand together in the shadow of a catastrophe that has shaken the very foundations of our nation. The Neutronium Bomb, a nightmare unleashed upon our West Coast, has left a trail of unspeakable devastation. Entire communities have vanished, with millions of our citizens missing or tragically lost. This is not merely an attack on our land; it is a brutal assault on our collective soul. We face an unknown enemy, The Confederation, shrouded in mystery yet bold in their claim of responsibility. As your President, I vow that in my remaining time as your leader, I will leave no stone unturned in our quest for answers and justice. Our nation's full might will relentlessly pursue those behind this heinous act.

In response to this national emergency, I have made the difficult but necessary decision to recall a quarter of our forces from overseas engagements. Our soldiers, our heroes, will now stand on the home front, aiding in rescue, recovery, and the restoration of order. This is a time of unity, a time to gather our strength and support one another. We will rebuild not just the cities and towns lost but the very heart of America.

We will rise from these ashes, for our resolve as Americans is unyielding. In our grief, let us find strength. In our despair, let us find hope. We are a nation not easily broken; we are a people of resilience and undying spirit. Together, we will navigate these dark times and emerge stronger, bound by our shared loss and our unwavering belief in the enduring spirit of America. God bless you all, and God bless the United States of America."

His words, meant to bring comfort and unity, also acknowledged the long road to recovery and justice ahead. Allison looked on with shock; she couldn't believe we had been attacked by a weapon so devastating that it killed millions of people.

A knock came at the door; it was Samantha. "Good Morning, Allison. I hope you had a good night's rest. I brought you some breakfast. Samantha laid the tray on the kitchen island and looked at the television.

"I can't believe we still don't know much about what happened. Dad has a meeting with some other governors in surrounding states this morning; maybe they will have more information." Samantha had an uneasy smile that crossed her lips.

Suddenly, a breaking news banner displayed across the screen.

"We interrupt this program with a breaking news alert. I'm Alex Martin, and we've just received urgent reports that Confederation troops have made a surprising landfall in British Columbia. This sudden military action has sent shockwaves through the international community. The Canadian Prime Minister has issued an urgent plea for support, calling on the United States and global allies to respond to this escalating situation. The full scope of the Confederation's intentions remains unclear, but this development marks a significant escalation in regional tensions. We will continue to bring you the latest updates on this rapidly unfolding situation. Stay with us for more details."

Samantha, visibly shaken by the breaking news alert, hastily grabbed her phone and dashed outside. "Dad, have you seen this? The Confederation, those who claimed the attack, they've launched a military invasion in British Columbia!" Her voice was tinged with urgency as she paced back and forth.

Jeremiah, on the other end of his phone, was equally alarmed. "Quentin Jamison has just briefed me. The troops that President Hastings is recalling haven't arrived, and our defenses are thin," he barked into the receiver.

Despite their political differences, Quentin Jamison, the Democratic Governor of Oregon and a presidential candidate, maintained a close relationship with Jeremiah. This bond was crucial now, more than ever, as they faced a dire situation. With the National Guard's ranks depleted due to extensive overseas engagements, the United States found itself in a precarious defense posture.

Jeremiah spun his chair around while still holding his phone tightly. Samantha broke the momentary silence, "I'll reach out to my contacts in the military later this afternoon. Maybe there's a way we can expedite the deployment or get some local support."

"We are in uncharted territory here, Sam. This Confederation threat—it's more serious than we could have anticipated. I am going to talk to the other Great Plains governors around us and see if we can form a local militia, just in case." Jeremiah quickly said, his heart beating tightly in his chest.

In the wake of the bombing, the election results were still being tallied, but no one was the clear victor yet. Troy Thomason, a populist member of the Republican party, had been ahead in the polls prior to the bombing. Still, Quentin Jamison was not far behind in the Electoral College vote.

Jeremiah paced in his office while the news played in the background. Miranda walked in with a pot of coffee. "Honey, it is still early; here is some coffee," Miranda said as the music on the newscast flashed a breaking news alert.

"We have breaking news coming in. The results are in, and it is official: Troy Thomason has won the Presidential election with 273 electoral votes to Quentin Jamison's 265. President-Elect Thomason is to become the 47th President of the United States,"

The clean-cut reporter said curtly,

"Joining his acceptance speech now in Raleigh, NC."

The screen was filled with red, white, and blue balloons and American Flag streamers as the Troy Thomason walked onto the stage with thunderous applause.

"My fellow Americans, tonight marks a turning point. I am deeply honored and humbled to be elected as your next President. However, our celebration is tempered by the enormous challenges we face as a nation, especially in the wake of the catastrophic Neutronium Bomb disaster. My first act as President will be to end our involvement in foreign wars and bring our troops back home. Our focus must be on strengthening our defenses and securing our borders. Furthermore, I am committed to ending the military draft implemented under President Arthur Hastings. It's time to heal, rebuild, and restore the soul of our nation. Together, we will face these challenges head-on and emerge stronger."

President-Elect Troy Thomason stood on stage and waved to the crowd; in his hands, he held a picture of his wife Julie, who was killed by the Neutronium bomb disaster, and beside him was his son Charlton, who waved ecstatically. The screen shifted back to the studio, where the reporter sat smiling before a commercial unexpectedly took over.

Jeremiah looked over at Miranda and smiled, "Maybe now we can get our entire military home to stop the advancing Confederation. Miranda nodded solemnly as she walked up and hugged Jeremiah; her attempt at consoling came after a week of nonstop meetings and obvious stress. Jeremiah let down his guard for a moment as he returned her gesture, "I love you, Miranda. I am sorry I've been so busy with everything."

Miranda returned a genuine smile and then kissed Jeremiah, "It's okay, honey; I knew when I married you that you were meant for great things." She grabbed the coffee pot and left the room as Jeremiah's phone rang. On the other end of the line was Davison Carey, governor of Wyoming.

"Jeremiah, have you spoken with President Hastings on troop placement?" Governor Carey asked as Jeremiah shook his head, "Unfortunately, I haven't been able to reach him. You know we 'red states' don't matter to him." Jeremiah chuckled slightly under his breath.

"I hear you," Davison said, letting out a slight laugh as well. I figure we need to call up our National Guard. I've talked to other governors, and they agreed. If this Confederation threat continues building momentum, we'll need to gather our resources and defend our territory."

Jeremiah's brows raised slightly, "you think this is that serious? You think the Confederation means to push into our borders?" Jeremiah knew the concerns were warranted, but with the political pressures of the last few years, he didn't want his fears to cause D.C. to think Montana was disloyal.

"I never imagined we'd be put into this type of position, but I've talked to Colorado, Kansas, Nebraska, and Missouri, and they are all on the same page. Our military is stretched too thin due to all of the wars we've been engaged in. Even with Troy winning the Presidency, it will be years before we can get all of our military members back home." Davison spoke with urgency in his voice.

"Davison, I was about to talk to the Dakotas, Minnesota, and Iowa. But I am waiting for the Governor of Idaho to get here. Maybe we need to all get together. We can meet at the Governor's Mansion in Helena. Can you come?" Jeremiah knew that the conversation would be more impactful if it were face-to-face.

"Let's plan to have a Governors' Summit. I'll reach out to the others."

2

SAMANTHA SAT IN HER Jeep after leaving Elkview Cabin. She maintained a fearless demeanor while around Allison and her kids, but here, in the quiet of her Jeep, her fears rumbled deep within her mind. She thought back to the men and women she fought beside in Afghanistan, all of the ones who were left behind in the tragic evacuation of forces in August 2021. She was fortunate to have been on leave when those orders were handed down, but closing her eyes, she saw their faces.

Her commanders would often say we fought there to keep the fight away from home. The younger version of herself agreed with that sentiment. Still, now, with the possible invasion of a foreign enemy on American soil, she found herself becoming increasingly disillusioned.

She turned her key, and the engine rumbled to life; letting out a sigh, she opened her eyes and started pulling forward. On her ride back to the main house, her mind began flashing with images of the rugged mountain terrains of Afghanistan. She remembered once driving a Humvee and leading her squad through an ambush; she was a young lieutenant quickly thrown into battle, where she first tasted the cost of leadership. She wasn't even supposed to be there, but at the last minute, she was ordered to lead a convoy to Bagram Air Force Base.

She remembered the young Ibrahim Linkin, who lost a leg in an ambush and was now a Senator for Illinois, with advanced prosthetics replacing his amputated limb. She smiled, thinking of him—a man whose family had fled Afghanistan during the Soviet invasion in the Eighties and sought refuge in the United States. Her thoughts snapped back to the present as her tires crunched against the gravel. The cool morning air reminded her of her time in the Russo-Ukrainian war, where she honed her skills as a field commander and tactician. She knew that war wasn't America's fight, but it was her duty that compelled her to participate. For morale's sake, she kept her doubts to herself.

The crisp air of the ranch reminded her of those chilled battlefields, where every decision could mean life or death for her or the members of those assigned to her. She recalled the weight of her rifle and the sound of gunfire, the grim satisfaction of a well-executed plan.

But the endless wars had taken their toll on America, and the wars she had been in had exacted a heavy price on her. Her youth was killed on those battlefields; she had been shaped by the conflicts, sculpted by duty and survival like a master sculptor fashioning a statue. Yet now, as the world teetered on the brink of another crisis, not long after the last, she wondered about her role in all of it. Would her past be a burden or an aid to the coming fight against this new enemy?

The large ranch house came into view as she pulled up the gravel driveway. In front of the house were several Sheriff's Deputy cars and her father's bulletproof SUV. She arrived just in time to see her dad exiting the house with a suitcase. Miranda, her mother, stood with her arms crossed on the porch, her breath fogging as she breathed.

She pulled her Jeep to the side of the driveway and jumped out. Jogging up to the house, she grabbed her father and hugged him. "Be careful, Daddy; if you need me in the upcoming fight, I am here to support you." Jeremiah smiled at Samantha and looked back up at Miranda.

"I'll be home in a few days," he said, putting on his cowboy hat and sliding into the big SUV. Deputy Andrew McAllister winked at Samantha as he turned to head back to the lead car. She rolled her eyes and smiled. She knew that Andrew cared about her, but high school was so long ago. He never could let her go, even after she had been gone with the Marine Corps for nearly a decade.

"He is a nice boy, Sam; it's a shame you don't pay him more attention." Miranda smiled as she returned to the warmth inside the ranch house.

"Mom, I know. But he doesn't know me like he did in high school. I am an entirely different person." Samantha said, brushing her long brunette hair from her eyes.

"You aren't getting any younger, sweetie, and your brother is no closer to settling down." Miranda poked Samantha in the ribs as she pretended the gesture hurt.

"Mom!" Samantha said, laughing loudly. It felt good to laugh, given the pressure building over the brewing chaos. Stepping over to the coffee, she poured herself a cup and leaned on the counter while sipping it.

"When is Jake getting home? Has he called?" Samantha asked while breathing in the fresh aroma of coffee.

"Haven't heard from him.", Miranda said, opening the dishwasher and putting some dirty dishes in.

Samantha's eyes darkened with concern as she fetched her phone from her coat pocket. When she dialed the phone, it immediately went to a busy signal. She hung up and tried calling again, with the same result.

"Mom. His phone is just going to a busy signal. I've tried a few times, but it just isn't going through." Samantha looked at her mom, who was now mirroring her concern. Both of their phones suddenly let out a loud alarm sound, and they both looked at their phones.

*****Presidential Alert*****

*****EMERGENCY ALERT****

States Affected: California, Oregon, Washington

Alert Type: Societal Breakdown & Protests

Issued: November 14, 2024-TBD

Message from the President: Due to escalating protests and signs of societal breakdown in California, Oregon, and Washington, all residents are advised to exercise extreme caution. Avoid unnecessary travel, particularly in urban areas. Stay informed on local news for safety instructions. Emergency services may be limited. Comply with local law enforcement directives.

For emergencies, dial 911.

Stay tuned to official channels for further updates.

*****End of Alert*****

Miranda's concern was palpable as she read the presidential alert. The sudden societal unrest in the western states was a grim reminder of the turbulent times they were living in. Samantha felt a familiar surge of duty, her instincts as a Marine kicking in.

"Mom, I need to check on the local situation," Samantha said, her voice steady despite the worry in her eyes. "I'll see what the local law enforcement knows about this. We need to be prepared."

As she left the house, Samantha's thoughts were with her brother, Jake. His unreachable phone added to her unease, fueling her need to take action. She drove towards the Sheriff's office, determined to gather information and help maintain order amidst the chaos.

Big Sky is situated between Madison and Gallatin counties, and the closest Sheriff's Department was in Bozeman. To the folks who stayed in Big Sky, Bozeman was considered the big city.

Arriving at the office, Samantha was greeted by a tense atmosphere. The local deputies were inundated with calls and reports of disturbances. She offered her assistance, drawing on her military experience to help coordinate their response. But the receptionist and deputies hastened by her, paying little mind.

Montana is a big state, and we are in the Southeast of the state near Idaho and Wyoming.

Her thoughts were a myriad of puzzled ideas as to what was going on. She looked over and saw her friend Tara, a bailiff in the Sheriff's Department. Walking towards her, Tara looked up and smiled an uneasy smile.

"What is going on, Tara? Why is everyone freaking out?" The expression on Tara's face went from unease to sadness.

"There was a bombing on the southwestern border of Idaho, an area around Washoe and Payette," Tara said. Samantha sensed more but waited as if another shoe was going to drop. She had driven through that area with Allison and her children the night before, and her mind immediately wandered to her brother's busy signal on his phone.

"They've found Jake's truck, and there were some human remains in the bed of the truck." There it was, the other shoe. It dropped solidly on the floor and caused Samantha's heart to sink into her stomach.

Samantha had seen war more than she cared to remember, but now it seemed there was a war coming home.

"But no Jake? Mike? Ray?" Samantha listed off the names of Jake's friends who had been hunting and fishing with him.

"Just that single set of remains—we aren't sure whose they are." Tara followed up, her voice cracking a little with concern. Samantha turned quickly and began briskly walking to the door.

"I have to find Jake. I have to. He wouldn't have been there if it weren't for me." Her voice trailed off as she ran out the door. Tara nodded as Samantha disappeared through the doors.

Jeremiah sat in his SUV, sipping his coffee while looking at his iPad. Scrolling through the news on his Vyber social media account, he saw there had been a bombing on the border of Oregon and Idaho and news of the Confederation crossing the border into Washington State. A press conference from the Governor of Washington began playing,

"I call on President Hastings to return our National Guard units from Ukraine and Israel war fronts to help our State Guard with pushing back the invaders from The Confederation. This is an unprecedented attack on our state sovereignty and the safety of our people. I have spoken with Governor Bradford of Idaho and Governor Nichols of Oregon, and they have committed their state guard also to reinforce the State of Washington. President Hastings, I know you are in your last few weeks of being President, but do your duty!"

A reporter cut the broadcast from the National News Desk of USNN. Jeremiah shook his head as he clicked off of the video and looked out of the windows; he tried calming his mind while leaning his head back.

His phone rang, displaying Samantha's name on the Caller ID. When he answered, he heard his daughter's frantic voice.

"Dad, Jake is missing; his friends are missing. Bombing." The voice went in and out because Jeremiah was driving through a large mountain pass, and his cell service was spotty. His face darkened as he realized what Samantha was saying; the bombing he had read about on the border of Idaho and Oregon had possibly claimed his son. Slapping the back of the driver's seat, he shouted,

"We need to hurry, Nick."

As the SUV hastened through the winding mountain pass, Jeremiah's mind was a whirlwind of strategy and personal concern. The meeting with the governors was not just another political rendezvous; it was a crucial assembly to confront an unprecedented crisis. The governors of Idaho, Wyoming, Colorado, Kansas, Missouri, Nebraska, and both North and South Dakota were gathering. As the host, Jeremiah felt the weight of leadership more heavily than ever.

The recent bombing on the Oregon-Idaho border and the alarming news of The Confederation's movements had cast a dark shadow over the region. The collective response of these states could shape the course of events in the days to come. Yet, amid these pressing matters, Jeremiah's thoughts kept veering back to his son, Jake. The personal and the political were colliding in a way he had never experienced before.

Nick maneuvered the SUV with expertise, sensing the urgency of their journey. The roads leading to Helena, usually familiar and uneventful, now felt like pathways to a pivotal moment in history. Jeremiah rehearsed potential strategies in his mind, balancing the need for strong defensive measures with the preservation of civil liberties. The decisions made in this meeting could set a precedent for years to come.

As they approached the Governor's office in Helena, the weight of the situation settled in. The building, typically a symbol of state governance and order, now seemed like a fortress in a rapidly changing landscape. Security was tighter than usual, a blunt reminder of the threats they were facing. Upon arrival, Jeremiah was greeted by aides and security personnel. He took a deep breath, steeling himself for the discussions ahead. His usual confident stride carried a hint of urgency as he made his way to the conference room where the governors were assembling.

The room was filled with a tense air of expectation as each Governor arrived, their expressions a mix of concern and resolve. They represented a diverse set of interests and perspectives, but today, they were united by a common threat. As Jeremiah took his seat at the head of the table, he was acutely aware of the eyes fixed on him, awaiting his leadership in this crisis.

"Thank you all for coming on such short notice," Jeremiah began, his voice steady but reflecting the seriousness of the situation. "The challenges we face are unprecedented, but together, we have the strength and the resources to respond effectively."

The meeting unfolded with discussions on coordinating state guard units, sharing intelligence, and protecting critical infrastructure. The atmosphere was one of collaborative urgency, with each Governor contributing to a rapidly evolving action plan. Yet, through it all, part of Jeremiah's mind remained with Jake, hoping against hope for some good news amidst the turmoil.

Governor Bradford of Idaho spoke up, "As many of you have heard, I have committed our state guard to assist Washington in pushing back against the Confederation. But I need help; Washington is tragically underfunded due to the racial riots and 'defunding the police' protests of the last several years. Some of their politicians are even applauding the invaders, and Antifa has been going to where the Confederation is breaking through the border and celebrating their arrival." Bradford recalled the last few days of events in tragic detail, the faces of the other governors reflecting concern and fear to the news.

"Some of their state guards have begun evacuating the northern parts of Washington and bringing them into Idaho. We don't have the infrastructure for it. Still, we Idahoans cannot turn our back on fellow Americans who are suffering." He continued as Governor Carey stood, his weary face showing exhaustion over the news of the last few days.

"These people ignited a super weapon off the coast of our country, and they invaded our close neighbors to the north and now one of our states. This is horrific, and we have to offer a response." He blustered and paced as Governor Beam stood,

"Listen, folks; I feel like we should trust our system of government. President Hastings is already recalling a portion of our troops to help with recovery efforts..."

"Oh, you Kansans feel like we should hold off?" Governor Kelly Lome interrupted, "How do you think the Washingtonians feel about being evacuated from their homes and their cities being burned?" she continued. The room erupted in loud jeers and shouting as the tensions flared.

"Okay, everyone, calm down." Jeremiah stood up and held his hand up, "That's the last thing we need to do is cause another Bleeding Kansas." A couple of laughs broke the tension.

Jeremiah's authoritative presence quickly brought the room to order. His eyes swept over the assembled governors, each grappling with the implications of the crisis in their own way. He understood their concerns, their fears, and their frustrations. But he also knew that decisive action and unity were crucial in these trying times.

"We are facing a threat that challenges the very fabric of our nation," Jeremiah continued, his voice resonant in the charged atmosphere. "We must rise above political divisions and focus on safeguarding our people and our sovereignty."

Governor Carey of Wyoming, who had been pacing, now stood still, nodding in agreement. His face, etched with lines of worry, seemed to soften slightly. "Jeremiah's right," he conceded. "Our first duty is to protect our citizens. We need a coordinated response, and we need it now."

Governor Beam from Kansas leaned forward, his expression serious. "I agree with a coordinated effort," he said. "But we must also consider the implications of our actions. We can't just react; we need a strategic approach that looks at the long-term impact as well."

Governor Kelly Lome of South Dakota, her voice still tinged with emotion, added, "Our people are scared. They need to see that we're doing something concrete. We can't just wait and hope for the best."

As the discussion unfolded, Jeremiah listened intently, weighing each point. The room was a microcosm of the nation itself – diverse, passionate, and facing a challenge that would define their era. He realized that their response would set a precedent, not just for this crisis, but for how the nation would handle future threats.

After much debate, a plan began to take shape. The council agreed on mobilizing additional state guard units, establishing refugee centers for displaced Washingtonians, and creating a joint task force to coordinate their efforts. They also decided to appeal to the federal government for more support, emphasizing the importance of the situation.

Governor Davison Carey of Wyoming stood up, his voice carrying a mix of determination and respect. "Given that Idaho was the first among us to respond decisively to this crisis, and considering Jeremiah's significant leadership in coordinating our efforts, I propose we name the joint task force the Montana-Idaho Militia." His suggestion was met with nods and a round of applause from most governors, acknowledging both Idaho's initiative and Jeremiah's pivotal role.

However, Governor Beam of Kansas remained notably reserved. The applause faded into a more somber atmosphere as he leaned towards his assistant, his voice barely a whisper yet laden with concern. "I'm worried," he confided, his words laced with a profound sense of unease. "The formation of this militia, while necessary, feels like a step towards the fragmentation of our nation. It's as if we're witnessing the end of the United States as we know it."

His assistant, equally pensive, nodded in understanding. The consequences of Governor Beam's statement hung in the air, reflecting a deep-seated fear that this crisis might irreversibly alter the fabric of the nation.

Jeremiah, sensing the shift in mood, addressed the room with a reassuring yet firm tone. "I understand the concerns about the long-term implications of our actions," he acknowledged. "But let us not forget that our first and foremost duty is to protect our citizens and uphold the principles of our union. This militia is not a symbol of division; it's a testament to our collective strength and unity in the face of a common threat."

Governor Kelly Lome of South Dakota chimed in, her voice echoing Jeremiah's sentiment. "We're not just fighting an external threat," she said. "We're fighting for the preservation of our way of life, for the values that define us as a nation. This joint task force, the Montana-Idaho Militia, is a symbol of our resilience and our commitment to those values."

The discussion continued, with each Governor contributing their perspective. The mood in the room was a complex tapestry of determination, apprehension, and a shared sense of responsibility. They all understood the historical significance of their decisions and the delicate balance they had to maintain in safeguarding their states while preserving the unity of the nation.

As the meeting concluded, the governors stood together, a united front ready to face the challenges ahead. They had come to an agreement on the structure and objectives of the Montana-Idaho Militia, and each Governor pledged their support and resources. The path forward was fraught with uncertainty, but they were resolute in their commitment to lead their states through these tumultuous times.

The weight of responsibility lay heavy on Jeremiah's shoulders as he prepared to address the media waiting outside.

The press conference that followed was a blur of camera flashes and pointed questions. Jeremiah, standing alongside the other governors, presented a united front. They spoke of the formation of a unified task force, the Montana-Idaho Militia, and the resilience of the states coming together to defy an invading enemy.

Jeremiah exited the conference room, his heart heavy yet driven by a newfound resolve. The establishment of the militia was a daring step, a ray of hope in guiding the region toward a semblance of stability. As he navigated through the hallway, his phone vibrated with an incoming notification. It was another update regarding the search for Jake. Pausing, he felt a tremor in his hand, a physical manifestation of the internal struggle between his paternal worry and his responsibilities as a leader.

Exiting the building, still immersed in his thoughts, the phone buzzed again. He glanced down at the screen, his pulse quickening. The message about Jake was more than just news; it symbolized the intertwining of his personal anguish with the broader crisis engulfing the nation. As he opened the message, Jeremiah stood at a crossroads where the personal and the political, the fate of his son and the fate of a country, were inexorably linked.

3

THE GLITTERING SKYLINE OF Raleigh, North Carolina, provided a dramatic backdrop to President-Elect Troy Thomason's campaign headquarters. Inside, a complex mood enveloped the room: one part celebration, two parts somber reflection. Troy, a figure of charisma and controversy alike, stood at the heart of the room, his eyes reflecting the city's lights yet shadowed by the weight of recent events.

The headquarters, usually a place of unbridled joy after such a significant victory, was subdued. The staff and supporters, while elated at their win, could not entirely escape the pall cast by the catastrophic event on the West Coast. Troy, ever the astute businessman turned politician, sensed the delicate balance of the moment. His victory speech had been a careful blend of triumph and tribute. Still, now, as the cameras had turned off and the crowd dispersed, the true urgency of the situation began to settle in.

A hush fell over the room as Troy received the call from Quentin Jamison, whom he had been anticipating yet dreading; the former governor of Oregon and his

Democrat opponent in the Presidential election was on the line to concede to him. The room's attention was fixed on Troy as he answered the call, the speakerphone broadcasting Quentin's voice, weary yet gracious in defeat.

"Congratulations, Troy," Quentin's voice echoed, embodying the tradition of peaceful power transitions, even amidst national grief. Quentin continued, "These are trying times for our country, and the road ahead will be challenging. I hope we can put our differences aside for the sake of the nation."

Troy, his expression a mix of appreciation and solemnity, responded with a nod that only his closest aides could see. "Thank you, Quentin. I fully intend to lead our nation toward healing and unity. We have much to mend, and I respect the role you've played in this democratic process."

As the call ended, a silence lingered in the room. Troy turned to his team, the weight of leadership settling upon his shoulders. "We have won the election, but now we face the greater task of leading a nation in mourning," he stated, his voice firm yet tinged with an understanding of the monumental task ahead. "Our responsibility tempers our celebration. It's time to prepare for the presidency, to address the wounds of our nation, and to guide us through this tragedy."

As Troy stopped speaking, the phone rang again. His assistant answered it quickly, "Yes, sir, right away, sir." Lisa Anderson said curtly as she looked up from the phone, her face betraying nervous energy, "Mr. Thomason, I have President Hastings on the line." Troy moved towards the phone; he had expected this call but wasn't sure when it would come.

"Hello, Mr. President," Troy said respectfully, the voice on the other end laughing slightly.

"That title is yours now; I am just keeping the seat warm for the next few weeks, President Thomason." Arthur Hastings said on the line, partly laughing but quickly shifting to serious.

"I want first to offer my condolences for the loss of your wife when we were callously attacked," Arthur said tenderly before picking up why he called. "Listen here, Troy, I am old, but I am not stupid. I know my party is putting me out to pasture. They wanted Quentin to carry on the Democrat banner, but frankly, we are in bad shape as a country." His voice trailed off as Troy nodded, "I am worried that, as a country, our days are numbered; my handlers would be furious if they knew I was having this conversation with you, Troy, but I am worried, and I want you to be prepared." Arthur grew silent, "I am going to transfer you to my private office; hold on one second."

"I need to take this call in private," Troy said as he parked the line in the system. Lisa and the other remaining office staff nodded as they returned to their duties of cleaning the office after their celebration.

A few moments later, Troy closed the door behind himself and picked up the phone on his desk, "I really appreciate your words about Julie; I will miss her. I felt like our conversation should be in my ears only." Troy said as Arthur spoke again.

"Troy, I just received word that a group of states in the Great Plains are creating a state militia to fight against the invasion of The Confederation. I have failed. I always wanted to be President. I always believed I would be a President of Peace, but under my watch, the world is at war, and we are involved. Our Southern border is in chaos, and now we are being invaded by a foreign power." Arthur's voice was emotional as he spoke, Troy's eyes showing weariness.

"What happened?" Troy asked.

"They happened…" Arthur's voice trailed off as the line died suddenly. Troy quickly tried dialing the number back, but it just rang on the White House switchboard.

Troy leaned back in his seat, frustrated. His face showed anger as he spun to look out of his office window at Raleigh's skyline.

"Who are they?" he asked himself as a knock came to his door. Spinning back around, he saw Senator Ulysses Mars standing at his door; Troy waved Ulysses into his office, a weary smile crossing his face. The Senator closed the door behind him and took the offered seat; his posture was relaxed yet attentive.

"Troy, you look like you've just seen a ghost," Ulysses observed his faded complexion, attempting to inject a bit of humor into the palpable tension.

Troy let out a heavy sigh, leaning back in his chair. "You could say that. I just got off the phone with President Hastings. The conversation took a turn I wasn't expecting."

Ulysses raised an eyebrow, concern etching his features. "Arthur? He's usually so guarded. What did he say?"

Troy rubbed his temples, gathering his thoughts. "He was... different. Almost like he was letting down his guard, you know? He said he's worried that as a country, our days are numbered."

"That sounds dire, even for him," Ulysses mused, leaning forward. "Did he say why?"

Troy nodded slowly. "He mentioned something about a group of states forming a militia to fight against The Confederation's invasion. It's like the whole fabric of the nation is starting to unravel."

Ulysses' expression turned grave. "This is serious, Troy. If Arthur's breaking protocol to warn you, we're in uncharted waters."

"Yeah, and then the line went dead. Just like that," Troy added, snapping his fingers. "He was about to tell me more, but we got cut off. And now, I can't help but wonder... who are 'they' that he was referring to?"

Ulysses leaned back, his mind racing. "This is more than just political maneuvering or international tension. It's as if we're on the brink of something much larger, something neither of us has seen before."

Troy met his friend's gaze, a mixture of resolve and uncertainty in his eyes. "Ulysses, I trust you more than anyone in this game. What's your read on this? How do we even begin to tackle something of this magnitude?"

Ulysses took a moment before answering, his thoughts carefully measured. "First, we need to understand the full scope of the threat. This militia formation is a symptom of a deeper issue. And The Confederation... we need intel, Troy. Real, actionable intelligence."

Troy nodded in agreement. "I was thinking along the same lines. We need to start pulling in favors and get a line on what's happening behind the scenes. And we need to do it discreetly."

"Discretion is key," Ulysses concurred. "But remember, Troy, you're not alone in this. You have allies, both seen and unseen. We'll rally the support you need."

Troy's expression softened, gratitude evident in his tone. "Thanks, Ulysses. It means a lot, especially now. I always knew this job would be tough, but this... it's like we're navigating a minefield in the dark."

Ulysses stood, placing a reassuring hand on Troy's shoulder. "If there's anyone who can lead us through this minefield, it's you, Troy. You have a way of bringing people together, of making them see the bigger picture."

Troy stood as well, the weight of leadership momentarily lifted by the bond of friendship. "We'll face this together, then. Step by step, we'll uncover the truth behind The Confederation, the militias, and whatever else is out there."

Ulysses smiled, a spark of determination in his eyes. "Together, my friend. And we'll start first thing tomorrow. For tonight, try to get some rest. Leaders need their strength."

Troy chuckled, a brief respite from the significance of their conversation. "Rest? That's a luxury I can't afford. But for you, Ulysses, I'll try."

As Ulysses exited, Troy felt a renewed sense of purpose. The challenges ahead were daunting, but with trusted friends by his side, the path forward seemed a little less daunting. The conversation with Ulysses had not only solidified his resolve but reminded him of the personal connections that would sustain him through the trials ahead.

"They happened..." Arthur said as one of his Secret Service Agents ripped the phone from his hand and hung up the line, acting with a decisiveness that bordered on aggression. The abrupt click of the line going dead echoed ominously in the grandeur of the room, marking an end to the President's clandestine conversation with President-Elect Troy Thomason.

Before Arthur could protest, the door swung open, and in strode Vice President Aleatha Morris, her presence as commanding as it was imposing. Her eyes, sharp and unyielding, immediately fixed on Arthur, who looked back at her with a mixture of frustration and resignation.

"Aleatha," Arthur began, his voice tinged with a weary defiance, "I was merely—"

"Merely what, Arthur?" Aleatha cut him off, her tone laced with scorn. "Undermining our position? Compromising our strategy? Or perhaps forgetting who is actually in charge here?"

Arthur's gaze dropped to the floor, a silent acknowledgment of the power shift that had occurred within
the walls of the White House. The once-revered office
he held was now little more than a ceremonial title;
the actual decisions were being made by Aleatha and
the cabinet she had meticulously assembled.

Aleatha continued, her words sharp as knives. "You
know the stakes, Arthur. Your little chat with Thomason is not just reckless; it's a liability. We can't afford
any deviations from the plan. Not now."

Arthur, finding a sliver of resolve, looked up at her.
"The people elected me, Aleatha, not a shadow government operating behind closed doors. What we're
doing... it's not right."

Aleatha scoffed, her expression unyielding. "What's
right is keeping this country from falling apart.
Do you think you're helping by spilling our secrets
to Thomason? You're endangering everything we've
worked for."

The tension in the room was palpable, a sharp contrast to the office's usual decorum. Arthur, once a figure of authority and respect, now seemed diminished,
his power eroded by the very people he had trusted.

"I believed I was doing what was best for the country,"
Arthur said quietly, more to himself than to Aleatha.
"I never intended to become a puppet."

Aleatha softened slightly, her demeanor shifting as she approached Arthur. "I know, Arthur. But times have changed. The world outside these walls is not the one you were elected to govern. We're at war in more ways than one. And in war, hard decisions must be made."

Arthur sighed, the weight of his presidency—and its apparent futility—bearing down on him. "And what of Thomason? What hard decisions will he have to make, Aleatha?"

Aleatha paused, her gaze drifting towards the windows overlooking the Washington Monument. "Troy Thomason will play his part, as we all must. But until he's sworn in, the course we've set remains unchanged."

With those final words, Aleatha turned and left the Oval Office, leaving Arthur alone with his thoughts and the daunting realization of his presidency's legacy. As the door clicked shut, Arthur turned back to the desk that had once symbolized the pinnacle of American democracy, now a vivid reminder of his diminished role.

The scene in the Oval Office laid bare the intricate web of power, loyalty, and ambition that defined the highest echelons of American politics, setting the stage for the tumultuous transition of power that awaited.

As dawn broke over the Washington border, a solemn scene unfolded. The battleground, caught between past tranquility and present turmoil, was strewn with the sacrifices of a fierce encounter. Soldiers from the State Guards of Washington, Oregon, and Idaho lay intermingled with remnants of the clash, their valor overshadowed by the harsh reality of insufficient resources and preparation.

Just beyond the front lines, a different kind of confrontation was taking place—a clash of ideologies. A multitude of protesters, donned in black symbolizing both mourning and defiance, converged at Oroville's main border crossing. Their presence was not in support of the State Guard but rather to express their vehement hatred for America, directing their anger and makeshift weapons not at the invading forces but at those tasked with the defense of Washington State. Caught in a tragic position, the Guards were compelled to shield themselves from their own citizens, resorting to non-lethal measures in a poignant effort to maintain order amidst the upheaval.

The protesters were fueled by a sense of celebration that the invading forces would bring about the Communist Utopia they had so dreamed of. They viewed the State Guard as defenders of the flawed systems they opposed.

Every advance by the opposing forces, each explosion that echoed closer to home, intensified their joy, creating a charged atmosphere where lines between friend and foe blurred amidst the smoke and chaos. Members of the black-clad protestors pounding on drums almost in unison with the explosions.

A young Guardsman from Idaho, fresh from adolescence, grappled with the essence of his duty as he stared in the direction of his fellow citizens chanting for his death.

"Sergeant Moss, why are they doing this?" the young man asked as he wiped sweat from his face. Streaks of soot intermingled with his tears and sweat as he looked at the elder Sergeant. Sergeant Moss was an experienced but retired sergeant in the Army, accustomed to distant battlefields. Now, he faced the alarming reality of conflict at his own doorstep and the disillusionment of being seen as an adversary by his fellow citizens.

"Son, I don't know. Some do not value what we have as a country and seek to see it destroyed as they wave their iPhones and tablets around, claiming to be oppressed. This gives them the perfect opportunity to rage against that stability," Sergeant Moss said to the young guardsman.

In the midst of the escalating chaos, the unexpected sound of gunfire shattered the fragile ceasefire that had momentarily calmed the front lines. As the bullet found its mark, the young Guardsman from Idaho fell, his dreams and doubts silenced in an instant. Sergeant Moss, his voice raw with urgency and fear, bellowed commands for his troops to take cover. The bullets, originating from the direction of the protesters, ripped through the fabric of the tents and the makeshift guard-house, sending splinters and shreds of material flying through the air.

The State Guards, trained for combat but not for this kind of internal strife, scrambled to find safety behind whatever cover they could. The chaos that followed was a grim dance of survival as soldiers ducked and weaved, trying to make sense of the source of the gun-fire. Amidst the confusion, it became apparent that a faction within the protesters had decided to escalate their aggression to lethal force, blurring the lines between peaceful demonstration and armed revolt.

Sergeant Moss, a veteran of conflicts far removed from the soil of his home in Oregon, quickly assessed the situation. His experience told him that retaliating with lethal force would only worsen the situation, potentially leading to a massacre. Instead, he ordered his troops to focus on non-lethal measures and to try to identify the shooters without escalating the conflict further. "Hold your fire!" he roared over the din, "Use tear gas and shields! We are not here to kill our own people!"

As the gas canisters were deployed, creating clouds of confusion and temporary barriers between the guards and the protesters, the immediate threat was momentarily suppressed. However, the damage was done. The trust that had been hanging by a thread between the State Guard and the civilian protesters was now severed, leaving a gulf of misunderstanding and fear in its wake.

The smoke from the gas containers was heavy as State Guardsmen pulled gas masks over their faces and rushed into the protestors to secure the members of the protest who opted for lethality. Sergeant Moss pulled his phone from his pocket and called for the local sheriff's department to dispatch their SWAT to apprehend the violent protesters. Still, while their focus was directed at the civilians, the sound of giant machinery filled the air.

Sergeant Moss turned his attention back to the border crossing. His eyes widened as he saw in the distance four tanks rumbling in their direction, flanked by what looked like thousands of soldiers marching toward the border.

"Listen up, folks, there is no fighting against four heavies and thousands of troops; we need to evacuate the area now!" Moss said as he gathered his things and grabbed the body of the young man killed by the protestors. He ran towards his truck, followed by the other Guardsmen, a large explosion rocking the area as the border crossing was targeted and destroyed by a large blast.

"Governor Lowery, we are evacuating the area. They have overwhelming force, and we don't have the manpower or equipment. We are falling back to the Spokane front," Sergeant Moss said, sliding into his truck and cranking it, his frustration bleeding through his voice as he spoke.

"I am doing everything I can, Sergeant. Get to safety so we can regroup." Governor Lowery said on the other end of the line. Hanging up quickly, he redialed the phone.

"Jeremiah, they have breached the border and are advancing; I don't know what to do. We are spread very thin." Governor Gary Lowery pleaded with Jeremiah on the line.

"Gary, We are working on it. President Hastings is worthless right now, and our Federal troops are still weeks away from returning home. How many military bases do you have in operation right now?" Jeremiah questioned, his voice filled with tension.

"We still have twenty or so. Why?" Gary questioned curtly.

"Don't worry about it. You'll know soon enough."

Jeremiah hung up the phone and turned to look at the other governors in the room.

"This is desperate, Jeremiah, but I know it is necessary." Governor Bradford Davidson said bluntly.

"Yes, but we need the equipment, and hopefully, the men and women stationed there will join us." Jeremiah picked up his cigar and puffed on it. He pressed a button on the intercom, "Send them in."

The door opened, and a group of soldiers walked in wearing camouflage and berets. They all stood at attention as Governor Jeremiah Johnson put his cigar back down and began to speak.

"Listen up, ladies and gentlemen. What I am about to ask you to do may be deemed treasonous by D.C., but frankly, I don't care. The lives of our citizens are more important to me than the political wrangling of the legions of bureaucrats in Washington D.C.," Jeremiah held a concerned look on his face, knowing what he was about to ask could cost the lives of the men he was about to order.

"You are to march into Fairchild Air Force Base and assume command. You may get resistance, but you are not to be lethal. We need to commandeer the base and equipment. We will continue taking over every military base and office along the way. Most of our Federal troops are overseas, so I expect much fewer numbers at the bases.

The lead soldier looked at Jeremiah, his face weary, "Sir, you want us to engage against our own people and take their bases?" The tension was heavy in the air, and the moments seemed to take years to pass.

"General Marcus Ross, you are the commander of the new Montana-Idaho Militia. I know I am asking a great deal from you and the men and women you command. Understand me, son, we are being invaded, and the members of the military still in the homeland have not been ordered to defend our states. That is unacceptable, and I know they are champing at the bit to join our defense. We have to give them a cause to rally to." Governor Jeremiah Johnson stood at attention and saluted as General Marcus Ross and the men who accompanied him returned the gesture. All of the other Governors in the room also saluted. The soldiers turned in unison and walked out of the room.

I hope I am doing the right thing. Jeremiah thought as the doors shut behind the soldiers who had exited. He turned back to the room of governors.

John Beam stood in the back and was the only governor who did not salute the soldiers. He spoke up, "You all are insane. God in heaven… you are insane." John shouted abruptly as he started walking towards the door. The other governors stepped in front of the door as Jeremiah pressed the intercom again, "Janet, send in security."

John's eyes were horrified at the implication and his being blockaded in the room.

"John, you had a chance to willingly stand beside your fellow states in the Great Plains against invasion, but since you won't, I cannot let you leave," Jeremiah said as three security guards entered the room. As they approached, John lifted his hands in the air. They cuffed him and took him away to a secure holding room.

Things were beginning to get real as Jeremiah looked at the other governors, "Are there any other governors who protest us defending our sovereignty?"

The room was silent as Gene Kyle, the governor from North Dakota, saluted Jeremiah. The others followed suit as Jeremiah returned the salute, "We have a lot of work to do." His voice boldly spoke as he sat down at the head of the table.

Fairchild Air Force Base, an extensive Air Force base in Washington State, brimmed with the routine vigor of military life as dawn unfurled its light across the vast runways. Home to the 92nd and 141st Air Refueling Wings, the base sheltered an impressive fleet, including the towering C-5M Super Galaxy planes and the slightly smaller C-17 Globemaster IIIs. Despite the morning's calm, an undercurrent of unrest stirred among its inhabitants. They had seen reports of a tragic bombing in the Pacific that claimed much of California. Now, the same forces responsible for that horrendous attack were invading United States territory from the north, bringing the war to their doorstep. The airmen stationed at Fairchild weren't permitted to complain about their commander-in-chief, Arthur Hastings. Still, it was evident that most hated him for hollowing out their military readiness by extending the draft and overextending them in more wars overseas. The quiet was a prelude to the storm that was intensifying on the northern horizon.

Within the cavernous belly of a C-5M, amidst the hum of machinery and the occasional roar of engines being tested, two figures stood dwarfed by the military helicopters and tanks surrounding them in the giant craft. Senior Airman Eliot James, his youthful optimism tempered by concern, and Technical Sergeant Hannah Martinez, whose determined eyes hinted at a wealth of experience, shared a quiet conversation about President Hastings and the conflict inching closer to their doorstep.

"It's like we're just spectators of our own fate," Eliot said, his voice barely rising above the ambient noise. "The news from the north... it's hard to ignore the feeling that we should be doing more."

Hannah nodded, her gaze lingering on a C-17 as it glided past them outside the massive bay door. "I hear you.

It feels wrong to stand by when there's a fight for our state, for our homes. We joined to defend, didn't we? Not to wait."

Eliot laughed a little, "That's the dream, right? Join to protect the freedom at home, then the draft 'to defend home.' When in reality, it is to protect the borders and governments from other countries while our country pays the price in our blood.

Their shared sentiment, a mix of frustration and a strong desire to contribute was symbolic of the mood that had taken hold of many at Fairchild. Yet, unbeknownst to them and the rest of the base, plans were already in motion that would challenge their convictions and alter the course of their lives.

The Montana-Idaho Militia, a collective forged in the fires of the impending invasion, had set their sights on Fairchild AFB. Led by General Marcus Ross, a figure both revered and feared for his strategic insight, the militia marched with a purpose that transcended mere conquest. They aimed to secure the base's assets and, if possible, enlist the support of its personnel in their quest to safeguard the Great Plains states from further encroachment.

As the militia neared, the base buzzed with a combination of rumors and official alerts. This chaotic symphony crescendoed with each passing hour. The airmen and commanders found themselves wrestling with the dilemma of how to respond to a force that, though potentially adversarial, shared a common nationality and, ostensibly, a common cause.

Militia members surrounded the entire border of the base, their presence a silent but formidable statement. They were heavily armed, yet their stance suggested they were holding back from immediate aggression. The tension in the air was palpable, a coiled spring ready to snap at any moment. In the main office, Colonel Alex Ford stood by the window, his gaze fixed on the encircling militia. He quickly assessed the situation, recognizing the precarious balance between potential confrontation and the slim hope of peaceful negotiation. Turning sharply, he barked orders to his second-in-command, "Get the quartermaster. I want every soldier on this base armed and ready."

The command center buzzed with sudden urgency. The base quartermaster moved with practiced efficiency, distributing weapons and ammunition. Soldiers, both men and women, ran with purpose, their boots pounding against the concrete as they hurried to their designated posts. Some took up positions behind sandbags and barricades hastily erected around the perimeter. In contrast, others manned lookout towers and strategic vantage points.

Sergeant Emily Hayes, a seasoned soldier with a reputation for keeping her cool under pressure, organized a squad near the main gate. "Hold your fire unless given the order," she instructed firmly. "We're here to defend, not provoke."

In the barracks, Private Jason Morales strapped on his gear, his hands trembling slightly as he loaded his rifle. He exchanged a glance with his bunkmate, Private First Class Megan Liu, whose determined expression mirrored the resolve shared by the troops.

Colonel Ford, returning to the command center, monitored the unfolding situation via a network of surveillance cameras. He could see the militia's calm but watchful eyes trained on the base, their leader standing at the forefront, silently conveying a message of resolve and readiness. Ford knew that any misstep could ignite the standoff into full-blown conflict.

Outside, the sun was setting, casting long shadows across the base. The scene was eerily quiet, save for the occasional bark of a command or the click of a weapon being loaded. The soldiers were ready, their faces a mixture of fear and determination, prepared to defend their home against an uncertain threat. The stillness before the storm was almost unbearable, each side waiting for the other to make the first move.

A standoff ensued as the base command tried calling the Pentagon, but their lines were cut, and their cell phones couldn't get a connection.

The silhouette of soldiers encroaching on the border became unmistakably clear. Colonel Alex Ford stood authoritatively among his airmen, issuing commands with precision. The air was charged with anticipation, each moment stretching into eternity as they prepared for what was to come. Suddenly, the loud ringing of the main phone cut through the tension, drawing every eye in the command center towards Staff Sergeant Liz Moon.

The room held its breath as Liz answered, her usual composed demeanor faltering as the color drained from her face. With a grave expression, she extended the receiver towards Colonel Ford. "Colonel," she uttered her voice a whisper against the storm of anxiety brewing within the command center.

Colonel Ford, his posture unyielding, accepted the phone. The voice that greeted him was direct, cutting through formalities with an urgency that demanded attention. "Colonel," it began, an echo of respect woven through the sternness.

"Yes, this is Colonel Alex Ford," he responded, his voice steady, betraying none of the apprehension that gripped him. "What do you want?" His question, posed with a blend of defiance and guarded curiosity, hung in the air, a challenge to the unseen caller.

"I want to talk, American to American, as brothers in arms." The sincerity in the caller's tone was palpable; a bridge extended across the divide.

The room fell silent, every officer and enlisted personnel within earshot fixed on Colonel Ford, awaiting his response. The proposition, unexpected as it was, opened the door to a potential resolution that Ford had been trained to navigate. His mind raced through scenarios, each decision branching into myriad outcomes.

"Very well," Colonel Ford replied after a moment that seemed to stretch into infinity. "Speak your piece."

The voice on the other end belonged to General Marcus Ross of the Montana-Idaho Militia, a man whose reputation had preceded him. As Ross outlined his vision for the defense of the Great Plains states and his reasons for approaching Fairchild AFB, Ford listened intently. The general spoke not as an adversary but as a fellow soldier concerned for the welfare of their shared country, presenting a narrative that challenged the black-and-white portrayal often depicted in briefings and reports.

Colonel Ford found himself at a crossroads. The proposition to collaborate with the Montana-Idaho Militia was filled with dangerous complexities, raising questions of loyalty, legality, and the broader implications for the nation's security. Yet, the underlying message, one of unity against a common threat of the Confederation, resonated with his core values.

The call concluded with an agreement to meet, discuss terms, and explore the possibility of cooperation as Colonel Ford set down the receiver, the weight of the decision ahead pressed upon him. Turning to his officers, he saw reflected in their eyes the same mix of uncertainty and resolve that he felt.

"Prepare for a meeting," he instructed, his voice carrying the authority of his rank and the gravity of the situation. "We will hear them out, assess their intentions, and decide our course of action. Remember, our duty is to protect and serve our nation in all its complexities."

As Staff Sergeant Liz Moon and the others sprang into action, Colonel Ford allowed himself a moment of contemplation. The path forward was uncharted, but his leadership would guide Fairchild AFB through the turbulence. In this pivotal moment, Alex Ford stood not only as a military officer but as a steward of peace, ready to navigate the delicate dance of diplomacy for the greater good.

4

"WHAT DID YOU DO, Dad?!" Samantha shouted into her phone while talking to her father, "My god, do you know what this means for me?" The tension in Samantha's voice sliced through the static of the phone call, her disbelief and frustration echoing off the confined space of her jeep. The news that Fairchild Air Force Base had sided with the Montana-Idaho Militia was not just a headline; it was a personal affront, a seismic shift in her reality. Her hand clenched tight around the steering wheel mirrored the tight knot of emotions within her.

"Honey, we did what we felt we had to do. Arthur Hastings was doing nothing, and Troy doesn't get inaugurated for another month." Jeremiah's calm and unwavering voice differed markedly from the turmoil swirling within Samantha. His conviction was clear, born of desperation and a deep-seated belief in the necessity of their actions.

"I am in the Marine Corps, and my own family has become traitors," Samantha retorted, her voice a mix of anger and pain. She turned the radio up, hoping to drown out the conflict, but the news only served as a reminder of the chasm that had opened between her duty and her family's actions.

The announcement that Fairchild had joined forces with the militia sent ripples through the military community, challenging loyalties and drawing lines that many, like Samantha, were unprepared to cross. Fairchild AFB, once a symbol of the United States, now stood as a testament to the partisan division happening in the country; its airmen and equipment pledged to a cause that placed them at odds with the official stance of the United States government.

"What next, Dad?" The question was loaded, a plea for some semblance of normalcy in a world that had turned upside down.

Jeremiah's response was measured, and his words were chosen with the precision of a strategist. "I want you to take a leadership position in the Montana-Idaho Militia. You are a decorated Marine, and when we call on the Marine Corps to join us, we will need your experience to help guide them." His respect for Samantha's military prowess was evident, yet it did little to bridge the gulf that was forming between them.

"Dad, I am not a traitor!" Samantha's protest was fierce, a declaration of her loyalty to the Corps and the country she had sworn to serve.

"Neither are we, honey. We are Americans doing something about the invasion where our government refuses to do so." Jeremiah's words were meant to soothe, to convince, but they landed like blows, deepening Samantha's turmoil.

Caught between her allegiance to the Marine Corps and her family's revolutionary stance, Samantha faced an impossible choice. To side with her father meant betraying the oath she had taken; to stand against him was to deny the blood that bound them. The road ahead was filled with difficulty, each step a potential minefield of personal and professional consequences.

As Samantha wrestled with her dilemma, the broader implications of Fairchild's allegiance to the militia began to crystallize. The base's strategic assets and manpower significantly bolstered the militia's capabilities, sending a powerful message to other military installations and personnel. The lines were being drawn, not just on maps, but in the hearts and minds of those who served.

As the news continued to play, a litany of updates and analyses on the situation at Fairchild AFB and its implications, Samantha's world felt as though it was splintering. Each word from the radio was a reminder of the widening gulf between her current reality and the life she had known. Her father's voice, once a source of guidance and strength, now seemed to emanate from across an insurmountable divide.

Samantha parked her car in a secluded spot near the Twentynine Palms base where she was stationed. Around her, the buzz of activity sharply juxtaposed the turmoil churning inside her. She needed a moment, a breath of clarity amidst the chaos. Her father's proposal echoed in her mind, a siren call to join a cause that resonated with the deepest fears and hopes of many Americans. Yet, to heed that call was to step into the unknown, risking everything she held dear.

The Marine Corps had been her home, a place where the values of honor, courage, and commitment were not just ideals but the very foundation of her existence. Her comrades her duties, represented a bond forged in the fire of shared trials and triumphs. To turn her back on that life, on the oath she had sworn, was unthinkable. And yet, the thought of standing idly by while her family and others took a stand against what they perceived as a failing government gnawed at her conscience.

The internal battle raged as Samantha considered her father's words: "Neither are we, honey. We are Americans doing something about the invasion where our government refuses to do so." Jeremiah believed in the cause and felt that action was necessary to protect the nation's future. Samantha understood and even admired this sentiment. But at what cost? And where did her true loyalties lie?

Her phone vibrated with incoming messages and calls, likely from colleagues and superiors curious about her prolonged silence. The reality of her situation was inescapable. Decisions needed to be made, and soon. Samantha knew that her next steps would alter the trajectory of her life. The thought of leaving the Marine Corps, of potentially facing charges of treason if she aligned with the militia, was a specter that loomed large. Yet, the alternative, to do nothing while her family fought for their beliefs, presented its own form of torment.

The sun began to dip below the horizon, casting long shadows that seemed to mirror the darkness encroaching on Samantha's heart. It was in this moment of solitude and introspection that she realized the truth she had been avoiding: the battle was not just between her and her family or even between differing factions within the country. It was a struggle for the soul of the nation, a test of principles in the face of unprecedented challenges.

With a heavy heart, Samantha turned off the radio, silencing the barrage of news. She reached for her phone, her decision crystallizing with each passing second. The call she was about to make would likely change her life forever. Whether she chose to stand with the Marine Corps or with her father and the Montana-Idaho Militia, there would be consequences. But Samantha understood now that inaction was a choice in itself, one she could not live with.

As she dialed, the weight of responsibility settled on her shoulders. She was about to step into the fray to define her stance in a conflict that would shape the future of her country. Everything ahead swirled with uncertainty, but Samantha was resolute. Her voice, when she spoke, would be that of a Marine, a daughter, and above all, an American determined to fight for what she believed was right.

The first ring on the other end of the line seemed to echo in the tight space of her car, a precursor to the conversation that would seal her fate. By the time the call connected, Samantha's resolve was an unbreakable fortress, her voice steady and imbued with the weight of her choice.

"Colonel Martinez," she began, addressing her superior officer with a respect that had been earned in the trenches of service and leadership. "I need to speak with you. It's urgent."

The brief pause before her superior's response was laden with anticipation. "Samantha, what's going on?" Colonel Martinez's concern was palpable; their relationship and camaraderie had been forged through the fires of many battles.

Samantha took a deep breath, the words she was about to utter marking a point of no return. "Sir, I'm aware of the situation unfolding with the Montana-Idaho Militia and Fairchild AFB. I also know that my family is deeply involved. I'm at a crossroads, and I've made a decision."

The silence that followed was a void, stretching between duty and conscience, waiting to be filled with her declaration. "I cannot turn my back on my oath to the Marine Corps, nor can I ignore the complexities of this conflict. I want to offer my services as a liaison—a bridge between the Corps and the militia. If there's any chance of understanding and mitigating further escalation, I believe I can help."

Colonel Martinez's reply came after a moment of consideration, his tone measured. "Do you understand the risks involved, Samantha? This is unprecedented. You're talking about walking a razor's edge."

"Yes, sir, I do. But if there's a chance to prevent further conflict within our United States and save lives while defending our country, then it's a risk I'm willing to take—that I have to take. I believe in the Corps, in our ability to lead with honor and integrity, even in the face of challenges that threaten to divide us."

The conversation that followed was a detailed negotiation of terms, of boundaries to be respected, and of the uncharted territory they were about to navigate. Colonel Martinez, while cautious, recognized the unique position Samantha was in to serve as a vital link between the conflicting sides potentially. Her mission would be unofficial, delicately balancing the line between her loyalty to the Marine Corps and her connection to her family within the militia.

As the call ended, Samantha felt the weight of her decision settle around her like armor. She was about to embark on a mission that could either bridge the divide or deepen the chasm, not just between the military and the militia but within the very heart of her family. The defense of the country, her home, was one she had to take on even if it was overflowing with danger, both physical and emotional, but Samantha's determination was unwavering.

In the midst of her preparations and the pivotal decisions she faced, Samantha's thoughts often drifted to her brother, Jake. Her search for him, driven by hope and desperation, had turned up nothing. The absence of news was a cold comfort, leaving her in a limbo of worry and wishful thinking. Ordered to return to base, she couldn't shake the concern for Jake, yet somewhere deep inside, a spark of confidence remained. Jake was hardheaded, resilient, and stubborn to the core. Despite the tension that clung to her every move, a faint smile cracked across her face at the thought of him somewhere out there, surviving against the odds.

As she started her car, the engine's roar seemed to echo her resolve, a battle cry for the uncertain journey ahead. Driving back to the base, Samantha's mind raced through a myriad of strategies and potential scenarios, each layered with complexities and brimming with risks. Yet, underlying the tumult of her thoughts was an unshakeable conviction. She was an American, sworn to protect and serve, committed to her duty above all else, even as she navigated the treacherous waters of her personal affiliations and the broader conflict engulfing her nation.

Samantha's path was illuminated by more than just the fading light of day; it was guided by a profound belief in the possibility of reconciliation, in the power of understanding to bridge divides. Her mission, born from a blend of duty and a deep-seated love for her country—and her family—was a bright light of hope in a landscape marred by strife.

The sun dipped below the horizon, painting the sky in a palette of gold and shadow; Samantha's silhouette merged with the fading light, a lone figure against the vastness of the challenge ahead. Her journey, intertwined with the fate of her brother and the future of her country, was a testament to the enduring spirit of those who serve. In a nation grappling with its identity and the path forward, Samantha's courage to seek a path of peace, to stand in the gap where others might falter, was a powerful reminder of the true strength of the human spirit.

She wasn't sure what the liaison duties would involve, but she vowed to do what she could to defend the United States while still supporting her family and her home.

A few days prior, the tranquility of morning just a little north of Payette, Idaho, was violently disrupted by an explosion on State Road ID-52. In the aftermath, a truck was found smoldering beside the road with human remains in its bed near the bridge that crosses the Snake River. Payette had small-town resources, so the local law enforcement was ill-equipped to manage an incident so unusual and severe. Sheriff Mark Hill decided to call for the help of the State Bureau of Investigation to tackle the situation.

The serene landscape, usually undisturbed except for the occasional wildlife and passing vehicles, had become the focus of intense scrutiny. The explosion not only disrupted the physical environment but also the lives of the tight-knit community in Payette. The Idaho State Police's Bureau of Criminal Investigation arrived promptly, their presence signifying the severity of the situation. Led by Detectives Alicia Wilson and Oliver Nelson, the team immediately set to work, cordoning off the area and beginning a thorough examination of the scene. Alicia stepped towards the windshield, snapped a photo of the vehicle identification number, and sent it in as Oliver examined the body.

"This is horrible, Sheriff Hill. Do you have any witnesses we can talk to?" Alicia asked while brushing her long blonde hair back out of her eyes. Sheriff Hill shook his head, "As far as we know, the explosion happened early in the morning. We have had some issues with Antifa-like protesters across the river starting fires and shooting firecrackers across the river at us, but that's Oregon over there, and we don't have jurisdiction."

Oliver stepped up, "Do you have a coroner we can get out here? I want to get this body back to the morgue so we can figure out who he is."

Mark nodded as he picked up his phone, "Andrea, send Asher Smith; we have a body."

"I will do that, honey. Are you okay?" Andrea said somewhat cheerfully on the line.

"I am fine, but this exploding truck thing has got me, along with the tension along the northern border," Mark responded, his nerves showing even though he was trying to maintain a level of calm.

"I'll tell Asher to be there in a jiffy," Andrea said as Mark disconnected the call. Looking at Alicia and Oliver, "We're a small town. My wife is my office manager."

He chuckled slightly as Oliver nodded and went back to the body; Alicia smiled, "It's good you get to work together."

Alicia's phone rang, and she answered it, the voice on the other end speaking on speaker, "It appears the truck is registered to Jake Johnson, son of the Governor of Montana.

"Oh my, that can't be a coincidence. Have you tried reaching the Governor?" Alicia asked while turning and looking back at the truck.

"We have, but apparently, he is tied up with the governors of several other states, including ours." the voice finished.

"Well, keep trying; he needs to know," she said as she hung up the phone, looking back at Mark. This information makes this potentially worse since Jeremiah is at the center of the creation of the Montana-Idaho Militia."

"I honestly don't pay attention to the national news. I have too much on my plate as the Sheriff of this small community. What is going on?" Mark asked, having never heard of the Montana-Idaho Militia but was keenly aware of the tragic Neutronium bomb explosion and the invasion by a foreign military.

"All I know is that it is essentially the State Guards and Volunteers from Great Plains States all the way down to Kansas, Nebraska, and Missouri that have enlisted in the defense of the United States since the US Military is at war overseas," Alicia said as Mark's eyes widened.

"Isn't that treason?"

"I mean, I don't know. It could be, but what are we to do while a foreign country is invading us? I am American as they come, an Army Veteran, and I agree that the states must take up the defense of our country where our own government cannot." Alicia said passionately, looking back at the truck, "in the meantime, we have a job to do—we need to find Jake."

With the revelation that the truck belonged to Jake Johnson, the son of Montana's Governor, the investigation took on a new urgency. The connection to Jeremiah Johnson, a prominent figure in the formation of the Montana-Idaho Militia, suggested complexities far beyond a simple case of vehicular explosion. This incident was now at the intersection of local crime and potentially significant political unrest.

Detectives Alicia Wilson and Oliver Nelson, alongside Sheriff Mark Hill, found themselves navigating a situation that stretched the boundaries of their usual duties. The small-town setting of Payette, Idaho, rarely saw crimes of this magnitude or with such intricate implications.

Alicia, with her background as an Army veteran, understood the solemnity of the situation. Her commitment to American values and the defense of the nation resonated deeply with the ethos of the Great Plains States' response to the invasion from the Confederation. Yet, as a law enforcement officer, she also recognized the fine line between defending one's country and the legal definitions of treason. The potential involvement of the Montana-Idaho Militia, in this case, hinted at a complex web of motivations and alliances that would need to be untangled.

As they awaited the arrival of coroner Asher-Smith, the team discussed their next steps. The identification of the body was crucial, as it could provide vital clues to the events leading up to the explosion. Was the victim connected to Jake Johnson, or was their presence at the scene merely a tragic coincidence? And where was Jake now?

The small-town dynamics, usually an asset to Mark in his role as Sheriff, now seemed like a hindrance. The lack of resources and personal connections within the community could complicate the investigation. Yet, Alicia, Oliver, and Mark's resolve was firm. They were determined to follow the evidence wherever it led, navigating the complexities of the case with professionalism and a keen sense of duty.

Their immediate task was straightforward: to piece together Jake Johnson's last-known movements and understand the motive behind the explosion. Was it an act of aggression related to the militia's activities or something more personal? Given the potential ramifications of the case, they would need to liaise with state and possibly federal authorities as they delved deeper into the investigation.

The peaceful backdrop of Payette, with its rolling hills and the serene flow of the Snake River, belied the turmoil that had unfolded. For Alicia, Oliver, and Mark, the challenge was not just to solve a crime but to do so while navigating the murky waters of political dissent and the passionate defense of American soil.

As they prepared to move forward, the weight of responsibility bore down on them. The explosion on State Road ID-52 had ignited more than just a fire—it had sparked an investigation that would test their limits and challenge their understanding of loyalty, legality, and patriotism.

Several miles from the chaotic remnants of the explosion on State Road ID-52, deep within the dense thicket of the Idaho forests, a desperate chase unfolded. Three men, Jake, Mike, and Ray, found themselves in a relentless pursuit, their bodies pushed to the brink of exhaustion. The wilderness around them, usually a haven of natural tranquility, had transformed into a difficult maze, with danger lurking behind every shadow.

The air was heavy with the tension of the chase. Every so often, one of the men would stop, breathing heavily, and aim his rifle back towards their unseen pursuers. The loud crack of gunfire would resound through the trees, a vivid reminder of their tragic situation. These fleeting instances of resistance, driven by adrenaline and a desperate will to survive, punctuated their relentless flight since the violent attack that reduced their truck to a smoldering wreck.

The trio's escape from the explosion had been narrow. They had managed to salvage only a single rifle before fleeing into the forest. Their pursuers, determined and relentless, seemed intent on ensuring no witnesses were left to tell the tale. Jake, Mike, and Ray, despite their growing fatigue, were driven by a primal instinct to survive. Each step forward felt like five backward as they weaved through the trees.

The forest, with its overgrown paths and dense underbrush, offered both concealment and obstacles. The men maneuvered through the terrain with a blend of haste and caution, aware that any misstep could give their position away or, worse, result in injury. The weight of the rifle felt heavy as their energy waned, often swapping to another of the men to carry for a while.

They had been on the run for what felt like days, though time had lost all meaning in their flight. The realization of their vulnerability now tempered their initial determination. Isolated, outgunned, and outnumbered, they understood the odds were against them. Yet, the alternative—capture or death at the hands of their pursuers—fueled their determination to keep moving, to find some way out of this relentless chase.

The pursuit was not just a physical challenge but a mental one as well. Doubts crept in with each step, each labored breath. Who were these people chasing them, and why? The explosion that had targeted their truck was no random act of violence; it was a message, a clear intent to kill. The reasons behind it, however, remained shrouded in mystery, adding to the fear and urgency of their escape.

As they navigated the rugged landscape, the bond between Jake, Mike, and Ray was their greatest strength. In the face of adversity, their friendship and mutual trust were unshakeable. Each man relied on the others not just for physical support but also for the courage to continue and to believe in the possibility of escape.

A thud sounded beside them as Mike looked over and saw what looked like a tranquilizer dart; as soon as it stuck in the tree, the dart disappeared.

"What the hell kind of weapon are they using?" Mike shouted as he ducked, and a dart whizzed above him.

He took the rifle and turned to shoot as one of the darts stuck him in the leg.

Ray and Jake stopped briefly. Jake grabbed the rifle, and all of a sudden, Mike screamed in agony and vanished. Only a pile of clothes remained where he had fallen.

Jake's eyes widened as he cocked the rifle, "Ray, we have to get out of here, NOW!" Jake ran in the direction of flowing water with Ray behind him. Darts flew around them as they finally reached a high bank overlooking Snake River. The water was flowing briskly, "This is our chance to lose them." Ray whispered as they hid in the brush. The darts stopped as they hid, so they weren't sure if they were seen.

"Jump!" Jake said as he ran and jumped down the large bank and into the water; Ray was right behind him. Plunging into the icy cold water, Jake swam underneath for as long as he could. As he surfaced, he looked back toward the bank, and he saw what looked like soldiers dressed all in black standing on the bank. Ray popped back up shortly behind him as a dart plinked into the water near Ray. Both men dove underneath the water, intent on staying out of the line of sight of their pursuers.

5

"HELLO?" ALTHEA'S VOICE WAS stern as she answered the desk phone in the Vice President's Office in the Eisenhower Executive Office Building. The building overlooked 17th St NW in Washington, D.C., nestled between the financial sector and the White House.

"They escaped." The voice on the other end said quickly, "We got one, but the other two disappeared in the river."

Althea's eyes curved in disgust, "Then go down the river and get them." Her voice was sharp and unyielding, "We need to punish Jeremiah for getting in the way of our plans." She slammed her phone on the receiver and opened a drawer, retrieving a folder; underneath it was a shiny white mask with a strange seal on the forehead. She looked at it quickly and smiled as she shut her drawer.

Opening the folder, she pulled out documents labeled Top Secret, one mentioning something called The Veil and others detailing plans from The Administration for Children and Families' rebranding. She looked up and saw a man standing in front of her desk: Chuck Gleeson. His suit was nicely pressed, and his thick-rimmed glasses hung on his thin nose.

"Madam Vice President." His posture was firm, and his eyes unwavering as he looked at Althea.

"What do I owe the pleasure of the Director of the Central Intelligence Agency's visit to my office?" Her smile was slight.

"We have to talk about what you have instructed us to do in light of the election not going according to plan." Chuck said as Althea stood quickly and flung her fingers over her lips, "We all have our part to play, so be wary; you remain to play yours." Althea threatened as Chuck bowed his head, "Yes, Madam Vice President."

"I have been studying the plans to bring the Head Start program into our organization," she said, walking out from behind her desk and to the conference table. "Not sure I want to make us that obvious."

"Ma'am, our marketers feel doing so might make it easier to move in our planned direction if the name is something they see and trust. Plus, the children will grow up trusting what we stand for, and it will make it more advantageous to..." Chuck was cut off in mid-sentence as Althea walked up and got into his face.

"I like the spunk, the desire to earn their trust. Let's commence with the plan." She turned and walked back to her desk. "If the United States is to survive, our next moves will be crucial."

"Speaking of which, I have our first commercial that we will roll out to the country." Chuck smiled, holding up a disk, and Althea sat back at her desk. She pressed a button, and a screen slid out of the ceiling.

Chuck slid the disk into the player, and the commercial started with a five-countdown with the test pattern. The speakers beeped as the countdown continued.

The screen fades in from black to a warm, glowing scene of a cozy living room decked out in holiday cheer. A sparkling Christmas tree stands in the corner, its lights twinkling merrily, and stockings hang from the mantle. Soft instrumental holiday music plays in the background, setting a tone of comfort and joy.

A cheerful, soothing voice begins to narrate, "This holiday season, as we cherish the warmth of family and the joy of togetherness, an exciting transformation is on the horizon for our nation's children and families."

The scene transitions to a bright, lively childcare center where children of various ages are engaging in festive activities: crafting handmade ornaments, singing carols, and laughing together. The decor is vibrant and welcoming, with drawings and educational toys visible, showcasing a nurturing and learning-focused environment.

The narrator continues, "The Head Start Program and The Administration for Children and Families are proud to announce a wonderful new beginning. We're coming together under a new banner, Consortium Child Care Centers, to bring all childcare facilities and public schools into one unified family."

Cut to a montage of various Consortium Child Care Centers across America being constructed: from bustling cities to serene rural areas. Computer imaging shows each center buzzing with activity and brimming with the spirit of community. Teachers and caregivers are seen interacting with children in classrooms, outdoor playgrounds, and during mealtimes, highlighting the comprehensive care and educational opportunities provided.

"With the spirit of the season guiding us, Consortium Child Care Centers of America is committed to nurturing every child's potential, ensuring that our future shines as brightly as the stars above. Together, we're creating a tapestry of support, education, and love, woven with the threads of community, dedication, and innovation."

The commercial shows a diverse group of children placing a star atop the Christmas tree in one of the centers, symbolizing unity, hope, and a bright future. The children's laughter fills the air, blending with the festive music.

"As we look forward to the new year, let's celebrate the gift of growth and the promise of a brighter tomorrow for our children. Consortium Child Care Centers of America is not

just a name; it's our commitment to a future where every child thrives, supported by a community that believes in their limitless potential."

The scene gently fades to the Consortium Child Care Centers logo, which is adorned with a bit of holiday flair—a wreath encircling it and the tagline "Nurturing Tomorrow's Brightest Stars."

The narrator concludes, "Join us in welcoming this new era of childcare and education. Consortium Child Care Centers of America—where every child is a star, and the future is bright with possibilities." The commercial ends on a high note with the logo sparkling like a star, and the screen fades to black.

The screen slowly rolled back into the ceiling as Chuck turned back to Althea, "thoughts?"

"I love it," she smiled widely, "I love it a lot."

"I'll roll it out to our Project Mockingbird partners, and it will be on the air starting on December 1st." Director Chuck Gleeson said, grabbing the disc out of the player and turning to walk towards the door. Althea walked to the window in her office.

"Remember, Chuck, the other project that was assigned to you needs to be done for the United States to heal." She spoke coldly, looking out of her window and towards the White House.

"Yes, madam." Chuck paused and then quickly left the room, closing the door behind himself.

Arthur Hastings paced in the residential wing of the White House; his wife, Dr. Gillian Hastings, sipped coffee while watching Arthur pace.

"Honey, I know you are anxious, but you are going to give yourself a stroke with all of that stress. Please sit down." Gillian said, continuing to sip on her coffee.

"Gillian, I have been in this political life since I was in my 30s, and now I feel like a damn puppet in my own Presidential administration. I finally became President at the cost of my soul." Arthur's words filled with disdain and frustration as he continued to pace.

"You knew the cost when you announced your candidacy. I warned you, but you wanted the Presidency to be the capstone of your legacy." Gillian said, leaning back in her seat, "You should have retired and let go of this life. You are 80 years old, for god's sake."

Arthur stopped and looked at his wife of thirty years, a curt smile crossing his thin and wrinkled lips, "I know, and I knew I would only get one term. I feel like I signed a deal with the devil."

"Althea and her people aren't the devil; they are just ambitious." Gillian laughed a little as she sipped on her coffee again.

"I wish you knew what I do, Gillian. They want to break the United States apart in order to gain more power. I did what they wanted, thinking I could distract them and postpone what they were doing. Little did I know they have been at this for much of the 20th century and almost a quarter into this one. Now we are being invaded by an unknown enemy in my administration, and I am powerless to stop them." Arthur's face creased in concern. In public, he pretended not to know what was going on, feigning dementia, but in private, he was very much aware of what was happening.

He was an old man who had run for the Presidency six times in his career. In his seventh run, Althea approached him to guarantee him the Presidency. Arthur knew better than most of the games in Washington, D.C., but he knew his dream had always been to occupy that office.

In the quiet of the residential wing, the distance between Arthur and Gillian seemed to expand, filled with the unsaid and the undone. Arthur resumed his pacing, each step slower, more deliberate than the last, as if he were measuring the time he had left—both in office and on this earth.

Gillian set her coffee down, her eyes following her husband. The man who had once stood before crowds, charismatic and commanding, now seemed diminished, his energy sapped by battles both public and private. "Arthur," she began, her voice softer now, "is there truly no way to turn this tide? Is there no action that can be taken?"

Arthur stopped and faced the window, looking out over the grounds that were a symbol of the nation's enduring strength—a strength he feared was waning. "I've considered every possible avenue, exhausted every potential ally. But the political machine I once mastered now moves of its own accord, driven by those who share neither my vision nor my concern for the republic." Arthur looked at his wife, tears filling his eyes, "even my attempt to warn Troy Thomason was cut short. The swamp is ever deepening, and he is about to step into a situation that will consume everything there is about himself."

The silence that followed was heavy, filled with the weight of a lifetime of service that was ending in uncertainty and fear for the future. "This nation is on the precipice," Arthur continued, his voice barely above a whisper. "A whisper on the horizon is not just a threat but an inevitability if we continue down this path. My Presidency, it seems, will be remembered not for its achievements but for its proximity to our country's unwinding."

Gillian rose, crossing the room to stand beside her husband. Her hand found his, a gesture of solidarity in the face of their shared despair. "We've weathered storms before, Arthur. Perhaps it's time to rally those who still believe in the Union, those who can see beyond ambition and greed."

Arthur turned to look at his wife, and her resolve a flicker of light in the gathering darkness. "Perhaps you're right," he conceded. "But I am 80, and I only have two months left in office; the challenge is monumental. Our adversaries are not just within our borders but within the very halls of power. Mobilizing a fractured populace, disillusioned and wary of more promises, more politics... It's a Herculean task that will consume me."

Yet, as they stood together, something akin to determination began to stir within Arthur. The thought of capitulating to the forces seeking to dismantle the country he loved was anathema to him. "If there is a chance, however slim, to stem this tide, then we must take it," he resolved. "For too long, I've allowed myself to be a puppet, reacting rather than acting. It's time to cut the strings."

Gillian squeezed his hand, her presence a reminder of the strength they had always drawn from each other. "Then let's begin," she said. "Together."

She turned and nodded to the Secret Service agent who had just walked into the room. Slowly, she turned back to her aged husband and kissed him on the cheek.

The Secret Service Agent left the room and closed the door silently behind himself.

Outside of the room, the agent lifted his phone, Althea's voice on the other line.

"Madam, it's clear that it is time to 25th Amendment President Hastings. He is going to make it very difficult to make the moves we are making." The agent said quietly into his phone.

"Agreed. I will meet with the Cabinet."

"Yes, ma'am."

"Great job, Agent Williams. We will reward you handsomely in the New Dawn." Althea said as the line disconnected. Agent Williams smiled as he stood rigidly guarding the door leading into the residential wing of the White House. A smile crossed his lips as he rocked on his heels.

Samantha crossed the barracks at Twentynine Palms, heading toward the office of her commanding officer. Nervously, she fidgeted with a lighter in her hand as she walked. She didn't smoke, but ever since she was a little girl, she kept a lighter to tinker with because she saw her father using the little torches often to light his cigars. She arrived at the door, took a deep breath, removed her cover, and stepped inside. A young man sitting at a desk quickly jumped to his feet and saluted, "First Lieutenant Johnson."

"At ease, Corporal Smith." She saluted back with a firm hand on her brow.

"The Colonel will see you now, ma'am." Corporal Alexander Smith said as he slowly returned to what he had been doing. Samantha walked down the hallway and up a flight of stairs to get to Colonel Zebulon Martinez's office. The door was closed, so she knocked lightly on it.

"Come in," the voice accompanied her knock as she slowly opened the door. Colonel Zebulon Martinez was a broad-shouldered man, tall and muscular. His dark hair was cut in the traditional high and tight buzz. Samantha stepped into the office, shut the door behind her, and saluted, "Colonel Martinez!"

Mirroring her salute, he returned to his usual posture, and his face changed into an uneasy smile, "Samantha, welcome back. I wanted to talk to you about this liaison thing because I just got off the phone with my daughter, who is stationed at Fairchild AFB."

Samantha's eyes took on a look of concern, "I am sorry, I had no idea."

"How would you know?" He asked as he picked up his iPhone and pulled up her Air Force Portrait on his phone, "I didn't want her in this life. I wanted her to be a lawyer or a doctor, but she chose the Air Force of all branches." He chuckled a little as an acknowledgment that the Air Force was the butt of every military branch joke, only recently replaced by the Space Force.

"She said they willingly aligned with the Montana-Idaho Militia and that they weren't betraying the Constitution but upholding their oath to defend the United States against foreign enemies. Samantha, reassure me that is the case." He sighed, putting his phone face down on the desk.

"Sir, I talked to my father on my way back to base, and he responded when I said that I wasn't a traitor, 'Neither are we, honey. We are Americans doing something about the invasion where our government refuses to do so.' I love my father, and I believe he has the best intentions in this situation, even if I don't particularly agree with the actions taken." Samantha nodded as she recounted her conversation with her father, her face revealing the exasperation of the moment, "the way the news makes it sound it was like the Montana-Idaho Militia muscled their way into Fairchild and that some battle took place. Nothing of the sort happened. My father would not have ordered an attack on our own people."

Zeb leaned forward, "are you sure about that?"

"Yes, sir, I am sure. If we would have attacked him, then I am sure he would have, but fortunately, it was a peaceful meeting, and I feel like a lot came out of it." Samantha said, quickly responding to the question.

"I am worried about my daughter most of all, but these events have me worried about our country. We are being invaded by what appears to be an organization made up of Russia, China, and Greater Korea. Most of our defensive capabilities have been sent overseas, and our President is inept." He stopped talking quickly, "I am sorry, that is not proper for an Officer in the United States Marine Corps to make judgments about our Commander in Chief."

"Sir, you can speak plainly to me. My father is a Republican Governor, so I hear it all the time." Samantha smiled.

Zebulon Martinez leaned back in his chair, the lines of concern etching deeper into his face. "Thank you, Samantha. Your reassurance brings some comfort, but these are unprecedented times. The very fabric of our nation seems to be unraveling, and it's hard to see where we'll end up."

Samantha nodded, her expression solemn. "I understand, sir. It's a confusing time for all of us. My father believes that the actions of the Montana-Idaho Militia are a necessary response to the current crisis. He's convinced that if the states don't stand up now, we might not have a country left to defend."

The room fell silent for a moment as both pondered the peril of the situation. Zeb broke the silence, his voice firm yet filled with an underlying worry. "I took an oath to defend this country against all enemies, foreign and domestic. It's an oath that I take seriously. Yet now I find myself questioning what that means in a world where the lines between friend and foe are blurred."

Samantha shifted slightly, her own convictions challenged by the complexity of the situation. "Sir, my loyalty to the Corps and this country is unwavering. But I also believe in my father's vision for a united defense against external threats. It's a delicate balance, trying to serve both."

Zeb nodded, understanding the delicate position Samantha was in. "Samantha, I trust your judgment. You know your father, Governor Johnson, and you believe he's a man of principle. If he's involved, he must think it's for the right reasons. But we must remain vigilant. Even the best principles can be twisted, and good intentions can lead to unintended consequences."

He stood up, signaling the end of their discussion. "I trust you, Samantha. Keep me informed about any developments with the militia in their defense of the Pacific Northwest. And about your father... be careful. These are turbulent waters we're navigating."

Samantha stood as well, a renewed sense of purpose strengthening her resolve. "Thank you, sir. I will. And I'll do everything in my power to ensure that his actions are in the best interest of the country."

As Samantha exited Colonel Martinez's office, the concern of their conversation weighed heavily on her. The corridors of the barracks, usually a place of routine and order, now seemed to echo with the uncertainty of the times. Her thoughts were a tumult of duty, loyalty, and the fear of what might come if the situation continued to escalate.

Colonel Martinez, meanwhile, turned his attention to an upcoming meeting that could potentially alter the course of their involvement in the unfolding crisis. Major General Kris Justice, a figure known for both his strategic acumen and his unwavering commitment to the nation, had agreed to a discussion about possible Marine assistance with the Montana-Idaho Militia. This meeting was not just a matter of military protocol; it was a delicate negotiation of allegiance, strategy, and the interpretation of their oath to defend the United States against all enemies.

The very idea of the United States Marine Corps collaborating with a militia was laden with legal and ethical complexities. Yet, in the face of an invasion by a coalition of foreign powers, the traditional lines of defense and allegiance were being challenged. Zebulon understood the necessity of adapting to the situation at hand, but he also recognized the risks involved. The potential for misinterpretation, the threat of escalating the conflict, and the implications for civil-military relations were all factors that needed careful consideration.

The meeting with Major General Justice was not just about seeking approval or support for the militia's actions; it was about ensuring that any involvement was strategic, measured, and, above all, in the best interest of the United States. Zebulon knew that the decisions made in the coming days would be scrutinized by history. The balance between acting decisively and overstepping their mandate was a fine one, and the consequences of getting it wrong were monumental.

As he prepared for the meeting, Zebulon reviewed the latest intelligence reports, the known capabilities of the invading forces, and the current state of U.S. military deployments. The traditional advantage of superior technology and firepower was mitigated by the fact that much of the U.S. military's strength was already committed to engagements overseas. The home front was vulnerable, and the Montana-Idaho Militia, with its knowledge of the local terrain and its commitment to defending the Pacific Northwest, represented a significant force multiplier.

Yet, the question remained: Could they ensure the militia's actions remained defensive, aimed solely at repelling the invasion? And how would they navigate the legal and ethical minefield of cooperating with a civilian and state-sanctioned militia?

As Zebulon Martinez pondered these questions, he was acutely aware of the weight of responsibility on his shoulders. The safety of the nation and the principles it stood for were at stake. The meeting with Major General Kris Justice was not just a discussion; it was a pivotal moment that could define the path forward in defending the United States against one of the greatest threats it had ever faced.

A few hours later, the dimly lit office of Colonel Zebulon Martinez buzzed with the tension of anticipation. The glow from his computer screen illuminated his focused expression as he initiated a secure video conference. Moments later, the screen flickered to life, revealing Major General Kris Justice, his face set in a stern visage that matched the acuteness of their conversation.

"Major General Justice," Zebulon began, nodding in respect. "Thank you for taking the time."

"Colonel Martinez," Kris acknowledged, his tone equally formal. "Let's get to the heart of the matter."

Zebulon wasted no time. "Sir, as you're aware, the situation in the Pacific Northwest is deteriorating rapidly. The Montana-Idaho Militia, under the command of Governor Johnson, has effectively taken a stand against the invading forces. Their request for our support is urgent."

Kris leaned forward, his eyes narrowing. "Zeb, you know as well as I do that without direct orders from the President, any military intervention on our part would be in violation of federal law. Engaging in an unauthorized operation, no matter the justification opens up Pandora's box of legal and civil ramifications."

The tension between the two men was palpable, a reflection of the broader conflict that threatened to engulf the nation. "I understand the legal constraints," Zebulon replied, his voice strained with frustration. "But are we to stand by while our country is invaded? Our oath is to protect the United States against all enemies, foreign and domestic."

Kris's expression softened slightly, the weight of their shared duty evident in his gaze. "Believe me, Zeb, I share your commitment. But we must consider the consequences. Any action we take without clear authorization could be construed as insubordination, or worse, treason."

The word hung heavy in the air, a reminder of the stakes involved. Zebulon felt the burden of the moment, the knowledge that their decisions could alter the course of history. "So, we're to wait for an order that may never come? What of our duty to the American people?"

Kris sighed; the lines of his face etched with the toll of command. "Our duty is to uphold the Constitution, Zeb. To act without the President's directive is to step onto a slippery slope. We risk not just our careers but the very principles we've sworn to defend."

The conversation veered into a tense silence, each man wrestling with the enormity of the crisis at hand. It was Zebulon who broke the silence, his voice carrying a hint of resolve. "What if there's another way? A means to support the militia indirectly, without overt military engagement?"

Kris's interest was piqued, and his strategic mind was already considering the possibilities. "Go on."

"We could provide intelligence, surveillance, logistical support... actions that fall within a gray area, offering aid without direct combat involvement. It's a fine line, but perhaps our best option under the circumstances."

The suggestion sparked a flicker of hope between them, a potential path forward that navigated the narrow space between duty and defiance. Kris nodded slowly, the gears turning. "It's a risky strategy, Zeb. But these are desperate times. I'll need to pull in legal counsel to assess the viability."

Zebulon understood Kris' commitment and the risk they were both willing to take for the sake of their country. "Thank you, sir. I believe it's our best chance to make a difference without crossing that line."

As the conference concluded, both men understood the difficult and morally ambiguous path that lay ahead. Yet, in the face of an unprecedented threat, they were prepared to navigate the shadowy margins of their duty, driven by a shared resolve to protect the nation they served.

The screen went dark, leaving Zebulon silently contemplating what was to come. The conversation with Major General Kris Justice had set the stage for a covert operation that blurred the lines of legality and loyalty. In the days ahead, their actions would either be vindicated by victory or condemned by defeat. The path forward was a murky and ultimately dangerous one. Zeb looked at his reflection on the monitor screen and then turned to open his curtains again.

He picked up his phone and dialed Samantha. Her voicemail picked up, and Zeb began speaking, "Samantha, I am trying to figure out a way to get the Marines into the fight as well; let your father know that there are quite a few on his side."

6

EXHAUSTED, RAY GRIZZLY CLAW did everything he could to keep his head above water; he could see Jake's head absently bobbing up and down in the rapids at a distance in front of him. His lungs burned, and his skin was ice-cold from the water. He tried shouting, but no sound escaped from his mouth.

Dammit, Ray. Get it together. Jake looks dead, and you are doing nothing.

Ray's thoughts swirled as he worked up the strength to try and swim towards Jake. He started stroking his arms and kicking. His hiking boots were adding extra weight, so he reached down and untied them, freeing his feet.

He kicked his feet and pushed himself closer to his friend Jake; as he got closer, he could see that Jake's face was turning blue. He grabbed his arm and began pulling him to the shore. Not sure how far they had gone and whether their pursuers would find them, he trudged through the rapids until his feet touched the ground. Using the newfound leverage, he pulled harder until he finally got Jake on the shore.

Ray Grizzly Claw's muscles screamed in protest as he hauled Jake's limp body across the shore and through the underbrush, seeking the scant cover it provided. The cold had seeped deep into his bones, but the urgency of the situation left no room for self-pity. He laid Jake down, checking quickly for any signs of life—a pulse, a breath, anything.

Finding Jake's condition more dire than he'd hoped, Ray's training kicked in. He positioned Jake carefully on his back, tilted his head to clear the airway, and started the CPR process he'd learned but never thought he'd use in such a critical situation. With each compression, Ray fought against the panic rising within him, focusing all his energy on the task at hand.

"Come on, Jake. Don't do this to me," Ray muttered between breaths, his voice a mix of determination and fear. The forest around them was eerily silent, the rapids' roar a constant reminder of the ordeal they'd just survived. Ray's hands worked methodically, pressing down on Jake's chest, then delivering rescue breaths with a precision born of desperation.

Minutes passed, each one stretching into eternity. Ray's arms began to tremble from the exertion, his breath fogging in the cold air. And then, miraculously, Jake coughed—a violent, sputtering sound that was the most beautiful noise Ray had ever heard. He rolled Jake onto his side, helping him expel the water he'd swallowed.

Jake's breathing was ragged, his eyes fluttering open to meet Ray's relieved gaze. "Ray?" he croaked, confusion and pain mingling in his voice.

"Yeah, it's me. You scared the hell out of me, man," Ray responded, his voice thick with emotion. He quickly checked Jake for injuries, noting a few cuts and bruises but nothing immediately life-threatening.

They were both soaked, cold, and vulnerable but alive. Ray knew they needed to get moving, to find shelter and warmth before hypothermia set in or their pursuers caught up to them. But for a brief moment, relief washed over him. They had survived the river, and for now, that was enough.

Ray helped Jake to sit up, supporting his weight. "We need to get moving, find someplace to hunker down for the night. Can you walk?"

Jake nodded weakly; the ordeal had drained much of his strength. "I think so. Thanks to you."

"Don't mention it. We're in this together," Ray said, offering Jake a small, reassuring smile. Together, they rose to their feet, Ray's arm around Jake for support.

The forest loomed large around them, its depths holding both danger and the possibility of refuge. With cautious steps, they began to make their way through the dense foliage, each supporting the other as best they could.

Ray looked around, not knowing where they were, but it was obvious they were outside of the grasp of civilization. They pushed deeper into the woods, cautiously listening to any noise around them. Continuing to walk, Jake pointed at what looked like a little hunting cabin.

It was common in the wilderness of Idaho and Montana to build little hunting cabins with sustenance and supplies in case someone was lost in the woods. Jake pushed in that direction with Ray. It was quiet like no one had been there in a while. They walked up to the little porch, where there were a couple of rocking chairs. Ray checked the doorknob, and it opened with ease. Inside were a couple of cots hanging against the wall, a little wood stove, and some blankets.

"We have to get out of these wet clothes so they can dry," Ray said, noticing what looked like a retractable clothesline on the wall. He pulled it out, hooked it to the other side, and removed his jeans and shirt, and Jake did as well. They hung their clothes on the line, and Ray stepped out onto the porch to grab some firewood.

He slid the firewood into the stove and began work with the pile of kindling and matches he found. Finally, the spark began to spread, and the fire started burning. It didn't take long for the heat to radiate and fill the small room.

As the warmth from the fire began to seep into their chilled bones, Jake and Ray settled into the two cots they found, the comfort of the cabin providing a welcome relief from the cold, wet river they had escaped. The silence between them was palpable. Each man was lost in his own thoughts until Jake broke the quiet.

"Mike... he just vanished," Jake said, his voice barely above a whisper as if speaking louder might make the reality of the situation harsher. "One moment he was with us, and then, after that dart hit him... it's like he disappeared into thin air."

Ray turned his gaze toward Jake, his expression filled with sorrow. The disbelief from the situation colored his words, "I saw it too. One second, he was shooting at our pursuers, trying to keep pace, and then... nothing. The scream he let out..." Ray stopped and took a deep breath, "No trace of him." The confusion and guilt were evident in Ray's voice. "In the blink of an eye, he just disappeared. We didn't even have time to grab the clothes that were left behind..."

Jake nodded, sharing in the torment. "Why were they after us? Why shoot at us with those darts? They blew up my truck, and we escaped, only to be shot at by darts. And how did they make him vanish like that?" The questions hung in the air, unanswered and ominous.

The mention of their pursuers reignited a spark of fear in both men. "Who are they, Ray? And what do they want with us?" Jake's gaze was fixed on the flickering flames, seeking answers in their dance.

Ray leaned back, staring at the ceiling of the cabin as he pondered Jake's questions. "I don't know, Jake. But it's clear they're not just some random group. That dart... it's military-grade tech, or I'm a fool. And their tactics, the way they moved through the woods... they're trained."

The realization that they were up against a formidable and mysterious enemy weighed heavily on them. "We're in deeper than we thought, aren't we?" Jake's question was rhetorical, the answer all too apparent.

"Yeah, we are," Ray confirmed, his tone grim. "But right now, we need to focus on staying alive and finding Mike, if we can. We can't let what happened tonight break us. We've got to be smart, lay low, and figure out our next move."

The conversation drifted into a planning session, both men pooling their knowledge of survival and evasion tactics. Despite the dire circumstances, the fire's warmth and the safety of the cabin lent them a temporary sense of security, allowing them to rest and recuperate.

As the night deepened and the fire burned down to embers, Jake and Ray knew that dawn would bring another day of running. But for now, they covered up with the sleeping bags they had found. Jake yawned and drifted to sleep. Ray finished dipping the beans he was eating from the can and then laid back as well.

He stared at the ceiling for a moment, the dancing light of the embers bouncing on the raw plywood ceiling. He closed his eyes and fell asleep as well in the comfort of the little hunting cabin in the woods.

Sergeant Nick Moss sat in his truck in front of a quaint little house in the small town of Weiser, Idaho. Exasperated, he placed his hands over his face as he let out tears of shame. He found the young Idaho State Guardsman's family to deliver the bad news after he had dropped the body off by the local morgue.

What has our country come to that we are being invaded, and this sixteen-year-old kid has to worry about his home? Now, he is dead as a result of my ineptitude!

Nick turned his key as he looked over at the mother and father standing on their porch, crying at the loss of their son. He lifted his hand and waved as he began driving down the road and out of the little subdivision. His journey back to Spokane would be a long drive, but he knew the advancing forces of the Confederation were expanding into the northern part of the state.

I need to breathe; I think I am going to drive the scenic route.

He thought to himself as he sped down the highway and turned off the exit to cross the Snake River into Oregon.

He turned his radio on as a breaking news report music began playing.

The anchor of the news desk began speaking in measured tones, "Good evening, listeners; we interrupt our regular programming to bring you this breaking news update. I'm Alex Reed, bringing you the latest developments from the northern border. In an unprecedented turn of events, the Montana-Idaho Militia, a state and civilian defense force, has made significant advances into Washington state. Reports coming in confirm that several military bases have decided to align with the militia in what's being described as a campaign to defend the northern border against what they are calling 'the invasion of the Confederation.'"

Nick turned the radio up and heard the sound of papers being shuffled around on the desk.

Alex Reed continued his report, "To provide some context, the Montana-Idaho Militia, initially formed as a defense group made up from several states spanning from Idaho all the way to Missouri, has rapidly grown in numbers and capabilities over the past few weeks. Their stated goal is to protect American soil against any and all threats, with a particular focus on what they perceive as an encroaching force from the north. This alignment with several key military bases marks a significant escalation in their operations and signals growing support within some sections of the armed forces."

Nick Moss smiled, knowing that this may be the weapon they needed to counter the Confederation's invading forces.

Alex Reed spoke again after a short pause, "Eyewitnesses near the affected bases report seeing military personnel and militia members conducting joint patrols and manning checkpoints together. This collaboration highlights a complex situation on the ground, with lines between civilian and military defense efforts becoming increasingly blurred." Alex mixed papers on his desk frantically as he started to speak again,

"Critics of the movement express concern over the legality and implications of military bases aligning with a state and civilian militia. However, supporters argue that extraordinary times call for extraordinary measures, praising the bases' personnel for taking a stand in what they believe is a fight for the nation's sovereignty. The federal government has yet to issue a formal response to these latest developments. However, sources within the Pentagon indicate that high-level meetings are underway to address the situation. The alignment of military bases with the Montana-Idaho Militia raises significant questions about command structures, legality, and the potential for further escalation."

Alex hesitated again, his voice overly stressed by the news report.

"As this story continues to unfold, we'll be here to bring you the latest information. Stay with us for updates on this devel-

oping situation. For now, this has been Alex Reed re-porting. We now return you to your regular programming, which is already in progress."

The breaking news jingle sounded, and the sound of Simple Man started playing again. Nick turned down another side road and sped up. Just as the first chords of "Simple Man" began to fill the cab of his truck, Nick's attention was abruptly drawn to the road ahead. Two disheveled men, appearing out of nowhere, ran into the road, waving frantically for him to stop. Instinctively, Nick hit the brakes, the tires screeching against the asphalt as his truck came to a halt mere inches from hitting the men.

Breathing heavily, both men approached the truck. One had features that hinted at a Native American heritage. The other carried the look of someone who had been through a harrowing ordeal, his eyes wide with a mix of fear and relief.

Nick, assessing the situation quickly, lowered his window. "You guys alright? What the hell are you doing running out into the road like that?"

The young white man leaned in, his breath fogging up the window. "Please, we need help. They're after us," he gasped, glancing over his shoulder as if expecting their pursuers to appear at any moment.

Nick's military instincts kicked in. "Get in," he ordered, unlocking the doors. As they clambered into the passenger seat, Nick noticed their soaked clothes and the bruises that marred their skin. It was evident they had been through a significant ordeal.

Once they were safely inside, Nick accelerated away from the scene, putting distance between them and any potential threat. "Mind telling me who you are and who is after you?" he asked, keeping his eyes on the road.

The two men looked at each other before responding. "It's a long story, but I am Jake Johnson, my father is the Governor of Montana, and this is Ray Grizzly Claw. My sister rescued a family after the Neutronium bomb explosion a few weeks ago, and my buddies Mike and Ray went with me to retrieve the body of the woman's husband, who had unfortunately died in the bombing. On our way back to Montana, we were being chased by an SUV that shot some type of explosive at us. We got out of the truck and ran before it exploded. We have been running from a group we couldn't exactly identify. They're well-armed, well-trained, and dangerous."

Nick's grip on the steering wheel tightened as the weight of Jake's story sank in. The Neutronium bomb explosion on Election Day had already rocked the nation, but now, learning about a high-speed chase with armed assailants added a new layer of danger to the situation. It sounded like something out of a thriller novel, but Nick knew it was all too real. After everything he had witnessed in the past month, nothing surprised him anymore. The fear in Jake's eyes and the urgency in Ray's posture confirmed the truth of their ordeal.

"Governor Johnson's son, huh?" Nick murmured, more to himself than to his passengers. The implications of what that meant—a direct attack on the family of a state governor—especially the one at the heart of this new militia were chilling. "And you said they shot something at your truck? An explosive?"

Jake nodded, his face pale. "Yeah, and that's not even half of it. Our friend Mike was hit by a dart by these guys, and he just disappeared. Vanished right in front of us."

Ray leaned forward, his voice low. "We jumped into the Snake River to escape. Spent hours in the water before we found a cabin to hide out and rest. We've been trying to make our way to safety ever since."

Nick was silent for a moment, processing their story. His years in the service had taught him that the world was full of unexpected dangers, but with the invasion to the north and everything else happening, he was growing numb to everything. "Well, you're safe for now," he finally said, casting a glance at his rugged companions. "I'm heading to Spokane, but I can take a detour to get you to a safer place. We'll figure out what to do once we're there."

The mention of Spokane seemed to reignite a spark of hope in Jake and Ray's eyes. "Thank you," Jake said, his voice laced with a mixture of relief and lingering fear. "We just want to get somewhere we can catch our breath and plan our next move. Maybe get in touch with my dad."

As they continued down the winding road, the landscape shifting from forest to farmland around them, Nick couldn't help but feel a growing sense of responsibility for the two young men in his truck. Their unexpected encounter had thrust him into a situation far larger and more complex than he could have imagined. Still, he couldn't turn his back on them—not when they were clearly in dire need of help.

The radio, now turned low, played softly in the background, contrasting the tension within the truck. Nick's mind raced with questions about the attackers, the mysterious disappearance of their friend, and what it all meant for the broader conflict unfolding across the state. But for now, his focus was on getting Jake and Ray to safety, away from the immediate danger that pursued them.

As the miles passed, the three men sat in silence, each lost in their thoughts about the ordeal behind them and the uncertain road ahead. Nick's truck became a temporary sanctuary, a moving bastion against the chaos of the outside world. But as they neared their destination, the realization that this was only the beginning of a much larger battle loomed large in their minds.

7

SEVERAL WEEKS HAD ELAPSED since Troy Thomason's victory in the election was declared, marking a pivotal moment in his journey to the presidency. It was during that time that his unexpected eye-opening conversation with President Arthur Hastings was terminated abruptly, ending with the phrase "They happened" hanging ominously in the air.

Now, Troy found himself seated in the office aboard his campaign airplane, a space that had become a temporary hub for his transition activities. Several members of the Raleigh, NC press had successfully petitioned to accompany the President-elect on his journey to Washington, D.C. Their aim was to provide detailed coverage of the transition process for the local news outlets, capturing every significant development and insight for their audience back home.

Troy Thomason was the first North Carolina-born person to be elected President since 1865. The irony wasn't lost on him, as the last President from North Carolina, Andrew Johnson, had been a Senator for Tennessee and was Abraham Lincoln's Vice President during the Civil

War. He had been the President during the tumultuous time of Reconstruction.

"There was an old proverb that said, 'History never repeats, but it certainly rhymes for those who don't know history.'" Troy sat back in his seat and looked at his press secretary, Amyleigh Hastings, who was seated nearby; she smiled nervously while looking at Troy.

"I know things are bad, but I don't know if they are that bad." Amyleigh said in her usual cheery voice, "I mean, do you really think that America will turn on herself again?"

"That's what President Hastings said, that we are on the verge of another Civil War and that he feels helpless." Troy recounted that odd conversation with Arthur Hastings, 'they happened...'. "Amyleigh, I just want to know what he meant by that. I am six weeks away from taking my oath, and I don't know who 'they' are..."

Troy's gaze drifted to the window, watching the clouds roll by as he contemplated the weight of his predecessor's cryptic warning. The plane hummed steadily, bridging the physical distance to Washington, D.C., but the distance between understanding and confusion felt insurmountable.

Amyleigh Hastings, no relation to the outgoing President, leaned forward, her expression a blend of concern and determination. "We'll figure it out, Mr. President-elect. You're not alone in this. The transition team in D.C. has been working tirelessly. We have meetings lined up with key figures, briefings, and a comprehensive review of all ongoing federal operations. Whatever or whoever 'they' are, we'll uncover it."

Troy nodded, taking solace in Amyleigh's words and the knowledge that a team was mobilizing around him, ready to tackle the challenges ahead. "You're right, Amyleigh. We've overcome every obstacle so far. This will be no different." He paused, his thoughts momentarily veering to the broader implications of his presidency. "America turning on herself... I can't allow that to happen. Not on my watch."

A bell sounded, and the pilot came over the intercom, "Hello, everyone; we are about to make our final descent into Ronald Reagan Washington National Airport. Please make sure you are seated with seatbelts on and seats in an upright position. You all know the drill. The high today will be a brisk 47 degrees." The bell dinged again as the airplane leveled off.

Troy looked out of his window again and saw the skyline of Washington, D.C., coming into view—the reality finally setting in that he was elected President. The transition period was crucial, a time to lay the groundwork for his administration's policies and strategies. Yet, amidst the logistical and procedural preparations, Troy knew that uncovering the meaning behind President Hastings's ominous words was paramount. Troy turned to his laptop again and filtered through the news stories. He looked at Amyleigh again, "I want a meeting with the governors of the Great Plains states as soon as we land. I want to learn about the Montana-Idaho Militia and talk with the various governors who are instrumental in setting up its charter." Amyleigh Hastings nodded, her fingers already dancing over her tablet to arrange the necessary meetings. "I'll get on it immediately. It's a big group, and their collective decision to form the militia is a significant development. Understanding their perspectives will be crucial."

The plane's descent sharpened, the capital's landmarks becoming clearer with each passing moment. Troy felt a mix of anticipation and responsibility. The transition from campaigning to governing was always complex, but the layers of urgency and mystery added a unique intensity to his imminent presidency.

"Also, arrange for briefings with the Department of Defense and Homeland Security," Troy continued, his mind racing through the potential implications of a civilian militia operating with the blessing of state governments. "I need to understand the federal government's current stance on this militia and any potential threats they're facing."

Amyleigh made notes, her demeanor professional and focused. "Consider it done. We'll have a detailed schedule ready for you by the time we land. The next few days are going to be packed, but we'll ensure you have all the information and support you need."

As the plane touched down, the reality of the moment hit Troy with full force. He was about to step into a role that would test him in ways he couldn't yet fully comprehend. The issues facing the country were deep and wide-ranging, from internal divisions to external threats. The cryptic warning from President Hastings and the formation of the Montana-Idaho Militia hinted at complexities that would require all of his resolve, wisdom, and leadership skills to navigate.

The cabin door opened, and Troy Thomason stepped out into the brisk Washington air, the press cameras immediately focusing on him.

Cameras clicked furiously as Troy stepped off the plane. He waved courteously to the members of the press, and they started shouting questions as his Secret Service detail pushed and pulled him towards the waiting SUV and entourage of vehicles.

The Secret Service quickly shut the door behind Troy and Amyleigh as they climbed into the SUV. The press pool outside moved closer, surrounding the vehicle, and pictures of the president-elect and his staff were taken. Reporters were still shouting questions about his commitments to end the wars in the various countries the United States had been involved with over the last four years.

"Mr. Thomason, the Raleigh press is requesting to follow the convoy to the transition office." The driver spoke over the intercom.

"Yes, they are permitted to follow; as for the rest, no. I promised the press from home they would get the exclusives on the transition of power." Troy smiled and leaned back while looking over to Amyleigh, who was sitting beside him.

"I wish my wife could be here and see this day," his smile turning forlorn and sad as he looked back towards the front. His wife had been killed in the explosion of the Neutronium bomb when she was campaigning at an election day breakfast in her home city of San Jose, California.

"Julie would be proud of you, Troy; I know that no amount of condolences can make up for the tragic loss of your beloved wife. But let us lead America into a greater American Century than ever before," Amyleigh said while trying to turn the topic of conversation back to the purpose of why they were here.

Troy nodded, the mention of Julie bringing a surge of emotions. Her absence was a void that couldn't be filled, yet her memory fueled his determination to make a meaningful change. "You're right, Amyleigh. Julie believed in a better future for America, and it's up to us to realize that vision."

As the SUV joined the convoy, weaving through the streets of Washington, D.C., Troy found his thoughts drifting to the challenges ahead. The formation of the Montana-Idaho Militia, the mysterious warning from President Hastings, and the divided state of the nation formed a complex puzzle that he was now responsible for solving.

When they arrived, the transition office was a hive of activity. Staff members, advisors, and security personnel moved with a sense of urgency that matched the significance of the moment. Troy was quickly ushered into a secure briefing room, where his immediate schedule, including the meetings with the governors and federal agencies, was laid out for him.

Over the next several days, Troy will be immersed in briefings, discussions, and strategy sessions. The first on his agenda was a meeting with the governors that made up the states supporting the Montana-Idaho Militia; he sat in his situation room mock-up in the office. A large screen at the front and center of the room lit up, showing the Presidential Seal. Quickly replaced by a room filled with the governors of the Great Plains region of the United States. Troy had met them all during his campaign and knew them all to be reasonable men and women, but his concern was palpable.

Jeremiah Johnson was the first to speak, "Congratulations Mr. President-elect. I know we are excited to see a man of great character and resolve to fill the office of the President. We are also sending our condolences for the loss of Julie in the attack on our West Coast."

Troy nodded, acknowledging Governor Johnson's condolences with a somber expression. "Thank you, Governor Johnson. Julie's memory drives me to ensure our nation is safe and united. That's why we're here today. I need to understand the motivations behind the formation of the Montana-Idaho Militia and how we can work together to address the threats facing our nation."

The governors shared their perspectives one by one, highlighting the challenges their states faced—economic hardships exacerbated by the ongoing conflicts, a perceived lack of federal support in critical areas, and the direct threat posed by the Confederation's advances. They spoke of the militia not as a separatist movement but as a necessary measure to protect their citizen's and states' sovereignty in unprecedented times.

Governor Davison Carey of Wyoming emphasized the strategic importance of their collective defense initiative. "We're not looking to secede or challenge the federal government's authority. This is about safeguarding our people and ensuring the continuity of our way of life."

Governor Emma Larson of Minnesota added, "The militia represents a united front against external aggression. It's a demonstration of our commitment to our states and to the nation. We hope to collaborate with your administration to address the broader security challenges we face."

Troy listened intently, understanding the depth of the crisis that had led these states to take such drastic measures. It was clear that the situation required a delicate balance — acknowledging the states' immediate security needs while reinforcing the importance of federal oversight and cooperation to ensure national unity.

"As President, my priority is the safety and welfare of all Americans. I believe in the strength of our union and the resilience of our people," Troy asserted, his voice firm yet open. "I propose forming a task force that includes representatives from your states, the Department of Defense, and Homeland Security. Together, we can develop a coordinated response to the threats we face, ensuring that actions taken by the Montana-Idaho Militia are in harmony with our national security objectives."

The proposal was met with nods of approval from the governors. Jeremiah spoke up as Troy finished his comments, "Sir, I would like for you to consider my daughter for the role of directing this task force. She is a Marine based out of Twentynine Palms and has already started in a role for the Marines as a liaison of sorts. Her name is Samantha Johnson, and her rank is First Lieutenant."

Troy leaned forward, intrigued by Governor Johnson's suggestion. The idea of appointing someone with direct experience in the field and a personal connection to one of the governors could provide valuable insights and bridge the gap between federal and state efforts. "Thank you, Governor Johnson. I appreciate your trust in recommending your daughter for such a crucial role. Her military background and relationship with you could be invaluable. I'll have my team review her qualifications and discuss how she could best contribute to our efforts."

The other governors nodded in agreement, acknowledging the wisdom in selecting someone familiar with the intricacies of the situation. The discussion then shifted towards the logistical and operational aspects of establishing the task force, with each governor expressing their commitment to providing support and resources.

As the meeting progressed, Amyleigh took meticulous notes, aware of the significance of these discussions in shaping Troy's administration's approach to domestic security. He recognized the delicate balance required to maintain national unity while addressing legitimate state concerns and security threats.

After the meeting concluded, Troy reflected on the enormous task ahead. The formation of the task force, potentially led by Samantha Johnson, marked the beginning of a comprehensive strategy to address the challenges posed by the Montana-Idaho Militia and the broader security landscape in light of the Confederation's invasion.

Turning to Amyleigh, Troy shared his thoughts. "This task force could be the key to navigating the complexities of our current situation. We need to ensure it's empowered to act effectively while maintaining transparency and accountability. Samantha Johnson's potential involvement could be a significant asset."

Amyleigh agreed, noting the importance of leveraging Samantha's experience and the symbolic gesture of unity it represented. "I'll coordinate with the Department of Defense and Homeland Security to facilitate her review. It's imperative we move quickly but thoughtfully to address these challenges."

In the days that followed, Troy's administration worked tirelessly to lay the groundwork for the task force. They held meetings with federal agencies, conducted security briefings, and engaged in discussions with legal experts to ensure the initiative's success. However, little could be done until Troy officially took the oath of office.

Troy retired to the secure living quarters set up in the transition office for him. Settling into the chair, he flicked on the television to watch the news. A commercial started playing Christmas music, and children made ornaments. Then, flashing across the screen was a new governmental logo he had never seen before that was wrapped in a wreath. He turned the volume up as the narrator spoke,

"The Head Start Program and The Administration for Children and Families are proud to announce a wonderful new beginning. We're coming together under a new banner, Consortium Child Care Centers, to bring all childcare facilities and public schools into one unified family."

Troy's eyes widened as one of his campaign planks was to remove burdensome bureaucracies and restore local control over childcare and education to the communities.

He picked up his phone and called Amyleigh, "Tell me about Consortium Child Care Centers..." Amyleigh quickly cut off his sentence, "Troy, turn to Complete News Network."

"That leftist nonsense?" Troy responded jokingly, but Amyleigh wasn't laughing.

"Troy, turn to the channel," she said, pointing out that Vice President Althea Morris was in front of the Chief Justice of the Supreme Court. He turned the audio up, and his jaw dropped.

The reporter on the television news network, in a shocked voice, spoke,

In a stunning and unprecedented move, Vice President Althea Morris and members of the Cabinet have invoked the 25th Amendment against President Arthur Hastings, effectively removing him from office just a month before the scheduled inauguration of President-elect Troy Thomason. This shocking development makes Althea Morris the 47th President of the United States, albeit for a brief tenure lasting only a few weeks. This extraordinary decision, announced earlier today, has sent shockwaves through the political landscape, raising numerous questions about its implications for the forthcoming transition of power. With President-elect Thomason's inauguration set for January 20th, 2025, political analysts and the nation alike are left grappling with the ramifications of this abrupt change in leadership. How this will affect the planned inauguration and the final days of the Hastings Administration remains to be seen as the nation watches this historic moment unfold with bated breath.

The camera on the news channel showed Arthur Hastings and his wife, Gillian Hastings, heading towards Marine One for the very last time as they headed home to their state of New Hampshire. Arthur turned and waved to the cameras as Gillian boarded the large helicopter, reporters shouting questions as the reporter showed again on screen.

In an update to the shocking news that has reverberated around the nation, sources close to the White House have

provided further details on the reasons behind the invocation of the 25th Amendment to remove President Arthur Hastings from office. It has been revealed that President Hastings suffered a minor stroke, which has significantly impaired his short-term memory and resulted in increasingly garbled and incoherent speech. Despite these concerning symptoms, which were evident in the weeks leading up to the stroke, medical staff had previously assured the public that the administration and the President were in fine health. However, just three days ago, the situation took a turn for the worse when President Hastings experienced a minor stroke, prompting Vice President Althea Morris and the Cabinet to take decisive action.

Describing the move as a "humanitarian decision," Vice President Morris and members of the Cabinet have emphasized that their primary concern was President Hastings' health and well-being. They stated that removing him from the pressures of office would allow him to focus on recovery at home while also ensuring the stability and continuity of government operations. This dramatic development leaves Althea Morris as the acting President of the United States, a position she will hold until President-elect Troy Thomason's inauguration on January 20th, 2025.

The news has sparked a flurry of reactions across the political spectrum, with many expressing sympathy for President Hastings' health struggles while also questioning the timing and implications of this transition of power. As the nation comes to terms with this unprecedented situation, all eyes are now on the Thomason transition team and how they will navigate the complexities of assuming office under these extraordinary circumstances.

Stay tuned to Complete News Network for this and more breaking news from across your country and the world. I'm David Reynolds, and this is the Complete News Network 24-hour coverage of Decision 24.

As the screen flickered with David Reynolds's breaking news, Troy Thomason sat in stunned silence, absorbing the heft of the report. The room was dimly lit, the only light coming from the television screen, casting shadows across Troy's thoughtful expression. Beside him, his phone lay with the speaker phone turned on, Amyleigh Hastings' voice coming through clearly, mirroring the shock and concern evident in Troy's posture.

"Did you hear that, Troy? This is... unprecedented," Amyleigh's voice broke the silence, her tone filled with a blend of disbelief and urgency.

Troy let out a slow breath, his eyes still fixed on the screen as the news report transitioned to a discussion on the constitutional implications of the move. "I heard it, Amyleigh. This changes everything," he replied, his voice steady but heavy with the weight of the moment.

"There's no playbook for this, Troy. Hastings' health ... I mean, we knew he was struggling, but the 25th Amendment? And just weeks before your inauguration?" Amyleigh's voice was filled with concern, not just for the political implications but for the personal toll on all involved.

Troy picked up the phone, pacing slowly as he spoke. "They said that it's a humanitarian move for Arthur's health. But the timing... It's going to raise a lot of questions. Questions we need to be ready to address."

Amyleigh was quick to respond, her mind already racing through the potential fallout. "We need to issue a statement. Something that shows our support for President Hastings during this difficult time while also reassuring the public about the transition."

Troy nodded to himself, appreciating Amyleigh's swift focus on the path forward. "Agreed. Let's emphasize our commitment to a smooth transition and the well-being of the nation. We can't let this shake the public's confidence, not when we're so close to taking office."

The conversation shifted to strategizing their next steps, discussing potential scenarios and how to navigate the political landscape that had shifted beneath their feet. Troy's leadership qualities shone through as he guided the discussion with a calm resolve, aware of the historic challenges they faced but unwavering in his commitment to uphold the democratic process.

As they concluded the call, Troy's gaze returned to the television, where analysts continued to dissect the day's events. The weight of leadership felt heavier at that moment, and the path ahead was more complex. Yet, amidst the uncertainty, Troy Thomason remained focused on the promise he made to the American people—a promise to lead with integrity, compassion, and an unwavering dedication to the principles that define the nation.

Turning off the television, Troy sat in the quiet room, allowing himself a moment of reflection. The challenges ahead were daunting, but he was not alone. With a team filled with people like Amyleigh by his side and the trust of the American people, he was ready to navigate whatever came next for the sake of the country he was about to lead.

8

SAMANTHA PACED IN HER living quarters, awaiting the outcome of the meeting between Colonel Zebulon Martinez and Brigadier General Kris Justice. It had been a few days since her meeting with Martinez, and she was nervous about the outcome of their meeting. Her mind raced with all sorts of thoughts about what a possible liaison between the Marine Corps and the Montana-Idaho Militia would look like in practice.

She loved her father and knew his intentions were pure, but the others in the military might see his moves as that of a secessionist traitor. She knew this wasn't the case but was worried all the same.

News had reached the base of Arthur Hastings being removed from office and Althea Morris being sworn in as the first female President of the United States; she wasn't sure what that meant, as she tried to stay apolitical even though she came from a politically inclined and active family. She did know something seemed fishy about the timing, but as an active Marine, her opinions had to be kept to herself.

Samantha's phone buzzed, breaking the silence of her quarters and momentarily distracting her from the whirlwind of thoughts. It was a message from Colonel Martinez, asking her to meet him in his office as soon as possible. Her heart skipped a beat.

This was it—the moment of truth.

Her mind swirled as she quickly grabbed her uniform jacket, ensuring she looked as presentable as possible before making her way to Martinez's office.

The base was alive with its usual activity, but Samantha hardly noticed. Her mind was focused on the meeting ahead. As she approached the office, she could feel the weight of the situation settling on her shoulders. This wasn't just about her future or her father's militia; it was about finding a path that could potentially bridge the divide between the military and the militia, ensuring a united front in the face of the nation's challenges.

Colonel Martinez greeted her with a nod as she entered, gesturing for her to take a seat. "Samantha, thank you for coming so quickly," he began, his tone serious but not unkind.

Samantha sat, her posture straight, her expression composed. "Sir, I'm ready to hear about the meeting with Brigadier General Justice."

Martinez leaned back in his chair, folding his hands on the desk. "The meeting was... productive," he started, choosing his words carefully. "General Justice and I discussed at length the situation with the Montana-Idaho Militia and your father's role in it. We also talked about the potential for a liaison between the Marines and the militia."

Samantha listened intently, trying to gauge from Martinez's expression the direction in which this conversation was heading.

"After much discussion, we've come to a decision. The Marine Corps will indeed establish a liaison with the Montana-Idaho Militia. And we want you, First Lieutenant Samantha Johnson, to take on that role."

Samantha's eyes widened slightly at the news. Relief, pride, and a hint of apprehension mingled within her. "Sir, I'm honored... and I understand the significance of this position. I won't let you down."

Martinez nodded, his expression softening. "I know you won't, Samantha. This is a delicate situation, and we need someone who understands both worlds. Your unique position makes you the ideal candidate."

Samantha took a moment to process the information. This role would place her at the forefront of a groundbreaking effort to unify the military's efforts with those of the militia. It was a challenge she never anticipated facing, yet here she was, ready to embrace it.

"As for President Hastings' removal and President Morris' swearing-in," Martinez continued, shifting the conversation, "it's a significant development. We're still assessing the implications, but for now, our focus remains on ensuring national security and preparing for any potential threats. Your role as a liaison will be crucial in navigating the complexities of this new political landscape."

Samantha nodded, her mind already racing with the tasks ahead. "I understand, sir. I'll do everything in my power to serve as an effective bridge between the Marine Corps and the militia."

As Samantha processed the responsibility of her new role, Colonel Martinez continued, his voice carrying a mix of concern and urgency that matched the tumultuous times they were living in. "There's more, Samantha. The situation on the ground is escalating. The Confederation has fully breached our borders, and their forces are pushing forward towards Seattle and Spokane. The Montana-Idaho Militia is doing what they can to hold them back, but they're outmatched and in dire need of more support."

The mention of the Confederation's advance sent a chill down Samantha's spine. Theoretical discussions about coordinating between the Marine Corps and the militia suddenly became immediately pressing. The conflict was no longer a distant possibility; it was unfolding now, directly threatening the nation's safety and security.

Samantha leaned forward, her military training kicking in, overriding the initial shock. "What's our plan, sir? How can we support the militia without official backing from the federal government? And how does this affect our stance with the new administration?"

Martinez sighed intensely, the weight of command evident in his eyes. "It's a delicate situation. Officially, the Marine Corps can't support a militia without direct orders from the top. However, your role as a liaison is now more critical than ever. You'll need to navigate these waters carefully, providing support in ways that align with our legal and ethical obligations."

He paused, looking directly at Samantha. "As for the administration, President Morris' position is still unclear. With the recent change in leadership, there's a lot of uncertainty. But we must proceed with the nation's best interests at heart, regardless of the politics involved."

Samantha nodded, her mind racing with potential strategies and the enormity of the task ahead. "Understood, sir," her smile was uneasy as she looked into the eyes of her commanding officer, "What of my brother? Has there been any news regarding the search?"

"I am sorry, Samantha, the only thing I know is what I have heard from you. The good news is that they haven't found any other bodies at the scene of the explosion except for the one that you believe to be the man named Neil.", Zebulon said with an air of grief peppering his voice, "I'll let you know, if anything changes."

"Thank you, sir. In the meantime, I'll establish contact with the militia leadership immediately and assess how we can best collaborate under the current constraints. It's imperative we find a way to bolster their efforts and push back the Confederation's advance."

Martinez stood, extending his hand across the desk. "I have every confidence in you, Samantha. This mission is unlike any other, and it's going to require all your skill, diplomacy, and courage. Remember, you're not just a liaison between two forces; you're a symbol of hope—a reminder that we're stronger together."

Shaking his hand firmly, Samantha felt a resolve hardening within her. The path ahead was fraught with challenges, both logistical and political, but she was determined to rise to the occasion. "Thank you, sir. I won't let you down. We'll find a way to turn the tide."

As she left Martinez's office, Samantha felt the weight of her new responsibility. The task was daunting but also clear. She was now a key player in a conflict that could define the future of her country. The road ahead would require all her tactical acumen, diplomatic skills, and steady heart. But she was ready—ready to bridge the gap between the Marine Corps and the Montana-Idaho Militia, ready to face the Confederation. She was prepared to do whatever it took to protect her nation.

The tension in the air was palpable as Sergeant Nick Moss maneuvered his truck through the desolate roads leading to Spokane. The usual hustle and bustle of civilian life had been replaced by a somber anticipation of what lay ahead. Nick's mind raced with thoughts of the coming confrontation, the weight of responsibility for his passengers heavy on his shoulders.

In the back seat, Jake Johnson and Ray Grizzly Claw were catching some much-needed rest. Their exhaustion was evident in the deep, steady breaths that filled the quiet cabin. These brief moments of peace stood in sharp relief against the chaos that awaited them. Nick glanced in the rearview mirror, his protective instinct for his two companions mixing with admiration for their courage and determination.

The radio, set to a low volume, crackled intermittently with updates from the front lines. Reports of skirmishes along the northern border painted a grim picture of the situation. The Confederation's forces, emboldened and well-coordinated, posed a significant threat to the security of the region. Nick felt a surge of resolve; he knew the importance of their mission and the role they could play in supporting the defense efforts.

As dawn broke, the silhouette of Spokane emerged on the horizon, the city's skyline a reminder of what was at stake. Nick's focus sharpened, his training kicking in as he mentally prepared for the tasks ahead. The truck slowed as it approached a checkpoint manned by the Montana-Idaho Militia. Nick rolled down his window, exchanging a brief update about his passengers with the guards before being waved through.

The streets of Spokane were eerily quiet, with sandbag barriers and makeshift fortifications dotting the landscape. The presence of militia personnel and vehicles underscored the seriousness of the threat. Nick navigated the truck through the city, making his way to a predetermined rendezvous point where they would meet with local militia leaders and coordinate their next moves.

Jake stirred in the back seat, rubbing his eyes as he took in the surroundings. "We're here," Nick announced, his voice steady despite the uncertainty that lay ahead.

"We need to get a hold of my father and let him know that Ray and I are alive," Jake said with a hint of weariness in his tired voice.

Ray sat up, scanning the area with a practiced eye. "We'll do that first thing. Let's find a secure location where we can establish contact," he suggested, his voice firm. He understood the urgency and the emotional weight the call would carry for Jake.

Finding a quiet corner in a commandeered building serving as the militia's temporary command center, Nick pulled out a satellite phone. The atmosphere was tense, the room bustling with activity as plans were hastily drawn and reports came in. Yet, in this corner, time seemed to stand still for a moment as Jake dialed his father's number, the weight of the call pressing down on him.

The line connected, and after a few tense rings, Jeremiah Johnson's voice came through, weary yet strong. "This is Jeremiah."

"Dad, it's Jake... I'm alive," Jake's voice cracked slightly, filling the silence that followed with a mix of relief and apprehension.

There was a pause on the line, a momentary quiet that felt like an eternity. Then, Jeremiah's voice, now laden with emotion, responded. "Jake? Son, is that really you? We thought we'd lost you..."

Jake swallowed hard, fighting back the emotions that threatened to overwhelm him. "It's me, Dad. Ray's here too, Mike... is gone."

"What do you mean gone, son?" Jeremiah's voice was piqued with concern.

"There were soldiers that shot something at us when we went to collect that lady's husband's remains, and my truck exploded. Luckily, the three of us got out and ran..." The crackling of the satellite phone interrupted for a brief moment, "struck in the leg by a weird dart and disappeared into thin air..." The audio crackled and buzzed again but eventually connected again.

"We were running through the woods, and then we met Nick. He told us that he was an Oregon State Guard who was helping Washington against the Confederation. We made it to Spokane with him."

Jeremiah's relief was palpable, even through the static of the satellite phone. "Thank God you're alive. I've been... We've all been worried sick. The reports, the uncertainty... it's been hell, son."

The room around Jake seemed to fade away as he focused on his father's voice, a lifeline amidst the chaos. "I'm sorry, Dad. We had no way of contacting anyone until now. It's been... tough."

"I understand, Jake. What matters is that you're safe. Tell me, are you alright? Are you hurt?" Jeremiah's concern was evident, as was the father in him taking over.

"We're tired, but we're okay, Dad. We're still standing," Jake assured, glancing at Ray, who offered a nod of confirmation.

Jeremiah took a deep breath, his next words filled with a newfound determination. "Listen to me, both of you. You need to stay safe; do you hear me? We're doing everything we can here to push back and end this. But I need you to promise me you'll look out for each other."

"We will, Dad. We promise," Jake responded, the significance of his words not lost on him.

"I don't want to put you in harm's way, but let the Commander there know that you are my son, and he will make sure that you and Ray are well-outfitted for the fight. Stay alive, son... I love you son..."

The satellite phone died. Jake handed it back to Nick, who returned it to the desk drawer. Nick glanced at Ray before looking back at Jake.

"Nick, thank you for picking us up. I know things here are probably much different than you thought," Jake spoke slowly, concerning how the Montana-Idaho militia was controlling the area and not the National Guard or State Guards. Nick nodded, "when I headed to Idaho to deliver the young man who had died at our border watch from the protestors, I heard radio news about the Montana-Idaho Militia moving into the area of operation and how our federal and state troops were joining them in their defense. I really didn't know what it looked like, but I am proud to say that we are better prepared than we were when we fell back from the border."

"Nick! Sergeant Nick Moss!" Someone shouted from across the room. As Nick turned, a big smile crossed his lips.

"Major Anderson!" Nick exclaimed, recognizing the figure approaching through the crowd of militia members and soldiers gathered in the command center. The Major, a tall, imposing figure with a presence that commanded attention, navigated his way toward them with a purposeful stride.

Major Anderson reached Nick and extended a hand, which Nick shook firmly. "I heard you just got into town. Brought some friends, I see," he said, nodding towards Jake and Ray. His gaze lingered on Jake for a moment, an unspoken understanding passing between them about the significance of Jake's presence.

"Yes, sir. Jake Johnson and Ray Grizzly Claw," Nick introduced. "They've been through quite an ordeal but made it here to contribute to our efforts."

Major Anderson turned to Jake and Ray, offering a nod of acknowledgment. "Glad to have you with us. Every capable hand is needed." Nick smiled along with Jake and Ray. It was an uneasy smile that reflected the uneasiness of the situation they were in. "Nick, thank you for carrying our young brother home and visiting his parents in Idaho. I know it was hard." Major Mark Anderson said while quickly looking at the two young men, "I understand you're Jeremiah Johnson's son," he said, addressing Jake directly. "Your father has been instrumental in rallying support. We're all in this fight together."

Jake nodded, feeling a surge of pride in his father's role and a renewed sense of purpose. "Thank you, sir. We're ready to do whatever it takes."

Major Anderson's expression hardened as he turned his attention back to Nick. "Sergeant, we have a situation developing on the western flank. Intelligence suggests a significant push by the Confederation forces within the next 24 hours. We need experienced personnel to reinforce the lines and coordinate with our units there." Nick's resolve solidified upon hearing the urgency in the Major's voice. "Understood, Major. We'll gear up and head out as soon as possible."

Major Anderson placed a hand on Nick's shoulder, a gesture of trust and confidence. "Good. I'll have the details sent to your comms. Time is of the essence, Moss."

Nick turned to Jake and Ray. "Looks like we're heading out soon. Let's prepare and check our gear. We need to be ready for anything."

Mark put his arm between Nick and the two young men, "I am sorry, Nick, we need to debrief these men about what happened in Payette, ID. You will be accompanying Company R-Squad," Mark pointed at a group of soldiers in camouflage cleaning their rifles. "I appreciate you for rescuing them and bringing them back here. We have Detectives Alicia Wilson and Oliver Nelson from the Idaho State Police here to ask some questions about what happened." Mark finished as Nick nodded. He placed both of his hands on their shoulders, smiled, and then shuffled in the direction of Company R-Squad.

Major Anderson nodded his head in the direction they were going to walk, "I know things are tense, but they found a body at the scene of your truck, and when Nick radioed in to tell us you were on your way, we contacted the State Police."

Jake and Ray followed Major Anderson to a secluded area of the command center, the gravity of the situation heavy in their hearts. The knowledge that they were carrying Neil's body back to his family when they were attacked brought a surge of grief and guilt. Neil had been a victim of the original Neutronium bomb blast, a man whose family was on vacation only to be evacuated and caught in the subsequent blast. His last heroic act was to wedge his wife and kids under the car so they could survive.

Detectives Alicia Wilson and Oliver Nelson were waiting with an air of solemnity fitting for the discussion that was about to take place. Detective Wilson, stepping forward, introduced herself and her partner with a respectful nod. "We're here to gather information about the incident in Payette, specifically concerning Neil's remains and the events leading up to the explosion of your truck, Jake," she began, her voice conveying the urgency of the conversation ahead.

Jake took a deep breath before speaking, his voice heavy with emotion. "Neil was... he was a hero. His last act saved his family during the Neutronium bomb blast on election day. We were asked by my sister, Samantha, to retrieve the body so she could get the family to safety. We happened to be close because we were hunting a couple of hours away when the attack happened. We were trying to honor a promise to my sister and his family to bring his body back to his wife, Allison, and their kids for a proper burial when we were attacked," he explained, the sorrow in his voice palpable.

Ray added details about the attack, describing the unknown soldiers and the peculiar, advanced dart that led to Mike's inexplicable disappearance. The detectives listened intently, their expressions blank as they gathered information. Oliver smirked at the science fiction nonsense of a dart that could cause their friend to disappear, but he did not let the disbelief shade his professionalism. Detective Oliver Nelson interjected with questions aimed at clarifying the sequence of events and the attackers' possible identities. "The level of coordination and the technology you've described... it's unbelievable. But so was the devastation of the Neutronium bomb, so as much as I am inclined to think this story is hogwash, I feel like your testimony could be key in understanding who we're dealing with here."

After providing a detailed account of their harrowing experience, Jake and Ray concluded their testimony, both emotionally drained but relieved to have shared their story. Detective Wilson assured them that their information was invaluable and would be treated with the utmost confidentiality and importance. "Your bravery in trying to honor this man's last wish under such dangerous circumstances is commendable. Rest assured, we'll do everything in our power to investigate this incident thoroughly and seek justice for Mike and all those affected by these attacks," she said, closing her notebook with a somber nod.

Major Anderson, who had been silent for most of the conversation, finally spoke. "Gentlemen, I want to extend my personal gratitude for your efforts and for making it back to share this crucial intelligence with us. The details you've provided give us a clearer picture of the enemy's capabilities and intentions." Ray cut off Major Anderson as he stood, "Sir, with all due respect, I don't think these people were agents of The Confederation. Why would they be after us? We weren't anywhere near the border."

Ray's interjection prompted a moment of contemplation from everyone in the room. Major Anderson leaned forward, his eyes narrowing in thought. "You make a valid point, Ray. It's peculiar that such advanced technology would be used in a seemingly random attack far from the frontline. This could indicate a more complex strategy at play, perhaps one aimed at sowing chaos or targeting specific individuals for reasons unknown to us at this moment."

Detective Alicia Wilson chimed in; her tone was reflective. "This raises several questions about the true nature of the conflict we're engaged in. If this wasn't the work of The Confederation, then we might be dealing with a third party with its own agenda or possibly a rogue element within. Your encounter might not have been as random as it seems."

Detective Oliver Nelson, who had been silently listening for a few moments, began channeling his fictional hero, Special Agent Fox Mulder, from The X-Files, and started adding his perspective. "Considering the strategic significance of your family, Jake, and the efforts your father has put into rallying support against The Confederation, it's plausible you were targeted to send a message or to disrupt those efforts."

The room fell into a heavy silence as the momentousness of Oliver's suggestion sank in. Major Anderson finally broke the silence. "We'll need to broaden our investigation and intelligence efforts. This incident might be a piece of a larger puzzle we've yet to understand. Jake, Ray, your experiences could be critically important in unraveling this mystery. For now, get some rest and keep us informed of any other details you may remember that might seem relevant."

With the meeting concluded, Jake and Ray stepped out of the room, their minds reeling with the implications of their discussion. The notion that their ordeal might have been part of a larger, more sinister plot was unsettling, but it also galvanized their resolve to contribute further to the defense efforts and to protect their loved ones.

As Jake, Ray, and Major Anderson left the room, the detectives shut the door behind them to continue their investigation. Just as the three men were walking down the hallway, a young Lance Corporal, Shane Michaels, hurried up to them and saluted. "Major Anderson, the Confederation... They've taken Seattle," he reported quickly. "Naval vessels are shelling coastal towns, and their forces appear to be moving on Portland."

Major Mark Anderson shook his head. "We need more support. Send this intel up to Governor Johnson and the Council of Governors. We need to mobilize everything we have."

9

PRESIDENT ALTHEA MORRIS STEPPED into the Oval Office alone. A wide smile crossed her lips as she looked at the office art, making a mental note of the busts and paintings she would replace with the ones she wanted. She walked over to the Thomas Jefferson sculpture that was placed there by Arthur Hastings, and her lips curled back in a snarl. For now, she knew that she had to keep up appearances, but ultimately, her benefactor was in charge of her actions, so the puppet show had to go on—for now.

She circled the desk, running her fingers along its polished surface, feeling the echoes of decisions that had shaped history. She paused, her gaze settling on the Jefferson sculpture once more, her thoughts drifting to the tumultuous path that led her here.

In the quiet of the office, Morris contemplated her next moves. The country was on the brink, its people divided, and its territories threatened by external forces. Yet, in this moment of introspection, Morris recognized the unique opportunity before her—to steer the nation through its darkest hours and into a new era.

An era in which her benefactor would control everything. She knew her part to play, but she knew that in that world, her power would grow exponentially. She pulled the chair out from the Resolute Desk, and sitting in it, she folded her hands on the desk and again smiled widely.

Her contemplation was interrupted by a discreet knock on the door. "Come in," she called, her tone composed.

Her Chief of Staff entered with a stack of briefings in hand, a reminder of the relentless pace of governance. "Madam President, your schedule," he began but paused upon seeing the contemplative look on her face.

"Is everything alright, Madam President?" he inquired with a mix of professional concern and personal curiosity.

Morris turned, her expression shifting to one of determined resolve. "Yes, everything is as it should be. Let's get to work. So many challenges we have to overcome, but we will navigate it with courage and determination."

"Madam President, I know your presidency is to be only a few weeks, but we need to name a Vice President in case something happens to you before the President-elect is sworn in." Chief of Staff Christopher Ward said as he laid a dossier of potential VP candidates in front of Althea. Her eyes curved in disgust as she saw several names before her. Some were the names of other presidential candidates who had run against her in the primary before Arthur won it and selected her as his Vice President.

Morris's eyes scanned the list, each name prompting a swift, internal calculation of their potential loyalty, usefulness, and, most critically, their alignment with the benefactor's grand plan. Her gaze settled on a name that sparked a fleeting sense of intrigue—a dark horse, less conspicuous, yet potentially malleable to her and, by extension, her benefactor's will.

"Christopher," she began, her voice steady, "I understand the necessity, but our choice must be strategic. We need someone who can be seen as a unifier yet remains under our influence. Someone who won't overshadow the short duration of my presidency but will stand as a testament to our 'dedication' to the country's stability."

Ward nodded, fully aware of the delicate balance his President sought to maintain. "Understood, Madam President. Do you have someone in mind?"

Morris tapped the dossier lightly with her finger, her decision clear. "Yes, I believe we do. This candidate," she said, pointing to the profile, "might be the perfect placeholder. Their background suggests a moderate stance that appeals to both sides of the aisle. Plus, their relative obscurity in the political arena could prevent any unforeseen power grabs."

She paused, considering her words carefully. "They have the right blend of experience and anonymity. This combination can be a strategic advantage, allowing us to maneuver without drawing too much attention."

Satisfied with her reasoning, she finished speaking and pulled out her phone. With a few swift taps, she sent a message to her benefactor, seeking approval for her choice. The response came quickly—unnaturally so. As if her benefactor had been anticipating this exact decision.

Morris glanced at the screen, a slight smile playing on her lips. The approval was more than just a green light; it was a signal that their plan was moving forward seamlessly. Looking at Christopher, she nodded, knowing her decision was the right one.

"Very well, Madam President. I'll begin the vetting process immediately," Ward responded, picking up the dossier and preparing to leave.

"Christopher," Morris called out just as he reached the door, causing him to pause and turn. "Make sure our choice understands the situation fully. They're to be a figurehead, nothing more. I won't have surprises."

Ward nodded, a slight smile playing on his lips. "Of course, Madam President. I'll ensure they're fully briefed on their role in our administration."

As Ward exited the Oval Office, Morris leaned back in her chair, her mind racing ahead to the myriad possibilities her brief presidency could unveil. For a fleeting moment, she allowed herself to ponder the legacy of her expected ascendancy to the highest office in the land. Yet, her thoughts quickly shifted back to the immediacy of her situation—the balance of power, the intricate dance with her benefactor, and the looming inauguration of Troy Thomason.

Unknown to many, Morris harbored her own ambitions, carefully concealed beneath a veneer of compliance. The upcoming weeks would be critical, not just for her political career but for the future direction of the nation as she saw it. As she gazed out the window, contemplating the sprawling grounds of the White House, a sense of purpose solidified within her. The puppet show, as she termed it, was far from over. It was merely evolving, and she intended to play her part to perfection.

Outside, the Washington skyline contrasted against the sky, a city braced for change, unaware of the machinations within its corridors of power. As the day progressed, the wheels of governance continued to turn, with Althea Morris at its helm, steering the ship of state through uncharted waters, her sights set on a horizon only she and her benefactor's organization could envision.

In the elegant confines of the American Consulate in Düsseldorf, Germany, Dr. Hal Bennett was addressing a gathering of concerned diplomats and staff. The consulate's grand meeting room, usually a scene of diplomatic functions and cultural exchanges, had taken on a more somber tone, not just because of the internal political upheavals back in the United States but also due to the escalating concerns over the Confederation's invasion and the unexpected transition of power to President Althea Morris.

"As we navigate these complex times," Dr. Bennett began, his voice steady against the backdrop of global concern, "our role here transcends our national interests. The world watches closely as the United States addresses its challenges—both from within the United States and the looming threat of the Confederation."

The room, filled with attentive faces from various nations around Germany, reflected the wider international apprehension. Amid this calculated calm, two figures entered the room—Daphne Holly and Yosef Bishara, members of the Presidential Steering Committee. Their arrival carried an urgency that paralleled the global anxiety surrounding the recent developments.

Dr. Bennett excused himself from the podium, moving toward the newcomers with a composed demeanor. "Dr. Bennett, we've come with a message from the White House," Daphne began, her tone reflecting the seriousness of their mission.

Yosef added, "The global community is deeply concerned about the Confederation's advances and the sudden change in leadership. President Morris believes your expertise and standing can help stabilize not only the national climate but also reassure our allies and partners abroad."

Dr. Bennett, absorbing the significance of the situation, responded, "I'm aware of the precarious position our nation finds itself in, both domestically and on the international stage. What is asked of me?"

"The President requests your immediate return to Washington to assume the Vice Presidency," Yosef explained, presenting Dr. Bennett with an official document. "Your role will be crucial in navigating the challenges ahead, both in addressing the Confederation's threat and in bolstering confidence in the United States' leadership at this critical juncture."

Accepting the document, Dr. Bennett recognized the dual responsibility laid before him—to mend the fractures within and to project a united front to the watching world. "I'll return at once. The task ahead is daunting, but with resolve and cooperation, we will uphold

the principles that define our leadership in the world."
He smirked while nodding and walking towards the
podium again.

Dr. Bennett resumed his address, his words now carrying an even greater significance. Unbeknownst to those
in attendance, he was poised to step into a role that
would test his resolve and dedication to his country and
its place in the global community.

"Ladies and Gentlemen, I have just been requested to
return to the United States to take on a new role, which
I am not at liberty to address yet, but we will have a
new Ambassador assigned in the next few weeks since I
am leaving I will leave Diplomat Martin Kuykendall, the
Minister Plenipotentiary, in charge until a new Ambassador is named and placed."

Dr. Hal Bennett paused, allowing his announcement to
resonate with the gathered audience. The diplomats and
staff, visibly surprised by the sudden turn of events,
exchanged glances, their expressions filled with a sense
of curiosity. The significance of Dr. Bennett's departure
at such a pivotal moment underscored the severity of
the situation facing the United States and its allies.

"I assure you," Dr. Bennett continued, his voice imbued
with a sense of purpose, "that our mission here remains
unchanged. The principles of democracy, liberty, and
international cooperation that have guided our actions
will continue to be our compass during these turbulent

times." He waved while stepping away from the podium towards the members of the steering committee. The room erupted into a polite but concerned murmur. Dr. Bennett turned and made his way back to the podium for a final address. "While I may be assuming a new responsibility, the bond between the United States and its partners remains steadfast. Our collective efforts to foster peace, security, and prosperity are more important than ever."

Turning to Daphne Holly and Yosef Bishara, he nodded in acknowledgment of their roles in conveying the urgent summons. Their presence in Düsseldorf underscored the interconnectedness of global politics and highlighted the importance of strong leadership during a crisis.

After the meeting, Dr. Bennett, accompanied by the Steering Committee members, prepared for his swift departure. The news of his appointment and the discussions that followed with embassy staff were conducted with the utmost discretion, yet the underlying urgency was palpable.

Martin Kuykendall, the appointed Minister Plenipotentiary, stood beside Dr. Bennett, offering assurances of continuity and stability. "Dr. Bennett, I will ensure that our operations here remain seamless and that the transition to new leadership is smooth."

Dr. Bennett offered a reassuring smile. "I have every confidence in your abilities, Martin. The work you do here is vital—not just for our nation but for the global community we serve. Keep the lines of communication open, and remember, diplomacy is our first line of defense."

With his final words to the consulate staff, Dr. Bennett stepped into the crisp evening air, his wife Lisa and their young daughter standing beside the car with their suitcases being loaded into the trunk by one of the drivers. The weight of his new role started settling on his shoulders as he looked at Lisa.

Lisa met his gaze, her eyes reflecting a mix of pride and concern. "It's a big step," she said softly, squeezing his hand. Their daughter, Holly, unaware of the significance of the moment, smiled up at them both, a picture of innocence in a complicated world.

Dr. Bennett knelt down to her level, brushing a strand of hair from her face. "Daddy has a very important job to do, but we're doing this together, okay?" His voice was gentle, imbued with the warmth of familial love.

The young girl nodded, wrapping her arms around his neck. "I know, Daddy. You're going to help a lot of people." Holly smiled as she turned to slide into the car.

Standing, Dr. Bennett embraced his wife one last time before they climbed into the car behind Holly. As the vehicle pulled away from the consulate, the city lights of Düsseldorf blurred into the night, marking the end of one chapter and the beginning of another.

Lisa broke the silence as they headed towards the airport. "Hal, are you ready for what's waiting for us back home?" Her voice was steady, but the underlying tension was unmistakable.

Dr. Bennett glanced at her, a resolve firming in his eyes. "I have to be. This is about more than just us now. It's about our country, our allies, and the principles we stand for. It won't be easy, but we've faced challenges before."

As they reached the airport, the reality of their imminent journey set in. Dr. Bennett checked his phone, noting several missed calls and messages from various officials and allies, all seeking guidance or offering support in the transition. It was clear that his new role as Vice President would be a challenge but also an opportunity to influence the course of national and international policy at a crucial time.

The flight back to Washington was a quiet one, each family member lost in their own thoughts. Dr. Bennett reviewed documents and briefings while Lisa watched over their daughter, her mind undoubtedly racing with concerns for their future and the impact of their new life on their family.

Upon landing, Dr. Hal Bennett immediately felt the weight of the task ahead. A security detail and a team of advisors awaited him, ready to brief him on the latest developments. The sense of urgency was palpable as they swiftly made their way to Washington, D.C.

As soon as they arrived, Dr. Bennett was escorted to the White House. The atmosphere was charged with tension, a clear reflection of the grave situation the country was facing. His family was taken to a secure and comfortable location, where they would wait for him, adding a personal layer of concern to his already heavy burden.

Walking through the familiar corridors of power, Dr. Bennett felt the enormity of his forthcoming responsibilities with each step. The weight of the nation's expectations and the critical decisions ahead pressed upon him as he approached the Oval Office. The stakes for him had never been higher, and the path forward was filled with challenges that would test his resolve and leadership like never before.

Entering the Oval Office, Dr. Bennett found President Althea Morris waiting for him, her demeanor composed yet unmistakably commanding. "Dr. Bennett, welcome," she greeted him, gesturing towards a seat. "Thank you for making the journey so promptly."

Dr. Bennett nodded, taking a seat. "Madam President, it's an honor to serve. The challenges ahead are significant, but I am ready to contribute to our nation's leadership in any way I can."

President Morris studied him for a moment, her gaze sharp. "I'll be frank with you, Dr. Bennett. Your role as Vice President will be... unique. Given the circumstances of my presidency, your appointment is as much about symbolism as it is about governance."

Dr. Bennett's brow furrowed slightly. "I understand the need for stability and unity at this time, Madam President. I am here to serve the best I can."

Althea leaned forward, her voice lowering. "Let me be clear, Hal. You are here to serve as a figurehead and an inoffensive member of this administration. Your reputation and expertise lend credibility to us, especially now. But the decisions, the real power, will remain with me and those I choose to involve directly."

The words hung heavily between them, clearly defining the power dynamics at play. Dr. Bennett paused, absorbing the implications, his initial shock evolving into a calculated determination. "I understand," he acknowledged. "While I had envisioned a more active role in tackling the challenges ahead, I am prepared to execute the responsibilities you have defined to the fullest extent of my capabilities."

President Morris smiled thinly. "That's all I ask, Dr. Bennett. Your cooperation and support are vital during these tumultuous times. Remember, the public image we project must be one of unity and strength."

Dr. Bennett nodded, his mind racing with the implications of their conversation. "Understood, Madam President. You can count on my support."

As the meeting concluded, Dr. Bennett was left to reflect on the conversation and his place within an administration that had already defined his role so narrowly. Exiting the Oval Office, he felt the weight of his new position more acutely than ever. The challenge was not just the external threats the country faced but navigating the internal dynamics of an administration where he was to be a figurehead.

Yet, within him stirred a quiet determination. Dr. Bennett understood the importance of public perception and the stability it could bring in uncertain times. But he also knew the value of his expertise and experience. The coming days would undoubtedly test his resolve and his ability to influence the course of events, even from the margins to which he had been consigned.

As Dr. Bennett emerged into the cool Washington evening, he inhaled deeply, steeling himself for the quiet comfort of home. His phone vibrated, and an unlisted number flashed on the screen. With a glance around, he answered, his stance shifting to one of taut attention. "Yes, it will be taken care of immediately. You do your part; I will do mine," he responded with a discreet nod.

As he ended the call, a hint of authority lingered in his tone, unbeknownst to those around him. He then smoothly stepped into the waiting car, disappearing into the bustling city night.

In the dim ambiance of his office in Helena, Montana, Jeremiah Johnson reclined in his chair, a sense of weary contentment washing over him. Before him, a crystal decanter gleamed, filled with amber bourbon distilled in the rolling hills of Kentucky—a rare find that he reserved for moments of reflection. With a practiced motion, he reached for the decanter, pouring the bourbon into a crystal glass, the liquid catching the light, casting a warm glow across the room.

A smile played across his lips, a mixture of relief and lingering worry, as he savored the aroma of the bourbon before taking a slow, deliberate sip. The richness of the drink spread through him, a comforting warmth amidst the storm of his thoughts. He then turned his attention to the cigar resting beside him, a luxurious complement to his drink. Striking a match, he lit the cigar, the glow briefly illuminating his rugged features as he puffed gently, coaxing the flame to life.

As the room filled with the rich scent of tobacco, the door opened softly, and Miranda Johnson entered, carrying a teapot with the grace of years spent navigating the highs and lows of their shared life. She settled onto the couch near Jeremiah's desk, pouring herself a cup of steaming tea with a delicate, almost ceremonial care.

"Honey, I am so glad Jake is okay," Miranda said, her voice filled with a combination of relief and maternal worry. She took a sip from her cup, the warmth of the tea a sharp contrast to the cool Montana evening.

Jeremiah swiveled his chair to face his wife, his gaze softening at the sight of her. Forty years of marriage had deepened their connection, a bond that weathered countless storms. "Yes, honey, very relieved," he acknowledged the weight of his responsibilities as a father and a leader, which was evident in his voice. "But I'm still concerned because he is in Spokane. However, it wouldn't be fair to the good people of the states who signed the Montana-Idaho Militia pact to pull him home. Jake and Ray are young and skilled men, capable of making a difference where they are."

Their conversation flowed a blend of personal worries and the broader concerns that came with Jeremiah's position. In the quiet of his office, with night pressing against the windows, the couple found solace in each other's company, a small island of calm in the ever-turbulent sea of their lives.

"When are you going to let John and his assistant out of lockup?" Miranda prodded as she spoke about how

Jeremiah and the other governors put John Beam, the governor of Kansas, and his assistant in a holding cell because of his wanting to leave at the formation of the pact.

"Honestly, honey, I just wanted to scare him, but if I release him, he could pull back the men and women he committed early on to the cause, and I fear that could hurt us." Jeremiah said while taking another sip of his bourbon, "I like John; he is a good man, and he had his reasons for objecting. If our roles were reversed, I would have done so, too, because we are walking a tightrope between patriotism and treason."

Miranda's eyes curved, "Jeremiah, you are a good man, too, and I know why we are doing what we are doing. I am concerned, though, that President Althea Morris might do something crazy."

"She is illegitimate, using the 25th Amendment a month before the President-elect is sworn in. There are ulterior motives. I can feel it in my bones." Jeremiah drew from his cigar again and knocked the ash from the end of it into the ashtray on his desk.

The tension in the room thickened as Jeremiah's words hung in the air, a sharp reminder of the troubling balance they were forced to maintain. The dim light from the desk lamp cast long shadows across the room, mirroring the uncertainty that shrouded their cause.

Miranda set her teacup down, the porcelain clinking softly against the table. "What's our next move, then?" she asked, her voice steady despite the storm of concerns swirling in her mind. "If Morris has other plans, we need to be two steps ahead."

Jeremiah leaned forward, resting his elbows on his desk, his gaze lost in the amber depths of his bourbon. "We strengthen our position. Ensure our pact is ironclad and that our allies are committed. As for John Beam, I'll have a talk with him tomorrow. Maybe it's time to extend the olive branch to help him see the bigger picture we are facing. We need unity now more than ever."

He stood, walking over to the window, peering out into the Montana night. "As for Morris, we watch closely. Gather intelligence. If she steps out of line or threatens the stability of the country, we'll be ready."

Miranda nodded, and her expression showed a combination of resolve and concern. "And our son, Jake, and his friend Ray... they're in the thick of it in Spokane. How do we ensure their safety?"

Jeremiah turned from the window, his features softened by concern for his son. "Jake knows what he's doing. He and Ray are more than capable. But we'll keep a close watch, ensuring they have all the support they need. They're not just fighting for the militia or Montana—they're fighting for the principles this country was built on."

"When will Samantha get here? Maybe she'll have good news from the Marine Corps." Miranda sipped from her teacup again.

"I am not sure; she has a heavy load to carry too, being a liaison between us and the United States Marines, and honey, while I am excited about her being in that position, she is certainly not 'on our side.'" Jeremiah's look of concern washed over his face as the intercom came to life.

"Sir, I have President-elect Thomason on the line. He wants to speak with you, but I'm not really sure about what." Janet's voice trailed off anxiously.

"Send him through," Jeremiah said quickly.

As Janet connected the call, Jeremiah straightened in his chair, his expression turning from one of familial concern to one of guarded readiness. The soft crackle of the line preceded Troy Thomason's voice, clear but carrying the weight of imminent responsibility.

"Jeremiah, it's Troy Thomason. I hope I'm not interrupting," Troy began, his tone respectful yet underscored with urgency.

"Not at all, Troy. To what do I owe the pleasure?" Jeremiah's voice was steady, masking the undercurrent of anticipation for the conversation's direction.

"I'll get straight to the point, Jeremiah. I'm aware of the situation in Spokane and the broader implications of the Montana-Idaho Militia's actions. I also understand your role and the delicate balance you're trying to maintain," Troy stated, the sound of papers shuffling in the background hinting at the depth of his preparations for this call.

Jeremiah listened intently, a flicker of surprise crossing his features at Troy's acknowledgment of the complexity of their position. "I appreciate your understanding, Troy. We're navigating through uncharted waters here."

Troy's sigh was audible, a brief moment of vulnerability in the political maelstrom. "I need your assurance, Jeremiah. When I take office, I want to ensure we're working towards the same goal—a united, secure, and prosperous nation. The challenges we face with the Confederation are unlike any other, and internal divisions will only weaken us."

Jeremiah nodded to himself; the urgency of the conversation was not lost on him. "You have my word, Troy. Our actions, while seemingly drastic, have always been in the interest of protecting our people and our way of life. But I'm also aware of the need for a unified front, especially now."

There was a brief pause as Troy considered Jeremiah's words. "I'm planning to set up a meeting with you and the other governors involved in the Militia pact. It's time we have an open dialogue about our next steps and how we can align our efforts with the incoming administration."

"That sounds like a plan. Open dialogue is the first step towards understanding and cooperation. Just say when and where, and I'll be there," Jeremiah agreed, the lines of worry on his face softening slightly at the prospect of a path forward.

As Jeremiah listened, Troy Thomason's voice took on a more serious tone, hinting at the undercurrent of unease that seemed to permeate the political landscape. "Before we conclude, Jeremiah, there's another matter that's been weighing on me," Troy said, pausing as if to choose his words carefully.

Jeremiah leaned in, sensing the weight of what was to come. "Go on, Troy. I'm listening."

"It's about Althea Morris and her use of the 25th Amendment to ascend to the presidency," Troy continued, his concern palpable even through the phone line. "It's unprecedented, and with only a month left before I'm sworn in, it's... troubling. I can't shake the feeling that there might be more to her intentions."

Jeremiah's hand tightened around his crystal glass of bourbon. This concern echoed his own misgivings. "I share your worries, Troy. It's a maneuver that's left many of us questioning the true motive behind it. The timing is more than just a little suspicious."

"There's an unsettling air of opportunism," Troy agreed. "And while I want to give her the benefit of the doubt, the situation demands scrutiny. We need to be prepared for any scenario, even the possibility that she might not step aside as smoothly as expected when my time comes."

Jeremiah nodded despite knowing Troy couldn't see the gesture. "Preparation and vigilance are key. We'll stand ready to support the constitutional process and ensure a peaceful transition of power. Your presidency represents a new chapter for our nation, and we can't let anything jeopardize that."

Troy's voice, though still laden with concern, carried a note of gratitude. "I knew I could count on you, Jeremiah. Let's keep the lines of communication open. I might need to lean on your counsel more than ever in the coming weeks."

"You'll have it, Troy. Together, we'll navigate these waters and keep our country on the course," Jeremiah assured him, the commitment ringing clear in his voice.

As they wrapped up their conversation with promises of further dialogue and collaboration, Jeremiah hung up the phone, a heavy sense of responsibility settling over him.

The challenges were daunting, but Troy's unwavering resolve and their shared commitment to their principles illuminated a path through the uncertainty. The office, now infused with the lingering aroma of bourbon and tobacco, felt like a sanctuary from the brewing storm outside. Yet, Jeremiah knew this tranquility was temporary—a brief respite before the inevitable tempest of political maneuvering and strategic planning awaited them.

Miranda watched her husband, sensing the gears turning in his mind. "Jeremiah," she said softly, breaking the silence, "you've always had a way of seeing through the fog. If anyone can navigate these troubled waters, it's you."

Jeremiah looked at his wife, her unwavering faith in him shining through the murky darkness of political uncertainty. "With people like Troy willing to listen and work together, maybe we stand a chance of keeping this country from splintering further," he mused aloud.

Miranda reached across to squeeze his hand, a silent pledge of her support. "And what about Althea Morris? Do you think she's aware of the storm she's steering us into?"

"That's the million-dollar question," Jeremiah sighed, gazing into the remnants of his bourbon. "Whether she's a pawn in a larger game or the mastermind of her own agenda, we'll need to be prepared. She's a wildcard, and wildcards are dangerous."

The clock on the wall ticked steadily, marking the passage of time in a world that seemed to stand still at the brink of change. Jeremiah stood, stretching his limbs, the weight of his upcoming responsibilities bearing down on him.

"The governors are still in town. If we are going to have a meeting with Troy, I need to catch them all up; hopefully, Samantha will be here soon as well. We have more military bases throughout Washington and Oregon that are joining us, and with the fall of Seattle, we are going to need all the help that we can muster."

Miranda nodded, understanding the urgency in Jeremiah's voice. "I'll make sure to have everything prepared for the meeting. I'll reach out to Samantha again and see if there's any update on her arrival."

Jeremiah appreciated her efficiency and how seamlessly she managed the complexities of their situation. "Thank you, Miranda. Your support makes all the difference. The cohesion among the governors and the support from the military bases could very well be the linchpin in our defense strategy against the Confederation."

Several hours later, Jeremiah sat at his desk pondering their next steps. His thoughts were interrupted by a knock at the door. Janet, his trusted aide, entered with a sense of purpose. "Sir, the governors are arriving in the conference room. They're awaiting your briefing." Taking a deep breath, Jeremiah nodded. "Thank you, Janet. Let them know I'll be there shortly." He turned to Miranda, who was still seated on the couch, scrolling through the news on her tablet. She looked at her husband, who was pacing the room, and saw that his resolve was clear. "We've been pushing back against the Confederation for a few weeks now with mixed results. We've lost Seattle, and the American Communist protestors are making things even more difficult for our men and women. I am not sure we can last until Troy is inaugurated; we are going to have to approach President Morris for support."

Miranda sat her tablet down on the coffee table next to the empty teapot, stood up, and walked over to Jeremiah. "Honey, are you sure? The tension between the parties these last few years has been at an all-time high, and I suspect she will turn your request for help into some referendum on Republicans."

Jeremiah nodded, his face weary with the weight of leading the offensive against the Confederation. Jeremiah was a proud American; his family played a part in the nation's founding, and he also descended from a member of Lewis and Clark's expedition. Montana flowed with decades of Johnson family blood, and he couldn't bear to see an invading force walk right in without trying to stop them. "Our situation is critical, teetering on the edge of catastrophe. Even a Californian thrust into the presidency must acknowledge her duty to secure our borders—a duty grossly neglected by the Hastings administration. We're vastly outmatched; simple farmers and blue-collar workers armed only with semi-automatic rifles stand little chance against the relentless tide of the Confederation. Our state and national guard units are desperately under-equipped, lacking the military technology needed to mount a substantial defense. Though we've garnered support from a few military bases, their resources are woefully insufficient. We're staring down the barrel of an impending disaster, scrambling for the supplies and support that could mean the difference between survival and annihilation."

Miranda's eyes began to show signs of tears as Jeremiah finished his statement; he caught himself and looked deep into those tearful eyes, "I am sorry, honey. I know you are worried about Jake and Samantha and our home, but I won't rest until we stop them." Jeremiah leaned down and kissed Miranda softly. "I love you."

Miranda smiled a tearful smile, "I love you more."

Jeremiah turned to leave the room; he grabbed his cowboy hat and long leather coat.

The government complex in Helena, Montana, extends over a vast and meticulously landscaped area encircled by a formidable wall designed to safeguard the state's officials and their operations. Jeremiah made his way out of the main building, navigating through the expansive grounds toward the designated conference room. Here, the governors from the states of the Montana-Idaho Militia Pact were already gathered, awaiting his arrival to strategize their unified response to the escalating threats. Jeremiah had made a decision a few moments earlier to petition the newly seated President Althea Morris for supplies and manpower; knowing it may be a fool's errand, he wanted to try anyway. He knew that part of the Marine Corps had already agreed to help with his daughter Samantha being a liaison between them, but he knew that would only get them so far, and if the President decided to pull back the support, it could strain relations even more.

Jeremiah's stride was purposeful, each step echoing his resolve as he approached the conference room. The atmosphere within the complex was charged with palpable tension, reflective of the critical juncture at which the Montana-Idaho Militia Pact found itself. The encircling wall, though a physical barrier meant to protect, also served as a constant reminder of the threats looming miles beyond its confines.

As he entered the conference room, the gathered governors—leaders from the pact's member states—turned their attention toward him. The room was filled with a mix of anticipation and apprehension, each governor acutely aware of the stakes involved. The unity of the pact was now a sign of resistance against both internal and external upheaval.

"Thank you for waiting," Jeremiah began, his voice steady, betraying none of the turmoil that churned within him. "As you are all aware, our situation is dire. Our collective defense against the Confederation's advances is hampered by a glaring shortage of resources and manpower."

He paused, letting his words sink in before continuing. "Despite the inherent risks, I've decided to petition President Althea Morris directly for additional supplies and reinforcements. I'm under no illusion about the complexity of this request, given the strained relations and her... unconventional ascent to power. However, we must explore every avenue available to us."

The room was silent, the gravity of Jeremiah's proposal hanging heavily in the air. "Samantha, with her connections to the Marine Corps, has already facilitated a critical alliance. But we're on borrowed time. The support from the Marines, while invaluable, is not a total remedy for our challenges. Should the President decide against our plea, or worse, withdraw existing military support, the consequences could be catastrophic."

Governor John Beam, recently released from his brief detainment, spoke up, his tone measured. "Jeremiah, while I share your concerns, how do you propose we ensure our petition is received with anything but disdain? Morris's presidency, legitimate or not, has so far been marked by decisions that, frankly, leave little room for optimism."

Jeremiah met Beam's gaze, acknowledging the valid concern. "John, I am sorry that we detained you. I felt it was necessary in light of the campaign at Fairchild. I am glad to see you have joined in with our resolve." Jeremiah lowered his head in acknowledgment of the mistakes that could have been avoided but weren't. "Now, to answer your question, it's a gamble, no doubt. But it's one we must take. We'll frame our request in terms of national security, emphasizing the broader implications of our failure to hold back the Confederation. It's not just about us or the pact—it's about the integrity of our national borders and the safety of all Americans, including Kansas."

He looked around the room, meeting the eyes of each governor in turn. "I won't pretend this is a guaranteed success. But silence and inaction are luxuries we cannot afford. I plan to leverage every bit of influence we have, including the media, to put pressure on Morris. We need resources, and even a Californian who has ascended to the presidency must acknowledge her responsibility for our nation's defense, especially in light of the destruction the Neutronium bomb wrought on her home state. Our current arsenal and manpower are insufficient for a prolonged engagement with the Confederation. We're not just defending our states; we're defending the principles this country stands for."

The governors nodded, a shared understanding of the stakes at hand uniting them. The meeting progressed into a detailed planning session, strategizing on the best approach to petition the President and preparing for the potential fallout of her decision, whichever way it might swing. Jeremiah's leadership, once again, proved to be the glue holding the Pact of States together as they navigated the uncertain waters that lay ahead.

10

A MONTH HAD PASSED since the tragic Neutronium bomb detonated off the coast of California, claiming Neil's life and casting a shadow over Allison's existence. Seated on the porch of the beautiful Elkview cabin, nestled amidst towering mountains, Allison found herself caught between the tranquility of nature and the tumult of her heart. The laughter and joyful screams of her children playing tag in the yard, under the watchful eyes of the Johnson family's golden retriever, offered a bittersweet respite from her grief.

The Johnsons had extended their welcome by letting Allison and her children stay in the cabin in this hour of need, a sanctuary as the specter of invasion crept ever closer to her doorstep back in Idaho. Their generosity illuminated her darkest times, yet the ache of Neil's absence remained a constant companion, reminding her in quiet moments that he was gone, forever beyond reach.

With each creak of the rocking chair, memories of Neil flashed before her, poignant reminders of a shared life abruptly severed. His last moments of tucking her and the kids under their station wagon to protect them, sparing his last moments to make sure they were safe. He was a hero, not just to her but to their young children. They would never understand his sacrifice or what came over their father, but she would never forget.

The cabin, the mountains, and even the laughter of the children contrasted sharply with the void Neil's death had left in her heart. Here, amidst the beauty of the Elkview cabin, Allison grappled with the reality that home was no longer a place but a memory, forever altered by the loss of her beloved Neil.

She snapped out of her thoughts as soon as she no longer heard her children giggling and playing. The golden retriever barked incessantly as she stood from the rocking chair. Walking to the edge of the porch, she saw her children talking to two men dressed in black uniforms. They had rifles hanging from their backs, and one was kneeling over talking to Luke, who was enamored by the armed men.

Allison's eyes opened wide, and her heart began to beat fast as she anxiously ran off the porch in the direction of her kids.

As she ran closer, the kneeling man stood and smiled, his dark hair and blue eyes creating a strikingly handsome expression. She thought to herself that he looked like a young Tom Cruise and the other one looked like a young Val Kilmer.

"You must be Mom; Luke here was telling us all about you," he said while extending a hand. "My name is Jack, Jack Ashby, and this here is Stephen Martenson." Jack said while Stephen nodded his head, "Ma'am."

"Who are you?" Allison quickly examined the men, finding no identification on their uniforms except for a single patch on their right arm.

The patch was circular with a blue border. Inside the circle, stars and stripes formed a familiar pattern, evoking a sense of American patriotism. At the center was an eye reminiscent of the all-seeing eye on the dollar bill, adding an air of mystery and authority. The design was both strange and familiar, and she couldn't shake the feeling that it was tied to something significant within American symbolism.

"We are part of the special forces attaché of the Montana-Idaho Militia. We were looking for two men from the Confederation that may have come through here." The one named Jack said, looking into her eyes with seriousness.

Allison's breath hitched at the mention of the Montana-Idaho Militia and the Confederation. The reality of the war, which had seemed distant, suddenly felt ominously close, right at her doorstep. She gathered her children closer, instinctively shielding them with her presence.

"What do you want with us? We haven't seen any-one," Allison said, her voice steadying despite the rapid drumming of her heart. She eyed the rifles slung over their shoulders, a harsh reminder of the danger that now lurked in the shadows of her serene refuge.

Jack held up his hand in a calming gesture, his de-meanor friendly but serious. "Ma'am, we're not here to cause any trouble. We're just sweeping the area for any signs of enemy activity. Your cabin is the last on our patrol today. We believe they might be heading towards populated areas to blend in."

Stephen, who had been quietly observing, added, "Your husband was a hero, Mrs..." He trailed off, not knowing her last name, "Adams, my husband was named Neil Adams..." she responded as if being questioned. "Mrs. Adams...We're just here to make sure his sacrifice wasn't in vain, and part of that is ensuring you and your family are safe."

Allison's guard remained up, but she couldn't help but feel a pang of gratitude mixed with sorrow at the men-tion of Neil's bravery. "We've been staying away from the news... trying to... cope," she managed to say, her voice thick with unshed tears.

Jack nodded understandingly. "We get it. But we need everyone to be vigilant. If you see anything unusual, or if anyone you don't know approaches you, please get in touch with us immediately." He handed her a small card with a radio frequency and a contact number. "We're not far, and we're here to protect this area."

The children, sensing the seriousness of the conversation, clung to Allison, their earlier playfulness replaced by a sense of wariness. Jack and Stephen took a few steps back, giving the family some space.

"We'll be on our way then," Jack said, tipping an imaginary hat. "Stay safe, Mrs. Adams. And remember, you're not alone in this."

As the two men turned to leave, Allison watched them go, their figures gradually disappearing into the thickening forest that surrounded the cabin. A combination of fear and relief settled over her. Neil's sacrifice, the men's visit, and the looming threat of the Confederation invasion reinforced the reality of their situation.

Turning back to her children, Allison mustered a smile. "Let's go inside, kids. It's getting chilly out here," she said, her voice steady, masking the turmoil within. As they entered the cabin, she glanced at the card Jack had given her, a lifeline in the vast uncertainty that now enveloped their lives.

Inside, she set about preparing dinner, her movements automatic as her mind raced. The peace of the Elkview cabin now felt fragile, a temporary haven in a world teetering on the brink. Allison knew they couldn't stay isolated forever. Sooner or later, the war would come knocking, and she would have to decide what her next move would be, not just for her sake but for her children's future.

Allison now felt a growing unease about the safety of the Elkview Cabin and the Johnsons' ranch, places she once thought were serene and secure. The recent events had shattered that sense of safety. Picking up her phone, she dialed Miranda Johnson's number, her fingers trembling slightly. She needed to share the disturbing news, hoping to find some comfort and perhaps a plan to ensure their safety. As the phone rang, Allison's mind raced with thoughts of what might come next, the tranquil memories of the ranch now overshadowed by a looming sense of danger. Miranda's voice answered, "Hey there, Allison," Miranda said nicely, "Sorry I had to leave so quickly; Jeremiah wanted me in Helena with him. Are you okay?"

"Miranda, it's... it's been a bit of a day," Allison started, her voice betraying a hint of the anxiety that had taken root in her chest. "We had some visitors—men from the Montana-Idaho Militia. They were looking for Confederation soldiers they thought might have passed through here."

Miranda's concern was palpable even through the phone. "Militia? At the cabin? Are you and the kids alright?" she asked, her voice tight with worry.

"Yes, we're fine. They were... polite, but it was unnerving. They gave me a contact number and said they were there to protect the area. But Miranda, it's made me realize just how close this all is. The war, the conflict... it's knocking on our doorstep," Allison explained, her gaze drifting towards the window, half expecting to see the militiamen still lurking among the trees.

Miranda let out a heavy sigh, a sound that carried a mix of frustration and resignation. "I know, Allison. I know. Jeremiah's been up to his neck in meetings and plans, trying to secure more support for the Militia. The tension's been thick enough to cut with a knife around here, too. But we don't have anyone operating even remotely in the area..."

Allison's heart skipped a beat at Miranda's last words. "What do you mean? If they're not with you, then who—" she started, her mind racing with the implications.

Miranda paused, the silence stretching between them, thick with uncertainty. "I'm not sure, Allison. It could be rogue elements or another group trying to take advantage of the situation. It's a chaotic time; people are using the confusion to their own ends. But I promise you, we'll look into it. Jeremiah will want to know about this."

Allison felt a chill run down her spine. A creeping dread now replaced the comfort she had taken in the men's presence. "I... I gave them nothing, Miranda. But they seemed so convinced we might have seen something," she whispered, clutching the phone tighter. "They knew about Neil; how did they know about Neil?"

Miranda's silence stretched for what seemed like hours, "Allison, describe the men to me, their uniforms and their names, anything that you remember."

Allison paced the length of the cabin's kitchen, her voice shaky as she recounted the details. "One was named Jack Ashby, and the other, Stephen Martenson. They wore black uniforms with no visible insignia except for a patch... it had a blue border, stars and stripes, and an all-seeing eye in the center. I've never seen it before."

Miranda was silent for a moment, presumably jotting down the information. "And you said they knew about Neil? That's... disconcerting. We've kept the details of Neil's heroism within a tight circle. If they're outsiders, it's worrying how they came by such information."

Allison stopped in her tracks, a sinking feeling in her stomach. "What should I do, Miranda? I'm scared for the kids. If these men aren't who they say they are..."

Miranda's voice turned resolute. "First, stay calm. We'll handle this. Jeremiah and I will alert our contacts to see if these names or that patch ring any bells. For now, keep that contact number they gave you, but don't use it. If they return or if you notice anything else unusual, call me immediately. And Allison," her voice softened, "we're here for you. If you feel unsafe at any moment, we'll find a way to get you out."

The conversation shifted to practical advice and plans for staying safe until they could figure out more about the mysterious visitors. By the end of the call, Allison felt a mix of reassurance and unease. The thought of unknown elements operating so close to her sanctuary was chilling.

After hanging up, Allison turned to find her children, once oblivious to the dangers lurking beyond their idyllic retreat, now watching her with wide, questioning eyes. She forced a smile, not wanting to frighten them with her own fears.

"Everything's okay, kids. Just some grown-up stuff I had to talk about with Miranda," she said, her voice brighter than she felt. "How about we make those chocolate chip cookies you love? We can even add extra chocolate chips."

As she gathered the ingredients, Allison's mind raced. The illusion of safety had been shattered, leaving her to wonder just how deep the tendrils of war had reached into their lives. The cabin, once a haven of peace, now felt like a fragile bubble, ready to burst at the slightest touch.

That night, after tucking her children into bed and ensuring the cabin was as secure as it could be, Allison sat at the kitchen table, the card with the radio frequency under the lamplight. The quiet of the night contrasted with the turmoil inside of her. The uncertainty of their situation, compounded by the mystery of the men's true intentions, weighed heavily on her.

With a determined sigh, Allison decided. She couldn't sit idly by, waiting for the unknown to come knocking. Tomorrow, she would head to her parents' home in Nebraska. She couldn't risk the lives of her kids being so close to the front lines, but she didn't have a vehicle to leave, and being so far out, there was no rideshare service or taxi that would come and get her family. She looked at her bank account and saw that the life insurance money had been added to the balance. She stifled a sob. The money couldn't replace Neil, but Neil saw to it that his life insurance was enough to support her and the kids for the rest of her life.

She dialed her father in Nebraska, Frank Harris; it was late, so she didn't expect an answer, but surprisingly, he answered.

"Hi, Allibug." His voice chipper as he called her by the name he had called her for as long as she could remember; she smiled widely.

"Daddy. The kids and I need you..." her voice trailed off as the powder keg of emotion and tears she had been holding back exploded, her voice now nothing more than gibberish.

Frank's response was immediate and soothing, a calm in the sudden storm of Allison's emotions. "Allibug, breathe. I'm here. Tell me what's wrong," he said, his voice steady and reassuring.

Through sobs, Allison explained the situation, from the appearance of the men claiming to be from the Montana-Idaho Militia to her conversation with Miranda and her realization they may not be who they said they were—that the tranquility of the Elkview Cabin might not be as safe as she once believed. Even though she had told him before, her emotion recounted Neil's heroism and the gaping hole it left in their lives, and now, the looming threat that seemed to edge ever closer.

Frank listened in silence, absorbing every word. When Allison finished, there was a brief pause, filled with the unspoken grief of a father who couldn't take his daughter's pain away. "Allison," he finally said, his voice firm, "you and the kids will come to Nebraska. I'll arrange for someone to come and get you. We'll keep you safe here. Neil... Neil did his part. Now, it's my turn to look after you and the grandkids."

Relief, mixed with a deep-seated sorrow, washed over Allison. "Thank you, Daddy. I... I just don't know if it's safe to wait here any longer. Those men, they knew about Neil. I'm scared they might come back."

"We'll act fast. I have a few trusted folks who can make the trip. They'll be discreet and quick. I'll call you back within an hour with details. Pack only what you need. We'll sort everything else out once you're here," Frank assured her, his tone leaving no room for argument.

After the call ended, Allison felt a flicker of hope amidst the fear. She began to pack, focusing on the essentials. She didn't have much aside from some clothes that were in their luggage and a few things the Johnsons had bought for her and the kids. The task gave her mind something to do other than spiral into worry. As she packed, she explained to her children that they were going to visit Grandpa in Nebraska, framing it as an adventure to ease their fears.

The night passed in a blur of activity and whispered assurances. When Frank called back, he relayed the arrangements he'd made. A trusted friend, a retired military man who'd helped Frank with the farm over the years, would be arriving by noon the next day with a secure vehicle to take them to Nebraska.

Allison didn't sleep much that night, her mind racing with what the next day would bring. But as dawn broke over the Elkview Cabin, she felt a resolve hardening within her. Neil had given everything to protect them, and now she would do everything to ensure their children's safety.

The sound of a vehicle approaching the cabin the next day brought Allison's heart into her throat. She peered out the window to see a nondescript SUV pulling up, dust swirling in its wake. A man stepped out, scanning the area before his eyes landed on Allison, who was watching from the window. He tipped his hat in a gesture of peace.

As she opened the door to greet him, Allison felt the chapter at the Elkview Cabin closing behind her. Ahead lay uncertainty but also safety and the warmth of family. With her children by her side, she stepped into the light of the new day, ready to face whatever came their way with the strength Neil had shown in his final moments and the love that would forever bind them together.

Jack and Stephen, shrouded by the dense undergrowth, kept a stealthy vigil over the Elkview cabin. The soft shutter sound of Jack's camera broke the silence, capturing not just the mundane details of an SUV and its license plate but also the intimate moment of Allison guiding Luke and Lily toward the vehicle. These photographs were far from ordinary; they were vital cogs in the machinery of a covert operation, serving purposes that extended beyond mere surveillance.

Their collection of data was intended for a particular audience—shadowy figures operating behind the scenes, capable of parsing through the gathered intel to identify threats and opportunities hidden from ordinary sight. The emblem they bore, a cryptic symbol unknown to Allison, marked their allegiance not to any recognized militia but to a covert organization working at the fringes of the known conflict. This organization excelled in the art of information warfare, skirting the boundaries of legality to further its undisclosed agenda.

As the sun rose higher in the sky and the SUV had already gone, Jack and Stephen withdrew deeper into the shadows of the forest. Trained to move unseen, they were ghosts in the landscape, leaving no trace of their presence. Unknown to Allison and her children, their watchful eyes represented not safety but a calculating assessment, measuring the potential impact of every piece of information on their covert operations.

Retreating to their hidden vehicle, equipped with state-of-the-art communication and surveillance gear, the pair uploaded the day's intel to a secure server. Their report would not only detail the day's observations but also provide an analysis of Allison's interactions, weaving her personal tragedy and protective instincts into the broader tapestry of their operations. This was intelligence gathering with a purpose, each piece of data a thread in the larger design of their organization's objectives.

The swift response from their command was encrypted, acknowledging the receipt of their report and suggesting further instructions were on the horizon. There was an unsettling acknowledgment of Allison's flight from the area, wrapped in the guise of concern for her safety. Yet, the directive was clear, they had to find Jake and Ray, and if that meant eliminating Jake's family or anyone else in the periphery, they would comply with the orders of their benefactor.

Ultimately, Allison wasn't important, but her orbit to the Johnsons made her a target of convenience. Jack and Stephen settled into the front seat of the RV-style vehicle that was used to hide their presence. Jack pressed the button, causing the engine to crank, "Phen, we have to find them before they tell everyone about our zero-energy technology." Jack said with a stern look on his face.

"Like anyone would believe them, there is no proof." Phen brushed his dirty blonde hair out of his eyes.

"Still, we are no closer to finding them, and we know the cost of failure." Jack looked towards the road in front of them as they entered the highway towards Boise, Idaho.

"We know it intimately."

11

IN THE SPRAWLING AMPHITHEATER of a commandeered community college, transformed into a makeshift briefing room, Jake and Ray found themselves amid a sea of fellow patriots who had answered the call to stand against the Confederation threat. The assembly was a vivid tapestry of the American spirit, representing a coalition drawn from fourteen northwestern states—each individual driven by a shared purpose to defend their homes and way of life against the encroaching darkness of the Confederation's advance.

The atmosphere was charged with palpable energy, a blend of determination and underlying tension. Men and women from Washington, Oregon, Nevada, Utah, Colorado, Kansas, Missouri, Iowa, Minnesota, North and South Dakota, Nebraska, Montana, and Idaho filled every available space. The unity of so many people in this gathering underscored the breadth of the crisis at hand, pulling together individuals from wildly differing backgrounds and beliefs towards a common cause.

At the heart of the amphitheater, the stage was transformed into a command center, where military leaders

from the Army, Navy, Air Force, and Marines presented a united front. These officers, each having taken
the extraordinary step to align with the Montana-Idaho
Militia, stood as symbols of the complex loyalties and
decisions forced by the unfolding conflict. Their presence, though unofficial, lent a gravitas to the proceed-
ings, bridging the gap between civilian resistance and
organized military discipline.

The room hushed as the briefing commenced, with the
lead strategist stepping forward. The screen behind him
flickered to life, displaying maps, troop movements,
and strategic points of interest. His voice, steady and
authoritative, cut through the silence, outlining the
current situation, the Confederation's tactics, and the
planned countermeasures. The presentation was meticulous, highlighting both the challenges and the opportunities ahead, underscoring the critical need for unity,
strategic intelligence, and tactical flexibility.

General Marcus Ross joined the General of the United
States Army on the stage, who had signed with the
Montana-Idaho Militia Pact.

"My name is Palmer Carlton, General of Western Defense Command. My home is Oregon, first and foremost, and I will defend her borders with my dying
breath, which is why I have aligned the WDC with the
Montana-Idaho Militia against the orders of the President of the United States. I am willing to face court
martial and lose my command to fight for our home-

land." General Palmer Carlton paused as applause from the whole amphitheater erupted; he held his hand up to silence the room.

"We have a lot of work to do, which is why we are gathered here today. The enemy has already taken control of over half of the state of Washington. Their soldiers seem to be unending, and their technology is superior to what a civilian force would have, which is why I am here. We are mobilizing our trained soldiers with the equipment we have to the Montana-Idaho Militia and to the men and women in those states that have chosen to stand up against this invading force." General Carlton finished his statement and waved his hand to the mass of men and women gathered. Thunderous applause as General Marcus Ross stepped to the microphone, "Thank you, General. Men and women of the Great Plains and Pacific Coastal regions of the United States, we are at a crossroads in this campaign to safeguard our sovereignty. The Confederation is moving rapidly towards Portland and Spokane. We will not survive a head-to-head battle with them, so we will make every acre of land they get a pain to hold." General Ross said, pausing as the speech got serious, "these are definitely hard times, and they will only get harder, but as Americans we are resilient. I have assigned everyone in this room to a squad in which we will commence guerilla warfare tactics. We don't have the resources to perform shock and awe attacks; instead, we have to be strategic." General

Marcus Ross paused, looking out at the faces of all the men and women placed under his charge.

His face turned defeated as an aide walked out on stage and whispered in his ear.

"The Confederation has now assumed control of Portland," General Ross continued, the weight of his words settling over the room like a pall. "Without firing a single shot, Portland has fallen, greeted by cheers from American Communist and Antifa protestors. This is not just a military defeat but a psychological one aimed at fracturing our resolve."

He clicked the remote, and the screen behind him displayed a live feed. The streets of Portland were filled with the flags of the Confederation, a sight that stirred a mix of anger and determination in the assembled crowd. "Our enemy has crossed the threshold of another state. The border of their control is expanding daily, and if we do not act, more cities will fall as Seattle and Portland have."

General Ross's gaze swept across the faces before him, each person mirroring the concern that the leaders gathered on stage showed. "We are dispatching contingents of Montana-Idaho Militia soldiers, alongside aligned US Military personnel, to strategic locations in Leavenworth and Yakima, Washington, as well as Northern California and parts of Oregon. Our mission is clear: to halt the Confederation's advance and, if we can, push back to reclaim our lands."

The room was silent, and the reality of the task ahead was sobering. Jake and Ray exchanged glances, understanding the enormity of the challenge they faced. They knew that they were going to be fighting in isolated skirmishes, but with the advance of Confederation soldiers, they were part of a larger, more desperate battle for the soul of their nation. They knew it was terrible, but this painted a far more ominous picture.

"As General Carlton mentioned, we're at a disadvantage in terms of technology and numbers," General Ross added, his voice firm. "But remember, we have the home-field advantage. We know our lands, our cities, and our people. This knowledge is our weapon, our shield. We will employ guerrilla tactics, hit-and-run attacks, and strategic retreats to bleed the enemy dry. Every inch they take will cost them dearly."

The generals outlined the tactical plan, emphasizing mobility, stealth, and the element of surprise. Training sessions were scheduled, and supply routes established, ensuring that every militia member and allied soldier was prepared for the unconventional warfare that lay ahead.

As the briefing concluded, the crowd was instilled with a sense of unity and purpose. Although they were a disparate group drawn from different walks of life and states, they were united in their determination to defend their homes, their families, and their freedom.

Jake and Ray, like everyone else, stood ready to play their part in the coming conflict. As they left the amphitheater, the sun had fully set, casting long shadows across the college campus. Ahead of them lie uncertain days, brimming with danger and the specter of loss. But within them burned the resolve to stand and fight, to push back against the darkness and to emerge, against all odds, victorious.

Ray looked at Jake with an uneasy smile across his lips, "I wish Mike were here; I miss our buddy." Jake acknowledged the pain in Ray's voice by grabbing and hugging him. It was almost Christmas, a month and a half since the Confederation bombed the coast of California, Oregon, and Washington with the Neutronium bomb, and nearly two months since things were—normal.

Jake's phone rang; he looked down and saw that Samantha was calling, "Hello?" Jake answered.

"Oh my God, Jake! Daddy told me you were alive and gave me this number. I can't believe you are safe! I thought you were dead!"

"Sam, it's so good to hear your voice," Jake responded, relief and a tinge of sorrow coloring his tone. "We've been through a lot, but yeah, we're still here. How are you holding up?"

Samantha's voice was a mix of excitement and exhaustion. "I'm okay, considering everything. I am on my way to Helena right now. The Brigadier General of the Marine Corps has agreed to align with the Montana-Idaho Militia. I have been selected to be a liaison between the two to ensure we have the legal authority to move. "

Jake's eyebrows rose in surprise at Samantha's revelation. "That's... incredible news, Sam. It sounds like you're playing a crucial role in all of this."

"Yeah, it's a lot of responsibility, but I believe in what we're doing. We're fighting for our homes, our families, and our future. I just wish it didn't have to come to this," Samantha replied, her voice tinged with determination and a hint of sadness.

"Agreed. It's been tough without Mike, and the situation on the ground is getting more intense by the day," Jake shared, feeling the weight of his own words. "We're about to start some intensive guerrilla warfare training. Things are escalating quickly."

Samantha let out a long sigh. "I heard about Portland. It's a tough blow, but we can't let it break us. We need to be smarter and more strategic. With the military expertise we're bringing into the fold, I'm hopeful we can make a difference."

The conversation shifted to more personal matters, with brother and sister catching up on lost time and shared memories, as well as a brief respite from the war that raged around them. Before they ended the call, Samantha's tone grew serious again.

"Jake, please, be careful. I know you and Ray are in the thick of it." The line was quiet for a moment as Samantha's voice reflected the emotion of the moment, "Just... make it back to us, okay?"

Jake nodded, even though Samantha couldn't see him. "I promise, Sam. We'll watch each other's backs. You do the same in Helena."

After they said their goodbyes, Jake stood there for a moment, phone in hand, staring at the darkening horizon. The reality of their situation had never felt more pressing. With the integration of aligned military forces and the looming threat of the Confederation's advances, the war had entered a new phase—one that would test their resilience and resolve like never before.

Gathering himself, Jake returned to where Ray and the others were gearing up for the night's operations. They were a makeshift family, bound together by circumstance and a shared resolve to fight for something greater than themselves. The road ahead was uncertain, and dangers lurked at every mile, but Jake knew one thing for sure: they wouldn't face it alone.

Under the cover of darkness, Jake and Ray climbed into the military transport headed for Yakima. Another truck was being loaded with personnel and gear heading for Leavenworth. Jake tipped his hat to one of the men climbing in, who returned the gesture.

Their guerilla training would begin at their destination, but Jake knew that the training would not be long, considering the Confederation was rapidly moving deeper into the states. Jake sat on the bench next to Ray and leaned back, pulling his hat over his eyes to try and get a little sleep on the ride, but he couldn't get the sight of Mike's face twisting in pain as the dart struck him, and he vanished. It was like a nightmare re-imagined; if Ray hadn't been there and seen it too, he wouldn't even believe it.

Just a few months ago, they had set out to hunt and fish; little did he know that just a few weeks later, he would be thrust into a war to protect his homeland. He finally started drifting off to sleep.

Jack Ashby and Stephen Martenson's journey toward Spokane was marked by tense anticipation, an undercurrent of unease threading through their otherwise silent preparation. As the highway gave way to the outskirts of the city, the sight of heavy military presence brought a palpable shift in the air, a tightening in Jack's chest that he hadn't anticipated. The checkpoint ahead, bristling with the activity of the Montana-Idaho Militia, was a fortress in its own right, a symbol of the escalated conflict that had drawn the nation's eyes westward.

The decision to pull off into the shadowed embrace of an abandoned gas station was mutual, a wordless agreement between the two men. There, concealed by the RV's innocuous exterior, they deliberated their next move with the gravity it deserved. The atmosphere within was charged, each breath a testament to the weight of the mission that lay on their shoulders.

"There's no way we're getting into Spokane with this level of security," Jack murmured, his frustration evident. Jack's frustration found a physical outlet against the RV's wall; his vulnerability cracked the veneer of their calculated calm and dented the wall of the RV. "Those are official Montana-Idaho Militia troops. They'll spot outsiders like us in a heartbeat, especially after our stint at the Johnsons' ranch. I know that woman called us in, which is why she left so quickly."

Stephen turned from the window, his face set in a grim line. "Maybe we could volunteer for the militia," he suggested, the idea forming as he spoke. "Reports said they're desperate for any able-bodied person. They might not look too closely at a couple of extra hands, even if it means we're stepping straight into the meat grinder."

Stephen's response, a suggestion to blend in with the militia by volunteering, was a gamble that carried the weight of their lives on its slender chance of success. Yet, in the silence that followed, a plan began to take root.

Jack paused, considering the proposal. He knew the risks involved, but their options were narrowing by the minute. "Volunteering could give us the cover we need, but it's risky. We'd be under their watch, embedded with their forces. If they discover who we really are..."

Stephen nodded, the weight of the decision pressing down on him. "It's a gamble, but it might be our only shot at staying close to the action without raising alarms. We blend in, gather what intel we can, and keep our heads down."

The RV was silent for a moment, save for the distant hum of military vehicles outside. Jack finally broke the silence, his voice firm. "Alright. We do it. We volunteer. But we stay alert, watch each other's backs, and get out at the first sign of trouble."

Stephen extended his hand, and Jack shook it, their agreement sealed with a look of determination. "To Spokane, then," Stephen said, a wry smile flickering across his face. "Let's hope our acting skills are up to par."

The transformation they underwent was methodical, a stripping away of their true identities to don the camouflage of ordinary men caught in extraordinary times. Their clothes bore no allegiance, blending into the environment with neutral tones. Their faces were scrubbed clean of any distinguishing marks, transforming them into anonymous defenders. The narrative they constructed was spontaneous, yet it resonated with the genuine desperation of people fighting to protect their homes. As they stepped out of the RV, the cold air bit at their skin, contrasting the stifled atmosphere inside. They approached the militia's checkpoint with rehearsed ease, their strides confident yet cautious. The closer they got, the louder the buzz of activity became, a cacophony of orders shouted and vehicles moving.

"Act natural," Jack whispered under his breath as they neared the first line of scrutiny, a pair of militia members who scrutinized every vehicle and person attempting to enter Spokane.

One of the militia members, a woman with sharp eyes and a no-nonsense demeanor, stepped forward. "Purpose of your visit?" she asked, her gaze flicking between Jack and Stephen.

"We're here to volunteer," Stephen responded smoothly, the lie tasting like ash on his tongue. "Heard you could use every pair of hands."

The woman eyed them, her suspicion a tangible thing. "Volunteer, huh?" She glanced at her companion, a silent exchange passing between them. "You got any military experience?"

Jack chimed in, "A bit. We're not soldiers, but we know our way around. Grew up hunting in these parts. Figured it's time to do our part."

Her scrutiny lingered a moment longer before she nodded, gesturing them through with a jerk of her head. "Fine. Head to the recruitment tent. They'll process you, get you sorted."

As they walked past the checkpoint, the weight of their deception felt like a heavy cloak around their shoulders. The militia's base was a hive of activity, with volunteers and military personnel moving in a choreographed chaos that spoke of urgency and determination.

As they walked past the pedestrian entry, several large military transports rumbled by, the ground vibrating beneath their feet. The vehicles were packed with soldiers and weapons, their faces grim and focused, heading deeper into Washington State. The sight was a vivid reminder of the escalating conflict, the air heavy with tension. Each transport underscored the gravity of the situation as the troops prepared to confront the unfolding crisis. They continued walking into the Spokane Forward Operating Base and looking around.

They found the recruitment tent easily enough, a large canvas structure with recruits ambling about. Inside, they were greeted by a burly man with a clipboard. "Names?" he barked, not looking up.

"Jack Smith and Stephen Jones," Jack replied, the names rehearsed, generic enough to be forgettable.

"Where are you from?" the man barked, still not looking at the two. Jack looked at Stephen and then back at the man, "We grew up outside of Omak; we were ordered out of our homes by the State Guard because the Confederation breached the Oroville border crossing. We brought our families to Coeur d'Alene, and we drove out this morning to volunteer."

The recruiter made a note on his clipboard, then looked up, finally giving them his full attention. "Alright, Smith and Jones. You'll start with basic training. If you've got any skills worth a damn, we'll find out soon enough. Welcome to the fight."

As they were ushered towards a group of other volunteers, Jack and Stephen exchanged a glance. They were now embedded within the very heart of the militia's efforts to defend Washington.

Their steps toward the training grounds were measured, and the weight of their decision settled in with each stride. The camp was a labyrinth of activity, the air thick with the scent of determination and the faint echoes of anxiety. Around them, faces blurred into a sea of resolve, each person there united by a common cause yet isolated in their own silent battles.

Stephen leaned in, his voice low, as they fell in line with the other recruits. "Keep your head down and eyes open. Remember, we're here to eliminate Jake and Ray. That's it, then we are to report back to the benefactor."

Jack's reply was a terse nod, his mind racing with the implications of their infiltration. The guise of Jack Smith and Stephen Jones was a thin veil, one that a single slip or an unexpected encounter could pierce.

As they reached the designated area for new recruits, a drill sergeant, a mountain of a man with a voice that could cut through the din of chatter and clattering equipment, barked orders, ushering them into formation. "Line up! Today, you start the journey from civilians to soldiers. It's not going to be easy, but it's necessary. You're fighting for your homes, your families, and your freedom."

The intensity of the drill sergeant's gaze swept over them, a challenge and a promise all rolled into one. It was here, among these would-be warriors, that Jack and Stephen would have to tread carefully, blending their fabricated identities with enough truth to avoid suspicion.

Their training began in earnest, a grueling regimen that tested their physical and mental limits. Yet, among the exhaustion and the endless drills, there were opportunities. Whispered conversations with fellow recruits revealed snippets of information, fears about the Confederation's advances, and personal stories of loss and defiance.

In these moments, Jack and Stephen gathered the intelligence they sought, piecing together a clearer picture of the militia's capabilities and intentions. Their dual role as observers and participants was a precarious balance, one that required constant vigilance to maintain.

As days passed, the initial suspicion that had greeted their arrival slowly ebbed away, replaced by a camaraderie born of shared hardship. Yet, beneath the surface, the tension never entirely dissipated, a reminder of the stakes involved and the consequences of discovery.

On a night enveloped in cautious silence, Jack Ashby and Stephen Martenson found themselves in a secluded corner of their temporary quarters, a repurposed high school classroom turned into a makeshift bunkhouse. The only source of light was a lantern, casting elongated shadows that danced across the walls, mirroring the covert nature of their hushed conversation.

"We've gathered enough intel to locate Jake and Ray, and then we can report back," Jack whispered, his eyes carefully moving over the scribbled notes and maps sprawled out before them. Their collected data was comprehensive: detailed accounts of the militia's strategic plans, troop movements, and even insights into potential vulnerabilities within their defensive lines.

Stephen, his face etched with the severity of their situation, nodded in agreement. "We need to establish contact soon, but stealth is key. Getting caught now would mean the end of everything we've worked for."

Their communication strategy was filled with the potential of detection—a coded message to be transmitted via the specialized equipment in their RV. This necessitated a daring departure from the heavily guarded militia encampment in Spokane under the cover of darkness, a venture that carried the weight of their mission's success or failure.

Understanding the urgency, they readied themselves to leave that very night. Staying would mean being dispatched to the Northern Front in California the following day, cutting off any chance to access their vital communication tools.

With practiced caution, Jack and Stephen navigated the dimly lit hallways of the school, each step deliberate to avoid any noise that might betray their presence. Their movements were synchronized, a silent dance of survival honed by years of experience. They quietly slipped through a door, inching closer to freedom with each silent movement.

As they reached the camp's perimeter, the fence loomed before them, a final barrier to their escape. With expert precision, they scaled it, their figures quickly swallowed by the shadowy embrace of the woods just beyond. Their escape into the night was a silent pact sealed with the urgency of their mission.

Once safely distanced from the camp, Jack glanced at Stephen, determination gleaming in his eyes. "Next, we send the encrypted message, then make it for Yakima," he said, the plan being clear in his mind.

Stephen, catching his breath, nodded in agreement. "The less the militia knows about zero-energy weapons, the better. Keeping that ace up our sleeve gives us an edge."

They covered several miles on foot, and the forest around them was a cloak of darkness and safety. Each step moved them away from the potential danger they had narrowly escaped and closer to their objective. The hidden location of their RV came into view, a sanctuary amidst the chaos. Climbing aboard, both men were hit by a wave of exhaustion.

Jack collapsed onto the couch, the adrenaline ebbing away, leaving him drained. Stephen found solace on the bed, his body aching from the exertion, but his mind still sharp and focused.

"Tomorrow, we will complete our mission," Stephen declared, his voice low but persistent. "And then, we can go home."

12

SAMANTHA'S JOURNEY FROM TWENTYNINE Palms
to Helena took several detours, eventually leading her
through Sheridan, Wyoming, as she navigated the series
of closed highways and roads enforced in the wake of
the Neutronium bomb's devastation throughout California. The aftermath of the attack had transformed
what should have been a straightforward drive into a
prolonged odyssey, with many main routes shuttered to
facilitate the passage of construction teams and FEMA
units working tirelessly to rebuild the affected areas.

Driving off Interstate 90, Samantha steered her Jeep
into a modest gas station nestled beside a quaint country pizza parlor,

Normalcy

She thought to herself as she sighed; the past few weeks,
she had been constantly running and trying to navigate
the intricacies of her father starting up a civilian militia
in response to the Confederation's invasion and her
duties as a Marine Officer in the United States Marine
Corps.

The pizza parlor was a piece of normal in the midst of uncertainty and an impending war on the United States home turf. The extended hours behind the wheel had taken their toll, and the prospect of stopping for gas and grabbing dinner in Sheridan offered a much-needed reprieve from the endless stretches of road that had characterized her journey so far.

The detour, though time-consuming, offered an unexpected chance to escape the monotony of the drive. Samantha paused to soak in the small-town charm of Sheridan, noticeably different from the scenes of destruction and upheaval she had witnessed elsewhere. Here, life appeared to proceed calmly, seemingly untouched by the chaos affecting much of the country.

Flyover country, as they call it, is so peaceful.

She smiled while thinking to herself and filling up her Jeep. Samantha relished the chance to stretch her legs and breathe in the crisp Wyoming air. The quaint setting of the gas station, with its adjacent pizza parlor emitting inviting aromas of freshly baked pies, was a welcome reminder of the simple pleasures often overlooked in the hustle and bustle of daily life in the military.

Samantha hopped back into her Jeep, pulled away from the gas pumps, and parked in an open parking spot.

The parlor seemed busy, which might be a good sign,

She mused to herself as she walked towards the parlor. The thought of a warm meal and the brief respite it promised injected a newfound energy into her steps. The journey to Helena was far from over. Still, the unexpected detour through Sheridan provided Samantha with a momentary escape, a chance to recharge before continuing on her way to meet with the council of governors in Helena. The prospect scared her, but she set her mind at ease for now.

As she walked in, the feeling of heat hit her across her cold cheeks. A smile crossed her face as she was greeted by a high school-aged girl named Abby.

"Welcome to Dwayne's Pizza Shack, dinner for one?" Abby grinned wide, revealing a mouth full of braces and colorful rubber bands.

"Yes, one, thank you, Abby," Samantha said, noting the girl's name on the little tag pinned to her apron. Following Abby through the pizzeria, Samantha passed several booths and tables where people were enjoying their pizza, immersed in lively conversations and laughter. As she settled into the booth, she marveled at the contrast. Here, in this small town, life seemed untouched by the war raging in the Pacific Northwest. The distant conflict felt like a world away, a harsh reality that these people appeared blissfully unaware of.

"What can I get you to drink?" Abby asked, pulling out her little notepad.

"I'll just have water," Samantha said, looking over the menu, "and... um... let me get some of your garlic knots."

"Comin' right out, sweetie." Abby quickly turned and disappeared into the kitchen. Samantha pulled her phone out and began to scroll through her Vyber account, clicking the like emoji on several photos and reading posts from her friends scattered all over the country. She got lost in her thoughts as Abby returned with the fresh and hot garlic knots and her water.

"What's for dinner, hon?" Abby asked with that same bright smile across her face.

"Let me get a Caesar salad and a meaty, cheesy calzone." Samantha laughed at the corny name as she handed her menu to the young girl.

"Good choice. You enjoy those garlic knots, and I'll be right back with the salad." Abby disappeared back into the kitchen as Samantha leaned back in her booth. She began taking a moment to savor the warmth and comforting hum of life around her. The garlic knots were perfect—golden, buttery, and fragrant with garlic. It was a simple pleasure, but at that moment, it felt like a rare luxury. As she enjoyed her appetizer, she couldn't help but overhear snippets of conversations from neighboring tables. People discussed everything from local events to the larger, looming concerns of the nation, yet there was an underlying current of resilience and community that Samantha found deeply reassuring.

The brief exchanges and Abby's cheerful demeanor served as reminders that there was a world outside the military and the ongoing conflict—a world that continued to thrive on small joys and connections. These moments of normalcy were precious, grounding her amidst the whirlwind of duties and the heavy burden of uncertainty that came with her role as both a Marine officer and the daughter of a man who had taken a stand to protect their home.

As Abby returned with the Caesar salad, Samantha thanked her and began to eat, the crisp freshness of the lettuce and the tangy dressing providing a welcome contrast to the measly snacks she had been subsisting on her drive. She allowed herself to relax, the stresses of her journey momentarily forgotten in the cozy atmosphere of Dwayne's Pizza Shack.

When her calzone arrived, steaming and laden with an enticing blend of meats and cheese, Samantha couldn't help but smile in anticipation. Abby lingered for a moment, making sure everything was to Samantha's satisfaction before darting off to attend to another table.

As Samantha dug into her meal, she realized that this pause, this simple dinner in a small Wyoming town, was exactly what she needed to gather her strength for the challenges ahead. It was a reminder of what they were all fighting for—not just the abstract ideals of freedom and sovereignty but the tangible realities of community, family, and the simple pleasure of a meal shared in peace.

The moment Samantha's knife pierced the crust of her calzone, the ambiance of Dwayne's Pizza Shack transformed. A ripple of applause and excited murmurs washed over the cozy space as five figures entered. She glanced up, her attention captured by the group's entrance. They were clad in a variant of the desert camouflage she recognized from her deployments in Afghanistan, yet this was deeper, tailored perhaps for the rugged terrains of mountainous or brush-laden areas. The fabric's subtle difference spoke of specialized operations, of environments far removed from the Afghan deserts she knew.

The crowd's enthusiasm swelled, a warm welcome for the three men and two women who moved with the assuredness of those well-acquainted with their uniforms. Abby, the ever-attentive hostess, quickly ushered them to a table, navigating through the suddenly energized patrons with ease.

Samantha observed the group discreetly, a sense of camaraderie threading through her at the sight of fellow service members. Yet, it was the patch they bore that truly piqued her curiosity—a simple yet unfamiliar emblem of a buffalo encased within a white circle. It was a mark of distinction, signaling a story, an identity she was yet to understand.

The soldiers' presence injected an unexpected layer of complexity into her quiet dinner, sparking a blend of professional interest and personal respect. She contemplated initiating conversation, eager for any insights they might offer into the evolving landscape of military alliances or operations. However, understanding the value of respite in their lives, she chose to observe in silence for the moment, respecting their moment of reprieve.

Finishing her meal amid renewed chatter and laughter, Samantha couldn't shake the intrigue the buffalo patch stirred within her. It symbolized a piece of the larger puzzle unfolding across the nation—a puzzle she was determined to understand.

She stood from the booth, grabbed her jacket, took a last sip of her water, and cleared her throat. Then, she approached the table with the soldiers sitting there.

"Excuse me, I just wanted to step over and say hello; my name is First Lieutenant Samantha Johnson of the United States Marine Corps, and I couldn't help but notice your uniforms; they don't look like standard issue." Samantha smiled at the men and women in uniform.

The group paused, their conversations tapering off as they turned their attention to Samantha. The closest to her, a man with closely cropped hair and an accessible authority, extended a hand in greeting. "First Lieutenant Johnson, it's a pleasure. I'm Lieutenant Harper, and this," he gestured to his companions, "is my team. We're part of a specialized unit aligned with the efforts in the Northwest."

Samantha shook his hand, noting the firm grip. "Your uniforms... and that patch," she nodded towards the buffalo emblem, "I haven't seen it before. Mind if I ask what it represents?"

Lieutenant Harper smiled with a hint of pride in his eyes. "Well," Harper began, "it's a bit of a long story, but in short, it symbolizes resilience and strength. We operate in some of the more challenging terrains, supporting both reconnaissance and direct engagement operations. The buffalo, well, it's an animal known for its toughness and its will to keep pushing forward, regardless of the storm. It embodies our spirit and determination."

One of the women, a corporal with sharp features and an observant gaze, chimed in. "We've been on assignment in Kansas for the last few weeks but are headed to Helena to meet with the council of governors."

Samantha's interest deepened. "I'm actually on my way to Helena to work as a liaison between the Marine Corps and the Montana-Idaho Militia. My father is Governor Jeremiah Johnson..."

Another member of the group jumped up and saluted, "Ma'am, if only we knew." The young man said quickly as Lieutenant Harper stood up and saluted, followed by the rest.

"Forgive the zeal of Private Waters; he was the reason we went to Colorado." He smiled as Samantha pulled a chair away from a neighboring table.

"Please, no need for formality," Samantha reassured them as she took a seat, gesturing for them to relax. "It's refreshing to meet others on their way to Helena. My journey's been... enlightening, to say the least."

Lieutenant Harper, resuming his seat, shared a knowing glance with his team. "Enlightening is one way to put it. The landscape is changing every day. Our mission's adaptability is crucial."

Samantha nodded, intrigued. "I've been somewhat out of the loop, dealing with the aftermath of the Neutronium bomb. My perspective's been, well, a bit singular. How are things shaping up in Kansas?"

The second woman, Sergeant Morales, leaned in, her tone earnest. "Kansas has been tough. The illegal immigrants that were coming up from Mexico were straining the state of Texas. Private Waters here was a new recruit who joined the Idaho State Guard and went to the Texas border to help when the Neutronium bomb happened. Now, Mexico is trying to keep Americans out of Mexico. The tide has changed quite a bit, but the charter of the Montana-Idaho Militia is that we fight for the sovereignty of the United States. If people want to leave, that is their choice." Morales laughed calmly, "Texas is sending their National Guard and State Guard up North to help out, too; it really is a weird turn of play." Morales finished.

Samantha listened intently, absorbing the complexity of Morales's description of the shifting dynamics. The world she was navigating seemed to invert traditional roles and expectations at every turn, painting a picture of a nation grappling with unprecedented challenges both within and beyond its borders.

"It's an abstract and chaotic painting of crises," Samantha mused, her thoughts briefly clouding with the weight of the situation. "But hearing about units like yours, coming together from different states, different backgrounds—it gives me hope. We're more interconnected than we realize."

Lieutenant Harper nodded in agreement. "Exactly. It's about finding common ground by leveraging our varied strengths. Take Private Waters, for instance," he said, gesturing to the young man who had eagerly saluted Samantha earlier. "His enthusiasm and willingness to jump into unknown situations have been invaluable."

Private Waters, a bit sheepish under the spotlight, managed a grin. "Just trying to do my part, ma'am. Every bit helps, right?"

"And then there's Sergeant Morales," Samantha said, turning her attention to the other woman. I like your gumption; you remind me of a young woman I fought with in the Russo-Ukrainian War."

Samantha's gaze shifted to the remaining members of the team, a man and a woman who had been quietly listening. "And you two are?"

The man, broad-shouldered with a calm demeanor, spoke up. "I'm Specialist Jensen, ma'am. Demolitions and engineering. Been working on plans to help with fortifying our positions in the Northwest, making sure we're ready for whatever comes our way."

The woman beside him, with keen eyes and a poised bearing, added, "Corporal Lee. Communications and tech. Keeping us connected, making sure information flows where it needs to, without getting intercepted."

Samantha was impressed. "You're exactly the kind of folks we need. It's reassuring to know you're headed to Helena as well."

As their conversation delved deeper into their military careers and personal stories, Samantha felt a kinship with these soldiers. They were all parts of a larger entity, each with a unique role in the unfolding narrative of their nation's fight for survival.

As the group finished their meal and prepared to part ways, Lieutenant Harper offered a final thought.

"First Lieutenant Johnson, we may come from different branches, different states, but we're all fighting for the same thing. Let's keep the lines of communication open. Who knows? Our paths might cross again in Helena."

Samantha smiled, feeling a renewed sense of determination. "I'd like that. Safe travels, Lieutenant. And to all of you," she said, addressing the team, "thank you for your service. Let's make sure we all make it through this."

Stepping out into the night's crisp embrace, Samantha's encounter at Dwayne's Pizza Shack lingered in her thoughts. The camaraderie she'd felt with Lieutenant Harper's team was a rare glimmer of unity in the tumult of her dual life as both a Marine and the daughter of a militia leader. The buffalo patch, emblematic of resilience, seemed now like a guidepost in the fog of war that had descended upon the country. Climbing into her Jeep, the weight of her responsibilities and the challenges ahead pressed heavily upon her.

With a few taps, Samantha reactivated her phone's screen, and the Vyber app was still open from earlier. Her curiosity piqued by the distinctive patch she'd seen, she typed "buffalo patch" into the search bar, not fully prepared for the flood of images and hashtags that would soon engulf her. The screen filled with photos and videos showcasing not just military personnel but civilians as well, all donning the white patch adorned with a blue circle and the distinct silhouette of a buffalo.

However, it was the hashtag #TurningInMyResignation that caught her eye and pulled her deeper into the rabbit hole.

Hesitation marked her finger's pause over the screen before she tapped the hashtag, bracing herself for what she might uncover. The content that unfolded before her sent shockwaves through her psyche. Video after video showed service members from the Pact states in a solemn ritual of removing the American flag from their uniforms to replace it with the buffalo patch. The symbolism was clear, a tangible sign of a divide that Samantha had hoped was not as profound or as broad as these posts suggested.

Each swipe brought more declarations of allegiance to this new symbol over the old, and with each post, Samantha's heart sank a little further. The buffalo patch represented more than resilience; it was becoming a symbol of a schism within the very fabric of the nation's military and civilian populations alike. The uneasy feeling that had been a mere whisper at the back of her mind now roared to life, a storm of doubt and confusion that threatened to overwhelm her.

For a moment, she sat frozen, the glow of the phone casting shadows across her face as she absorbed the significance of what she was witnessing. The posts weren't just expressions of individual choice; they were markers of a seismic shift in loyalty and identity, reflective of the deep turmoil tearing at the seams of the United States.

The Vyber feed, once a source of casual browsing, now felt like a portal into a rapidly changing landscape where the certainties of duty and patriotism were being questioned and redefined. Samantha felt a chasm opening beneath her, a gap between her understanding of her role and the reality of the shifting allegiances around her. How could she navigate this divide, torn between her sworn duty to the United States Marine Corps and the undeniable pull of the cause her father and now seemingly many others had taken up?

With a heavy heart, Samantha locked her phone and set it aside, the echoes of #TurningInMyResignation haunting her thoughts. The drive ahead would be long and filled with more than just the miles between Sheridan and Helena. It would be a journey through her own doubts, fears, and loyalties, a path she would have to navigate with no clear map or guide. The night air, once refreshing, now seemed to carry a chill of uncertainty, a prelude to the challenging days ahead.

She turned the key to her Jeep, and the vehicle roared to life. Pushing her gas pedal, she shifted her manual and pulled back onto Interstate 90 towards Helena, her emotions swirling inside of her as her thoughts raced a mile a minute.

She reached over and grabbed her phone, looking through the text messages to get Jake's phone number, which her mom had sent earlier. Finding it, she tapped on it, and the ring picked up on her Bluetooth system.

Jake picked up the phone, "Hello?"

"Jake?" Samantha asked quickly,

"Hey, Sis." Jake chuckled a little at hearing his sister so soon after their last conversation.

"I just can't—I still can't believe you are okay," Samantha said, her emotions getting the better of her as her mind teetered between the safety of Jake and the whole experience she just had with the rabbit hole she had fallen into.

"Jake, I saw this white patch with a blue circle and a silhouette of a buffalo. Do you know anything about that?" She asked as she read a sign that said Three Forks was 297 miles.

"Yeah, it's a patch that was created by the daughter of the Wyoming governor, Davison Carey. It's a patch that all of the members of the militia have taken to wear in solidarity with our Great Plains Sovereignty and so that we are easily able to identify each other." Jake explained as Samantha nodded in silence, "Speaking of being able to identify each other, I hear you got the Marine Corps coming to help, finally." Samantha's grip on the steering wheel tightened as she processed Jake's explanation, the patch now a tangible symbol of the growing movement that her father and Jake were part of. The revelation that it originated from Davison Carey, the governor of Wyoming's daughter, only added layers to the complexity of the situation she found herself entangled in. "It's all happening so fast," she murmured, the illuminated signs blurring past her as she navigated the dark roads.

Jake's voice brought her back from her fantasy. "Yeah, the Marine Corps alignment is a big step. You going to Helena is crucial, Sam. Your role as a liaison could really bridge the gap between the military and the militia. There's a lot of tension and misunderstandings that need clearing up. Not to mention, we need the extra manpower," Jake said as voices in the background started singing random songs.

Samantha exhaled a mix of apprehension and resolve settling in her chest. "I'm on my way, Jake. But I won't lie; it's a lot to take in. This patch, the militia, and our family are directly in the middle of it all—it's overwhelming. Where are you, by the way?"

"I wish I could tell you, but I get it, Sis. Remember, we're doing what we believe is right for our state, our people, and our region. This patch," Jake paused, choosing his words carefully, "it's more than just fabric. It's a commitment to stand for what we believe in, even when it's hard."

The conversation shifted as Samantha shared her experiences at Dwayne's Pizza Shack, the soldiers she met, and the intriguing buffalo patch. Jake listened intently, his occasional questions a comforting presence as the miles stretched on.

As they delved deeper into the implications of the Marine Corps' involvement and the militia's actions, Samantha felt the weight lifting slightly. Jake's understanding and encouragement served as a clear guide, illuminating her path through the fog of her doubts.

"Look, Sis, when you get to Helena, we'll sit down on a conference call with Dad and the others. You'll see the bigger picture, how everything fits together. We're on the right side of history here," Jake assured her, his confidence a comfort to the uncertainty that had clouded Samantha's thoughts.

The sign for Three Forks grew nearer, marking the distance to her next turn. As she continued on the highway that would eventually lead her closer to Helena, Samantha found a semblance of peace in the knowledge that she was not navigating this journey alone. Her family, despite the turmoil and the looming challenges, remained united in purpose.

"Thanks, Jake. I really needed to hear that," she said, a smile touching her lips for the first time since leaving Sheridan. "I hope to see you soon; I have about fifteen hugs and a few punches saved up for you."

Jake laughed uncomfortably as voices in the background started making smooching and kissing noises. "It's my sister, idiots!" He said at a distance from the microphone on the phone.

"Where are you, Jake?"

"Don't worry about that, sis. You just get to Helena in one piece, safe and sound; I will see you soon." Jake said quickly, then hung up in the middle of Samantha, telling him that she loved him.

She was puzzled by the voices. The last time she had spoken to Jake, he had been in Spokane, straightforward and clear about his whereabouts. Now, however, his tone had shifted to one of evasiveness, which set off alarm bells in her mind. He was being unusually cagey, dodging her questions and offering vague answers that only heightened her concern. The change was unsettling, and she couldn't shake the feeling that something was terribly wrong. Her worry grew with each ambiguous reply, and she felt a gnawing sense of dread about what he might be hiding.

"Yo Vyber." She said as her phone's assistant lit up, "Play The Black Keys radio." Shortly after the music began playing on her radio, she smiled slightly and settled in for the long drive.

13

TROY'S OFFICE WAS A sanctuary of solitude, save for the meticulous scratching of pencil on paper. Engrossed in the task at hand, he crafted the words of a speech that marked a pivotal transition not just in his life but potentially in the history of the nation. Scheduled for the following Wednesday, January 15th, this address to the public and press was not just any speech; it was to be his final one as a private citizen. The acuteness of his words weighed heavily on him, knowing that his subsequent speeches would be delivered from the most distinguished platform in the country — that of the President of the United States.

As the CEO of Thomason Estates, a national real estate conglomerate, Troy had wielded considerable influence in the business world. Yet, this new role required him to pivot from corporate strategies to steering the ship of state. In this quiet moment, he was no longer the executive dictating terms but a leader contemplating the future of his country. His eldest son, Charlton, had recently taken the reins of Thomason Estates, assuming the mantle of CEO and allowing Troy to dedicate himself to his upcoming responsibilities fully.

The weeks leading up to this moment had been a whirl-wind of preparations for office, juxtaposed against the backdrop of Althea Morris's contentious ascension to the Presidency. Troy harbored deep reservations about the legitimacy of her claim, perceiving her actions and the rapid expansion of her administration as overly am-bitious, perhaps even underhanded.

With each word Troy penned, he outlined a vision for an America reborn, a nation he believed was teetering on the precipice of decline due to decades of mismanage-ment and aggressive foreign policies. His rhetoric was bold, promising to herald a new era of prosperity and to bring an end to the invasion of the Confederation. He pledged that within the first ten days of his Presidency, he would declare victory, a statement that underscored the ambitious nature of his forthcoming tenure.

This speech was more than a declaration of political intent; it was a manifesto for change, a commitment to guide America back to a path of unity and strength. As Troy crafted each sentence, the weight of the re-sponsibility he was about to assume settled upon his shoulders. This was his commitment not only to those who would hear his words on January 15th but to all Americans whose futures were intertwined with the decisions he would soon be responsible for making.

A soft knock on the door interrupted Troy's thoughts, pulling him out of his reverie. He set the pencil down on the desk, the unfinished speeches and doodles before him reflecting his distracted state. Leaning back in his chair, he watched as the door creaked open and Amyleigh's head peeked through the gap. Her curious eyes met his, a small, tentative smile playing on her lips.

"Hey, Amyleigh," Troy greeted, trying to mask the tension in his voice. "Come on in.

"I am sorry to disturb you. Senator Robert Sinclair from Texas is here to see you," she said, smirking slightly. What would you like me to do?"

"Amyleigh, send him on in." Troy smiled as he flipped the paper over on his desk and slid the pencil into his top drawer.

Amyleigh slowly closed the door, but Troy knew where the smirk had come from. Bob is a Democrat State Senator from Texas. Some would call him a blue-dog Democrat, but in 2025, conservative Democrats were hard to find.

Moments later, the door slowly opened as Amyleigh walked in with Senator Sinclair. She smiled and then exited the room, shutting the door behind herself.

"Mr. President-elect. Thank you for agreeing to see me." Bob said as he sat his big, brimmed cowboy hat in the seat next to the one Troy motioned for him to sit in.

"To what do I owe the pleasure of a Texas Senator's visit today?" Troy sat after Bob took the seat he was offered.

"Honestly, sir. I am not really sure why I've come other than to tell you privately how much I am excited you have won, especially in the fashion you did.", he remarked, pointing at a poster on the wall showing that Troy had won every state in the Electoral College except for Hawaii and Rhode Island, "even winning the popular vote by a significant margin.", he continued. It was apparent that his visit was that of a supporter and not a rival, but Troy didn't know for sure.

"I am sure the attack on the homeland on election day really helped." Troy nodded, his face showing signs of humility and sadness in light of that possibility.

"Well, sir, that is the reason why I am here." Bob's face turned from amused to serious. "You know, once the Democratic National Convention gets their teeth into a narrative, this is hammered everywhere, and I wanted to warn you." Bob adjusted his bolo tie slightly.

"Oh?" Troy was confused as he took a sip from his coffee cup.

"Yes, it appears that the attack is going to be peddled throughout the media and official channels... that you were involved in the attack so that you would gain the positive vote of the electorate," Bob said. At the same time, Troy turned his television over to the Complete News Network and started turning the volume up. Bob slid his chair back and turned to look at the television.

They looked on as Quentin Jamison, the Democrat candidate for the Presidency, spoke to one of the commentators.

"Yes, I think that Troy had business dealings in China and Korea; it is apparent that he may have been directly linked to the financing of the formation of the Confederation," Quentin said as the camera zoomed out to reveal a panel of commentators and reporters.

"What does that mean, Governor?" a woman reporter asked casually, referring to the highest office Quentin had served in as Governor of Oregon.

"I don't know what that means other than to say that the Confederation chose my state and my state neighbors to attack. California has been obliterated, and whether or not it ever recovers is a mystery. Washington has fallen, and half of my state has been taken over by... by our enemy. Thomason supported our enemy."

Troy's face showed signs of anger as he flipped the TV off. Bob turned to look at him again, "I am sorry, I just found out in the appropriations committee in Texas. It seems they are trying to defame you at the state level as well. I would have communicated this with you sooner, but they are moving at lightspeed to defame you."

The revelation struck Troy with the force of a physical blow, the fabric of his envisioned Presidency beginning to fray even before he could officially step into office.

His contemplative solitude shattered, replaced by a tu-multuous storm of thoughts and emotions. The accusations laid out on national television, painting him as a conspirator with foreign powers, threatened not just his political future but the very fabric of his integrity and dedication to the nation he was poised to lead.

Bob Sinclair's presence, initially a curious anomaly given his political alignment, now felt like a lifeline amidst the brewing storm. The Senator's frank disclosure underscored a sense of shared concern for the country's direction, transcending the usual partisan divides.

"Thank you, Bob, for bringing this to my attention," Troy managed, his voice steady despite the turmoil within. "This... this is a serious allegation. One that not only undermines the democratic process but also endangers the unity and security of our nation."

Bob nodded, his expression somber. "I figured you should hear it from someone who sees beyond party lines; besides, a state Senator visiting is less obvious. There are a lot of us who believe in what you stand for, Troy. And this," he gestured towards the now silent TV, "this is not the America we fight for."

The two men sat in contemplative silence, the urgency of the situation wrapping the room in a palpable tension. Troy's mind raced, analyzing the potential fallout, the necessary countermeasures, and the implications for his impending Presidency. The charges, baseless or not, would need to be addressed head-on, with transparency and unwavering resolve.

"We need to respond to this, and soon," Troy finally said, breaking the silence. "But not in the way they expect. We'll use this as an opportunity to unify, to show that this Presidency is about the American people, not about unfounded accusations or political maneuvering."

Bob's gaze met Troy's, a spark of determination lighting his eyes. "You've got allies, Troy. More than you might realize. It's time we bring this country back together to focus on healing and progress. Let me know how I can help." Bob stood up from the chair and picked up his cowboy hat, nodding as he walked toward the door.

As Bob Sinclair departed, leaving Troy to the silence of his office once more, the president-elect knew his path wouldn't be easy. Yet, the resolve that had driven him to seek the highest office in the land now fueled his determination to defend his honor and the principles upon which his campaign was built.

He flipped his sheet of paper back over and grabbed his pencil from the drawer. He sat to write a different speech, one that vowed that enemies, both foreign and domestic, would be brought to justice, not just for himself but for all American people.

Jeremiah Johnson found himself trapped in a relentless march of worry and strategic contemplation in the dimly lit ambiance of the Governor's Mansion in Helena. Each step he took across the ornate living room seemed to echo the weight of dire reports from the battlefield. The recent engagements in Leavenworth and Yakima, Washington, had been disastrous, with the militia suffering devastating defeats at the hands of the Confederation forces. The situation could have spiraled into an even graver catastrophe had it not been for the timely intervention of the Marines—a silver lining in a sky burdened with storm clouds. Yet, this assistance came without the official sanction of the United States government, a fact that did little to ease Jeremiah's deep-seated concerns. It was Samantha's hard work that guaranteed the Marines would come to help, and he was thankful for her being a liaison between the Pact States and the United States Marine Corps.

He paused, catching his reflection in the antique mirror above the fireplace. The lines on his face spoke volumes, each one a testament to sleepless nights and the heavy burden of leadership in times of crisis. As he massaged his temples, trying to dispel the shadow of exhaustion that clung to him, Miranda approached with a grace that seemed almost incongruous with the grimness of their situation.

Her hands, soft yet steady, began to ease the tension in his shoulders. "Jake is okay, honey," she whispered, her voice a soothing balm against the cacophony of bad news. "He just has a concussion. Ray managed to get him to safety." Her words were meant to comfort, to offer radiant warmth to counter the cold pain. Miranda, ever the pillar of strength and optimism, knew all too well the heft of their plight, yet she refused to let despair take hold.

The news of Jake's injury, while distressing, was a flicker of light in the pervasive gloom—the knowledge that their son had survived, albeit wounded, was a reminder of the personal stakes involved in this conflict. The involvement of the Marines, operating in a gray area beyond the direct approval of the government, under-scored the complexity and desperation of the situation.

As Jeremiah absorbed Miranda's words, swirling relief and resolve settled over him. The fight was far from over, and the path ahead bristled with challenges. Yet, in this moment of quiet solidarity, the couple drew strength from each other, their bond a fortress against the encroaching despair.

The Governor knew that the successes in Dorris and Hornbrook, California, while significant, were but small victories in a much larger and more brutal campaign. The strategic landscape was overflowing with peril, and the alliances they had forged with various military factions were tenuous at best.

Washington had fallen, Montana-Idaho Militia members in Spokane fell back to the border of Washington and Idaho, while members in Oregon were fighting a desperate fight to keep from losing Oregon, too. Jeremiah picked up the patch given to him by Davison Carey, whose daughter made the symbol under which the entire militia was fighting this fierce fight for the soul of their nation.

People from all over the United States were rushing to wear the patch and fight against the invading force. Althea Morris didn't make it any easier when she signed an executive order ending funding to military members who wore the patch in solidarity with the Montana-Idaho Militia. That didn't stop thousands from resigning their military position to rush to the aid of the Great Plains, a fact that Jeremiah would never forget.

Jeremiah turned to Miranda and kissed her, "I love you. Thank you for trying to bring me to my senses," he said, smiling at her, "Things aren't as bad as my mind is making them; we are starting to turn the tide in several places." Jeremiah tried to look at the positives even though every fiber of his being screamed otherwise.

Samantha walked in, saw her parents kissing, and started to turn around to leave. Jeremiah stood up and looked at Samantha.

"Hi, honey," Miranda said, her cheeks blushing a little when she saw Samantha.

"I didn't mean to walk in on you two. I just wanted to let you know that our reconnaissance drones are picking up some interesting things." Samantha said as Miranda backed away from Jeremiah to leave the room.

"This is official talk, and I need to be ready when Jake and Ray arrive to care for our son." Miranda smiled as she walked out of the room.

Samantha grinned wide as her mom passed by her; she pulled out a tablet and tapped the screen a few times to pull up the information she wanted to share.

Jeremiah held up his hand, "Can we talk for a few minutes, Samantha?" Jeremiah smiled a pained smile and motioned for her to sit on the couch. As soon as she did, he sat beside her. He put his arm around her and pulled her close, "You are so grown up; every time I see you, it's hard not to see you as that beautiful newborn baby 28 years ago." Jeremiah reminisced briefly, probably brought on by the stress of her older brother Jake getting injured and the tension all around.

"Daddy, I am a woman now..." Samantha said as Jeremiah cut her off, "You'll always be my little girl, no matter how old you get." Leaning over, he kissed her cheek and hugged her.

Samantha smiled. She knew her father was under immense pressure, and she knew this was his way of dealing with it.

"I know, Daddy," she said as her eyes welled in tears.

They sat for a moment in the quiet with nothing but the sound of the fireplace crackling.

"Now, First Lieutenant Samantha Johnson, tell me what your reconnaissance drones picked up." Jeremiah pushed his emotions down and got back to the business of leading the Great Plains Pact.

"Right, Governor." She said, picking up her tablet and flipping to some pictures of large aircraft carrying large slabs underneath them. There were thousands of these aircraft in the photos and on the reports.

"What are we looking at?" Jeremiah asked as he pinched his fingers on the tablet to see what looked like tank treads on the bottoms of the slabs they carried.

"We aren't really sure; they don't look like weapons of any kind. Brigadier General Justice thinks they might be some kind of barricade. He thought we should warn you so that maybe you can pull back the Militia to Idaho, Nevada, and California; we suspect they are trying to build some sort of wall so that we cannot directly engage the Confederation." Samantha said, grabbing the tablet and laying it back down on the table. Looking at Jeremiah, her lips began to smirk gently. "I love you too, Daddy." Her response to their earlier conversation was delayed, but Jeremiah accepted it while expressing the tenderness that only a father could provide.

Jeremiah took the buffalo patch that he had in his shirt pocket, the one gifted to him by Davison Carey after the Wyoming Governor's daughter created it. Slowly, he handed it to Samantha.

"I am not going to turn in my resignation, Daddy."

"I am not asking you to. I want you to have the original patch that was gifted to me by Davison's daughter."

Handing the patch to Samantha, Jeremiah reinforced his earlier sentiment. "Keep this as a reminder of what we're fighting for and of the unity it represents among all who stand with us. It's more than a piece of fabric; it's a symbol of our indomitable spirit."

Samantha accepted the patch, her face showing a combination of pride and fear for what the patch meant for the United States as a whole. "I will, Daddy." She slid the patch into her uniform shirt pocket, the very same design that had fascinated her for weeks now.

The conversation between father and daughter, though centered on the immediate tactical challenges, was imbued with a deeper understanding of the stakes involved. As they parted ways to attend to their respective duties, the shared commitment to their cause and each other remained an anchoring support in the tumultuous storm of war enveloping their nation.

As Samantha stepped out of the warmth of the living room and into the cool night air, the weight of their conversation lingered on her shoulders. The tablet, now tucked securely under her arm, felt heavier with the responsibility it symbolized. The patch felt like it radiated heat, but she was convinced the heat was coming from her shame of accepting it in light of President Morris' executive order, which up to now had not affected them because no Marine under her watch took the patch. The night was quiet, a converse to the turmoil brewing hundreds of miles beyond the peaceful façade of the Governor's Mansion and the lands it overlooked.

The sky was a canvas of stars, a reminder of the world outside their immediate conflict. Samantha lifted her gaze to it, finding a moment of solace in its vastness. It was a brief respite, allowing her to gather her thoughts and steel herself for the actions to come. The decisions made in the warmth of her family's presence would ripple out into the cold reality of war, affecting countless lives.

Returning inside to another part of the Governor's compound, Samantha made her way to the makeshift operations center that had been established within the mansion. The room buzzed with activity, illuminated by the glow of computer screens and the hushed tones of strategic discussions. Maps covered the walls, dotted with markers indicating troop movements, potential targets, and now, the locations of the suspected barricades flying in from Canada.

Samantha's entrance drew the attention of several officers and strategists, their expressions a mix of respect and anticipation. She dialed Brigadier General Justice on the large screen. "General, the reconnaissance data we discussed," she began, her voice steady despite the fatigue tugging at the edges of her resolve.

Justice nodded his head as he acknowledged receipt of the data, his eyes quickly scanning the images and data. "Thank you, First Lieutenant Johnson. This confirms our suspicions. We'll need to reassess our approach, perhaps even consider unconventional tactics to breach these defenses, if that is what they are," Brigadier General Justice said while sending more data to the makeshift Marine Operations Center in Helena, MT.

"I am heading into a meeting with the President and the Department of Defense on Thursday this week. I will keep you apprised of anything we need to do going forward. Stay safe, ma'am, and happy hunting." With that, the screen flickered off, and Samantha turned to all of the Marines and other military members who had joined in on their efforts.

"I spoke with Governor Johnson, and he agreed to pull Militia troops back to the neighboring states. We also need to facilitate this as well. Send this out to the field command." Samantha said as she heard the beating of helicopter rotors outside. Running back outside, she saw an army Chinook landing on the helipad.

That must be Jake and Ray. Hopefully he is okay.

She thought to herself as she turned to head back inside the operations center.

The heavy thud of the helicopter's landing reverberated through the chilly air of Helena, its massive rotors slowly coming to a halt as the aircraft touched down on the helipad nestled within the Governor's Mansion compound. The moment the helicopter's side door slid open, a team of Army Medics sprang into action, their movements precise and coordinated under the artificial lighting of the helipad. They gripped the sides of a gurney with urgency, upon which Jake Johnson lay, his condition a silent testament to the harsh realities of the battlefield from which he had just been extracted.

As the medics efficiently moved Jake towards the mansion, Ray stumbled out behind them, his body bearing the fatigue and scars of combat, yet his spirit buoyed by the sight of the familiar and safe haven they had reached. Behind him, two figures emerged from the helicopter, their presence on this flight unexpected but profoundly significant.

Ray turned to address them, his voice a mixture of relief and welcome. "Jack Smith, Stephen Jones, welcome to the free state of Montana." His introduction carried a weight of gratitude and camaraderie forged in the hot fires of conflict and survival against a formidable enemy.

Jack and Stephen, known to Ray by their assumed names, exchanged glances. The weight of their secret, the real reason behind their presence, remained locked behind their composed exteriors. To Ray and the medics bustling around the helipad, they were allies who had fought bravely alongside Jake, heroes of the same cloth. But beneath the surface, their true allegiance to an organization with far-reaching influence and objectives withheld a complex narrative of espionage, loyalty, and the murky waters of wartime alliances.

As they stepped onto the grounds of the Governor's Mansion, the gravity of their situation settled in. They were deep within the stronghold of the Montana-Idaho Militia, a key faction in the struggle for sovereignty against the Confederation's aggression. Their journey here was marked by battles fought, alliances tested, and identities concealed. The mansion itself, a bastion of resistance leadership, loomed large as a symbol of the conflict that had torn through the fabric of the North-west and the nation as a whole.

Ray, oblivious to the layers of deception, led the way with a sense of homecoming. The mansion was not just a political command center; it was his friend's child-hood home, imbued with memories of a life before the conflict had reshaped their world. For Jack and Stephen, however, the compound represented a critical juncture in their mission, a place where the lines between friend and foe, truth and deception, were blurred by the chaos of war.

Each step Jack and Stephen took deeper into the heart of the compound entangled them further in a web of military strategy and political intrigue. Their true iden-tities had the power to either unravel alliances or forge new ones, impacting their benefactor's authority in the fight for freedom. They knew their mission: finish the job and kill Jake and Ray before anyone would believe the story of their zero-energy weapons.

They watched as Ray limped ahead, trying to keep up with the medical personnel. Jack looked over at Stephen, "We have to finish this job, or the benefactor will have our heads."

Stephen nodded while pulling a cigarette from his pock-et and lighting it up.

"I miss home."

"You and I both."

14

ON THE BRISK MORNING of January 15th, 2025, Washington, D.C., was abuzz with a sense of purpose and anticipation. The nation's capital, always a nexus of political energy, felt even more charged as it counted down five days to the inauguration of Troy Thomason. But before the ceremonial swearing-in, a pivotal event was slated for the evening: Troy Thomason's speech at the foot of the Washington Monument.

As the sun began its ascent, casting a soft glow over the monuments that stand as silent guardians of American history, a team of dedicated individuals worked tirelessly. They were constructing a stage that faced the Capitol, an intentional positioning that served as a powerful symbol of Troy's imminent journey toward the epicenter of American political power. This stage, set against the backdrop of the Washington Monument, was not just a physical platform but a symbolic statement of the direction in which Troy aimed to steer the country.

This speech, meticulously planned for the evening of January 15th, was more than a prelude to the inauguration; it was Troy's opportunity to lay out his vision for a presidency committed to pursuing justice against all enemies, both foreign and domestic. In the shadow of one of the nation's most iconic landmarks, Troy expressed his commitment to upholding the principles of democracy and the rule of law, presenting his upcoming term as a symbol of hope during a time of division and uncertainty.

Seats were arranged in neat rows, facing the stage and the distant Capitol, inviting citizens and dignitaries alike to witness a moment of historic significance. The symbolism was profound, with the stage's orientation towards the Capitol serving as a reminder of the path that lay ahead, not just for Troy Thomason but for the entire nation. This setting, chosen for its historical and visual impact, underscored the urgency of the message Troy was set to deliver.

As the day unfolded, the area around the Washington Monument transformed into a hive of activity. Security protocols were meticulously reviewed, and final checks were conducted to ensure that every aspect of the evening's event would proceed without a hitch. The air was filled with a palpable sense of expectation as attendees began to gather, drawn by the promise of hearing a vision for America's future directly from its soon-to-be leader.

This was to be a defining moment for Troy Thomason, a chance to address the nation from a place steeped in the legacy of those who had shaped America's past. His speech would not only set the tone for his presidency but also serve as a declaration of his commitment to lead with integrity, courage, and an unwavering pursuit of justice. His speech would also dispel the talking point that Troy was involved in financing the Confederation in light of the accusations being levied at him by his political rivals.

As the stage was set against the grandeur of the Washington Monument, with the Capitol in its sight, it symbolized a bridge between America's storied past and its hopeful future. Troy Thomason stood ready to address the nation and share his vision of a united America, fortified against its adversaries and steadfast in its quest for justice. On this January evening, as the nation looked on, Troy would articulate his pledge to be a president for all Americans, guiding the country towards a new era of leadership and resilience.

Troy nervously walked back and forth, straightening his tie. He had put the finishing touches on his speech, and now he was reading over it to make sure that it flowed correctly. Julie was always his proofreader, and he worried that he would mess up somehow in her absence. He imagined she was standing at the window, and his eyes started welling up in tears.

"I am sorry, Julie.", he said as his imaginary Julie turned to look at him. He saw her mouthing words, but his imagination was not filling them in.

Amyleigh walked in behind him, and Troy jumped from being startled out of his imagination.

"Troy, I understand that you miss Julie; there is nothing wrong with you talking to your memory of her, especially since it happened only a few months ago." Amyleigh approached and touched a tender hand to his shoulder. Troy looked back at Amyleigh, and his face relaxed as he looked at her.

"I'm sorry to interrupt, but Charlton has come from Raleigh specifically to hear your speech tonight, and he's here to see you now," Amyleigh said, her expression marked by a mix of concern and unease. She was acutely aware of the heavy burden Troy was shouldering—grappling with the loss of his wife, facing the immense responsibilities that lay ahead, and now, unexpectedly, confronting the arrival of her former fiancé.

"Hi, Dad!" Charlton popped into the office behind Amyleigh and came over to hug his father. Troy returned the hug as Amyleigh looked at Charlton and then at Troy. She slowly began to sneak out of the office, shutting the door behind herself.

"It's okay to miss Mom; I miss her too." Charlton tried comforting Troy as he backed away, "It's good to see you."

"Son, it's good to see you." Troy nodded with a tearful grin, "I know it's a little off-topic, but I see the stock is dropping because of the claims the Democrats and Media are making right now." Troy started speaking to change the subject.

"Yeah, I want you to be proud, but I am not going to lie that it's hard to do with these unfounded lies floating around in the media and Vyber. I have nominated a member of the board to research ways to turn the tide, but until we stop this lie about your involvement with the Confederation..." Charlton said, sitting on the couch as Troy sat behind his desk.

As Troy and Charlton delved deeper into their conversation, the topic inevitably swung back to the forthcoming speech. The weight of the moment wasn't lost on either of them; this speech wasn't just a rebuttal to the swirling allegations but a declaration of Troy's vision for the future of America.

Charlton noticed his father's nervous pacing and tried to offer some words of encouragement. "Dad, you've always had a way with words. Remember, it's not just what you say but how you say it. People believe in you, not just because of your policies but because of the man you are."

Troy paused, the advice hitting closer to home than he expected. He glanced at the speech laid out on his desk, each word a promise, each sentence a step towards the presidency he envisioned—one based on justice, integrity, and unification.

The conversation shifted as they discussed the speech's key points. Troy aimed to address the nation's division head-on, to acknowledge the challenges they faced without shying away from the hard truths. Yet, he also planned to highlight the strength found in unity, the resilience of the American spirit, and his commitment to lead the country into a brighter, more glorious future.

"As you stand before the Washington Monument tonight, remember you're not just speaking to those in attendance or even just the people watching at home," Charlton continued, his voice firm and encouraging. "You're speaking to history, to the future generations who will look back on this moment. You're laying the foundation for what you want this presidency to represent. You have no idea what impact you are going to have on the future."

Troy nodded, absorbing his son's words. The enormity of the task ahead was daunting, yet in Charlton's unwavering belief, he found a reservoir of strength. "You're right," he said, the resolve in his voice growing. "This speech is more than a declaration of policy. It's a commitment to our principles, to the ideals that have guided this nation through its darkest times and brightest days.

It's no different to the dark times we are facing today!" Troy's face lit up with the knowledge that his legacy would be one of bringing a nation together and making that nation stronger.

As the afternoon waned and the time for the speech drew closer, Troy reviewed his notes one last time. Each line felt like a pact between him and the country he was about to lead—a vow to uphold the virtues that the United States was built upon.

The setting sun cast long shadows across the room, revealing the fleeting nature of time and the urgency of the tasks that lay ahead. Troy stood, straightening his suit jacket, a final gesture of preparation. Charlton offered a supportive smile, a silent acknowledgment of the challenges and triumphs that awaited.

Amyleigh entered the office, radiant in a sequined red dress that hugged her figure gracefully, paired with high heels that accentuated her posture. Her long brown hair flowed over her shoulders like a waterfall of silk, capturing the room's attention. Charlton, upon catching sight of her, couldn't mask the flicker of old feelings her presence ignited. Despite the passage of years and the closure of their chapter together, the bond they once shared left an indelible mark on him. Every memory, every shared moment, seemed to etch itself deeper into his heart. Amyleigh, sensitive to the unspoken emotions of their past relationship, she felt a warm flush of color that rose to her cheeks under Charlton's appreciative gaze. His eyes held a mix of nostalgia and admiration, reminding her of the connection that had once been so strong between them.

As Charlton looked at her, he couldn't help but recall the countless nights they had spent talking about their dreams and fears. Those memories lingered, woven into the fabric of his being. For Amyleigh, the flush on her cheeks was not just a reaction to his gaze but also a response to the resurfacing of those intimate moments they had once shared. She could feel the silent conversation between them, a dialogue that spoke of affection, regret, and the undeniable impact they had on each other's lives.

Standing there, in that fleeting moment, the air between them was charged with the echoes of their past. Charlton's gaze softened, and a small, wistful smile played on his lips. Amyleigh's eyes met his, and for a brief second, they were transported back to a time when the world had seemed full of endless possibilities, and their hearts had beat in unison.

Their bond, once defined by romance, now resurfaced with a deeper, more profound connection—proof of their shared history and the ways they had shaped each other. The warmth in Amyleigh's cheeks was more than just a reaction to Charlton's gaze; it was the rekindling of an emotional attachment that had never truly faded, even with time.

Troy looked at his son and Amyleigh and cleared his throat loudly. "Watch it, son. She is off limits now." Troy's voice cut through the moment, a lighthearted but firm reminder of the boundaries that now defined their interactions. Charlton glanced at his father, a mix of emotions playing across his face—a cocktail of nostalgia, respect, and a tinge of regret for the feelings that were resurfacing and thoughts of what might have been.

"Let's head to the monument," Troy redirected the focus with a voice imbued with resolve and anticipation. "It's time to share our vision with the nation." As they prepared to leave for the monument, the air was charged with a mix of professional purpose and the unspoken histories that intertwined their lives. The journey ahead was not just about shaping the future of a nation but also about navigating the complex human relationships that underpinned their shared mission. As father, son, and Amyleigh left the room, stepping into the evening's cool embrace, they joined the convoy that would take them to the site of the speech. The streets of Washington, D.C., were lined with anticipation. Supporters and protestors yelled both messages of support and hate as the convoy passed them by. The city paused at the cusp of a new chapter in its storied history.

The journey to the monument was short in distance but meaningful; each mile traversed was symbolic of the change Troy aspired to bring. The city's iconic landmarks passed by their windows, each a silent witness to the history Troy hoped he would be able to make.

Arriving at the monument, Troy was greeted by the sight of thousands gathered, a sea of faces reflecting the numerous people of the United States and showing the strength of the nation he was poised to lead. The Capitol loomed in the distance, a reminder of the responsibility and governance it symbolized.

Secret Service agents surrounded the stage and cleared a path for Troy to assume his place on the stage. He slid out of the car, and cameras began flashing. People shouted to get his attention in order to ask him questions that would end up in the papers and on the internet.

Troy slowly walked the path while waving and smiling; camera flashes illuminating the area every few seconds like lightning striking in the clouds. He reached the stairs and started to walk onto the stage. Troy Thomason looked out over the crowd, then up at the towering figure of the Washington Monument, feeling a profound connection to the leaders who had navigated the nation through its tumultuous past. Tonight, he stood on the precipice of history, ready to share his vision for an America united in its pursuit of justice and prosperity.

"Ladies and Gentlemen," Troy held up both arms in an effort to silence the crowd's noise. American flags were situated around the stage, and he stood there with his arms in the air. Cameras relentlessly continued to take pictures.

"I know that picture is going to be everywhere tomorrow." Troy chuckled, and the crowd laughed with him.

The crowd hushed as Troy continued to speak, his voice clear and resonant, carrying across the National Mall.

"Tonight, as we stand in the shadow of the Washington Monument, a symbol of our nation's founding ideals and enduring strength, I speak to you not just as your President-elect but as a fellow American deeply concerned about the fabric of our society and the future of our great nation." Troy paused for effect because he knew that he would be speaking on important topics that the nation faced.

"In recent weeks, a narrative has been constructed, one that seeks to undermine the unity and resolve of our people. Allegations have been levied against me, suggesting affiliations and conspiracies that not only distort the truth but also threaten to distract us from the pressing issues at hand. I stand before you to categorically deny any association or affiliation with the Confederation. These accusations are not just unfounded; they are a deliberate attempt to weaken our collective resolve at a time when our nation needs strength and unity more than ever." His face grew somber as he spoke, and filled with determination, he continued with his speech.

"The Democrats and certain media outlets have pedaled these lies, not to illuminate the truth, but to sow division, to hurt my ability to govern, and to hamper our collective efforts to repel the invasion from the Confederation and to rebuild California in the aftermath of the devastating Neutronium bomb. This strategy of division does not serve the American people; it only serves the interests of those who would see our nation falter." Troy stopped speaking once more as he grabbed the microphone and left the podium. There was no sound by anyone in attendance, and everyone in attendance hung on to his words.

"However, tonight, I call for a new direction—a direction where we put aside political enmity and work across the aisle for the good of all Americans. The challenges we face as a nation—rebuilding our cities, defending our borders, and restoring our global standing—demand that we come together, irrespective of party lines.

To those who have been misled by the falsehoods spread about my campaign and my intentions, I ask you to look at the actions and policies that I advocate for. They are focused on unity, rebuilding, and resilience. My commitment to America is unwavering, and my allegiance is to its people alone. I pledge to bring all of our military members home to take the burden off of my friends in the Northwest fighting a war on American soil. It is unacceptable that our military has to act in defiance of the Commander in Chief. I ask President Morris to rescind her awful executive action that is gutting our military and forcing so many to turn in their resignation to join the fight for our country. If she does not, that will be my first action in office on January 20th. I will not sit by and allow a foreign adversary the ability to invade unanswered by the most powerful military in the world.

In my administration, I pledge to pursue justice against all enemies, foreign and domestic, with every tool at our disposal. But to be effective in this endeavor, we must first rebuild the trust that has been eroded by divisive rhetoric. We must remember that our strength lies in our unity, in our ability to work together towards common goals, and in our shared love for this country.

As we look towards the inauguration and beyond, I urge every American, regardless of political affiliation, to join me in this mission. Let us commit to ending the cycle of division and hostility, to focusing on what brings us together rather than what tears us apart. Together, we can overcome the challenges before us and build a future that reflects the true spirit of America—one of hope, courage, and enduring freedom. "Troy paused and pointed towards the Capitol Building.

"I want to restore honesty and integrity to the United States. I want our citizens who have fled to Mexico after the horrific attack to feel safe enough to go back to their homes. I want to restore America to the city on a hill whose light may never be extinguished." Troy hesitated and looked over the entire crowd.

"Thank you, and may God—"Troy's speech was interrupted by an explosion of blood from his head and another from his chest as bullets struck him, the origin of which was indeterminable. Secret Service agents ran on stage and pulled their guns as the crowd screamed in terror and scattered all over the grounds. Charlton jumped on top of Amyleigh to protect her, his instinct to get as close to the ground as he could.

The Secret Service pulled Charlton and Amyleigh back to the car, and they climbed in. The door shut behind them.

"Oh my God, Charlie, Troy... Troy..." Amyleigh struggled to get her words out, and Charlton tried to comfort her the best he could, but he struggled to find the words he wanted to speak. Looking out the window, he saw his father's body lying in a lifeless heap on the stage. A wave of disbelief washed over him. He had always been taught to remain stoic, never to show his tears. Yet, as he stared at the tragic scene, the weight of his sorrow became unbearable.

Tears began to blur his vision, falling freely down his cheeks. It was the second time in months that he found himself overwhelmed by grief. The first had been when he lost his mother, her passing a wound that had barely begun to heal. Now, the brutal assassination of his father ripped that wound wide open, leaving him raw and exposed.

Memories of his father's strength and guidance clashed with the stark reality of his lifeless form. He felt a profound emptiness, a void where his parents' presence once provided comfort and security. His cries were a mix of anger, sadness, and helplessness—a young man mourning not just his parents but the loss of a part of himself.

The sharp echoes of the shots still hung heavily in the air, a grim reminder of the violence that had just unfolded.

Charlton, huddled protectively beside Amyleigh in the car, suddenly felt a surge of disbelief and horror wash over him. His mind refused to accept the reality that his father, Troy Thomason, a voice of hope for so many, the President-elect, lay motionless on stage. His father's words about unity and justice, still ringing in his ears, now seemed like a distant dream shattered by the harshness of reality.

Amyleigh, her voice trembling with shock and fear, could barely articulate her thoughts. The image of Troy's collapse, so sudden and violent, was etched into her mind, a haunting vision she knew would never fade. Charlton's comfort, though earnest, felt like a fragile shield against the magnitude of their loss.

As Secret Service agents and medical personnel rushed onto the stage, their movements were swift and coordinated, standing out sharply against the surrounding disarray. The crowd's screams and cries filled the air, a collective outpouring of grief and terror. Cameras continued to flash, capturing the tragedy from every angle, ensuring that the world would witness the horror of the moment.

Charlton's tears, unbidden and unrestrained, marked a departure from the stoicism he had always been taught to uphold. In this moment of profound loss, the façades of strength and composure crumbled, revealing the raw, unguarded pain of a son who had just witnessed the assassination of his father.

As the reality of the situation settled in, Charlton's mind raced with questions and fears. Who would commit such a horrifying act? What would this mean for the nation his father dreamed of uniting? And how could they move forward from such a devastating blow?

Amyleigh's hands trembled as she cupped Charlton's face, her gaze locked onto his, conveying a depth of sorrow and confusion that words could never articulate. In the silence between them, a chorus of sirens began to wail, underscoring the emotional turmoil that gripped both their hearts.

Without a word, she drew him closer, and their lips met in a kiss that was heavy with the weight of the painful loss. It was a moment where grief, pain, and anger were intertwined, each emotion amplifying the other. As their past, filled with memories both bitter and sweet, flashed before Amyleigh's eyes, the pain of Charlton's sorrow merged with her own, deepening the ache in her soul.

In the aftermath of the kiss, they remained close, their foreheads pressed together as they sought comfort in each other's presence. The chaos around them seemed to fade into the background, if only for a moment, as they found solace in the familiarity of each other's touch. Amyleigh's eyes, glistening with unshed tears, searched Charlton's face for any sign of the strength they would need to navigate the storm of emotions that awaited them.

Charlton, his own eyes blurred by tears he had been taught to hold back, found himself overwhelmed by the magnitude of their loss. The man he had admired, the father he had loved, was gone, leaving a void that seemed insurmountable. The kiss was heavy with the memories of their past relationship, a momentary escape from the pain. Still, it also served as a poignant reminder of the fragility of life and the bonds that tied them to one another.

As the sirens grew louder, signaling the rapid approach of emergency responders, the reality of their situation began to sink in. They were on the precipice of a new and daunting chapter, one without Troy Thomason's guiding hand. In the midst of their grief, Amyleigh and Charlton found themselves grappling with the uncertainty of the future, the responsibilities that now lay on their shoulders, and the pressing need to uphold Troy's legacy.

In the tender silence of their embrace, Charlton and Amyleigh found a silent oath weaving between them—a promise, unspoken but deeply felt, to be each other's anchor amidst the brewing storm. The memory of their broken engagement, a decision marred by forgotten justifications, seemed trivial and distant in the shadow of current events. The past, with its joys and sorrows, was momentarily eclipsed by the urgent need for comfort and connection.

Despite Troy's warnings, the bond that once propelled them toward marriage—a bond Charlton had been told to sever and forget—was quietly reigniting. It wasn't about defying advice or revisiting what was lost; it was about the instinctive human need to hold onto something real and reassuring in a world suddenly plunged into chaos.

In that charged moment, protection became Charlton's sole focus, a primal drive that superseded all else. His hand, acting on a mix of fear and determination, found the back of the driver's seat. It was a gesture that signaled the need to move, to escape the palpable danger that lingered in the air, but it was also an acknowledgment of his renewed commitment to Amyleigh. Not just to shield her from harm's way but to be by her side, facing whatever the future held together. "Get us to the airport, please," Charlton ordered; the driver nodded and started to maneuver between the emergency vehicles to leave.

Charlton and Amyleigh looked out of the window as their car sped away from the scene. Charlton looked at Amyleigh, "I am not sure what to do except to get us out of D.C."

As the city landscape blurred past her window, Amyleigh's tears flowed anew, each one a testament to the shock and sorrow engulfing her. Beside her, Charlton wrapped his arms around her, his own eyes not immune to the sorrow that had enveloped them both. In this overwhelming moment of grief, their emotions became a silent understanding intermingled with verbal cries because of the loss of a great man.

Beneath the towering gaze of the Statue of Freedom, high within the Tholos of the Capitol, a shadowed figure worked methodically. Cloaked in black, the man dismantled his rifle with practiced ease. Each piece—the barrel, the stock, the spent casings—vanished into the depths of his backpack. The precision of his movements underscored the weight of his actions. Each component secured away as if it were a piece of a dark puzzle he was keen to conceal.

Nestled in the shadows, the figure leaned against one of the aged pillars holding up the Statue of Freedom. His concealed actions clashed with the ideals proclaimed by the statue overhead. Casting a last look over the vast expanse of the Capitol, he pulled a phone from his coat and dialed a number with practiced ease, each press of the button echoing a routine both familiar and ominous.

The phone connected, and a cool and detached voice answered. "Hello, Agent Reed."

With a voice devoid of emotion, he replied, "It's finished. Please inform the benefactor and the President." The words fell into the silence, heavy with implication, hinting at a conspiracy woven into the very fabric of power.

Without a moment's hesitation, he dropped the phone, the device shattering beneath his boot with a finality that echoed ominously in the secluded space. The act of destruction was not just a physical severing but a symbolic disconnection from the deed he had executed.

As he vanished into the access hatch, the shattered remnants of the phone lay scattered, but not for long. Gradually, they began to disintegrate, turning to dust that vanished into the air, erasing any trace of their existence. Agent Reed had executed an act shrouded in secrecy, a crime hidden from view and beyond discovery. The events that transpired in the shadowed recesses above the city remained obscured, unknown, yet profoundly altering the arc of history.

15

PRESIDENT ALTHEA MORRIS LOOKED out of the Oval Office window at the flashing emergency lights and vehicles rushing to the area. She leaned against the arm of her chair, and a wry smile crossed her lips.

"Thank you, Troy, for playing your part," she said under her voice so that she wouldn't be heard in case anyone walked in.

A knock came to the door, and Chuck stuck his head into the opening, "Hello, Madam President."

"Come in, Chuck," she said as the man stepped in and shut the door behind himself.

"It is finished." He said in a whisper.

"I gathered that, by all the emergency vehicles surrounding the monument. I need to get a statement together. Is his Vice President on board?" Althea asked, coyly spinning to look outside again.

"Rice folded as soon as we told her, ever the politician." Chuck's lips parted in a sinister grin. Althea opened a folio on her desk and began reading aloud the body of the contents.

"I, President Althea Morris, 47th President of these United States, have authorized the Central Intelligence Agency to operate fully within the borders of the United States. Thereby allowing the Central Intelligence Agency, Federal Bureau of Investigation, the Bureau of Alcohol, Tobacco, Firearms and Explosives, and all associated agencies to coordinate together and investigate the Assassination of President-elect Troy Thomason. This order operates into perpetuity unless Congress rescinds it with a 2/3 vote. "She stopped reading and then looked up at the Director of the Central Intelligence Agency, "this is what our benefactor wants, so I will sign as I speak about our country's sadness at the intense tragedy of Troy's assassination." Althea studied Chuck's eyes as he nodded.

"Will Lisa Rice be a problem for us?"

"She understands that we were never going to let them take office, no matter how effective their campaign was. She will be here on camera with you tomorrow urging Americans to support your continued Presidency until a special election can be had." Chuck spoke plainly as Althea continued with her dark expression.

Althea's gaze lingered on the chaos unfolding outside, reflecting on the intricacies of the plan that had now reached its crescendo. "And the media?" she inquired, her tone shifting to a more pragmatic concern. "How are we managing the narrative?"

Chuck, ever the strategist, leaned slightly forward, his voice a blend of confidence and calculated calm. "We've already initiated contact with key figures across major networks. The story is being framed as an unprecedented attack on democracy, an act that demands unity and resilience from the American people. Your statement will be the linchpin, calling for calm and leadership in these turbulent times."

The President nodded, absorbing the magnitude of their actions. "And the opposition?" she prodded further, knowing full well the political landscape was about to undergo seismic shifts.

"There will be an outcry, of course," Chuck admitted, acknowledging the inevitable backlash. "But with the Vice President-elect aligning with us, dissent within the ranks will be minimal. Those who voice their opposition too loudly will find themselves under scrutiny for obstructing national security during a crisis."

A silence fell between them, each lost in the weight of their scheme. Althea, with a deep breath, broke the quiet. "Ensure our allies in Congress are briefed and ready to support the narrative. I don't want any surprises. As for our benefactor, arrange a secure line for tonight. I want to confirm his satisfaction personally."

Chuck's acknowledgment was a simple nod, a gesture that sealed their commitment to navigating the storm they had conjured. "Consider it done, Madam President. By this time tomorrow, the nation will be looking to you as its guiding light through this darkness."

Chuck paused, waiting for more instructions. Althea patiently and methodically gathered the dossier lying in front of herself.

"And what of our problems with the Johnson family?"

Chuck paused for a moment, looking at the tablet in his hand. "It looks like our men have successfully embedded into the Montana-Idaho Militia. We have to be careful that we don't move too fast regarding the Confederation invasion. Americans were already depending on Troy to put an end to the invasion."

"Yes. Instruct our military contacts that they may assist them for now. I will rescind my executive order, removing funding from the defectors so that it looks like I care. Ultimately, the benefactor wants to maintain control by any means necessary." Althea tapped her chin as she wrote the task down, "For all the American people know, Troy's assassination could have been a member of the Confederation or a sympathizer... I want to play into that."

"What of the Johnson boy and his Native American friend?" Chuck asked calmly.

"Plausible deniability, Chuck. I don't want to know." Althea said, spinning to look at the activity at the Washington Monument once more.

As Chuck exited, leaving Althea alone with her thoughts, the oppressive weight of leadership bore down on her. The decision to orchestrate such a drastic measure had not been made lightly. In the ruthless chess game of political power, sacrifices were inevitable. Troy Thomason's assassination was a grim necessity. For Althea and Chuck, it was a pivotal move in securing power for their enigmatic benefactor. Though they deemed it essential, their planned display of concern was nothing more than a sinister facade, concealing their true motives and thwarting a perceived threat to the nation's trajectory.

Sitting down at her desk, Althea began drafting her address to the nation. She spoke of the tragedy but framed it in unity and strength. She mourned the loss of Troy Thomason, a "leader taken too soon, a great man," and outlined the steps her administration would take to ensure justice and safety for all citizens. She didn't believe a word of it, but politics.

Beneath the polished rhetoric and calls for unity, Althea Morris knew the truth. Her now-secured Presidency was built upon the promise of a new world, one where control and authority would win over freedom.

Opening her drawer, she pulled out the shiny metal mask. Engraved on the forehead was a triangular seal, one that represented her rank in the benefactor's board. She turned it over and read the mantra laser engraved on the inside of the mask, the one only members of the board knew.

"Bearer of the mask, keeper of the secrets,

In shadows, we thrive; in unity, we conquer.

We are the architects of fate, the puppeteers of destiny,

Bound by the oath of silence, we shape the world unseen.

By the ancient code, we wield power unseen,

Guided by the Ten, we bring forth the New Dawn."

She recited it out loud as she slid the mask over her face; it was a badge of honor; it meant more to her than the office of the Presidency.

Althea stood before the mirror, the metal mask reflecting a cold, emotionless version of herself. The symbol of her true allegiance stood out distinctly against the backdrop of American flags and presidential emblems that decorated her office. It underscored the dual life she led: outwardly, a grieving and unifying leader; privately, a committed member of the shadowy group orchestrating a new world order.

Removing the mask, she placed it carefully back into the drawer, locking it. Her thoughts then shifted to the broader implications of her actions. The Confederation's invasion, a crisis manufactured to justify drastic changes in national policy and security measures, served as the perfect backdrop for her administration's aggressive consolidation of power. The American public, already weary from political unrest and the promise of change that Thomason's campaign had represented, would now look to her for guidance and security. It was a calculated risk, but it was one she believed was necessary for the greater vision the benefactor had laid out.

Turning back to her desk, Althea contemplated the Johnson boy and his Native American friend, recognizing them as potential loose ends in a meticulously woven tapestry. They posed a significant threat to her benefactors' organization. She knew that if they exposed the existence of the experimental weapon used to kill their friend, it would lead to questions she wasn't prepared to answer.

As she pondered the layers of misinformation and manipulation at play, Althea felt confident in her ability to steer the narrative. However, she remained cautious of unforeseen variables. She trusted the agents assigned by Chuck Gleeson to handle the situation, but the implications of stirring up trouble weighed heavily on her. Her actions during her tenure as Vice President under

Arthur Hastings had already poked the hornet's nest, and any further moves could escalate the risks.

As the night deepened, Althea focused on preparing for her address to the nation. She refined her speech, infusing it with appeals to patriotism, resilience, and the collective mourning of a nation betrayed by unseen enemies. She planned to rescind her previous executive order as a necessary step toward national security. This rallying call would, she hoped, unify the country under her leadership and stop the military members who were resigning by the thousands to join Johnson and his illegal defense of the Northwestern border.

Her address would also subtly sow distrust toward the Montana-Idaho Militia and its sympathizers, leveraging the assassination and the ongoing invasion to justify her administration's upcoming actions. She believed this narrative would galvanize public support for her expanded surveillance and military initiatives, framing them as patriotic responses to a national tragedy. Moreover, the reversal of her previous executive order was a strategic move to regain the trust of the military and the public, painting her as a flexible and responsive leader in the face of emerging threats.

In the solitude of the Oval Office, Althea Morris rehearsed her speech, the weight of her office, and the decisions she had made pressing down on her. She understood the importance of her role, not just as President but as a key player in a larger, shadowy agenda. The path ahead was overflowing with moral ambiguity and potential peril, but Althea was resolute. Her commitment to the benefactor's vision was unwavering, and she was prepared to face the consequences of her actions, whatever they might be.

Early morning light washed over the nation's capital, bringing with it a day that would be marked by a significant pivot in the course of its leadership. President Althea Morris was prepared to step before the nation. Her heart, as hard as if it were cast in steel, knew well the weight of the words she was about to deliver. This was a day for history books, a moment where the path to a "New Dawn" required sacrifices not all were prepared to make. She looked into the mirror again as she straightened up her jacket, focusing on her eyes. She knew her identity and that everything she was—belonged to the benefactor's organization, which she sought to elevate.

In the solitude of the Oval Office, before the cameras would capture her poised image, Althea reflected on the urgency of her upcoming address. She wondered if she could successfully portray the sorrow necessary to fool the American people; she also wondered if she could convince herself of that sorrow. She understood that her speech would need to weave a delicate tapestry of grief but still offer hope—a narrative strong enough to rally a fractured nation to her side and thus to the side of the benefactor.

The reversal of her previous executive order, a move some would view with skepticism, was to be presented as a strategic retreat in the face of a cunning and elusive enemy. This adjustment, she reasoned, was necessary to reclaim the trust and morale of the military, a vital component in the stability of her administration. After all, the organization needed soldiers, and if they all left to fight for Johnson's militia, she would be at a disadvantage.

She heard a slight knock at the door and turned to face it as Dr. Hal Bennett stepped in, wearing a blue suit with a red tie. His hair was neatly combed to the side, and his thick-rimmed glasses sparkled under the sharp lighting inside the Oval Office.

"Madam President, it is time to head to the Rose Garden. We have a large turnout of people waiting to hear from you," Vice President Bennet said, turning to look out the window behind the resolute desk. It's hard to believe such a tragedy happened last night, just over there." He continued, turning back towards the door.

"Yes, Hal, it is horrible. Troy was a good man," Althea said, straightening her hair a little. She played her cards close to her chest because she knew that Hal was part of the same organization she was but didn't know what role he played or how much he knew.

"I am ready," Althea said, grabbing the dossier containing her speech and executive order. Hal walked out first as the Secret Service surrounded both of them on their way to the Rose Garden.

Every person in the nation, glued to screens in living rooms, offices, and public spaces, awaited her words. President Morris walked toward the podium, and the press and everyone in attendance began snapping photos and screaming questions.

Standing behind the podium with Hal standing right behind her and Lisa Rice standing on her other side, Althea began to speak,

Ladies and gentlemen, my fellow Americans,

Today, I stand before you in the Rose Garden, a place of beauty and serenity. It is with a heavy heart that I address you as we mourn the loss of President-elect Troy Thomason, a man of vision and unwavering dedication to our country. His untimely passing is a loss not just to his family and loved ones but to every American who believes in the promise of a brighter future.

In these moments of collective grief and uncertainty, it is imperative that we, as a nation, come together in solidarity. We must rise above the divisions that seek to tear us apart and unite under the banner of our shared values and ideals. The

fabric of our democracy is strong, woven through centuries of challenges and triumphs, and it is this very strength that will guide us through the current turmoil.

As your President, I am fully committed to ensuring the security and prosperity of our nation. It is with this commitment in mind that I have decided to reverse a previous executive order, acknowledging the need for adaptability in the face of new and evolving threats. This decision was not made lightly, but it is necessary to protect the sanctity of our democracy and the safety of our citizens.

In response to the tragic events that have unfolded, I have authorized the full cooperation and coordination among our intelligence and law enforcement agencies. This unprecedented collaboration is crucial in our pursuit of justice for President-elect Thomason and in safeguarding our nation against any and all threats. Let there be no doubt: we will leave no stone unturned in our quest to uncover the truth and ensure that those responsible are held to the fullest account.

In response to this tragic and horrifying event, I have taken it into my executive authority to cancel the upcoming inauguration. Troy's Vice President-elect, Lisa Rice, has agreed not to challenge my staying in office until a Special Election can be conducted.

Gasps from the audience in attendance gained momentum as President Morris spoke, and shouts could be heard from the audience, "That is something that has never been done." Althea just smiled and held up her hand gracefully to quiet everyone down.

Moreover, in these trying times, it is vital that we reaffirm our commitment to the principles that define us. Liberty, justice, and the pursuit of happiness are not just ideals; they are the cornerstones of our American identity. We must defend these principles, now more than ever, against the forces that seek to undermine them.

I also call upon our citizens to stand together, to support one another, and to remember that our strength lies in our unity. It is through our collective will that we will overcome the challenges before us and emerge stronger.

In honor of President-elect Thomason and all those who have dedicated their lives to serving our country, let us renew our pledge to uphold the values of our republic. Let us work together, across all divides, to build a future that is bright with promise for all Americans.

I assure you my administration is unwavering in its dedication to this cause. We will navigate these turbulent times with resolve and determination, guided by the principles of justice and the rule of law.

To the Thomason family and to all who are grieving in this moment of national sorrow, you have my deepest sympathy and unwavering support. Together, as one nation, we will honor the memory of Troy Thomason by continuing the work he so passionately pursued.

May God bless you all, and may God bless the United States of America.

Thank you.

As President Morris concluded her address, a palpable tension hung over the Rose Garden. The assembled press corps, who had been silent during her speech, erupted into a cacophony of questions, their voices rising in anger and disbelief. "President Morris, how can you justify canceling the inauguration?" one reporter shouted, trying to rise above the din. "Isn't this an unprecedented grab for power?" another called out, echoing the sentiment of confusion and suspicion that permeated the air.

Vice President Hal Bennett and Troy's Vice President-elect Lisa Rice, both flanking Althea, remained stoic, their expressions unreadable amidst the storm of inquiries. The Secret Service, sensing the growing unrest, moved closer, forming a protective circle around the trio.

Althea, maintaining her composure, nodded to her security detail, signaling it was time to leave. She did not answer any questions; her smile was tight, revealing none of the inner turmoil that the questions might have provoked. The Secret Service efficiently ushered them away from the podium and back toward the safety of the Oval Office. Their path, so somber and controlled, was in noticeable contrast to the surrounding vibrant garden, now merely a scenic yet silent witness to a nation's escalating tension.

Behind them, the press corps continued to shout, their questions turning to frustrated exclamations as they realized no further answers would be forthcoming. The sounds of their discontent faded as the doors to the West Wing closed behind President Morris and her companions.

Inside, the atmosphere was charged. Hal broke the silence first, his voice low, "That was quite the gambit, Althea. Do you think the country will stand behind us?"

Lisa Rice, her face a mask of political calculation, added, "I did what was commanded of me. Now leave me and my family alone." Lisa growled furiously at Althea; she pulled her resignation out of her jacket pocket and slapped it against Althea's shoulder.

Althea caught the resignation letter swiftly, her expression unreadable as she met Lisa's furious gaze. The tension in the room thickened an almost palpable force that seemed to slow time itself. Vice President Hal Bennett watched the exchange, his analytical mind calculating the potential fallout from this unexpected confrontation.

"Lisa," Althea began her voice, a controlled blend of authority and reassurance. Your feelings are understandable, given the circumstances. However, we are at a critical juncture for our nation, a point where personal grievances must be set aside for the greater good." Althea's eyes looked into Lisa's with stern authority. "I needed your resignation so that I could make the moves I have to in order to protect the United States of America."

Lisa's anger, however, was not so quickly quelled. "The greater good?" she spat, her voice laced with contempt. "You call this manipulation and power grab the greater good? I cannot, in good conscience, be part of this any longer." Lisa turned to leave as Hal pulled a small gun from his pocket, striking Lisa in the back with a dart. Her face contorted in pain as Lisa began to vanish. A few moments passed, and all that was on the floor was Lisa's clothing and shoes. Althea looked at Hal dumbfounded, "I, too, am working towards the New Dawn." Hal said with a sly look on his face.

Althea stood frozen, her gaze locked on the spot where Lisa Rice had been just moments before. It was hard to comprehend what had just transpired, even within the context of their clandestine operations and morally ambiguous mission. Hal's revelation about his connection to the benefactor's deeper agenda and the demonstration of the experimental weapon—something she had only heard about but never seen—made her realize the extent of their willingness to go.

"Hal, what have you done?" Althea's voice was barely above a whisper, colored with shock and disbelief. The implications of Lisa's disappearance were vast; it would be hard to explain if anyone asked questions. Althea had been deeply involved in a web of dangerous activities, trying to eliminate Jake Johnson and his friends and orchestrating the assassination of Troy. And now, Lisa.

She had always prided herself on being in control and managing every detail with precision. But now, things were beginning to spiral out of the control she thought she had. Every new complication added a layer of risk, and Lisa's sudden absence was the latest in a series of escalating crises. Althea felt the weight of it all pressing down on her, the once-clear path now obscured by uncertainty and fear.

"Hal, answer me," she insisted her tone a mix of desperation and command. "Why did you use the weapon on her?"

Hal looked at her, his face a mask of defiance. "I had no choice," he said, his voice barely audible. "She knew too much. It was only a matter of time before she exposed everything."

Althea's mind raced, the gravity of the situation sinking in. She had to find a way to regain control, to navigate the chaos that threatened to consume them both. But with each passing moment, the task seemed more daunting, the consequences more dire.

Hal, placing the small gun back into his jacket, turned to Althea with a calm demeanor that belied the severe nature of his actions. "Althea, our commitment to the New Dawn necessitates actions that, while difficult, are essential for our ultimate goal. Lisa's refusal and her potential to destabilize our efforts made her a liability. The benefactor's resources include solutions for such... complications."

Althea's mind raced as she processed Hal's words. The organization they were involved with had always demanded loyalty and discretion. "And what of the aftermath, Hal? How do we explain Lisa's sudden absence?" Althea was as intelligent as she was cunning. She knew the answer to the question but didn't know how much Hal knew.

"Neither can the assassination of Troy, or the murder of Mike in Idaho, or what of the 25th Amendment ploy you pulled to take the office of President? I thought you were smarter than that, Althea. "Hal's words served as a reminder of the deep waters Althea had waded into. Each action, each decision she had made during her ascension to power, had been a step further into a realm of moral ambiguity and political machinations far beyond the ordinary bounds of governance.

The significance of Hal's involvement and the benefactor's far-reaching influence suddenly became oppressively clear to her. She realized she wasn't just a participant in this game; that she wasn't just a member of the benefactor's inner circle, but she was deeply entangled in its web, with every action closely observed and orchestrated by those who wielded true power from the shadows. If they would go as far as to eliminate Troy, start a war to destabilize the country, and cause Lisa to disappear, how much further was she from that political calculus?

Althea took a moment to collect her thoughts, her resolve hardening. "We say Lisa resigned for personal reasons. She left with an entourage on the other side of the White House. The details outside of that are her own to disclose, should she choose to return," she said, her voice steady, betraying none of the turmoil that churned within. It was a lie, a fabrication as thin as paper, as if Lisa would just come walking through the door any moment. The truth was far more dangerous than any lie they could tell.

Hal nodded, a grim understanding passing between them. "I'll handle the family and communications. The benefactor will be pleased with how we're managing the situation. As for the public and the press, they'll be too caught up in the narrative we present to question it too deeply."

But Althea wasn't so sure. The events of the past days had unfolded with a speed and intensity that left little room for reflection, but now, in the aftermath, the total weight of their actions began to press down on her. Lisa Rice's disappearance, orchestrated in such a chilling and final manner, would inevitably leave a void that could not be easily explained away. The narrative they spun would have to be meticulously crafted, leaving no room for doubt, yet Althea understood that the truth had a way of surfacing, often at the most inopportune times.

"The benefactor's methods..." Althea began, her voice trailing off as she considered the implications. "They're becoming more extreme. Disappearing Lisa won't just go unnoticed. What of her twin daughters and her husband? What lengths are they prepared to go to ensure compliance?"

Hal's expression was unreadable, a mask of professionalism and loyalty to their unseen puppet masters. "The lengths that the benefactor is willing to go is far beyond anything you have seen. The organization has been working towards these ends since the end of World War 2. You and I... well, when our usefulness is used up, we, too, will be removed from the board. Sometimes, that removal requires sacrifices."

"Sacrifices..." Althea echoed, the word tasting bitter on her tongue. She had entered this alliance believing in a shared vision of change, of steering the country through a period of upheaval to emerge stronger and more unified. Yet, the path they were on seemed increasingly paved with secrecy and manipulation. She had gone to great lengths to get where she was now, only now realizing that she was only a tiny player.

Turning away from Hal, Althea gazed out the window, contemplating the city spread out before her. The nation's capital, with its monuments to history and progress, seemed oblivious to the dark currents flowing beneath its streets. "We're crossing lines that I'm not sure can be uncrossed, Hal. The New Dawn... Is it really worth the cost?"

Hal approached, placing a reassuring hand on her shoulder. "It's natural to have doubts, Althea. But remember, we're not just reshaping policies or legislation; we're reshaping the destiny of the nation. The benefactor's vision is clear, and the outcomes will justify the means. Trust in the process."

Althea nodded, though Hal's words did little to quell the storm of doubts raging within her. Trust in the process, she thought. But at what point would she be removed from that metaphorical board?

As Hal left the Oval Office, Althea remained at the window, a solitary figure silhouetted against the backdrop of a city on the brink. She thought she was a bigger player, only now realizing that even the President of the United States is controlled. She helped orchestrate it, and now she would continue to play her part.

16

NESTLED WITHIN THE RUGGED embrace of the Appalachian Mountains lies Martinsburg, West Virginia—a city where the echoes of history blend seamlessly with the quiet stirrings of modern life. It was here, amid the verdant hills and timeless streets, that Lisa Rice's journey began. Before the national spotlight beckoned, Lisa devoted her heart and intellect to the people of Martinsburg, serving two terms as their Mayor with a zeal matched only by her commitment to the people of her community.

Her leadership, marked by an uncanny ability to bridge divides and envision a brighter future for her constituents, propelled her into the broader political arena. Lisa's voice, once confined to the council chambers of Martinsburg, found a new stage in the West Virginia House of Delegates. Over three terms, she championed policies that echoed her early promises—unity, growth, and a steadfast dedication to the public good. It was a tenure that caught the eye of Governor Campbell, who saw in Lisa not just a politician but a visionary capable of greater influence. Her appointment to the United

States Senate was a testament to her unwavering service and the trust she had earned.

In the Senate, Lisa's path crossed with Ulysses Mars, the distinguished Senator from North Carolina. Their partnership, built on their conservative values and desire to make America freer, opened new doors to new people. It was through this political tapestry that Lisa was introduced to Troy Thomason, a man whose ideals resonated with her own and whose vision for America sparked a flame of possibility in her soul. When Thomason chose her as his Vice-Presidential running mate in the 2024 election, it was not just a political decision; it was a declaration of shared purpose, a joint venture into the unknown for the sake of their nation.

Behind the public figure of Lisa Rice was a life rich with personal joys and challenges. Thomas Rice, her husband, navigated the complex world of real estate in Martinsburg, balancing the demands of his career with the responsibilities of family life. Their seventeen-year-old twins, Eve and Eden, were a constant source of wonder for Lisa. With their fiery red hair and vibrant green eyes—a mirror image of their mother—they embodied the spirit of their heritage, a reminder of the roots that kept Lisa grounded amid the whirlwind of politics.

Thomas sat at the table of the family's Martinsburg home, sipping on his coffee and reading the paper. He was saddened to hear that Troy had been assassinated, and according to the 12th Amendment, Lisa would be

inaugurated as President. He was both thrilled and saddened by this turn of events.

"Daddy!" Eve ran into the kitchen, her long red hair
flowing behind her. Thomas looked up and smiled. His
girls had him wrapped around their fingers, and he
would do absolutely anything for them. She had her
tablet in her hands, "Look, Mom is standing with President Morris." He took the tablet and turned the volume
up to listen to the speech being delivered. How the
President was suspending the inauguration and that
Lisa had resigned for the 'good of the nation.'

As the pundits dissected President Morris's address
and the camera captured the hurried departure of Lisa
alongside Hal Bennett, Thomas stared at the screen,
disbelief etching his features. The notion of Lisa stepping down, let alone endorsing another day under
Althea Morris's leadership, was unfathomable. This
wasn't the Lisa he knew, the woman who fought tirelessly for her beliefs and the betterment of their nation.
The events unfolding seemed to belong to an alternate
reality, one far removed from the principles and dreams
they had nurtured together in Martinsburg. At that
moment, Thomas felt the ground shift beneath him,
heralding a new chapter fraught with uncertainty and
the daunting task of navigating the tumultuous waters
of a nation in transition.

He immediately picked up his phone and dialed Lisa.
The phone rang several times, and then he went to

voicemail. He couldn't escape the sinking feeling in his heart that something terrible had happened. He tried calling again, but it just kept ringing, and again, he went to voicemail. His anxiety was piqued even more after calling again and getting the same result. He knew that even if Lisa were busy, she would text back. Eden walked into the room, brushing her hair as she looked on at her father with stress etched across her features.

"What's wrong, Daddy? Eve?" Eden asked as Thomas stood up, "Something is wrong. I know it."

The tension was suddenly pierced by a sharp, insistent knock at the front door, breaking the anxiety that had taken over the Rice household. With a sense of curiosity mingled with a hint of trepidation, Eden, her green eyes wide with surprise at the unexpected interruption, hurried to see who it could be. The house, usually a haven of tranquility, felt overwhelmingly charged with horror as she approached the door.

As Eden swung the door open, her gaze was met by an imposing sight. Standing before her were two men, their stature tall and commanding, dressed in meticulously tailored black suits that seemed to absorb the light around them. The afternoon sun glinted off the polished surface of their sunglasses, hiding their eyes and adding an air of mystery and intimidation to their already striking appearance. Each wore an earpiece, a clear indication of their professional vigilance and connection to something beyond the quiet street on which the Rice family lived.

Eden dropped her brush as Thomas ran up behind her. The men appeared to be members of the Secret Service. Thomas felt a lump swell in his throat as the men stood perfectly still. Their expressions were unreadable behind the dark lenses that shielded their eyes. There was a sense of authority emanating from them, the kind that suggested they were not merely visitors but bearers of news or directives that could alter the course of the day—or perhaps even life itself. In that moment, as Eden took in the sight of these unexpected guests, a flurry of questions raced through her mind. Who were they, and what brought them to their doorstep? Were they government agents, security personnel, or messengers from some powerful entity tied to her mother's political career?

The air seemed to thicken with anticipation as Eden stood there, the threshold between her familiar world and the unknown intentions of these strangers. The quiet of the neighborhood, with its distant sounds of life going on as usual, felt suddenly very far away, as if she and these two men were caught in a bubble of heightened reality.

"Can I help you?" Eden's voice broke the silence, her tone steady despite the rapid beating of her heart. She was unaware of the significance of this encounter, the sense that whatever message these men carried, it was connected to the whirlwind of events surrounding her mother's ascent to national prominence and the shadowy figures that moved behind the scenes of power.

The men exchanged a brief, almost imperceptible glance before one of them spoke; his voice was strong and authoritative and carried the undercurrent of urgency. "Is this the residence of Senator Lisa Rice?" he inquired, his tone formal yet expecting affirmation.

Thomas pushed Eden aside as Eve stood in the doorway to the kitchen, "Who are you?"

In a rehearsed manner, the men pulled out their badges, sure to show the guns neatly holstered underneath their jackets.

"I am Agent Chris Williams, and this is Matthison Reed. Are you Thomas Rice?" Chris asked while simultaneously flashing his badge. Thomas looked at the men coldly, "Well, Agents Williams and Reed, how can I help you?"

"May we come inside to talk?" Matthison asked as Thomas nodded, inviting them in. The door shut behind them, and Thomas showed them to the living room.

"May I get you something to drink?" Eve asked from the entryway to the kitchen.

"No, thanks," Chris said as Thomas leaned back in the recliner. The men sat on the couch, and the girls sat on the loveseat, "We have a lot to say, and it is something you as a family need to hear."

"Is this about Lisa?" Thomas looked suspiciously at the men.

"I am afraid so."

Thomas' heart sank into his stomach with their answer. He wasn't sure what to think; he couldn't get ahold of Lisa, and the news wasn't painting a rosy picture either.

"We are afraid we have bad news. Your wife has re-signed her claim to the Presidency after Troy Thoma-son was assassinated and has... disappeared." Matthison nodded his head in a manner that was condescending but sympathetic, "Chris, the package?"

Agent Chris Williams reached into his jacket and fished around for a moment. Thomas looked at his girls with concern etched into his features. A sharp twinge of pain struck him in the chest as he quickly looked back at the agents and realized Chris had shot him with a dart from a little gun he pulled out of his jacket. Searing pain coursed through his veins where the dart had injected into his chest, Thomas' face disfigured in anguish, and his body began to fizzle into nothingness. Thomas had no time to scream before vanishing, leaving only his clothing where he once sat.

Startled from their relaxed posture on the loveseat by the abrupt chaos, Eve and Eden scrambled into action. The shock of seeing their father disappear before her eyes provoked Eve into letting out a piercing, raw scream that cut through the air. In the midst of this turmoil, Agent Matthison Reed reacted with quick precision. With a deft movement, he retrieved a small sphere from his pocket and threw it toward the sisters, marking the beginning of yet another unexpected and alarming turn of events.

The moment it made contact with the ground, the ball erupted, releasing a dense cloud of fog that enveloped the room. Caught off guard and unable to see or react, the fog's effects swiftly overcame Eve and Eden, their bodies succumbing to the engineered sedative. Within seconds, they collapsed onto the floor, rendered unconscious by the agent's calculated maneuver.

Chris pulled his phone out and dialed a number, "It is finished. We have the girls."

He nodded while looking over at Matthison, "We need to take the girls to Shepherdstown. Our benefactor has a site there."

Matthison walked out the door and pulled their car up to the garage as Chris opened the garage door.

Chris and Matthison moved with a silence that only seasoned operatives could muster, each action precise and calculated. The ordinary act of driving into the garage suddenly took on a dramatic weight, transforming it into a gateway to an unknown and daunting future for Eve and Eden. The shadows of the garage seemed to swallow the car whole. Matthison looked down at Eden and smirked, "I wonder what the benefactor has planned for these girls."

"Watch it with the questions, Matthison," Chris warned, still calm and collected as he picked up Eden. Her head rested limply on his shoulder; she was out cold. Matthison did the same with Eve, her bright red hair contrasting against his dark suit. Just a minute ago, the girls were full of energy. Now, they were caught up in a dangerous game, silent and unaware.

Sliding the two girls into the hatch of their black SUV, they closed the door and climbed into the front seats. Chris pushed the starter button, and the vehicle roared to life.

The journey to Shepherdstown was brief, spanning just 20 minutes over winding back roads and state highways. Throughout the drive, the agents maintained a silent vigil in the front seats. Their destination was a newly established facility under the umbrella of the Consortium Child Care Centers, located in Shepherdstown. This was where they had been directed to deliver the girls, marking the next phase of their covert operation.

Approaching their destination, the vehicle left the main road, winding its way along seldom-used dirt tracks. Eventually, they arrived behind an imposing structure

affiliated with the state college. This building, crafted to mimic the appearance of a higher education
institution, buzzed with activity beneath its serene
facade. Unlike typical colleges, this facility did not
enroll local students; instead, it functioned as an ex-
clusive establishment where the affluent sent their
offspring, maintaining its operations discreetly away
from public scrutiny.

Chris and Matthison pulled up to the loading bay
as several scientists meandered around the entrance.
The agents pulled the girls from the back and laid
them on the gurneys provided. Rolling them inside,
they began passing through layers of security with an
ease that spoke of their familiarity with the premises.
The interior was stark and functional, with a cold
efficiency that mirrored the purpose of those who
operated within its walls. They moved through the
corridors, the sound of their footsteps echoing off the
sterile walls until they reached a room equipped for
containment and observation.

Gently, they placed Eve and Eden on separate cots,
their unconscious forms splayed out onto the cots. As
the agents stepped back, a figure emerged from the
shadows—a person of authority within this hidden
world, someone who held the strings to the puppets in
this grand political theater. He wore a blue suit with
a red tie, a plain white mask that covered his entire
face, and his eyes covered with blue lenses.

The two agents immediately stood at attention and then slapped their left hand to their right shoulders.

"Sir, we were not aware you would be here." Agent Matthison Reed looked on, his face full of respect and admiration.

The masked man hissed a response, "Speak only if spoken to, Agent." Both men bowed their heads, "Now that Lisa Rice and her husband Thomas are out of the picture along with Troy Thomason being eliminated, we can consolidate our power even more." He hissed as he approached the girls, observing them with a calculating gaze. "Ensure they are comfortable and secure," the figure directed, their voice devoid of emotion. "They are valuable pieces in a much larger puzzle—a puzzle that is nearing completion."

The agents saluted again and began to leave the room, "Which one of you shot the bullet that killed Troy?" The man hissed again, his voice devoid of emotion.

"I did, sir, for the glory of our organization." Agent Reed said, saluting again, "Well done, Agent Reed, you will be at my right hand as we continue to reveal ourselves."

"Yes, benefactor. It would be an honor, sir."

"You two can call me Chairman..."

The title 'Chairman' fell into the silence of the room like a stone into still water, sending ripples through the air that carried with it a weight of authority and foreboding. Chris and Matthison, now more aware than ever of the gravitas of their mission and the implications of their actions, exchanged a glance that spoke volumes of their newfound understanding and commitment to the cause.

The Chairman, a figure shrouded in mystery and power, turned his attention back to the unconscious forms of Eve and Eden. "These girls are not merely pawns in our grand design," he mused aloud, his voice carrying an edge of something that might have been construed as respect—or perhaps something darker, a sense of ownership over the fates of those entangled in his plans. "They represent the future—a future that we will shape according to our vision. Along with the others." The Chairman said, opening his palm and waving it around the room. The agents took note of hundreds of identical rooms, with children and teenagers from all over inside.

With that, the Chairman made his way out of the room, his steps measured and confident. Chris and Matthison left in the wake of his departure and felt the enormity of the task ahead. They had been part of operations before, but nothing that bore the weight of such significant consequences. The realization that they were instrumental in the unfolding of events that would reshape the political landscape was both exhilarating and daunting.

As they exited the facility, the quiet of Shepherdstown enveloped them—closing the door to the storm of activity and ambition brewing within the walls they had just left behind. The drive back was contemplative, with each agent lost in thought over their roles in the Chairman's grand scheme. The road stretched before them, a metaphor for the path they had chosen—a path brimming with secrecy, danger, and the promise of power.

"I cannot believe we finally met the Chairman. I've heard rumors, but he is quite the leader." Agent Matthison Reed gushed over their meeting as they walked down the hallways past all of the identical rooms occupied by children of all ages.

"We can finally go back to the city." Agent Chris Williams smiled; relief washed over his face as they climbed into the SUV.

Chris started the engine, the low hum breaking the eerie silence that had settled over them. The path back to Washington D.C. stretched ahead, a familiar route that now seemed different, charged with the weight of their recent encounters and the knowledge of the Chairman's broader plans.

Chris eventually broke the quiet in the car. "Matthison, the Chairman's vision... it's larger than anything we've been part of before. These kids, the political moves, it's all interconnected in ways we're only beginning to understand."

Matthison nodded, his mind racing with possibilities and the implications of their actions. "Yeah, it feels like we're part of something historic. But it's also... daunting. We're shaping the future, Chris. The responsibility is enormous."

The agents drove through the darkening landscape, the setting sun casting long shadows over the road. The conversation turned to the logistics of their next steps, the operational details that would need to be ironed out, and the ongoing surveillance and security measures that would ensure the success of their mission.

As they neared the city, the lights of Washington D.C. emerged ahead, a bright display against the evening's deepening shades. The transition from rural darkness to the illuminated cityscape underscored the dual nature of their existence: one foot in the visible world of politics and power, the other in the clandestine realm of secrets and strategies.

Pulling into the secure, underground parking of an unmarked government building, Chris and Matthison were swiftly enveloped in the efficiency of their covert operations. Driving deeper into the garage, they reached what appeared to be a dead end. Chris pulled his phone out and connected it to a secure network, then tapped a few buttons. The bricks slid apart, revealing a long subterranean road leading deeper underground. As they pulled inside, the bricks sealed behind them.

They drove further through the twists and turns and finally reached a security booth. "Welcome home to Consortium City, Agents." They pulled through the security doors and out onto sunny streets with a rich blue sky. The sun was hanging high in the sky as people walked up and down the sidewalks, and kids played in the park as they drove by it.

"Home sweet home." Agent Matthison Reed smiled as Chris nodded.

"It's good to be home."

Eden woke up on the cot in the little room that she and Eve were placed in. The room was sterile and cold. The walls were floor-to-ceiling mirrors; the only thing contrasting was a white door with a small window in it. Her eyes adjusted to the lighting in the room, and she noticed Eve still out cold on another cot. "Oh my god, Eve," She put her feet on the cold cement floor and ran to her sister's unconscious body. Shaking it furiously, she could not rouse her awake. She looked around the room, ran to the door, and beat her hands on it, screaming as loud as she could, "Help us! Please, someone!" Eden's voice echoed off the mirrored walls, amplifying her desperation but meeting no response. The sterile environment of the room, with its clinical cleanliness and lack of personal touch, felt like a prison crafted from cold logic rather than steel bars.

After several fruitless minutes, Eden's breaths became ragged, her fists sore from pounding against the unyielding door. She sank to the floor, her back against the door, pulling her knees close as tears began to stream down her face. The realization of their predicament sank in; they were captives, they witnessed their father disappear into thin air right in front of them, and now they were trapped in this place. Her tears were hot on her face, and she wiped them away with her sore hand.

She sat there, and as time passed, Eden's despair turned to determination. She wiped her tears, stood up, and surveyed the room once more, searching for any overlooked detail that might offer a hint of escape or at least communication with the outside world. The room's design left no such allowances; it was a perfect cell designed to isolate and contain. But she was determined to try. She dug her nails into the seams between the mirrors and pulled furiously. She pulled so hard that her cuticles began to tear and bleed.

Nothing. She turned her attention back to Eve. Eden checked her sister's pulse and breathing, and she was relieved to find both steady. "I won't let this be the end for us," she whispered, more to herself than to Eve. With renewed resolve, Eden began to explore the room's boundaries, running her fingers along the seams where the mirrored walls met the floor, hoping to find a hidden latch or weakness. She smeared blood all over the mirrors from where her cuticles were bleeding.

A click suddenly broke the silence of the room, and the small window on the door slid open, revealing a pair of eyes that observed them quietly for a moment before the window shut with another click. Eden rushed to the door again, "Who's there? Why are you doing this to us?" But there was no answer, only the retreating sound of footsteps on the other side.

In that brief encounter, Eden felt the weight of observation, the realization that their every move was likely being monitored. It was a chilling thought, but it also sparked an idea. If they were being watched, there might be a way to communicate, to plead for empathy from someone on the other side who might see them not as pieces in a game but as human beings in distress.

Eden tore the sheet on her cot and used it to wrap her hands tightly.

Eve coughed and shifted a little on her cot, which prompted Eden to run to her side again.

"Sis, wake up. Are you okay?"

Eve's eyes opened a little before, and here they focused on Eden's face, "Where is Daddy?"

"Eve, you saw the same thing I did," Eden answered as her eyes opened wider; looking around, she noticed the clinical room they were in.

"Daddy disappeared." Eve's voice cracked from dryness as tears began pouring from her eyes, "I thought that was a bad dream." Sitting up, Eden hugged her identical twin's neck.

As they clung to each other, the harsh reality of their situation settled around them like a suffocating blanket. Eden's steady yet laced with fear voice tried to offer a semblance of comfort: "We're together, Eve. We'll figure this out. We have to be strong for Dad... for Mom."

The sisters sat in silence, their minds racing through the series of events that led them to this strange, mirrored prison. The questions loomed large in their thoughts—Where was their mother? What had happened after their father's disappearance? Who were these people holding them, and what did they want?

Determined not to let despair take hold, Eden stood up again, her gaze fixating on the door. "We need to make them see us as people, not just... whatever they think we are." Her voice carried a newfound resolve. With Eve's help, they began to write a message with the blood from Eden's injured hands, spelling out "HELP US" in large, desperate letters across the mirror directly opposite the door, hoping it would be visible to anyone observing them through the small window.

As they worked, Eve's voice was a whisper, "What if they don't care? What if nobody comes?"

Eden, finishing the last of the letters, stepped back to look at their work. "Then we'll make them care. We'll make so much noise they can't ignore us. We have to try." She knew the odds were against them, but the act of defiance brought a small glimmer of hope.

Hours turned into what felt like days, with no indication of time other than the occasional dimming and brightening of the lights overhead. Their only interruptions were the sliding open of a small panel at the bottom of the door, through which trays of food and water were silently delivered twice. Each time, the sisters rushed to the door, trying to catch a glimpse of their captors and plead their case, but they were met with silence and the retreating footsteps of whoever was on the other side.

In these moments of brief interaction with the outside world, Eden and Eve understood the importance of maintaining their strength. They ate despite their lack of appetite, drank the water to stay hydrated, and used the time in between to strategize, support each other's spirits, and remind themselves of the life they were fighting to return to.

They had spent what felt like days screaming, banging, and crying for help, only to realize this was probably where their lives would end. They lost track of time in this place, and their hope waned.

Suddenly, there was a click at the door, and as they both wearily looked at each other, a man wearing a hazmat suit walked in, his identity obscured by the mirrored panel over his face.

"Six and Twelve."

He walked to Eden, who nervously looked at the man shielded from view. He grabbed her arm forcefully, and every attempt for her to pull back was met with a resistance she could not explain.

"Twelve, Specimen Alpha Charlie 12-31." He plunged a needle into her vein and drew a vial of blood. A little printer on his belt printed a label that he wrapped around the vial. He took out another syringe and injected it into the arm he still held in his hand. Eden attempted to pull away, but her strength was absent; she felt groggy and then collapsed to the cot.

The man's attention shifted to Eve; Eve's body didn't respond to her desire to move away either. He grasped her arm, pulling it closer to himself; he stuck the needle into her vein and drew blood, also labeling it.

"Six-Specimen Alpha Charlie 6-31." Following the same procedure, he injected another needle with a neon green liquid inside. Injecting it, Eve collapsed into her cot as well.

The man in the hazmat suit meticulously noted each procedure on a digital tablet, his movements precise and devoid of unnecessary motion. As he finished, he scanned the room once more, ensuring that his tasks were completed to satisfaction. Then, without a word or glance towards the sisters, he exited the room, leaving behind a heavy silence that quickly enveloped the space once again.

In the aftermath, the room felt even colder, the mirrored walls reflecting the vulnerability and fear that Eden and Eve were experiencing. As the drugs began to take effect, their minds raced with questions about what had just been injected into them and what it was for. The labels, 'Specimen Alpha Charlie 12-31' and 'Specimen Alpha Charlie 6-31', resonated ominously in the sterile air, suggesting they were part of some experiment or study they had no control over.

Hours passed, or so it seemed, before Eve began to stir. Her eyelids fluttered open, struggling against the weight of drowsiness that threatened to pull her back into unconsciousness. Eden was slower to awaken, her body fighting the sedative's lingering effects with every shallow breath. When they finally managed to sit up, the reality of their situation came crashing down once more.

"Eden... what are they going to do to us?" Eve's voice was barely above a whisper, her fear palpable in the dim light of the room.

"I don't know, Eve, but we have to stay strong. We have to find a way out of here," Eden responded, her voice steadier than she felt. Her mind raced with possibilities, each more desperate than the last. They needed a plan, but first, they needed more information.

More time passed as the routine continued; the girls would wake up and stare at their reflections in the mirrors, and food would be slid into the slot of the door twice a day.

Unbeknownst to them, the Chairman watched from his office, a slight smile playing across his lips as he observed the sisters' resilience. "They have spirit," he murmured to himself, considering the implications of their latest test results. Let's see how they adapt to being separated." With a flick of his wrist, he closed the feed, already plotting the next steps in his grand design.

As the days melded together in a blur of monotony and despair, Eden and Eve clung to each other for comfort and strength. Their silent meals became the only markers of time, punctuated by the occasional, distant sounds of movement beyond their mirrored cell. Despite the grimness of their situation, they forged a quiet resolve, a determination not to be broken by their unseen captors.

One morning, or what they assumed to be morning, the routine was shattered. The familiar click of the door lock disengaging was followed by the entrance of two figures in hazmat suits, identical to the ones who had previously administered their injections. Without a word, they approached Eve, who instinctively reached for Eden's hand, gripping it as if to anchor herself to the only constant she had left.

"Subject Six, it's time," one of the figures announced, his voice muffled through the mask. Eden's heart raced, panic seizing her as she realized what was happening. They were going to be separated.

"No, please! Please don't take her! Take me instead!" Eden pleaded, her voice cracking with desperation. But her pleas fell on deaf ears as the figures efficiently and coldly disconnected Eve from her side, ignoring Eden's sobs and protests.

Eve, still weak but fueled by a sudden surge of fear and determination, struggled against the grip of the figures. "Eden!" she cried out, turning to lock eyes with her sister one last time before being forcibly led out of the room.

The door slammed shut, leaving Eden alone with her reflection and her fears. Her sister's absence was a tangible void, a silent scream that echoed off the mirrored walls. Collapsing onto the cot, Eden allowed herself a moment of grief. Her tears poured from her eyes, bitter sobs that she would never see her sister again.

Yet, as the initial shock wore off, Eden's despair morphed into a fiery resolve. She wiped her tears, her jaw set with determination. "I will find you, Eve," she whispered into the silence, a promise to herself and to her sister. "No matter what it takes."

In the facility's depths, Eve was taken to a similar room, the door locking behind her with an ominous click. Alone, she felt the weight of their separation, a hollow ache that seemed to consume her. Yet, Eve's thoughts echoed her sister's determination. "I'll find a way back to you, Eden," she vowed, her voice steady despite the quiver of fear that threatened to overcome her. "We're not done fighting."

The Chairman, observing the scene from his office, nodded in approval at the display of resolve. "Separate but not broken," he mused, considering the implications for his experiments. "Let's see how this new variable affects the outcome."

As Eden and Eve faced their isolation, their spirits remained unbroken, each sister holding onto the hope of reunion. Unaware of the Chairman's plans, they sat in their separate cells, staring at their reflection.

Time was losing all meaning.

Life was losing its meaning.

Alone.

17

"SIR, THEY ARE DROPPING barriers!" Private Prescott screamed into his radio. He and his company were falling back to the Snake River bordering Oregon and Idaho.

"Fall back, fall back!" another militia member said as they ran harder towards the river. Airplanes flew overhead, dropping payloads on their previous positions. The huge barriers landed with a thud, shaking the ground and shooting out grenade charges on the outer edge of the wall as they crashed into the battlefield. The explosive charges erupted into curtains of explosions as the walls landed.

Private Prescott looked on as the walls began to roll into place. Like puzzle pieces, they connected to each other and then expanded in height and length.

"Captain. They are cutting us off! The rats are cutting us off!" Prescott shouted into his radio once more, referring to the Confederation and their advance.

"They are doing the same at the border of Washington and Idaho. These wall things are ridiculous!" Captain Walker responded over the radio.

A Marine chopper landed behind the militia soldiers on the Oregon side of the border.

"Come on, guys, let's fall the hell back!" A Marine gunner shouted from the side of the chopper.

"Get to the Chopper!" Captain Shaw said as he ran towards his militia members. "The Marines are going to help us fall back." He hollered as they all retreated.

"Are they going to have enough room for us?" Prescott shouted, trying to keep up with his fellow militia members.

"Trust me, that horse is big enough to carry three times our numbers; they don't call it a Super Stallion for nothing." Captain Shaw laughed nervously as more of the massive barriers landed, accompanied by the curtains of explosions rippling through the air.

As the Militia raced towards the safety of the Super Stallion helicopter, the air was thick with the smell of smoke and the echoes of distant explosions. The ground beneath their feet trembled with each impact as the barriers deployed by the Confederation continued their relentless expansion, severing any hope of retreating to their former positions. The once familiar landscape was rapidly transforming into a fortified border, an imposing testament to the Confederation's resolve to halt their advance.

Private Prescott, his lungs burning with exertion, cast one last look over his shoulder at the chaos they were leaving behind. The sight of the barriers, now fully integrated and imposing in their newfound stature. The Montana-Idaho Militia and the Marines that were assisting looked at the walls constructed in front of them, realizing this shifted the tide of the conflict. "This changes everything," he thought, the decisive blow heavy in his chest.

The chopper's blades sliced through the air, whipping up a storm of dust and leaves as the militia members piled in. Inside, the space was loud with the hum of the engine and the intermittent crackle of the radio, relaying updates from the front. Captain Shaw checked his men as they boarded, ensuring no one was left behind.

"We're going to need a new plan," Captain Walker's voice crackled over the radio, a sentiment echoed in the tight expressions of the men around Prescott. The walls, a technological marvel of warfare, represented a new kind of enemy—one that couldn't be outflanked or outgunned.

"Send a report back to the Pact governors." Captain Shaw said, looking at one of his other Privates, "We are going to need a new plan."

As the Super Stallion lifted off, gaining altitude with its precious cargo of retreating Militia, the view from the windows painted a grim picture of the battlefield they were leaving. The barriers stood unyielding, a physical and symbolic divide that marked the new front lines of a war that had just escalated in complexity and danger.

Below, the Confederation moved in, securing the area around the barriers. Their presence was a dark swarm of activity against the backdrop of destruction. It was clear that the Confederation was staking its claim, solidifying its control with each section of the barrier that autonomously locked itself into place.

The flight back was tense, filled with silent contemplation and whispered conversations. Plans were already forming, alliances were being considered, and strategies revised. This was no longer just a battle of territories but a war of innovation and adaptation.

"We'll regroup and reassess," Captain Shaw announced, his voice firm over the din of the helicopter. "This isn't the end. It's a new beginning. We adapt, we overcome."

"What if we bombed our side of the wall to keep the walls from being able to expand their territory? If we build a big enough trench around it, any movement outward will cause that wall to fall," Engineer Snell said while looking out the windows and observing how the walls were moving.

"That might work. But how are we going to do that?" Captain Shaw asked with a perplexed look on his face.

"Can't we get a bunch of bunker busters and bomb the landscape to create an artificial canyon." Private Prescott looked at Engineer Snell and Captain Shaw.

The Super Stallion's rotor blades churned the air into a frenzied whirlwind. Private Prescott's suggestion seemed to hang in the balance, oscillating between desperation and ingenuity. The concept of creating a physical barrier against the advancing technological walls of the Confederation sparked a flicker of hope among the weary soldiers.

"The idea of using bunker busters to forge a trench isn't without merit," Captain Walker's voice broke through the radio static, contemplative yet cautious. "But we're talking about an operation that requires precision and an arsenal we might not have access to."

Engineer Snell nodded, his gaze fixed on the retreating landscape below. "The key would be targeting strategic points along the projected path of the barriers. If we can disrupt the terrain enough, we might prevent further expansion, at least temporarily."

"I want it to be permanent." Captain Shaw interrupted.

"If we disrupt enough with big enough bombs, we might just be able to do that." Snell tapped his fingers on the surface of the table he sat at.

The cabin was filled with the muted sounds of the men, considering the feasibility of such a daring counter-measure. It was a plan fraught with risks and uncertainties, yet the alternative—watching helplessly as the Confederation solidified its control with unbreakable barriers—was unthinkable.

"We'll need to coordinate with the Pact governors, military engineers, and anyone who's got a stake in keeping the Confederation at bay," Captain Shaw said, his voice firm and sharp. "It's going to require a unified effort like we've never seen before."

As they flew towards their temporary base, the men aboard the Super Stallion were united in a singular focus. The conversation shifted to logistics, potential allies, and the daunting task of gathering the necessary munitions for such an unprecedented offensive.

Jeremiah threw his decanter of whiskey into the wall; the amber liquid sprayed as the crystal shattered into chunks. "Men and women of the Pact of Governors, our duly elected President of the United States has been murdered in an assassination, and his Vice President resigned, leaving room for President Morris to postpone elections for the foreseeable future. Not to mention, the Militia had to fall back into the surrounding states while the Confederation erected a huge wall in our United States. We have ceded the states of Oregon and Washington to the Communists." Jeremiah's voice was raw and unfiltered, usually a man of calm composure; he was furious that things were not going the way they should.

"What do we do?" Davison Carey of Wyoming asked while lowering his glasses onto his nose. He looked around at all of the other governors, but no one moved to answer. The hits just kept coming in a manner that was devastating to the cause of the Militia.

An awkward quiet filled the room; no one had any answers; they all just looked around. John Beam of Kansas leaned forward, breaking the heavy silence that had enveloped the room. His voice, though calm, carried an urgency that matched the seriousness of their situation.

"We have fought a hard battle and spilled a lot of blood for our homeland. We cannot let that be in vain, no matter what President Morris says."

Gene Kyle of North Dakota added, "Our militias are doing what they can, but they're outmatched in terms of technology and strategy. We need a new approach, one that leverages our strengths and the spirit of our people."

Mark Matthews of Nebraska offered a strategic perspective: "We need to secure our borders and ensure the safety of our citizens. Perhaps it's time we looked into developing our own technological defenses, some-thing to counteract those walls."

Jeremiah looked around the room as the various solu-tions were coming in, "listen, people, we are reliant on the United States Military in this fight. If Althea pulls support, it would be devastating."

Bradford Davidson, who had remained quiet up until now, stood, "We have to have a plan in case that happens. Our combined states make up a significant portion of the United States' GDP. I am not suggest-ing we secede, but we have been fighting our federal government's fight for months now. It is our sons and daughters dying for the Great Plains."

"Careful, Bradford, that bridges on outright treason." Jeremiah looked at his neighboring state's Governor.

"They already see what we are doing is treason, and the only reason they are standing with us now is because Althea thinks it helps her image after the assassination of Troy." Bradford stepped away from the table and started walking towards Jeremiah, "We fight for our home and uphold the Constitution against all enemies, foreign and domestic."

Suddenly, the door was kicked in by the Marines and other military soldiers who were present on the Gov-ernor's compound, their rifles drawn to low ready.

They walked around the room fanning out, their rifles trained on each of the Pact governors.

"What are y'all doing?" Jeremiah ordered with his hands over his head.

"We are under orders from the President of the United States of America, who has invoked the Insurrection Act. The Montana-Idaho Militia ends now, and the federal government assumes its sovereignty once more!" One of the lead soldiers said, aiming his rifle in the face of Governor Jeremiah Johnson.

Just as the room began to tense further, on the brink of what seemed like an inevitable violent clash, the doors burst open once again. This time, First Lieutenant Samantha Johnson, Jeremiah's own daughter, stormed in, her face a mask of righteous fury. Her voice boomed across the room, her Marine officer training kicking in despite the turmoil within her heart.

"Stand down! All of you!" she commanded, her gaze fierce as it swept over the soldiers, meeting the eyes of friends and comrades she had served with. Confusion and hesitation flickered in the eyes of some of the soldiers, torn between their orders and the authority with which Samantha spoke.

As the soldiers hesitated, unsure of how to react to Samantha's command, the room filled with the sound of more footsteps. Montana-Idaho Militia soldiers filed in;

their weapons were also drawn, but their presence was not aggressive toward the governors. Instead, they were there to support Samantha, backing her stand against what they saw as a betrayal of their cause.

The standoff was tense, with each side waiting for the other to make a decisive move. Samantha, realizing that words were her most potent weapon at this moment, continued, "You are turning your guns on the very people you swore to protect, on the very principles we all vowed to uphold. This is not what our country stands for!"

In the heat of the moment, with her conviction as strong as the steel of her resolve, Samantha did something that symbolized her complete commitment to her cause. She peeled off her American Flag patch from her arm, the very symbol of her service and allegiance to a country she believed in. In its place, she affixed the Buffalo Patch, given to her by her father just days earlier—a symbol of the Pact Governors' unity and resistance.

The symbolic act was not lost on those present. For some soldiers, it was a wake-up call, a reminder of the values they were supposed to fight for. The tension began to ebb as murmurs of dissent spread among the ranks of the military personnel present.

As the Montana-Idaho Militia soldiers moved in, the standoff came to an abrupt but bloodless conclusion. The United States Military members, now in a clear minority and facing the combined will of the governors and their own comrades' hesitation, were taken into custody by the Militia. They were disarmed respectfully, with Samantha overseeing the process, ensuring that no further escalation occurred.

Samantha, standing tall amidst the chaos she had quelled, turned to address the governors. "We need to act and act now. Unity and resolve are our greatest assets. Let's use this as a turning point, not just for our states, but for the principles we believe in."

Jeremiah looked at his daughter with a mixture of pride and sorrow for their position and nodded.

"As much as it breaks my heart to say this, I propose that we declare independence from the failed government of the United States!" Jeremiah spoke, looking reluctantly over at Bradford and then at the rest of the governors.

All of the governors of the Pact voted in favor except for John Beam of Kansas, his face filled with shame, "We can't turn our backs on the United States, even if she turned her back on us." John Beam's words hung in the air, a poignant reminder of what that decision meant. The room fell silent, each Governor grappling with the enormity of the moment. To declare independence was to cross a line from which there could be no return, setting them on a path of war against their own country and the foreign invaders of the Confederation. Yet, the

urgency of their situation and the betrayal they felt from
the federal government weighed heavily on their hearts.

Jeremiah, sensing the hesitance and conflict within his
fellow governors, stood once more, his voice steady but
heavy with emotion. "I understand the reservations, the
fear, and the weight of this decision. But consider where
our loyalty lies — with the principles upon which this
country was founded or with those who would betray
those principles for power? We stand at a crossroads,
not just for our states, but our states and for the very
soul of The Great Plains Nation."

Silence enveloped the room, heavy with the importance of their imminent decision. Among them, First
Lieutenant Samantha Johnson stood as a monument
of resolve, her mind echoing with her father's impassioned speech. The realization of what lay ahead —
the inevitable sacrifices, the risks to their very lives —
weighed heavily on her. Yet, the peril of doing nothing,
of watching their way of life disintegrate under external pressures, loomed even more prominent. Her hand
subconsciously brushed the buffalo patch now adorning
her arm, the irreversible step she had just taken.

At that moment, Samantha grappled with the enormity of her actions. She had forsaken her allegiance to
the United States, a decision that set her heart racing
with fear and defiance. She pondered the ramifications,
aware that she had crossed a line from which there was
no return. Her commitment to her family, her commu-

nity, and the ideals that had been threatened propelled her forward. Yet, the knowledge that she had breached her military oath cast a shadow over her resolve.

The drama of her internal conflict was a microcosm of the broader struggle facing the governors. Samantha's betrayal of her official oath for a higher cause underscored the dire situation they all encountered: a choice between the safety and sovereignty of their people or allegiance to a government they felt had abandoned them. In this charged atmosphere, the air thick with anticipation, dread, and uncertainty filled the path before them, but they were driven by a fierce determination to protect their homes and way of life.

Finally, Bradford Davidson broke the silence, "Jeremiah is right. We've reached the point of no return. Our people, our homes, our way of life are under threat. We must stand united for our families, for our communities, and for the future of our states. If that means declaring our independence, then so be it. For the glory of The Great Plains Nation!"

The governors voiced their agreement one by one, their resolve hardening with each affirmation. The decision was made not out of a desire for power but out of a necessity to protect and preserve their way of life.

As the meeting adjourned, plans began to take shape. Messages were sent, rallying the Militia and informing the citizens of their new course. The Pact of Governors, now the interim leaders of a fledgling nation, worked into the night, laying the groundwork for what would come next.

Outside, under the vast Montana sky, Samantha stood beside her father, looking out over the land that had been her home her entire life. Now, it was the heart of a new nation, born from the strife of invasion and the abandonment of its people by the government to which they swore allegiance.

Jeremiah placed a hand on her shoulder, "This will be our hardest battle yet, Sam. But we'll face it as we've faced all others — together."

Samantha nodded. The buffalo patch on her arm symbolized her commitment to this new cause. "Together," she echoed, her voice firm with resolve. The birth of their new nation was upon them, and though the road ahead was uncertain, they would walk it together for freedom, justice, and the hope of a better tomorrow.

In the distance, the American flags were lowered; in their place, the Montana flag flew high, the fabric catching the wind and crackling in the air.

"Daddy, I don't want to reinvent the wheel. I want all of the documents we use in the formation of this new federal government to be the same as those that founded our former home but with stronger protections to prevent people like Althea from rising to power." Samantha said, laying her head on her father's shoulder.

"I agree with that. We will definitely model our society around what the founders of the United States imagined because the United States isn't abiding by those things anymore." Jeremiah chuckled, his heart still beating fast at the revelation that he and his fellow Pact Governors were now the founders of a new nation.

The Great Plains Nation.

Althea walked into the Oval Office and slammed the door behind her. Hal caught the door and walked in behind her.

"Damn that Jeremiah and his Montana-Idaho Militia, damn him and his whole family." She shouted as Hal stood there quietly, "This is my time, Hal, my time. I was supposed to stop the invasion, and I was supposed to bring the entirety of the country to The New Dawn. "Her anger furiously steamed as she walked around the room length. She picked up the bust of Abraham Lincoln and threw it across the room; it broke into pieces as it landed on the ground.

As the shattered remnants of the Lincoln bust lay scattered across the floor, a symbol of a nation divided, President Althea Morris paced the room, her fury palpable. Her breath came in short, angry bursts, each step echoing her escalating frustration. Vice President Hal Bennett stood by the door, his presence more like a shadow than a comforting ally, absorbing the storm of her wrath without a word.

"This was not how it was supposed to unfold," Althea seethed, turning to face Hal with eyes that burned with a mix of betrayal and determination. "Jeremiah Johnson, that insufferable man, has taken it upon himself to fracture this nation further in the name of what? Freedom? Sovereignty?" She spat the words out like venom, her disdain for the actions of the Pact of Governors, and particularly Jeremiah, evident in her tone.

The letter, that damned piece of paper that proclaimed the birth of The Great Plains Nation, lay on her desk, an insult to the vision for America laid out by her benefactor's organization. Eleven states declaring their independence under the leadership of Jeremiah Johnson was not just a political maneuver; it was a direct challenge to her authority and her plans for the New Dawn she was envisioning for the country.

Hal, ever the voice of reason, finally spoke, his voice calm yet firm. "Madam President, we must approach this with strategy and precision. Your leadership is needed now more than ever. Reacting in anger will not—"

"Strategy?" Althea interrupted, her gaze sharp as she turned to him. "My strategy was clear, Hal. Unite the country and guide it to a New Dawn. But how can I do that when the ground is literally being split beneath us?"

"Althea, you did this to yourself by invoking the Insurrection Act against them. Did you think they would just lie down?" Hal asked, trying to center her focus back on the actions that caused it.

She walked over to the window, gazing out at the Washington Monument, where the man Troy was put to death. She imagined Troy's blood still on the base of the memorial as she seethed with her anger. "Jeremiah Johnson thinks he can just rip apart this country and start anew? He underestimates the resolve of this administration. He underestimates me."

Turning back to Hal, her expression softened slightly, a new resolve taking shape amidst the anger. "We need a countermeasure, Hal. Something that will bring the Great Plains Nation to its knees and force them back into the fold. I will not stand idly by while separatists carve up this country."

Hal nodded, understanding the urgency of the situation. "I'll convene with the defense and intelligence teams immediately. We'll need every asset at our disposal if we're to address this swiftly."

"We have to be careful; our relationships with other states are tenuous at best. We need to be calculated." Althea took a deep breath, her mind racing with potential strategies and outcomes. "Make it clear, Hal. The Great Plains Nation is an act of rebellion, and we will respond accordingly. I want options on my desk by morning. And get someone to clean this up," she added, gesturing to the broken statue on the floor.

As Hal left the room to carry out her orders, Althea turned back to the window, her reflection mingling with the view of the capital. The challenge laid before her was immense, but her determination to preserve the union and bring about the New Dawn was unwavering. The formation of The Great Plains Nation was a setback, but in her mind, it was far from a defeat. It was a call to action, a test of her resolve, and she was ready to answer it.

18

MIRANDA WALKED DOWN THE hallway towards where Jake was recovering, and the news that the Pact Governors had decided to declare independence from the United States was fresh in her mind. She was disturbed that it had gotten to this point. Still, the idea that they had been fighting a war for the United States without the assistance of the military for such a long time before they were able to get it sanctioned showed her that it may have been inevitable.

Miranda walked around the corner and noticed that none of the Militia were posted at the door. She immediately felt like something was wrong, so she quickened her pace and ran as she got to the door where Jake was recovering. The door was cracked, so she gently pushed it open.

In the bed where Jake had been recovering was just his clothing that he had been wearing; beside the bed was a pile of clothes haphazardly clumped on the floor. Her heart beat faster as she picked the clothes up from the floor, only to realize it was the uniform that Ray Grizzly Claw had been wearing the last time she saw him.

She didn't know why they would leave the clothes piled on the floor like that. She picked up the uniform and folded it, sitting it in the chair beside the television.

When she went to the bed and grabbed Jake's clothing, which was spread out on it, the bed felt hot, like it was on fire, but it wasn't burning.

Miranda's mind raced as she processed the bizarre scene before her. The absence of Jake and Ray, coupled with the peculiar heat emanating from the bed, felt like pieces of a puzzle she couldn't quite put together. The air in the room was thick, with tension that made her skin crawl. The situation was odd, and she had no answers. The last she saw Jake, he was still unconscious. Why would he get up and leave with no clothes on?

As she stood there, trying to make sense of it all, she noticed something else out of place—a faint, almost imperceptible mark on the wall opposite the bed. Squinting, she moved closer and saw that it wasn't just a mark but a series of pinpricks, like something a thumbtack would leave.

The absence of the militia guards, the mysterious heat, the clothes left behind, and now these tiny holes—each element added layers to the mystery, suggesting that what happened here was no ordinary event. Miranda felt a surge of apprehension and curiosity. Where were Jake and Ray, and what caused these peculiar occurrences?

She stood up and noticed a lamp on the floor, shattered like there had been a struggle of some sort. There were no immediate answers in sight, but Miranda knew she needed help. She pulled out her phone to call Jeremiah but stopped herself, knowing that he was busy with meetings and trying to form the new government of the Great Plains Nation.

She started to walk out of the room and noticed that there was another pile of clothes next to the door with a handgun lying on the side of it. When she picked up the uniform, she realized that it was Private Lucas's uniform. She grew up in Montana and knew a pistol with a chambered round meant something far darker than she realized. Grabbing her phone again, she dialed Jake's phone and heard the ringing, but she couldn't tell where it was coming from. She called Ray's phone and heard the ringing in the room.

Miranda's heart skipped a beat as the realization dawned on her—the ringing was coming from another pile of clothes by the door. Frantically, she dug through the garments until she found Ray's phone, its screen lighting up with her call. The discovery sent a chill down her spine. Why were their phones left behind, and where had they gone without them?

The room felt like a scene from a mystery she was unprepared to solve. With Ray's phone in one hand and the gun in the other, Miranda knew she had to act fast. The absence of guards, the unexplained heat, and the struggle—all pointed to a sudden and violent event that had occurred.

She pocketed the phones and, with a determined breath, stepped out into the hallway, now eerily silent. The lack of activity and the missing militia members only added to the growing sense of unease. Miranda moved swiftly, her mind racing with possible scenarios, her military training kicking in as she assessed her surroundings for any clues or threats.

As she made her way through the corridors, Miranda's thoughts were interrupted by a faint sound. Stopping in her tracks, she listened closely, trying to identify the noise. It was a muffled voice, barely audible, coming from a direction she couldn't immediately discern. Following the sound, she found herself standing before a door she hadn't noticed before, slightly ajar.

Pushing the door open with caution, she stepped into a dimly lit room that appeared to be an old storage area repurposed into a surveillance room. She ducked immediately behind the shelf as she noticed the two Militia soldiers that accompanied Jake here from Yakima, Jack Smith and Stephen Jones. They were erasing what looked to be surveillance tapes; in the video playing on the screen, she saw that Jack and Stephen had shot some type of weapon that caused Jake, Ray, and Private Lucas to vanish, and now they were trying to cover their tracks.

Her eyes welled in tears at the revelation of seeing her son and two others apparently vaporized by a technology that she didn't know existed.

As Miranda stood hidden, her heart thumped wildly against her chest, the shock of the situation paralyzing her with fear and confusion. She was a mother, not a soldier; her world was one of care and comfort, not covert operations and betrayals. Yet, there she was, witnessing a scene that seemed ripped from a spy thriller, far beyond her comprehension.

Her first instinct was to rush in, confront them, demand answers—but she knew that would be foolish. Instead, she pressed herself further into the shadows, her mind racing for a solution. The realization that her son, Jake, along with Ray and Private Lucas, were vaporized into nothing left her with a sharp pain in her chest.

As she watched Jack and Stephen erase what appeared to be crucial evidence, a desperate idea formed. Quietly, she pulled out her phone, not to record evidence—she had no such training or presence of mind for that—but to call for help. Her hands shook so violently that dialing was nearly impossible. The fear of being discovered was overwhelming, yet the fear for her safety propelled her forward.

Miranda barely managed to send a message to Jeremiah, her husband, before Jack and Stephen backed away from the bank of displays.

"That's enough thermite to set the whole mansion on fire; be careful," she heard as one of the men spoke to the other. She looked behind her where there were some shelves. She proceeded to slowly move some of the boxes aside so that she could squeeze behind them.

Miranda moved silently, her breaths shallow to avoid detection. The word "thermite" sent a wave of terror through her. Thermite, capable of burning at temperatures intense enough to cut through steel, suggested a plan far more sinister than merely erasing evidence. They were planning to destroy everything, eradicating any trace of what had transpired, potentially along with anyone who could bear witness.

She carefully slid behind the boxes, making no noise other than her breathing, which she tried to keep as quiet as possible. Her mind raced. The thought of sending another message to Jeremiah was now a distant option; she was deep in enemy territory, and her only immediate goal was survival.

Miranda had just turned on 'Do Not Disturb' mode, hoping to silence any further alerts. However, in her haste and trembling state, she hadn't completely silenced her phone. As she slid behind the boxes, trying to make herself as small as possible, her heart pounded against her chest with the terror of being discovered.

The room was almost silent, save for the sounds of Jack and Stephen methodically searching. They were thorough, their intent clear: leave no evidence behind. The air was thick with tension, the only light coming from the dim bulbs overhead and the glow of the monitors they were scrutinizing.

Jack started to light the thermite to destroy the evidence of their surveillance when suddenly, the eerie silence was broken by a soft but unmistakably audible beep from Miranda's phone. It was a notification she had forgotten to silence—a low battery alert, of all things, betraying her presence. Her heart stopped for a moment; the fear was so intense it was as if time had frozen around her.

"What was that?" Jack's voice cut through the silence, sharp and alert. The sound had drawn their attention, their footsteps now moving towards her hiding spot with purpose.

"Someone's here. Check it out," Stephen's voice commanded, closer now than ever. Miranda's mind raced, panic setting in as she realized her mistake might have just cost her the chance to escape.

The footsteps grew closer, the inevitability of discovery pressing down on her like a physical weight. In a desperate bid for survival, she knew she had to distract them, to give herself a chance to flee. With trembling hands, she reached for anything she could throw—a small, heavy book on a nearby shelf seemed like her best option.

With all the strength she could muster, Miranda hurled the book towards the far end of the room, opposite the direction she intended to run. The book hit a stack of metal boxes, creating a loud clattering noise that echoed through the storage area.

Both Jack and Stephen immediately turned towards the source of the sound, their weapons ready. "Over there!" Jack shouted, and they both rushed towards the noise, giving Miranda the precious seconds she needed.

Using their momentary distraction, Miranda pushed herself out of her hiding spot and darted towards the door, her footsteps as silent as a ghost's. She didn't look back, knowing that any second wasted could lead to her capture.

As she slipped out of the room, her heart pounding in her chest, Miranda couldn't help but feel a mix of relief and dread. She had escaped detection, for now, but the realization that she was involved in something far bigger and more dangerous than she could have imagined was overwhelming.

Miranda knew she needed to find help and fast. She ran as fast as she could down the corridor, not daring to look back.

Jack turned back to light the thermite to destroy the computer gear. As Stephen ran out of the room, he looked frantically back and forth, but the person who had seen them was nowhere to be found; knowing that they had little time, Stephen looked back at Jack, "I think our cover is blown; we have to get out of here."

Jack nodded, lighting the thermite quickly. The incendiary material sparked to life, casting an ominous glow over the room. They both knew the consequences of leaving evidence behind were far worse than the risk of starting a fire. The thermite began to burn through the surveillance gear, its intense heat melting metal and circuitry with ease, eradicating any trace of the incriminating surveillance.

Miranda, meanwhile, had managed to make it a considerable distance away from the surveillance room. Her heart still raced with adrenaline, her mind replaying the moment of escape over and over. She knew she needed to alert someone, anyone, about what she had witnessed. The realization that Jack and Stephen were not just erasing evidence but willing to destroy everything to cover their tracks was terrifying.

As she rounded a corner, she heard the faint crackle of fire behind her. The thermite had done its job too well. Panic surged through Miranda as she realized the fire was spreading beyond the intended surveillance equipment. Smoke began to fill the hallways of the east wing, a clear indication that the fire was burning through more flammable materials within the governor's mansion.

Miranda knew she had to act quickly. She pulled out her phone, now on its last bits of battery, and sent a frantic message to anyone in the militia command structure who would listen, warning them of the fire and Jack and Stephen's treachery. Her message was like a warning flare, a desperate plea for help as the situation escalated beyond her worst fears.

Back in the surveillance room, Jack and Stephen were acutely aware of the growing fire. Their mission to erase their tracks had backfired, the thermite igniting a huge flame that threatened to consume the mansion. "We need to get out, now!" Stephen shouted, grabbing Jack by the arm.

They raced through the smoke-filled hallways, coughing and sputtering as they tried to find the nearest exit. Behind them, the fire roared like a living beast, hungry and unrelenting. The mansion, the seat of the Pact Governors' resistance, was now a blazing inferno, its flames visible against the night sky.

Miranda, having sent her message, looked for a way out. The smoke was getting thicker, making it difficult to see and breathe. She wrapped a cloth around her mouth and nose, moving as quickly as she could towards what she hoped was an exit. The heat from the fire was intense, and the crackling sound was a constant reminder of the danger she was in.

Outside, the first responders were already on their way, alerted by Miranda's message. The Montana-Idaho Militia mobilized; their focus shifted from defending against external threats to saving their own from a disaster of their making.

As the mansion burned, the betrayal of Jack and Stephen, the disappearance of Jake, Ray, and Lucas, and the declaration of independence from the United States all converged into a singular moment of crisis. Miranda, caught in the midst of it all, was a testament to the resilience and determination of those fighting for their homes, their families, and their freedom.

Miranda crawled along the floor in the smoke-filled hallway, her eyes watering and her throat burning. Each breath she took was a struggle, her nose stinging from the acrid fumes. Determined to find an exit, she kept moving, inch by inch, despite the overwhelming smoke. The air grew thicker, making it harder to see or breathe.

Her vision blurred, and her movements became sluggish. Just as she thought she saw a glimmer of light ahead, her strength gave out. The toxic smoke enveloped her completely, and with a final, desperate gasp, Miranda passed out, collapsing onto the cold, hard floor of the hallway.

Jack and Stephen, realizing the urgency of their situation, made a beeline for the side exit, weaving through the labyrinth of corridors with a single-minded focus: escape. The fire they had inadvertently unleashed was spreading rapidly, and they hoped the chaos it caused would divert the Montana-Idaho Militia's attention away from them.

As they burst through the exit, the cool night air hit them, contrasting the suffocating heat and smoke they had just fled. They didn't pause to catch their breath; their mission now was survival and evasion. The sprawling governor's compound lay before them, eerily silent but for the distant crackling of the fire consuming the mansion.

Their destination was clear: a helicopter parked on a helipad at the far edge of the compound. It was a desperate gamble, but they knew it was their only chance to escape undetected and return home. The helipad, usually well-guarded, appeared deserted, likely due to the militia members being mobilized to respond to the emergency.

Jack and Stephen advanced cautiously, aware that the slightest noise could betray their presence. The vast grounds of the compound, bathed in the glow of the fire, seemed to stretch on endlessly, making their objective feel farther than ever.

Each step they took was measured, and their senses were on high alert for any sign of the Militia. The tension was palpable, a tangible force that drove them forward even as their muscles screamed for rest. They moved with the stealth of shadows, avoiding illuminated areas and sticking to the cover provided by the landscape.

As they neared the helipad, the sight of the helicopter offered a glimmer of hope. But their relief was short-lived; the sound of voices carried on the wind, coming from the direction of the mansion. The Militia was closer than they thought, their search likely expanding as the fire continued to rage.

Jack and Stephen exchanged a look. They would have to slow down and proceed with even greater caution to avoid detection. Their pace became painstakingly deliberate, each movement calculated to minimize noise.

The final stretch to the helicopter felt like an eternity, every second stretched thin by the adrenaline coursing through their veins. They were so close, yet the possibility of capture loomed large, a constant threat that kept their nerves taut like a drawn bowstring.

As they finally reached the helipad, their escape within grasp, Jack and Stephen knew the most challenging part was yet to come. Starting the helicopter and taking off without drawing attention would require finesse and a bit of luck. They approached the aircraft, their minds racing with plans and contingencies; Stephen kept watch at the machine gun on the side as Jack pushed the starter switch.

The tail rotor began to spin, making the most noise as the blades on top got up to speed.

In the distance, the Militia guards could be heard, "Someone is stealing the chopper!" The rotors spun slowly at first and then faster as they began to spin up fully.

"Jack! We gotta go!" Stephen yelled as Jack looked out of the window back towards the compound, seeing about a dozen militiamen running down the hill towards the helicopter.

Jack and Stephen's escape was marked by urgency as the helicopter flew off the ground, the rotors cutting through the night with growing intensity. Unbeknownst to them, their situation was even more dire. As the helicopter lifted into the air, neither of them noticed the subtle hiss of fuel escaping from a bullet hole in the tank—a silent countdown to a potential disaster they were blissfully unaware of.

Stephen, manning the machine gun, laid down suppressive fire to cover their ascent while Jack's focus remained locked on piloting the helicopter away from the compound. The chaos below, highlighted by the advancing Militia and the orange glow of the fire, seemed to recede with every heartbeat, replaced by the vast, open sky that offered a semblance of freedom.

The helicopter's ascent was shaky but successful, the craft gaining altitude and distance from the immediate danger. Inside the cockpit, the adrenaline of their escape began to mingle with the relief of survival, even as the aircraft shuddered under the stress of rapid takeoff and gunfire.

As they cleared the compound's walls, the sound of bullets against the helicopter's body became a distant memory. Jack and Stephen allowed themselves a moment of breath, the tension in the cockpit easing slightly. However, their relief was short-lived, as the reality of their escape and the next steps began to set in.

"Okay, we're clear... for now," Jack said, glancing at the instrument panel, unaware of the silent threat leaking away beneath them. "We need to find a safe place to regroup and figure out our next move."

Stephen nodded, scanning the dark horizon for any signs of pursuit or danger. "Yeah, let's just get as far away from here as we can," he agreed, his voice carrying the weight of their narrow escape.

The helicopter wasn't as responsive as Jack had expected; he could feel shudders in the engine as if it were spontaneously losing power. Stephen stuck his head out of the side of the chopper and looked back towards where they had come from, fully expecting the Militia to scramble the jets they had received from the Air Force in Idaho, but he saw nothing. Holding onto one of the bars, he reached out and ran his hand along the body of the vehicle, feeling a few of the bullet holes.

"Jack, we got hit pretty hard." Stephen pulled his arm back inside the helicopter and sat in one of the jump seats.

"Yeah, the fuel gauge is bouncing around like we are losing fuel. I don't know how far we will make it, and I am sure if we landed, we'd have a welcome party."

"Push as long as we can, bro!"

As the helicopter pressed on through the night, Jack's grip on the controls tightened, determination and concern etched into the features of his face. The dimly lit cockpit illuminated the concentration and worry that played across both men's features. Stephen, after alerting Jack to the bullet damage, kept vigil at the side, scanning the skies and ground below for any sign of pursuit or a safe haven to make an emergency landing.

The further they flew, the more erratic the fuel gauge behaved, its needle swinging with alarming unpredictability. The realization that they were leaking fuel at a rate that could soon render them powerless in the sky hung over them like a dark cloud.

"We need to make a decision," Jack shouted over the noise of the rotors, his eyes flicking between the instruments and the landscape unfolding below. "We can try to make it to an area where we can disappear or put down in a secluded spot before we run dry."

Stephen weighed their options, his mind racing. "I would rather have an area where we might have a chance to refuel and repair... but if we don't make it?"

Jack nodded, understanding that gravity was pulling their injured vehicle to the ground, which only intensified their tension. The risk of being stranded, or worse, captured, if they couldn't reach safety was a gamble. Yet, flying until they ran out of fuel wasn't an option either. They had to find a middle ground, a place secluded enough to attempt a safe landing but close enough to escape the Montana-Idaho Militia.

As they deliberated, the engine's occasional shudder became more pronounced, a subtle reminder of their dwindling time. Decision made: Jack adjusted their course slightly, aiming for an area known to be less patrolled and, hopefully, more forgiving for an emergency landing.

The landscape below was a patchwork of shadows and moonlit clearings, the terrain unfamiliar and unwelcoming. The fuel gauge's warning light flickered on, a silent alarm that their time was running out. The cabin started beeping repeatedly, an audible alarm, "emergency," repeated over and over.

"Brace for landing!" Jack called out, his voice steady despite the tension that gripped him. Stephen secured himself as best he could, his eyes fixed on the rapidly approaching ground.

Jack's piloting skills were put to the ultimate test as he maneuvered the helicopter towards a less dense part of the forest they were flying over. Trees and terrain rushed up to meet them, the ground a blur of motion and darkness.

With a final, desperate effort, Jack eased the helicopter down, the aircraft's skids scraping against the earth in a rough, graceless landing that jolted them both. The aircraft lurched a groan of stressed metal and whining engines filling the air before coming to a sudden, eerie silence. All that could be heard was the steady beeping from the helicopter's computer.

They had made it to the ground, but the battle for survival was far from over. The leaking fuel tank, now evident by the strong smell of aviation fuel, posed an immediate danger. They had to move quickly before the helicopter became a magnet for anyone who might be searching for them.

As Jack and Stephen exited the crippled craft, they ran deeper into the woods, "We have to figure out where we are." Jack's stressed voice spoke as Stephen stepped up beside him.

"We are probably still in Montana. We weren't flying for long."

19

TAMARA HOLLIS CLIMBED OUT of the news van in Washington, D.C., where thousands of people gathered at the National Mall. Troy Thomason supporters wandered aimlessly around the area with flags, with the bold words Thomason/Rice 2024 with the motto 'Small Town America is the Best America' flapping in the wind. Tamara looked over at Joel Prescott, her cameraman and on-site producer.

"I have a bad feeling about this, Joel." She said, looking into the mirror at the back door of the van while cleaning up her makeup. Her hair was fixed in bouncy curls, and she wore a purple suit and a fuchsia blouse. Joel looked over at her and back at the growing crowd, "Yeah, it feels like what happened a few years ago here, but honestly... worse."

Tamara nodded and grabbed her microphone; she was smart this time to wear sensible shoes because last time, she broke a heel and ended up in the hospital for a week when the two mobs violently clashed in front of the White House after the last election. She was not looking forward to today.

When the station manager assigned her, she fought back because of what had happened last time, but she was known as the 'Face of Balanced Political Reporting.'

After Thomason was assassinated at the Washington Monument on Wednesday, January 15th, political tension in America reached an all-time high. The nation was in turmoil on Inauguration Day: the President-elect had been murdered, and the Vice President and her family had vanished without a trace. To make matters worse, the Confederation had claimed victory over the Pacific Northwestern states of Washington and Oregon, and nearly a dozen states had declared independence. These were far from normal times.

Althea Morris, the acting President, was set to give a speech from the inauguration stage that had been set up, but that was looking less and less likely as the crowd grew.

Tamara bowed her head and began to pray that there wouldn't be violence today; Joel laid his hand on her shoulder and feigned to pray himself. As Tamara finished, she looked up, and she could already see the beginnings of a giant clash at the White House and at the Washington Monument. Sighing, she gathered the things that they needed and began to walk towards the White House. Joel closed the van and locked all of the doors, then rushed to keep up with Tamara.

Walking down Pennsylvania Avenue, she noted two particular groups, some from what called themselves the American Communist Brigade, ACB for short. The other group consisted of small-town American folks and farmers with their bull horns and Thomason flags.

On both sides, people were armed with rifles and handguns against the laws of D.C., but by the thousands, they merged in the National Mall, staying mainly on their sides with other like-minded people. In between, a large contingent of National Guard descended to try and keep the peace; they, too, were armed.

Tamara looked over at Joel, concern etched across her face. "I don't like this; it feels like a powder keg is about to explode." She stopped and motioned for Joel to start filming.

As Joel adjusted the camera, focusing on Tamara with the swelling crowd in the background, the tension in the air was palpable. The National Guard soldiers, positioned strategically throughout the area, eyed the crowds warily, their fingers never far from their triggers.

Tamara cleared her throat, readying herself for the live broadcast. "This is Tamara Hollis, reporting live from the National Mall in Washington, D.C., where supporters of Troy Thomason and concerned citizens from across the country have gathered in what is rapidly becoming a highly charged environment," she began, her voice steady despite the underlying tension.

The camera panned to capture the sea of people, the Thomason/Rice 2024 flags waving amidst signs of protest and defiance. The two groups, divided by the National Guard, began pushing against the National Guard members, resembling the raging rapids of a river. The camera moved around, capturing angry faces. Joel then focused back on Tamara.

She continued, "In the wake of the assassination of President-elect Troy Thomason, and with the disappearance of Vice President Rice and her family, America finds itself at a crossroads. The Confederation's claim over the Pacific Northwestern states and the declaration of independence by almost a dozen states have only added fuel to the fire."

Joel zoomed in on Tamara as she gestured towards the Washington Monument, where minor skirmishes were already breaking out, the tension escalating with every passing moment. "The acting President, Althea Morris, is expected to address the nation shortly, but as you can see, the likelihood of violence looms large."

Just then, a shout erupted from the crowd, followed by a loud pop, causing a ripple of panic. Tamara and Joel instinctively ducked, the camera still rolling, capturing the sudden chaos that ensued. National Guard soldiers moved in, trying to contain the situation, but the crowd's agitation was palpable, a volatile mix of fear, anger, and determination.

As Tamara and Joel maneuvered through the crowd, trying to keep a safe distance while continuing their report, it became clear that the day would not pass without incident. The National Mall on Inauguration Day was a powder keg ready to explode, and the entire nation watched with bated breath as the drama unfolded.

Tamara's voice rose above the chaos, a source of calm amid the turmoil. "We urge everyone watching to stay safe as we continue to report on this historic and tumultuous day in our nation's capital. The world is watching as America grapples with its identity and its future."

The camera captured a panoramic view of the Mall, the historic setting now a battleground for the soul of a nation. Tamara and Joel, in the midst of the chaos, remained committed to their duty, providing a window into the heart of a divided America.

Amidst the burgeoning tumult, Tamara raised her voice, struggling to be heard over the raucous din. "The atmosphere here is charged with an intensity I've seldom seen," she declared, her expression grave as the camera captured a wider angle of the escalating confrontation. The crowds of people, once separated by mere ideology, now teetered on the brink of physical conflict, their chants and cries melding into a single, ominous roar.

Suddenly, the situation deteriorated further. A loud bang echoed across the Mall, followed by a series of rapid pops. The crowd surged like a wave, panic and aggression colliding. The National Guard outnumbered and under immense pressure, formed tight ranks and raised their shields as they attempted to stem the tide of oncoming protestors.

Tamara, maintaining her professionalism amidst the chaos, continued her live broadcast. "Violence has erupted at the National Mall," she reported, her voice steady despite the apparent danger. Joel's camera swiveled, capturing the scenes of conflict—protestors clashing with guards, flags, and homemade signs becoming makeshift weapons.

The sound of sirens filled the air, a jarring symphony to the visuals of chaos and division unfolding before the nation. The police and FBI reinforcements poured into the area, their efforts to restore order only adding fuel to the fire of rebellion and dissent.

Some of the law enforcement officers began choosing sides and clashing with each other as the shouting and screaming became louder. Tamara grasped her ears as Joel kept the camera focused on her. He really didn't think this would be worse than a few years earlier, and his mind was set on a Pulitzer. He zoomed in on Tamara's terrified face, tears streaming from her eyes.

"This is excellent footage! Let's keep going, Tamara!" Joel shouted as Tamara looked perplexed at his request.

"What the hell is wrong with you, Joel? This is the day America dies." Her voice was raw as she screamed, but Joel kept filming.

The air crackled with the electricity of an imminent catastrophe. Tamara Hollis, amidst the escalating unrest, felt the weight of her responsibility as a journalist more acutely than ever. The center of American politics had now transformed into an arena of division, the ground beneath her feet vibrating with the unrest of a nation torn asunder.

Joel, camera in hand, captured every moment with professional detachment; his concern for Tamara was outweighed by his desire to be recognized with a journalistic award. The crowd's energy, volatile and unpredictable, surged around them, a living entity of collective anxiety and defiance. Shouts and cries for peace mingled with the roar of anger, an auditory representation of America's fractured soul.

The escalation was rapid, and the initial clashes between protestors and the National Guard quickly spiraled into a broader conflict that consumed the Mall. Some law enforcement officers were caught between their duty to maintain order and their sympathies for the protestors, while others joined in the burgeoning conflict. National Guard members found themselves in a moral quagmire, and their decisions in these moments were critical to the unfolding events.

Tamara's reporting, her voice battling the chaos, continued unabated. "As we stand here on the precipice of history, the actions of those gathered today will forever shape the narrative of our nation," she intoned, her words slicing through the raging voices and shouting. Her face was streaked with makeup and tears, her once new hairstyle now soaked with sweat and a mix of water and tear gas that had been sprayed through the area. The camera panned to capture the vast expanse of the Mall, now a battlefield of conflict and passion. In the distance, the Capitol was in flames as the American Communist Brigade used the opportunity to burn the symbols of American governance.

The sound of gunfire, sporadic at first, became a terrifying constant; the echo of bullets was a grim punctuation to Tamara's live report. Joel's camera, unflinching, recorded the descent into violence, the screen a window into the heartbreak unfolding before it. The National Guard, their presence a thin veneer of control, was quickly overwhelmed, and their attempts to mediate met with resistance from all sides.

An explosion near the Washington Monument sent a shockwave through the crowd, the force of the blast knocking protestors and law enforcement alike off their feet. Smoke billowed into the sky, a dark cloud over the nation's capital, as screams of terror and confusion filled the air.

Tamara, momentarily stunned, regained her composure with remarkable speed. "We've just witnessed an explosion near the Washington Monument," she reported, her voice trembling with emotion. "The situation here is deteriorating rapidly. We implore everyone watching to seek safety immediately."

The camera, now shaky in Joel's grasp, captured the aftermath of the explosion, the ground littered with debris and the injured. Law enforcement and protestors, their differences momentarily forgotten, rushed to aid those affected, a fleeting glimpse of humanity in the midst of despair.

In a moment of clarity, Tamara gathered her thoughts and stood, the White House over her shoulder. She pushed her messed-up locks of hair from her eyes and motioned for Joel to focus on her.

"Our brave police forces and National Guard, armed only with rubber bullets and tear gas, found themselves outnumbered and under attack by political dissidents on both the right and the left." She spoke as what appeared to be soldiers in black uniforms began filing out of the White House. They uttered no words but began firing strange weapons at the combined crowds. Tamara looked behind herself as people began disappearing and vanishing; all that was left behind was their clothing.

Thousands began turning to run from the scene on both sides of the altercation, abandoning their flags and signs, some returning fire on the strange soldiers.

Tamara turned back to the camera; fear flickered on her face as she began to repeat herself.

"Our brave police force, armed only with rubber bullets and tear gas, found themselves outnumbered and under attack. They were no match for the strange weapons wielded by their faceless aggressors. Their retreat sent a shockwave of horror among the onlookers as several officers and protestors seemed to disappear, leaving no trace, no sign of their once steadfast presence.

"I am Tamara Hollis, reporting to you from chaos and uncertainty..." Her words were cut off as a bullet hit Joel's camera, knocking it from his hand and to the ground. The crowd ran in their direction, trampling on the camera and pushing Joel and Tamara onto the ground. More of the strange weapon projectiles struck several people running through the area where Tamara and Joel were being trampled. Their faces twisted in agony and then vanished as their clothes fell on top of Tamara and Joel. Tamara looked over at Joel, who wasn't moving. She slid her uncooperative body over to Joel. She shook him, but there was no response. Her hands grasped his face and turned it towards her; his lifeless eyes were glassy, blood trailing from his nose and mouth.

"Oh God, Joel, Oh God. Oh, God." She lowered her head onto his chest and began to cry bitter tears as she realized he had been trampled to death. She began to pray again, her bitter tears mixing with the blood streaming from the wounds on her own head.

Firm hands grabbed her shoulder and flipped her over. She looked up at the man who had flipped her; it was one of the strange soldiers; he was wearing a plain white mask, and on his arm was a patch she had never seen. It looked like a mix of a CIA shield and the All-Seeing Eye on the back of the dollar bill. Her eyes widened in terror as the masked man aimed his weapon at Joel; pulling the trigger, Joel's lifeless body vanished. Tamara's terror overtook her as she began to plead for her life. The faceless masked soldier turned his weapon onto her.

"Please, don't." Those were the only words that escaped her lips as the trigger was pulled. As soon as its projectile struck her, she screamed in agony, her body dematerializing into nothingness, leaving behind nothing but her purple suit, skirt, and fuchsia blouse.

Philip Buchanan sat in the hospital room, holding the hand of his father, the beeping of the machines tracking his father's heartbeat. He grasped the remote control and turned the television on, turning it over to Monday

Night Football. He smiled as he saw his dad's favorite team playing, the Packers against the Cowboys, in one of the NFC Playoff games of the 2024-25 season. His dad loved the Packers; they had season tickets and went to as many games as they could growing up. He looked over at his unconscious father, and a tear traced his cheek. The morphine dripped constantly, keeping him in a state between life and death. He came home to Green Bay from Seattle, Washington, right before Election Day and the craziness of the last few months.

Philip knew that he could never go home now that the Confederation had invaded and his state had fallen. Wisconsin was now part of another country that had declared independence from the United States, so he wasn't sure how to feel about anything. Luckily, football, the great American escapism, continued chugging along. He wasn't sure how any of that worked behind the scenes, but he was glad it was.

As the game progressed, Philip's attention drifted from the screen to the window, where the world outside seemed so distant, so removed from the sterile confines of the hospital room. He wondered about the changes sweeping across the nation, the political upheaval, the formation of new countries, and what it all meant for the simple pleasures in life, like watching a football game with his father.

The hospital room felt like a bubble, insulated from the chaos that had enveloped the country. Here, life was measured in heartbeats and breaths in the quiet moments between the nurse's visits. Philip squeezed his father's hand tighter, wishing for a sign, any sign, that he could hear him, feel him.

The Packers scored a touchdown, and instinctively, Philip turned to share the moment with his father, only to be met with silence. He missed the shared cheers, the high fives, the heated debates over plays. Now, the sounds of the game echoed vainly in the room, a reminder of what was lost.

The game was interrupted by a report from Tamara Hollis; she looked disheveled and agitated. It was a distinction from her usual crisp and professional image. There was an air of chaos in the image Philip saw on the television playing out in front of him.

He noticed that her short bob, usually perfectly styled in tight, bouncing curls, was now a disorderly mess. Strands of hair stood out in various directions, hinting at her hurried, possibly frantic preparations to appear before the camera. One look at her face further underscored her distress—her makeup was smeared across her cheeks, an unusual sight for a reporter known for her immaculate presentation. The streaky blush and mascara told a story of rushed application and perhaps a lack of time for necessary touch-ups.

The seriousness of her disorderly appearance was not lost on him. No one had ever seen her like this. It was immediately apparent that something extraordinary was unfolding, something so urgent that it warranted neglecting her impeccable appearance. The game, which had held everyone's attention only moments ago, was now forgotten as all eyes turned to the visibly flustered reporter, anxiously waiting for her to reveal the cause of her evident distress. "In the heart of our nation's capital, downtown Washington D.C., a chilling scene of violence unfolded today. Anti-government activists, fueled by rampant hostility, made Pennsylvania Avenue their battlefield. The once peaceful street echoed with the whistle of Molotov cocktails and the harsh snap of bricks hurled at parked vehicles from the Presidential motor pool. The arrival of an unidentified armed militia worsened the widespread unrest." Her announcement was matter-of-fact and plain, she continued,

"Our brave police force, armed only with rubber bullets and tear gas, found themselves outnumbered and under attack. They were no match for the strange weapons wielded by their faceless aggressors. Their retreat sent a shockwave of horror among the onlookers as several officers seemed to disappear, leaving no trace, no sign of their once steadfast presence.

I am Tamara Hollis, reporting to you from chaos and uncertainty... "But just as she was about to continue, the T.V. feed waned, the screen fizzled, and Tamara's voice was lost. Flickering text appeared on the screen, a cold, impersonal message replacing the live reporter,

"The station is experiencing technical difficulties". At that moment, Tamara was no longer there, and we were left in silence, waiting and wondering what would come next.

Philip sat in stunned silence, the remote dangling from his hand. The shift from the vibrant energy of a football game to the chilling news report was abrupt and disturbing. The flickering message on the screen, "The station is experiencing technical difficulties," seemed a feeble effort to gloss over the severity of events that, though distant, had been thrust into the hospital room yet so vividly brought into it through Tamara's report.

The variation between the serene hospital room and the chaos on the T.V. screen was stark. Philip's father lay unaware of the turmoil, his breaths steady amid the beeping machines. Yet, Philip felt a deep unease in his chest. The country he knew, the very fabric of its society, seemed to be unraveling, torn apart by internal strife and division, compounded by an invasion and attack on the West Coast.

He looked back at his father, wishing more than anything that he could share his thoughts and seek his wisdom. They had often discussed politics and the state of the world, debates that could last hours. Now, in the silence of the hospital room, Philip felt the absence of those conversations more acutely than ever.

The sense of powerlessness was overwhelming. There was nothing he could do from the confines of the hospital room, nothing but watch as the country he loved faced an uncertain future. The realization that the political turmoil had reached a boiling point, capable of igniting violence in the heart of the nation's capital, was chilling.

Philip turned off the television, and the room was now filled only with the sound of the medical machines and his father's steady breathing. The contrast between the internal peace of the hospital room and the external chaos of the world outside was bleak. He was reminded of his conversations with his father, who often spoke about the fragile balance that held society together, a balance that now seemed to be teetering in the direction of collapse.

He leaned closer to his father, speaking softly as if trying to bridge the gap between them with words. "Dad, I wish you could see what's happening. I wish we could talk about it and figure it out together." The words were a whisper, lost in the expanse of the room, but they carried the weight of his concern, his fear for the future.

Philip remained by his father's side, lost in thought as the night deepened. The uncertainty of the times, the fear of what lay ahead, and the longing for guidance in a world that seemed to be losing its way consumed him. In the quiet of the hospital room, Philip Buchanan faced the reality of the changing world outside, armed only with the memories of better times and the hope that somehow, someway, things would find a way to mend.

His phone rang, and he went to answer. The voice on the other end was one he hadn't heard for a long time: his mom's brother, Uncle Jack Ashby.

20

SENATOR ULYSSES MARS SAT in his North Carolina Senate Office, which was established in Raleigh, NC. His eyes continued to watch the news of the chaotic event in the Capital of the United States. He was thankful that he had come to his home before the protest on Inauguration Day that he had seen advertised on Vyber; he wanted no part of a repeated event from a few years earlier after the virus shut the country down.

The news spread like wildfire throughout the remaining states; news replays of the protests and violence played on every newscast, and the last few minutes of Tamara Hollis' broadcast repeated as reporters dissected the events.

Ulysses stared with glassy eyes at the screen as Samuel Burris peeked around the corner. Ulysses shook from his stupor, acknowledged Samuel, and motioned for him to enter.

"Hey there, Governor. What do I owe this pleasure?" Ulysses smiled, holding up his half-drunk glass of scotch.

"Hello, Senator, I just wanted to swing by and chat about what happened yesterday in D.C. and North Carolina's response.", the Governor said, walking into the door fully as Ulysses leaned forward and flipped the television off with the remote.

"What do you mean 'North Carolina's response?' Like we can even respond?"

"Well, I have been talking to surrounding governors, and no one is happy with the response after the Neutronium bomb, Confederation invasion, the assassination of the first North Carolina native president in two centuries..." Samuel's words were cut off abruptly by Ulysses as he spoke up, "Don't pretend you liked Troy. I expected you to celebrate his assassination with your political action committee and your Democrat friends."

"I am sorry. I know you were close with Troy, and I am sorry for your loss. You are right. I didn't like him, but I didn't want him dead. Not to mention, I couldn't bite the hand feeding me from the Democratic National Committee." Samuel's face creased in an uneasy smile.

"What do you want, governor?" Ulysses' tone was a mix of curiosity and apprehension. He was aware that a visit from Governor Burris, especially under such tumultuous circumstances, could only mean significant political maneuverings were afoot.

Samuel took a deep breath, choosing his words carefully. "Senator, I think it's time for us to seriously consider the future of North Carolina and, indeed, the entire South. The formation of the Great Plains Nation has set a precedent, one that could provide us the political cover we need to pursue our own path."

Ulysses raised an eyebrow, the glass of scotch momentarily forgotten. "Secession? Is that what you're hinting at, Samuel?" His voice was calm but carried an underlying note of incredulity.

Samuel nodded, the weight of his proposal evident in his demeanor. "Yes, secession. It's not just me thinking along these lines. I've been in discussions with other governors from the South. The events of the past few months—the Confederation's bold moves, the assassination, the chaos in D.C.—have only highlighted the deep divisions within our country. We need to think about protecting our people, our way of life."

Ulysses leaned back, processing the importance of the situation. The notion of secession was radical, fraught with legal and moral complexities, yet the unfolding national crisis lent it a veneer of legitimacy he found deeply unsettling.

"And what about the people of North Carolina? How do you propose we bring them along on this journey?" Ulysses asked, his skepticism thinly veiled.

Samuel's response was measured, betraying the careful consideration he had given the matter. "We start by laying out the facts and the reasons why we believe secession is the best path forward. We talk about self-determination, about preserving our rights and freedoms in the face of an increasingly authoritarian federal government. We highlight the success of the Great Plains Nation as an example of what can be achieved."

Ulysses considered Samuel's words, the potential implications spinning through his mind. The Senator was no stranger to political battles, but the scale and consequence of what Samuel proposed were unlike anything he had encountered before.

"Governor, this is a monumental decision, one that could redefine the very fabric of our nation. Have you considered the risks, the potential for conflict, the economic implications?" Ulysses prodded, seeking to gauge the depth of Samuel's commitment to this course of action.

Samuel met Ulysses' gaze squarely, his resolve apparent. "I have, Senator. And I believe the risks of inaction, of remaining passive observers in a country that's tearing itself apart, are far greater. This isn't about politics or power—it's about the future of our state and our people."

The room fell silent, the magnitude of their discussion hanging heavily in the air. Ulysses swirled the scotch in his glass, contemplating the uncertain path ahead. The road to secession, should they choose to embark upon it, would be fraught with challenges. Yet, in the face of a nation divided, the allure of charting their own destiny was undeniably powerful.

Ulysses laughed under his breath ironically, "History seems to be rhyming!"

"What do you mean, Senator?"

"Well, Democrats seceded back in the 1860s, then spent two centuries accusing Republicans of trying to tear the country apart." Ulysses chuckled at the irony.

"Well, I may have been a Democrat for a long time, but there is a new grassroots party forming called the Unionists that I have changed my affiliation to. A lot of Democrats are abandoning ship for it since the Democrats have become increasingly socialist." Samuel's face creased with stress, "Regardless, I want you with me when I meet with the governors of Virginia, South Carolina, Georgia, Alabama, and Florida."

"What? No Tennessee, Kentucky, or the rest of the former Confederate States?" Ulysses strained to find humor in all of it, even though the conversation he was engaged in was horrific.

Samuel shook his head, a small smile at Ulysses' attempt to lighten the mood. "Tennessee and Kentucky are considering their options, but they're on the fence.

This isn't about rehashing the Confederacy, Ulysses. It's about carving a path forward for our people, one that respects our history but isn't bound by it. We're trying to build something new here, something that reflects the values and needs of our citizens today."

Ulysses sighed, placing his glass down. "Samuel, you know this is going to cause a stir, not just here but across the country. Secession is a loaded word, full of historical baggage. You're talking about fundamentally altering the course of our state and potentially setting off a chain reaction across the South."

"I understand that, Ulysses. And I don't take it lightly. But consider this—across the nation, we're seeing movements of self-determination gaining momentum. People are questioning whether the federal government truly represents their interests anymore. In North Carolina, we've always prided ourselves on our independence and our resilience. Maybe it's time to channel that spirit into something tangible, something that can protect and preserve our way of life."

Ulysses nodded slowly, the gears turning in his head. "If we go down this path, Samuel, we need to ensure we're doing it for the right reasons. It can't just be about political power or escaping federal oversight. It has to be about securing a better future for our people, about ensuring their rights and freedoms are safeguarded."

Samuel stood up, extending his hand to Ulysses. "That's exactly why I came to you first, Ulysses. I knew you'd understand the stakes. Let's work together on this, make sure we're considering all the angles, ensuring that if we do decide to take this step, we're doing it with the best interests of North Carolina and her people in mind."

Ulysses took Samuel's hand, the weight of their potential decision heavy on both of them. "Alright, Samuel. Let's see where this conversation leads us. But whatever we decide, let's ensure it's done thoughtfully, with the full understanding of what it means for our state and for the nation."

As Samuel left the office, Ulysses turned back to the muted television; the images of unrest saddened him deeply. The idea of secession, once unthinkable, was now a topic of serious consideration. The world was changing, and North Carolina was poised at the edge of history. They wouldn't be the first to secede, but they would be ready to make a decision that could alter its course forever.

Nestled in the heart of the American Midwest, the quaint town of Independence, Kentucky, was a picturesque embodiment of rural charm. An hour's drive from the bustling streets of Cincinnati, Ohio, it was a world apart—a serene expanse of farmland dotted with barns and stables, where the gentle whinny of horses mingled with the rustling of crops. This pastoral landscape was the birthplace and retreat of Kenneth Chandler, the esteemed Governor of Kentucky, who found solace among its rolling hills and verdant fields.

Governor Chandler's horse ranch, a sprawling estate tucked in the flourishing countryside of Independence, was more than just a home; it was a sanctuary from the tumult of political life. Here, amidst the meticulously fenced paddocks and the stately oak trees that had stood sentinel for generations, Chandler found peace. The ranch was renowned not just for its beauty but for its distinguished residents—the sleek, powerful thoroughbreds that galloped across its pastures, embodying the spirit of Kentucky's storied racing heritage.

Yet, even in this idyllic setting, the echoes of discord from the wider world intruded. The fabric of the United States, formerly a melting pot of unity, was breaking apart at its foundation, broken apart by forces that Chandler had scarcely imagined possible in his earlier years of public service. States declaring independence, alliances fracturing, and the very idea of a united nation seemed perilous and uncertain.

As Chandler stood on the wooden porch of his ranch house, the early morning mist weaving through the fields like wraiths, he couldn't help but feel the weight of the moment. The crisp air filled his lungs, the dew-soaked earth beneath his boots grounding him in the reality of his surroundings. Yet, his mind was adrift, caught in the turbulent currents of political upheaval that threatened to engulf his beloved Bluegrass State of Kentucky.

The sound of hooves on the soft earth pulled him back from his morning daydream. He watched as one of his prized horses, a majestic bay with a coat that shimmered in the sun's first light, galloped freely along the fence line. In its grace and power, Chandler saw a symbol of what he fought to preserve—a legacy of freedom and dignity, not just for his horses but for the people he served.

But as the horizon blushed with the dawn, painting the sky in hues of orange and pink, Chandler knew that the day ahead would demand more of him than reflections on beauty and heritage. The challenges facing Kentucky, and indeed the entire nation, were daunting. Yet, amidst the uncertainty, Chandler's resolve was unwavering. He witnessed the United States turning its back on the states being invaded and refused to help the states fight back until it was politically expedient. His friend Troy Thomason was murdered before he took the oath of office, and the way the traitor Althea Morris took power violated the principles on which he believed were the foundation of the United States.

Samuel Burris, the Governor of North Carolina, had reached out to see if they would be on board with setting their own path separated from the United States. This idea terrified him, but he got to thinking about it more and more after Governor Kelly Moss of Tennessee called. She was worried about the fracturing nation, but she knew they couldn't do it on their own, and politically, she didn't see joining with the Southeastern states as viable.

Kenneth Chandler found himself entangled in a web of introspection and doubt as he pondered the future of Kentucky and its place in an America fraying at its edges. The early morning tranquility of his ranch, usually a source of solace, now served as the backdrop to a storm of internal conflict that mirrored the chaos unfolding across the nation.

The Governor's rugged hands, so accustomed to the reins of power and the tactile connection to the earth and its creatures, trembled slightly as he contemplated the calls from his fellow governors. The notion of secession, a word heavy with historical consequence and laden with the blood of forebears, seemed to hang over him like the mist that shrouded his fields. Could he, a man who had dedicated his life to the service of his state and its integration within the Union, now consider a path that would sever those bonds?

His gaze drifted across the paddocks, where the morning light played on the dew-laden grass, revealing nature's serene beauty despite the turmoil that filled his mind. The sight of his horses, symbols of Kentucky's proud heritage, evoked a deep, almost primal connection to the land and its history—a history rich in struggle, resilience, and an unyielding spirit of independence.

Yet, the echoes of the past did not offer solace but instead served as a reminder of the bloodshed and division that had once torn the nation asunder. The Civil War, a specter that lingered in the collective memory of the South, cast a long shadow over Chandler's deliberations. The parallels were unnerving, the implications profound. Could they chart a course that would avoid the pitfalls of their predecessors, or were they doomed to repeat the mistakes of history?

As the morning waned and the sun climbed higher in the sky, casting long shadows across the ranch, Chandler's internal battle raged on. The ideals he held dear—the unity of the nation, the collective endeavor towards a more perfect Union—clashed with the sad reality of a country divided, a government that seemed increasingly alien to the principles upon which it was founded.

The sharp ring of the telephone pierced the stillness, a shrill ringing that snapped Chandler back to the present. The voice on the other end was terse, conveying the urgency of the situation. "Governor, you're needed back in Frankfort immediately. It's been confirmed—the United States is sending military forces to the Great Plains Nation to quash their secession."

The words hung heavy in the air, a harbinger of the conflict to come. The decision before him, once theoretical, was now immediate and laden with consequences. As he set down the receiver, Chandler knew that the days ahead would test the very soul of Kentucky and its people.

"They are not sending our Kentucky sons and daughters to fight their damn fight." Kenneth's face was filled with rage, and, with a heavy heart, he gazed once more upon the land that had shaped him, the land he was sworn to protect. Then, with a resolve born of necessity and a deep love for his state, he turned towards the house to prepare for the journey to Frankfort. One thing was clear: the world he knew was changing, and he would not allow Kentucky blood to be spilled for a war the United States caused.

The simmering tensions along the southern edge of the United States had reached a boiling point, transforming the landscape from a source of hope for millions into a symbol of a nation in turmoil. The Gulf of Mexico to the Pacific Ocean, a vast stretch of land that witnessed the dreams and despair of countless souls, now bore the scars of a country unraveling. The cataclysmic detonation of the Neutronium bomb off the West Coast ignited a series of catastrophic events, leading to an unprecedented exodus in modern history. As despair gripped the heartland, waves of Americans, along with those who had once sought refuge within its borders, fled the chaos, seeking solace in Mexico.

But peace was a fleeting dream. The desperate tide of humanity clashing at the border culminated in a tragic confrontation, a bloody testament to the depths of the crisis. Thousands perished in the ensuing conflict, the dark reminder of the cost of desperation. International pleas for restraint fell on deaf ears as Mexico, over-whelmed and defiant, began erecting a formidable bar-rier, a wall that mirrored the divisions tearing through the heart of America.

It was against this backdrop of division and despair that Governor Gerald Martinez stood before a joint session of the Texas House and Senate. The chamber, usually a place of lively debate and discourse, was shrouded in an anticipatory silence, every Senator and representative keenly aware of the severity of the moment.

Governor Martinez approached the podium with a grav-itas that silenced the whispers of dissent. His gaze swept across the gathered assembly, who at this time were united in their desire to break away from the coun-try they once claimed to stand with proudly. But the recent attack on the United States, the invasion, and the murder of the President-elect had hardened their hearts to the possibility of staying in the Union. "Ladies and gentlemen of the Texas Legislature," he began, his voice echoing through the hallowed halls, "today, we stand at a crossroads, not just as a state, but as a light of freedom for our nation and for the world. The events that have unfolded along our southern border, the tragic loss of lives, and the disintegration of the Union compel us to take decisive action."

The chamber hung on his every word, the air thick with anticipation.

"It is with a heavy heart but unyielding conviction that I stand before you to announce the unanimous support for the Restore Texas Independence Act. This is not a decision we make lightly, but out of necessity, for the preservation of our liberties, our values, and our way of life."

A murmur of approval rippled through the chamber as most agreed with the move, all except for State Senator Robert Sinclair. He stood in the chambers, his voice rising in fury, and Governor Martinez fell silent.

The outcry from State Senator Robert Sinclair cut through the chamber like a knife, silencing the ripple of approval and drawing all eyes to him. "How can we consider such drastic action without thinking of the consequences?" Sinclair's voice boomed, raw with emotion and tinged with disbelief. "Are we so quick to abandon what our forefathers built, to fracture even further in a time when unity is our greatest need?"

The room, charged with the energy of historic decision-making, suddenly became the stage for a profound debate on the future of not just Texas but the very idea of the United States. Governor Martinez, a seasoned politician well-versed in the art of discourse, regarded Sinclair with a mix of respect and solemnity. "Senator Sinclair," he responded, his tone firm yet empathetic, "I understand your concerns, and believe me, this decision was not made lightly. But the Union, as we knew it, had already begun to unravel. Our primary duty is to the people of Texas, to ensure their safety, their freedom, and their prosperity."

The Governor's words resonated in the silence that followed; the silence started being replaced by applause smattered about the room. The senators and representatives, men and women elected to lead, found themselves cheering for defiance and division. The air was thick with tension, with the unspoken fears and hopes of a state on the brink of a new beginning.

Senator Sinclair, still standing, his stance defiant but his expression betraying a hint of doubt, looked around at his colleagues, his voice softening. "I fear for the path we are about to embark upon, for the division it will sow, not just among states, but within our own communities. Is independence from the United States truly the answer, or are we stepping into a chasm from which there is no return?"

Governor Martinez nodded, acknowledging Sinclair's words. "These are questions we must all ask ourselves," he conceded. "But consider this—perhaps in taking this bold step towards independence, we are not stepping into a chasm but crossing a bridge. A bridge towards a new destiny, where we can redefine what it means to be Texan, and by extension, what it means to be free."

The chamber erupted into a loud applause as a large portion of the elected leaders stood to their feet, applauding and shouting. The applause began to crescendo into a deafening roar, the chamber alive with the sounds of cheers and stamping feet, a palpable wave of excitement washing over the assembled legislators. Yet, amidst this tumult of jubilation, Senator Robert Sinclair realized that he stood isolated, a lone figure amidst the sea of exultant faces. His concerns, so passionately voiced, seemed to dissipate in the air, overwhelmed by the thunderous endorsement of Governor Martinez's call for independence.

As the fervor continued, Sinclair's expression grew stoic, his disappointment palpable. He had hoped for a deeper reflection, a consideration of the long-term repercussions of such a seismic shift. Instead, the chamber had erupted in a near-unanimous display of support for the Governor's proposal, a clear signal that the path to secession was not just considered but was now being embraced with open arms.

The celebration around him felt foreign as if Sinclair had found himself adrift in a sea of unfamiliar faces. Colleagues with whom he had worked for years were now seemingly strangers in their unbridled enthusiasm for a future he feared was fraught with uncertainty and division. The air, thick with the spirit of rebellion, suffocated him with its zeal, the echoes of applause a reminder of his solitary dissent.

Governor Martinez, buoyed by the overwhelming support, looked out over the chamber, his eyes briefly meeting Sinclair's. There was a moment of silent acknowledgment, a fleeting connection in the midst of the chaos, before the Governor turned his attention back to the assembly, his voice rising above the din to call for order.

As the noise gradually subsided, Sinclair made his way through the crowd, his departure unnoticed by most, a shadow passing through the light of the assembly's newfound resolve. The whispers that followed him spoke of betrayal and defiance, casting him as an outlier in a legislature united by a common goal. In the hallways of the Capitol, his name became synonymous with dissent, a byword for opposition to the tide of independence that was sweeping through Texas.

Yet, Sinclair's conviction remained unshaken, a steadfast belief in the Union that had once been unbreakable. As he exited the building, the weight of his solitude was a heavy cloak around his shoulders, a burden he bore with a quiet dignity. He knew the road ahead would be lonely, his voice perhaps drowned out by the clamor for independence, but he also knew that history would judge their actions for better or worse.

The celebration was cut short as the news had broken—the United States, in a bid to quell the burgeoning secessionist movements, was sending military forces to the Great Plains Nation. The implications were immediate and grave. The decision to pursue independence, once a distant possibility, was now hurtling towards an inevitable confrontation, setting the stage for a conflict that would test the resolve of all who had chosen to stand on the side of the newly proclaimed Republic of Texas.

21

BOB SINCLAIR EXITED THE Texas State Capitol, his steps heavy as he made his way to his truck. Climbing in, he let out a deep sigh, his emotions overwhelming him—a single tear streaked down his cheek. He glanced at the empty passenger seat next to him, where he pictured his late wife, her presence a comforting memory in times of distress.

"Honey," he murmured softly, turning the ignition. The truck roared to life, cutting through the silence of his sorrow. He pulled onto the street, the mental image of his wife silently accompanying him.

"It's finally happened," he said to the empty seat, his voice a mix of resignation and disbelief. "The United States is no more." The weight of his statement hung in the air, as heavy as the humid Texas heat.

As he merged onto the main road, Bob glanced in his rear-view mirror and noticed several black SUVs tailing him closely. His pulse quickened, a surge of adrenaline rushing through him as he realized he wasn't just being followed—he was being chased.

His foot pressed harder against the accelerator, the engine growling in response. The SUVs fanned out behind him, one making a bold move to overtake him. As it pulled alongside, Bob saw the unmistakable emblem of the Texas Rangers on its side. Red and blue lights started strobing, slicing through the dimming light of the evening.

Bob's grip tightened on the steering wheel, his instincts screaming at him to drive faster, to escape the looming threat. He pushed the gas pedal to the floor, the landscape blurring past him as the speedometer needle climbed. The pursuit was on, and Bob Sinclair, the irony that he was once a staunch defender of law and order, now found himself in a desperate race, the outcome of which could redefine his very existence.

Texas still recognized property rights, so he thought to himself that if he could only make it to his ranch, they would have to get a warrant. He turned down an access road only to find his property surrounded by Texas Rangers and State Troopers. They blocked his entrance, so he decided to stop and see what happened next.

Ranger Jim Gillis exited one of the black SUVs and walked over to Bob's truck. The window was still rolled up, so Ranger Gillis knocked gently. Bob pressed the button to roll the window down, but his right hand was gripping his pistol between his seat and console.

"Robert Sinclair, let me see both hands, sir," Gillis said forcefully.

Bob reluctantly lifted his hands from the steering wheel, making sure to keep them visible as he slowly rolled down the window. His heart pounded in his chest, the thrumming almost deafening in the eerie silence that followed the high-speed chase. Ranger Jim Gillis, whom Bob recognized from numerous law enforcement gatherings, stood just outside, his expression unreadable.

"Bob, what are you doing running from your own?" Gillis's voice was stern yet carried an undercurrent of concern. He peered into the truck, his eyes narrowing slightly at the sight of Bob's drawn face.

"I'm not running from you, Jim. I'm running from what I don't understand anymore," Bob replied, his voice cracking slightly under the strain. The weight of his actions, the seriousness of political upheaval—it all seemed to crash down on him at once.

Gillis sighed, stepping back as he glanced over his shoulder at the other officers who had quietly formed a perimeter around Bob's truck. "Look, Bob, things are changing fast, and we're trying to keep up. But running isn't going to solve anything. Why don't you come out, and we can talk this through?"

Bob hesitated, his gaze drifting to the rear-view mirror where the flashing lights painted the dusk in strokes of red and blue. The thought of abandoning his truck and stepping into the unknown was daunting. Yet, the familiar face of Gillis, a man he had known and respected, offered a sliver of reassurance.

Slowly, with a deep breath to steady his nerves, Bob opened the door and stepped outside. The evening air was cool against his skin, a relief from the intense heat that had built up inside him during the chase. As he stood there, the reality of his isolation sank in; the wide-open spaces of his ranch, once a sanctuary, now felt confining.

Gillis approached, his hand resting casually on his belt, not far from his own firearm—a reminder of the delicate balance between peace and conflict. "Bob, let's talk. What's got you so spooked that you'd flee into the night?"

Bob shook his head, a mix of defiance and desperation etching his features. "It's the whole damn situation, Jim. The country's falling apart, and what are we doing? Drawing lines, pointing guns at each other. I stood for something once, for law, for order. Now? I don't even know who we are anymore."

Gillis nodded slowly, understanding dawning in his eyes. "I get it, Bob. But this isn't the way. You know as well as I do that this chaos won't last forever. We need level heads, now more than ever."

As Bob and Gillis exchanged words, the tension between them was palpable. Bob's deep-seated fears about the direction of their country and state seemed to echo in the empty fields surrounding them. Just as Bob was about to respond, the crackle of the radio on Gillis's belt interrupted their brief standoff.

The dispatcher's voice was clipped, urgent. "All units, be advised of priority orders from Command. Immediate apprehension and property seizure under the Texan Constitutional Article One is authorized for Robert Sinclair. Proceed with caution."

Bob's heart sank as the words sliced through the tense air. He knew the accusation being thrown at him: he was being branded as someone aligning with the enemies of Texas. The betrayal felt brutal. The realization that his own government now saw him as a threat hit him harder than he had expected. He glanced at Gillis, searching the Ranger's face for any hint of what was to come.

Gillis's expression hardened as he listened to the transmission. Turning to face Bob, the regret in his eyes was unmistakable, but so was the resolve. "Bob, I..." His voice trailed off, the weight of the situation rendering him momentarily speechless.

Bob swallowed hard, his mind racing for options. "Jim, you know me. I've served this state and our people all my life. You think I'd really betray Texas?"

"Bob, it's not about what I think," Gillis responded, his voice firm yet filled with a tinge of sadness. "Orders are orders, and these come from the top. But it doesn't have to get ugly. Come in quietly; let's sort this out the right way."

The silence that followed was heavy, filled with the pain of the accusation. Bob looked around at the assembled officers, the men and women he had once commanded when he was Police Chief, now positioned to take him into custody.

With a heavy heart, Bob nodded slowly. "I'll come in. But not for them," he said, pointing towards the other officers. "For you, Jim. Because I trust you still stand for what's right."

Gillis gave a curt nod, signaling the officers to lower their weapons. He approached Bob, his movements deliberate, radiating a calm authority that had always commanded respect. "Let's go, Bob. We'll do this by the book. I promise you'll get a fair hearing."

The sun dipped below the horizon, casting long shadows across the land he loved. Bob was escorted to one of the vehicles, and the other officers maintained a respectful distance. The drive back to Austin was quiet; the hum of the engine reminded him of what was happening. Bob was once a proud member of the state government, but now, he is a prisoner because he believed in the Union of the United States.

Arriving at the Ranger Headquarters, Bob was led into a holding area, the finality of the door closing behind him echoing ominously. He was alone now, left to ponder the unraveling of his world. Bitter tears flowed as he stared at the wall; his anger and resentment percolated under the surface.

After what felt like hours, he heard the door open into the holding area and turned to look at the door. His eyes widened as he saw Gerald Martinez walk in, his suit nicely pressed. In his hand, he held a folder; he sat at the table as Bob stood to join him.

"Governor." Bob still maintained respect for his Governor even though he bitterly disagreed with how things were going.

"Bob, I am sorry things had to turn out this way." Gerald opened the folder. The first page was the Republic of Texas Constitution of 1836, which Bob had hung up on his office wall.

"We have decided to throw off the government of the United States and re-establish the Republic of Texas. As such, we have re-ratified the Constitution of 1836 as our standard until we are able to reevaluate things. So, you see Bob? We still love Freedom and Liberty, but most of all, we want to be in control of our legacy, our future."

Bob sat motionless, his hands clasped tightly together, the lines of strain etched deeply into his face. He stared at the document with a mixture of reverence and sorrow. "Governor, with all due respect, this isn't the legacy or the future I envisioned when I swore to uphold our laws and protect our people."

Governor Martinez's eyes met Bob's, holding a glint of sympathy mixed with firm resolve. "I understand your concerns, Bob. Really, I do. But the times have changed. We must adapt and do what's necessary for the survival and prosperity of Texas. We cannot let external chaos dictate our fate."

Bob shook his head, the weight of his disillusionment palpable in the heavy air of the holding room. "Adapting doesn't mean we should abandon our principles, Governor. What about the oath we took? What about the United States Constitution? Does this mean that we abandon the United States in 2025 and expect them to do nothing?"

Martinez sighed, closing the folder and pushing it slightly to the side. "Sometimes, Bob, the hardest decisions are the ones necessary to safeguard our future. You know as well as I do that Texas has always had a spirit of independence. This is simply us taking control of our destiny, and I dare the United States to try anything."

As they spoke, the room seemed to close in around Bob, the walls echoing back his fears and doubts. The discussion was no longer just about legalities or governance;

it was about the moral compass of a state he'd served his entire life.

"The Texas Supreme Court has already reached a verdict on your case," Martinez continued, his voice steady. "You've been found guilty of treason against the State of Texas under the Texas Constitutional Law of Treason by offering aid and comfort to the enemy. The choices before you now are severe—execution or exile."

Bob's breath caught in his throat, the finality of his situation crashing down upon him. Execution or exile—it was a choice that encapsulated the tragic depths to which their society had sunk.

He looked up, his eyes hollow yet resolute. "Exile," he whispered, the word tasting bitter on his tongue. "I'll take exile. At least that way, I might live to see the day when reason returns to our land."

Martinez nodded, his expression unreadable. "Very well. Arrangements will be made. Adequate compensation will be granted for the property we have seized because we are not savages, and we still believe in property rights. Upon receipt, you will leave Texas and not return. This is your home no more."

The words echoed through his heart, 'This is your home no more.' It had always been his home; he was a third-generation Texan, and his birthright was being stolen from him. As the Governor stood to leave, Bob remained seated, the reality of his exile washing over him in painful waves. The door opened and closed with a soft click, leaving him in solitude once more. A man sentenced not just to leave his home but to abandon everything about himself, his son, his wife's grave, and his very identity.

In the bleak confines of the holding cell, Bob Sinclair confronted the harsh reality of his unraveling life. The walls around him seemed to close in, each one echoing back the profound loss of everything he held dear. Alone and stripped of his rights, the oppressive weight of his impending exile bore down on him. As he sat there, memories of his family in Western Pennsylvania surfaced—a distant connection he hadn't nurtured in years, perhaps the only refuge left to him now.

Overwhelmed by the peril of his situation, Bob buried his face in his hands, his body shaking as deep, wrenching sobs escaped him. These were the tears of a man who had lost not just his wife to cancer back in 2017 and his son to suicide in 2021 but now, everything else that defined him. Texas, his home, where he had poured his heart into the land and its people, had turned its back on him. He was utterly alone—no wife, no children, no property, nothing but the haunting specter of a life he once knew.

Bob Sinclair's deep descent into despair marked a significant change in his life. Within the dismal confines of his cell, the harsh reality of exile weighed heavily upon him, a relentless force that seemed to drain the very spirit from his soul. The news of his sentence—a choice between death and banishment—echoed in his mind like a dire prophecy fulfilled. Alone, his thoughts spiraled into the depths of his own sorrow, each one a painful reminder of the home he was being forced to leave behind.

"I don't want to leave you, Texas; I have no choice," Bob whispered to the unfeeling walls, his voice thick with emotion. He lay on the narrow cot; his gaze fixed on the blank, white wall opposite him, the impersonal chill of the cell seeping into his bones. The weight of his grief was palpable, a heavy cloak that smothered his thoughts and left him gasping for the faintest trace of hope.

As the hours stretched into the night, Bob's emotional turmoil deepened. Memories of happier times—laughter shared with his late wife, proud moments with his son—paraded through his mind, each one a cruel reminder of all that had been ripped away. His family, his land, and his very identity were all casualties of a political storm that showed no mercy.

Outside the solitude of his cell, the Ranger headquarters was a hive of activity. Ranger Jim Gillis, who had once stood by Bob as a friend and colleague, now found himself navigating the murky waters of duty and personal loyalty. He sat at his desk, the latest edition of the Texas Sentinel open before him. The headlines screamed of secession, of impending conflicts, and of the United

States preparing to invade the newly declared independent states of the Great Plains Nation—a nation on the brink of civil war.

He continued reading and saw that Texas wasn't alone in its desire to separate after the invasion of the Pacific Northwest, Virginia all the way to Florida was announcing its intentions, and Tennessee all the way North to Michigan was also in talks. Jim's mind reeled as the complications continued compounding. Looking up, he saw a familiar face walking down the hallway.

Jim sipped his tea, the bitter taste mingling with his growing unease. "Alice, can you believe the U.S. is drafting soldiers to invade all the states that joined the cause to prevent the Confederation from invading?" he called out, his voice a mixture of disbelief and frustration.

Alice, the office administrator, paused at the doorway, her expression one of weary cynicism. "Jim, I don't really involve myself in politics, and frankly, as long as whatever government is in charge leaves me alone, I'm fine," she replied, her tone laced with a dry humor that did little to mask her underlying concern. With a dismissive shrug and a roll of her eyes, she vanished down the hallway, leaving Jim to his thoughts.

The following day, as the first light of dawn crept across the sky, Bob was roused from a fitful sleep by the clanking of keys and the heavy tread of boots outside his cell. The door swung open, revealing a group of Texas Rangers, their faces stern and resolute.

"Time to go, Sinclair," one of the Rangers announced, his voice devoid of emotion.

Bob rose slowly, his movements stiff with apprehension. He was led outside, where the early morning air was crisp and the heat biting, conversely contrasting the stifling atmosphere of the cell. The sky was a pale wash of blue, the sun just peeking over the horizon, casting long shadows on the ground.

An SUV awaited him, its engine idling softly. A somber Ranger handed Bob Sinclair a thick folder, his expression severe yet not without sympathy. "Sinclair, the governor, recognizing your years of dedicated service, has arranged for your personal belongings to be shipped wherever you decide to settle," the Ranger explained, his voice low.

Bob was then escorted to the black SUV, his heart heavy as he took one last lingering look at the Capitol building and the land he had known for so long. The door closed with a definitive thud, sealing his fate.

Once inside the vehicle, the Ranger handed Bob a folder from the front seat as they began to drive. "This contains an inventory of items from your home—your heirlooms, the contents of your safe, including your gun collection and other valuables, and all personal effects from your residence on the ranch."

Bob's hands trembled slightly as he accepted the folder, opening it to reveal the detailed lists and photographs of his possessions, each item a sharp reminder of the life he was being forced to leave behind. Among the papers was a cold and impersonal cashier's check. It was compensation for his hundred-acre ranch—$1.25 million. The amount was a fraction of what his property was truly worth, a harsh consolation for the loss of land that had been in his family for generations.

With the folder in his lap, Bob leaned back against the seat as the SUV continued its journey away from the life he knew. The familiar landscape of Texas, with its vast fields and sprawling skies, slowly disappeared behind him. Each mile they covered was a searing line drawn between his past and his uncertain future.

The silence in the SUV was suffocating, punctuated only by the steady hum of the engine and the occasional crackle of the radio. Bob's mind was tumultuous, a vortex of regret, anger, and profound sorrow. These feelings merged into a deep, pervasive ache that seemed to echo the barren expanse they passed.

He gazed out the window, watching the sun ascend in the clear Texas sky, its rays illuminating the road ahead. This journey was more than just a physical relocation—it was a forced march into exile, a punitive severance from all that he had held dear. The severing of his ties to Texas marked the end of a significant chapter in his life, one defined by dedication and service to his state.

As the vehicle crossed county lines, heading towards the border of the newly declared Republic of Texas, Bob felt the finality of his departure. The road stretched endlessly before him, a tangible symbol of the long, uncertain path ahead. Resolute yet resigned, Bob Sinclair faced the horizon, prepared to embark on a new chapter, one filled with unknowns but driven by the faint hope of eventual redemption or return. The land he loved was now a part of his past, and as the border approached, the reality of his exile settled heavily upon his shoulders, a burdensome cloak of solitude and displacement.

22

"THE LINES ARE BEING drawn faster than we can respond, Chairman!" Althea shouted into her phone while standing in the privacy of the Oval Office. "In less than a month, we have lost about thirty-eight states. Twenty-seven states are leaving in response to your urging me to send in troops to fight against our own citizens." Her anger seethed through her voice as her benefactor, now revealed to be the Chairman, who has been pulling the strings behind the scenes for decades.

"I created you, President Althea. The least you can do is show me respect as the Chairman of our Consortium of Power." The deep voice chided her as Althea sat at the Resolute Desk and put her head between her hands in frustration; she dared not respond.

"I made you President, and just like the others before you, I can remove you as well." The voice boomed through the phone again. Althea sat there silently as she began to realize her hands were all over the Chairman's actions; her doubt began to creep as she remained silent while holding the phone.

"All is according to plan. Smaller countries are easier to control. Have you learned nothing, Althea?"

Althea Morris, the current acting President, felt the walls of the Oval Office close in on her as the menacing tone of the Chairman resonated in her ear. The shadowy figure at the helm of the Consortium—a covert group that had orchestrated the political landscape from the shadows for decades—was not one to be disobeyed or questioned. She had knowingly been a part of it, but she saw the power that she felt she earned being pulled from her fingers. His revelation of control was a reminder of the precariousness of her position.

"The United States was never meant to be a monolith," the Chairman continued, his voice as cold as it was calculating. "By breaking it apart, we can install regimes that are more manageable and aligned with our interests. This chaos, Althea, is by design."

Althea's grip tightened around the phone. "And the people? What about the lives that are being torn apart? Our nation is fragmenting!" Her voice was a mix of desperation and defiance, challenging the Chairman's ruthless logic. She knew the answer because when she signed the dotted line swearing loyalty to them, she knew what her allegiance meant, and she didn't care as long as her legacy could be that of the President of the United States.

"Collateral damage is inevitable; you're starting to sound like Arthur," the Chairman replied dismissively, hinting that if Althea stepped out of line, she too would be removed from office, leaving her vice president to take control. Althea now realized Hal Bennett was more dangerous than she had imagined. "Focus on securing the regions that are still loyal. Let the others go for now. We can always reclaim them later, under different terms, under different flags."

Althea's mind raced as she grappled with the chilling implications of the Chairman's words. Over the years, she had willingly helped put numerous plans into action, manipulating events and policies from the shadows. She had played a pivotal role in orchestrating the draft for the Russo-Ukrainian War. She internally supported the Confederation's invasion, facilitated the ouster of President Arthur Hastings, and even played a part in the assassination of Troy Thomason. Each move had been calculated, part of a grander scheme she believed she controlled.

But now, as the full scale of the Chairman's ambitions to reshape the geopolitical landscape became apparent, a sense of dread settled over her. This was not just about power or control of a single nation anymore—it was about fundamentally altering the balance of global power. The reality of her actions, once justified in her mind as necessary for greater strategic goals, now haunted her. Althea realized that what she had helped to unleash had spiraled far beyond what she had envisioned or intended. The gravity of her complicity weighed heavily on her, sparking a conscience she hadn't felt in years. She understood now that the situation had escalated too far, far beyond her original intentions or understanding.

Hanging up, Althea paced the room, her mind racing. The Consortium had its agents embedded everywhere—politics, military, corporate sectors—all working in sync to execute a vision that was now becoming clear. They had engineered economic crises, manipulated elections, and even instigated conflicts to serve their agenda. It was the New Dawn that she had been striving for, but now that the veneer of the goal was being washed clean by the blood of patriots, she realized that her part had been on the side of tyrants.

Outside, the sun was setting, casting long shadows across the Resolute Desk. Althea knew she was no more than a pawn in a much larger game—a game that was about to enter a new phase. With a deep sense of foreboding, she realized she had to play along, but on her terms, to protect what remained of the country she had sworn to serve.

Drawing in a shaky breath, Althea paused, her hand hovering over a drawer of the Resolute Desk. Slowly, she pulled it open and retrieved a smooth, white metal mask—a symbol of the Consortium's invisible governance and her allegiance to their cause. This mask, once a representation of her power and connection to the shadow government, now felt like a chain around her neck.

She stared at the mask, its cold metal surface reflecting the dimming light in the Oval Office. It had been a gift from the Chairman upon her initiation into the higher echelons of the Consortium, a symbol that she was part of something larger than herself. But now, it was a dark and evil reminder of the path she had chosen—a path paved with manipulation, betrayal, and blood. Millions of souls perished, and she played a part.

With a sudden surge of resolve, Althea stood and moved to the center of the room. Her arms trembled as she lifted the mask, staring into its hollow eyes. "No more," she whispered, her voice gaining strength. "I won't be a part of this destruction any longer."

In a dramatic flourish, fueled by a newfound determination to right her wrongs, she hurled the mask to the ground. The impact sent a loud, jarring clang through the room as the metal bent and twisted under the force. With her heel, she stomped on it repeatedly; each strike was a catharsis for her years of complicity. The mask crumpled under her assault, its once smooth surface now marred and twisted—a ruined symbol of a ruined allegiance.

Breathing heavily, Althea stepped back and surveyed the damage. The broken mask symbolized a commitment, a symbolic breaking away from the Consortium's grip. She had been pivotal in orchestrating events that led to the nation's fracture, but now she sought redemption, even if it meant facing dire consequences.

Her next steps were clear but perilous. She needed to expose the Consortium, shine a light on their manipulations, and rally the remaining fragments of the government to restore what had been torn apart. It would be her redemption or her downfall, but she was ready to face whatever came.

The battle lines were drawn not just across the states but within herself. Althea realized she might very well lose her life in this endeavor, but the thought of continuing as a puppet was intolerable. If her actions could steer the nation back toward unity and away from the brink of complete dissolution, it would be worth any personal cost.

Later that evening, Althea drafted a memo in secrecy, revealing who the Consortium was and their tenets, which were engraved on the Georgia Guidestones in the open, even though everyone thought it was purely art. She wrote the memo in order to prepare herself to go public with her knowledge. This would be her final act as President, one that could either ignite a war against the shadows or see her extinguished by them. But before she could set her plan into motion, she had one more task—to ensure that any traces of her collaboration with the Consortium were destroyed.

She worked through the night, deleting files and burning documents. She took a knife, carved a hollow place inside the Resolute Desk, and folded the memo tightly. Sliding it inside the secret hollowed-out area, she then began preparing a cache of evidence against the Consortium that she would reveal in her forthcoming address to the nation.

Hal Bennet sat in his Vice President's ceremonial office as his phone rang in the Eisenhower Executive Office Building, the phone's ring slicing through the quiet like a well-aimed dart. He answered with a casual cheer. "Hey there, Charles," he greeted, reclining further into his chair, his gaze idly tracing the lines of a Dwight Eisenhower portrait.

"Hello, sir," came the clipped reply, formal as always.

Hal chuckled, his grin spreading wide across his face. "Ease up on the formalities, Charles. We're beyond that now," he said, his fingers playing over a peculiar object on his desk—a mask of pristine white marked with a symbol of intricate design.

He held up the mask, its eyeholes vacant yet somehow watchful, the forehead adorned with an emblem of cryptic origins. It featured two concentric circles suggesting a secretive unity, each inscribed with symbols that whispered ancient secrets and timeless influence.

Centered within the mask was a bold, assertive triangle pointing skyward, while another, smaller one nestled within it, offering a layered mystery. At its core, an eye-shaped emblem commanded attention, an eternal observer of the dance of power and shadows.

Encircling this enigmatic core were delicate marks, points of light resembling stars, and connecting lines that could be a celestial map or a cryptic code known only to those who were initiated. The mask and its symbol, resting there on Hal's desk, were more than mere decoration; they were a testament to the hidden reach of the man who now held it, a tangible link to a realm of influence that stretched far beyond the walls of his ceremonial office.

As Hal handled the mask, the eye-like figure at its center seemed to gaze into the very soul of the room, an all-seeing eye presiding over unseen machinations. "Our plan is unfurling as expected, isn't it?" he mused aloud, addressing both the empty room and his unseen confidant.

"Indeed, sir. But there is the matter of Althea. She's becoming... unpredictable," Charles's voice crackled through the phone, laced with concern.

Hal's expression didn't waver. "I'm aware. Althea thinks she's playing her own game, but she forgets — she's a piece on our board," he said, his voice now edged with steel.

"The American people are growing weary, Charles. They clamor for stability, for the comfort of the familiar. Althea's moves will only serve to alienate her further. We've already laid the groundwork to turn the tide of public opinion against her," Hal continued, setting the mask down with respectful care. The act felt almost ceremonial, as if the mask was a sacred artifact, its placement upon the desk a rite that could summon or quell storms at will.

Charles's acknowledgment was a mere whisper, yet it held the weight of armies. "And the Consortium's assets?"

Hal leaned back, the leather of the chair creaking softly under his movement. "In position and ready to act at a moment's notice. The media, our politicians, even our corporate friends—they will all play their part. Althea's desperate truth will be spun into a web of lies so intricate, she'll be trapped without even realizing it."

Outside, the faint sounds of the capital's evening hustle filtered through the walls, a distant and almost foreign cacophony to the silent intensity within the Vice President's ceremonial office. Hal rose from his seat, pacing slowly, his footsteps silent upon the plush carpet.

"We must also consider the global implications," he said, his tone now contemplative. "The world watches, and while they may not see the full extent of our reach, they sense the shift. We must be delicate yet decisive."

"Agreed, sir. Our international chapters are on alert, ready to capitalize on the unfolding chaos," Charles responded, the undercurrent of his voice suggesting movements on a chessboard far larger than any one nation.

Hal stopped before the window, hands clasped behind his back as he gazed out over the twilight-draped city. "Chaos," he echoed softly, "is but a ladder. And we, Charles, are its architects and its climbers. Althea's faltering steps will be her undoing, and we shall ascend to heights unseen, shaping the new world from the shadows."

He turned back to the desk, the mask once again drawing his gaze. "Prepare the next phase. Once Althea plays her hand, we will make our move, and the nation—no, the world—will be forever changed."

"Yes, Chairman," Charles said as the call ended with a quiet click, leaving Hal Bennet alone with his thoughts and the mask that was both his armor and his standard. The darkness of the room seemed to converge around him, a physical manifestation of the influence he wielded. And at that moment, the Vice President, the Chairman, was the eye at the center of the storm, watching, waiting, and ready to command the storm.

In recent weeks, the Capitol building had been set on fire, leaving smoldering ruins and ash as evidence. The House of Representatives chamber, once a place of debate, had transformed into a cauldron of dissent and disarray, far more chaotic than in previous decades. Under the looming shadow of conflict, an emergency session was convened, holding the fate of the entire United States in its hands. Speaker John Marks stood at his podium, trying to navigate the tumultuous sea of impassioned voices that filled the historic room.

"Order! I call for order!" Speaker Marks' gavel struck down with force, the sharp pounding vying for attention above the clamor. But the importance of the decision at hand—the funding of a military operation against the newly formed Great Plains Nation, a coalition of former states and military units—was too volatile to be tamed by parliamentary procedure.

From the corners of the chamber, a cacophony of protests rose like wildfire. The representatives of the seceding states, their faces set in lines of defiance, stood as a united front. Among them, Representative Jacob Miller from Montana's second district commandeered a microphone, his voice ringing out with a mixture of accusation and bitterness.

"We stood alone against the Confederation, abandoned by this government!" Miller bellowed, his fist slamming down on the lectern. "When we needed you most, you faltered, and now you expect us to bow down as you marshal forces against us? Against your own people?"

His words struck a nerve, and the chamber erupted. Other representatives from the Great Plains Nation joined in, their voices rising in a chorus of outrage. Across the aisle, objections and arguments were hurled back with equal fervor, the ideological divide cutting deep.

"It's all about subjugation; it's about destroying the unity we had as a nation; we should be ashamed as Americans!" a representative from Virginia retorted, his Southern drawl cutting through the noise.

The Speaker's gavel struck down once more, desperate to restore some semblance of control. But the rules of decorum were no match for the tempest of emotion that engulfed the room. The murmurs and outcries grew louder, the air crackling with the electricity of a storm about to break.

Representatives from a multitude of states, now standing on the cusp of forming their own sovereign nations, convened in clusters scattered throughout the chamber. They were a mosaic of defiance and resolve, each group a distinct entity yet united in a common purpose. As they prepared to exit the House floor, their steps were measured and deliberate—a collective action that would echo through the annals of history.

Among them were the delegates from the burgeoning Bluegrass States Republic, a fellowship of lawmakers bound by shared traditions and a vision of self-determination. Close by, members of the newly proclaimed United Alliance of America conversed in hushed, urgent tones, their camaraderie fortified by the extraordinary circumstances that had brought them together. Not far from them, the stalwarts of the Republic of Texas stood tall, their Lone Star emblems a proud declaration of their intent to reclaim their legacy of independence.

This was no mere protest or partisan walkout. This was the culmination of a political cataclysm that had been brewing beneath the surface for years, now brought to the forefront by the actions of a federal government they felt had lost its way. Their movement toward the grand doors was a choreographed statement, a silent symphony of dissent that resonated with the urgent nature of their conviction.

As the delegates from the Great Plains Nation joined the procession, their numbers swelled, each step resonating with the mounting desire for independence that had spread among the states-turned-nations. The grand doors of the chamber, steeped in history, once welcomed lawmakers from multiple generations of a united country. Now, they stood as the threshold to a new geopolitical era.

Each step taken by the representatives was a thread unraveling from the fabric of the Union, their synchronized departure not just a rebuke but a proclamation of a new era. The doors of the chamber, which had once symbolized the gateway to collective governance, now became the exit from a union that was, for these states, no longer tenable.

As the representatives from the Great Plains Nation, the Bluegrass States Republic, the United Alliance of America, and the Republic of Texas filed out, the atmosphere within the chamber shifted. It was a moment of profound realization for all present—the Union was not merely fracturing; it was being remade, with new borders drawn not just on maps but within the hearts and minds of those who sought to redefine the meaning of self-governance and liberty.

Yet, as they reached the threshold, a chilling halt was called to their protest. In a harrowing turn of events, the National Guard and Capitol Police stood barring the way. The representatives halted, confusion and alarm spreading through their ranks.

"What is the meaning of this?" Representative Miller demanded, his voice carrying the authority of his office.

The reply came not in words but in the stark, unforgiving sound of safety catches being released. The echoes of gunfire that followed reverberated through the halls of democracy, shattering the silence that had fallen.

In a matter of seconds, the world outside the chamber fractured. The representatives from all of the seceding states fell, one by one, as bullets found their marks. The hallowed ground of the House was desecrated by an act of violence that would resonate through history.

Amidst the chaos, the Speaker looked on, aghast. The gavel slipped from his hand; its wooden clatter was lost in the chaos. Around him, representatives ducked, screamed, and scrambled for cover. Some rushed to aid their fallen colleagues; others stood frozen, witnesses to a tragedy that would sear itself into the nation's collective consciousness.

Speaker Marks found his voice, a lone voice of humanity amidst the madness. "Cease fire! Cease fire!" he yelled, rushing forward. But his words were too late; the deed had been done, and the proverbial Rubicon had been crossed.

As the gunfire ceased and a heavy silence descended, the air was thick with the acrid smell of gunpowder and the weight of consequences yet to unfold. The chamber had become a stage for an act of suppression that would change the course of history; there was no returning from it.

"You fools, we were on the right side of history until you did this!" Speaker John Marks yelled angrily as the National Guard Soldiers and Capitol Police stood in silence.

Surviving representatives emerged from their cover, their eyes wide with shock and horror. In the gallery, staff and journalists began to comprehend the gravity of what had transpired before them. The images and sounds of this day would be broadcast to a nation already on edge, igniting a flame that no words or promises could extinguish.

And in the center of it all stood Speaker Marks, his hands trembling, his ideals shattered. Around him, the principles of a nation lay in tatters, and the path forward was shrouded in uncertainty and fear.

The aftermath was an immense tragedy—the fallen representatives, the stunned survivors, and the armed officers, who realized too late that they had been pawns in a much larger game. The echoes of the shots fired would ring out across the land, heralding the end of an era and the beginning of an uncertain new chapter in American history.

Samantha stood on the balcony of the Governor's compound in Helena, Montana, overlooking the rubble of the burnt East Wing. She scrolled through videos of the Capitol Massacre on Vyber, her eyes filling with pain. Among the portraits of the killed representatives, she saw her childhood friend, Sarah Childress, from the First District of Montana. A bitter and salty tear trailed down her cheek. Her heart panged with anger as her tears became more frequent.

Samantha's father, Jeremiah, emerged from the stately double doors, his stride purposeful yet heavy with sorrow. His keen eyes found his daughter's grief-stricken form, and a profound sadness creased his weather-beaten face. "Daddy, Sarah is dead," Samantha's voice broke as she spoke, the words feeling alien, impossible. "I knew... I just knew something terrible would happen..."

Before she could finish, Jeremiah was by her side, his large hand, worn from years of statesmanship, gently squeezing her shoulder in a gesture that spoke volumes of their shared loss. "I know, Honey," he whispered, his voice a mix of anguish and resolve.

He knelt beside her, his presence a tower of strength amidst the turmoil. With a tenderness that belied his towering figure, he placed a kiss atop Samantha's head, the fatherly gesture a small token of comfort in the storm of their reality. "They will answer for this travesty, this massacre," he said, his tone steeled with the promise of justice. "It was uncalled for—a senseless act that has torn the heart of our community."

"Everything is falling apart, Daddy. We've lost Jake, and I still can't wrap my head around it. It feels like a piece of my heart has been ripped away. And now, we're about to fight a war against the United States." Samantha's voice trembled as she looked down at the American flag patch on her knee, the one she had replaced with the buffalo patch, a symbol of her new allegiance. Tears welled up in her eyes. "How is Mom?"

"Still the same, Honey, she hasn't left the bedroom in a week." Jeremiah nodded his head slowly as he pressed his forehead to Samantha's head.

Together, father and daughter sat on the balcony, their gaze extending beyond the compound's physical boundaries to the mountains, which stood as silent witnesses to the seismic shifts within their infant Great Plains Nation. The world around them was changing so rapidly that the newly drawn borders felt fictional. After losing Washington and Oregon, other states had seceded, and now the President of the United States was declaring war.

23

PHILIP PULLED UP TO his father's house on South Wisconsin St. in De Pere, Wisconsin. His drive was interesting coming back from St Buren Hospital. American flags were being pulled off of poles and replaced with a white flag, a circle in the middle with a buffalo on it. He had seen the news about Wisconsin aligning with The Great Plains Nation and how most Wisconsinites were furious with the United States' response to the Northwest Invasion. He sat in his car for a moment with the news playing on the radio; not only did he witness the horrific White House Riot that turned into a chaotic event where thousands vanished, but he also saw strange soldiers and that poor reporter Tamara Hollis knocked down, but now he heard about the Capitol Massacre where hundreds of representatives from the United States Legislature were gunned down trying to leave.

Philip was stressed already about his dad, but now everything he knew and loved was taken from him. His home in Seattle is now behind what the news is calling the Great Wall of America; he tried calling his girlfriend Tracy but couldn't get through. It just went straight to voicemail. His dad was on death's door, and now the state he grew up in had seceded from the same United States his dad fought for in Vietnam.

Philip's hands trembled slightly as he switched off the engine, the radio's last words echoing in his mind like the lingering notes of a somber eulogy. He sat there, enveloped in the stillness of the car, staring at the house that had been a constant symbol in his life. It was the home where his father, a Vietnam veteran, had taught him the values of loyalty and patriotism. Yet now, as he looked upon the fluttering American flag—an emblem of the divided loyalties that now tore at the fabric of his world—he felt unmoored from the past he cherished.

Outside, the street was abuzz with his neighbors' activity, their faces etched with the same confusion and concern that gnawed at him. Philip watched as the familiar red, white, and blue were lowered, a poignant end to an era that no one had foreseen. The sight of the buffalo within the circle on the new flag sent a clear message: Wisconsin was charting its own course, aligning with the Great Plains Nation, a conglomerate of states that had turned their backs on a federal government they felt had failed them.

Philip stepped out of the car, his legs stiff from the drive and his heart heavier with every step he took towards his father's doorstep. The house, once filled with the sounds of his family's laughter and debate, stood silent—a testament to the upheaval that had claimed even the most intimate spaces of American lives.

As he reached for the door, a familiar voice broke his memory. "Philip?" It was Jack Ashby, his uncle, his mother's brother. The man stood there, his face a map of the same weariness that Philip felt in his bones.

"Uncle Jack?" Philip's voice was a mix of surprise and relief. He hadn't expected to see family, not when the world seemed to be collapsing around them. But here he was, standing alongside another man who introduced himself as Stephen Martenson. They both wore a dark uniform of sorts that looked familiar, but Philip couldn't place where he had seen it before.

"Philip, we have been walking for days now and need to get some food, water, and rest. Can you help us out?" Jack's weary face looked gaunt now that Philip was really looking.

"Of course, Uncle Jack, come on in." Philip reached for the doorknob and turned it. The door squealed as it opened to a room illuminated by the sun filtering through the curtains.

"Man, I haven't been here since Tammy died, what three years ago?" Jack looked at Philip, studying his nephew's movements.

"Yeah, that damn virus. I still can't believe it took her." Philip said as both men entered, and he closed the door behind them.

In the dim light of the living room, dust particles danced in the streams of sunlight like a slow, silent ballet. Philip led the way, navigating through memories that clung to every piece of furniture, every picture hanging on the wall, every knickknack that had been part of the fabric of his upbringing. The house, once his home where he felt safe and secure, now felt more like a mausoleum, each step an echo of a past that seemed as distant as a half-remembered dream.

"Sorry for the mess," Philip muttered, though the house was orderly—just quiet, the kind of quiet that spoke of absence and loss.

Jack glanced around, his eyes briefly touching upon a framed photograph of Philip's mother. "Tammy was a force of nature," he said, a wistful smile creasing his face. "The world's dimmer without her light."

Philip nodded, his throat tight with emotion. He guided his uncle and the stranger, Stephen, into the kitchen, the heart of the home, where his mother's laughter once rang out, and the scent of her cooking filled the air.

"Make yourselves comfortable," Philip motioned towards the small kitchen table as he busied himself with fetching glasses of water and whatever food he could find. The cupboard was sparsely stocked, but he managed to pull together a modest offering of cheese, crackers, and a can of Spam.

As they sat down, the quiet was broken by the sound of utensils on plates; the simple act of eating created some normalcy in the surreal situation. Philip watched as his uncle devoured the food with a ravenous intensity born of days on the road.

Stephen, meanwhile, remained quiet, his gaze distant, as if lost in thought or burdened by things unsaid. The uniform he wore—dark, with insignias Philip couldn't quite recognize—gave him the air of a soldier, but not one that Philip could identify.

"Uncle Jack," Philip began, his curiosity overcoming his reluctance, "where have you been walking from? And what's going on with that uniform?"

Jack wiped his mouth with the back of his hand, his gaze meeting Philip's. "We've come a long way, Philip, from the Great Wall between Washington and Idaho. We fought with the Idaho-Montana Militia, and then, when trying to return home, we faced an unexpected disaster. Our helicopter was forced to crashland in the rugged mountains of East Montana. The terrain was unforgiving, the cold biting, and we had to rely on every ounce of our training to survive."

Jack's voice grew somber as he continued, "Things are changing, collapsing fast. We aren't sure what caused the crash, but it's clear that trust and stability are in short supply." Jack's lie was so convincing that even Stephen believed it, nodding along as if it were the absolute truth.

Stephen nodded in confirmation, his voice low and rumbling. "It's a new world, Philip. We're not allies anymore, but they allowed us to leave—to go home to D.C., but somehow, I think they may have betrayed us."

Philip absorbed their words, the story weaving a tapestry of chaos and betrayal that seemed to stretch far beyond the boundaries of the home he had once known. The mention of the Great Wall—a glowing reminder of the deepening divides within the country—painted a picture of a new America, fractured and distrustful.

The room fell into a lull as the men finished their meager meal, each lost in their own thoughts about the rapidly shifting landscape outside. Philip's gaze kept returning to Stephen's dark uniform, noting the insignia that he couldn't place—a circle with what looked to be an American flag on its left side and an eye in the center surrounded by barbs of some sort. It was not the emblem of any military branch Philip recognized; it seemed to belong to a different force altogether.

Breaking the silence, Stephen finally spoke up, his voice edged with a hardness that hinted at recent struggles.

"We need to lay low for a while, Philip. There are eyes and ears everywhere, and the wrong word to the wrong person could mean more than just trouble—it could be fatal."

Philip's thoughts were interrupted by a sudden, urgent knocking at the front door, rhythmic and persistent. The three men exchanged wary glances. In these turbulent times, an unexpected visitor could mean anything from a friendly neighbor to a harbinger of doom.

Philip rose from the table and approached the door with cautious steps. Through the peephole, he saw a figure he didn't recognize—a woman with sharp, searching eyes, her hair tied back in a tight bun, and a demeanor that suggested she was not there for a social call.

His hand hesitated on the lock. "Who's there?" he called out.

"Mr. Buchanan? My name is Agent Bethany Shaw. I need to speak with you regarding a matter of national security," came the firm, clear response.

A chill ran down Philip's spine. National security? Here? Now? He turned to look at Jack and Stephen, silently questioning what to do. Jack gave a slight nod, an unspoken agreement to face whatever was coming head-on.

Philip opened the door to Agent Shaw, who stepped into the house with a brisk, professional air. Her eyes quickly scanned the room, taking in Jack and Stephen before settling back on Philip.

"Thank you for seeing me, Mr. Buchanan. I'm with the newly formed Homeland Continuity Service, and I believe you can help us with some critical information about recent activities in the Northwest. Specifically, regarding a helicopter that went down under suspicious circumstances," she explained, her voice devoid of any emotion.

Philip felt a knot form in his stomach. The truth about the helicopter crash—Jack and Stephen's real story—was dangerously close to being exposed. They were on the brink, a precipice that could either lead to safety or plunge them into an abyss from which there was no return.

Before he could respond, Jack stepped forward. "Agent Shaw, If this is about our involvement with the Militia, we were auxiliary members of the Militia before they decided to secede, and now we are just trying to return back home. Whomever you are looking for, we are not them."

Her gaze flicked to Jack and then to Stephen. "We have reason to believe otherwise. But this isn't an accusation, Mr..." Her voice trailed off in an invitation for the two men to identify themselves. "Carmichael, Sean Carmichael, and this is Nick Samuels." Jack concealed their identities because he knew this HCS was looking for them since they had murdered Jake, Ray, and Mike. They stood at an angle so that their patch was not seen. "Mr. Carmichael—It's an opportunity for cooperation, for clarification. We need to understand the players, the loyalties, and the intentions if we're to navigate this crisis." Agent Shaw stood silent for a moment, waiting for someone to say something. Two other men stood with her, armed.

"Well, I don't know anything about a helicopter crashing anywhere; where did you say it happened?" Jack's face creased in concern as he tried acting like he cared to reveal anything.

"I didn't." Agent Shaw rebutted quickly, "Mr. Buchanan, there were two men running operations for an unknown assailant. They murdered the Governor of Montana's son and best friends. They also burned down part of the Governor's compound and stole a Montana-Idaho chopper from the grounds. These men are dangerous."

Philip stared at Agent Shaw, the information hitting him like a physical blow. His father's home had turned into a stage for a thriller he never wished to be part of. His gaze shifted between Jack and Stephen, trying to decipher the truth beneath the façade.

The room tensed as the implications of Shaw's accusations hung thick and oppressive in the air. Philip's mind raced, trying to reconcile the uncle he knew with the figure Shaw depicted—shadowy, dangerous, potentially murderous. The disconnect was jarring.

Jack maintained his composure under Shaw's scrutinizing gaze. "Agent Shaw, you must understand your information is incorrect; we aren't who you are looking for. We've been merely trying to survive, like everyone else affected by the chaos." His voice held a steady calm that contradicted the gravity of the accusations against them.

Stephen, who had remained silent until now, finally spoke. "We've seen things go wrong on all sides, Agent. Misunderstandings can lead to tragic mistakes. We're just trying to get home safely."

Agent Shaw nodded slowly, her expression unreadable. "I appreciate your cooperation, Mr. Carmichael and Mr. Samuels. However, we'll need to verify everything. In the meantime, I must ask you not to leave town. Consider yourselves under discreet surveillance until further notice."

As she turned to leave, Philip felt a chill run down his spine. The stakes were higher than he had imagined, and now, his family was involved in a narrative much larger than he had anticipated. Shaw paused at the door, turning back with a final, piercing look. "Mr. Buchanan, we'll be in touch. Please keep this conversation confidential. The less panic we cause, the better."

Once the door clicked shut behind the agents, an uneasy silence fell over the room. Philip turned to his uncle, the question evident in his eyes. Jack sighed, a deep, weary exhalation that seemed to acknowledge the weight of unseen burdens.

"Philip, there's a lot you don't know. It's complicated—more than you can imagine," Jack began, his voice heavy with a mixture of regret and resolve.

"This...all of this wasn't supposed to involve you."

"But it does now," Philip angrily retorted as he turned around to face his uncle and the man who was with him, "what were you thinking coming here, Jack? My dad is dying, my mom died years ago, the world is changing, and you are placing me in the middle of everything. I can't believe you. Mom would be so disappointed." Philip's face contorted into an angry display as Jack and Stephen stood there.

Jack's face softened, lines deepening with each word Philip spoke, but there was a deceptive edge to his seeming gentleness. "I know, Philip. I know it's the last thing you need. But there's nowhere else to go. And there's more at play here than just survival. It's about setting things right."

Stephen, his tone equally somber yet tinged with a hidden urgency, added, "We're not just running from our past deeds, Philip. We're trying to unearth secrets—secrets that could supposedly change everything. It's not just our own survival at stake. It's about exposing what we call a 'conspiracy' that seemingly runs deeper than you can fathom."

Philip's anger simmered as he tried to digest the enormity of their story. "Conspiracy? What are you really talking about?" His voice, a mix of intrigue and skepticism, filled the quiet room.

Jack exhaled, sharing a loaded glance with Stephen before locking eyes with Philip again. "There's a group, a powerful one, manipulating the chaos you're seeing—the secessions, the unrest. They're orchestrating it for their gains, pushing America into turmoil." Jack knew his words were closer to the truth than he wanted to get, but it was his only way to distract Philip because right now, Jack and Stephen were between a rock and a hard place,

"And we're the ones—we're the good guys fighting against them," Stephen chimed in, his gaze intense. "But the truth is, they want us silenced because of what we know." Steven joined Jack in the narrative, spinning, knowing that Philip was even more cautious than before. The weight of their narrative hung heavily in the air, dense with the scent of deceit. Philip felt an uneasy duty stir within him, a conflict between the values his father had instilled and the murky reality his uncle presented.

"How deep does this go? What are we really up against?" Philip's voice steadied as he turned; he knew something was off as his resolve began to harden. He walked to his father's easy chair and sat down. Jack and Stephen watched him as Philip asked more and more questions about what they were up to.

"It goes right to the very top," Jack whispered conspiratorially. "To people with enough power to start wars and topple governments. We have 'evidence' that can expose them, documents we need to get to the right people."

As Philip processed the gravity of what was being asked of him, the room seemed to contract, the walls inching closer. While they spoke, Philip's hand felt for the pistol that his dad had hidden in the cushion of the easy chair. He realized that the discussion wasn't just about family or survival anymore; it was about something that stank of lies and deceit. He knew his uncle had been in military intelligence, and he knew they were lying. A lump began to swell in his throat as Jack and Stephen began walking closer. Stephen looked out the curtains to see if the Homeland Continuity Service was still nearby. Philip's hand felt around for the pistol but couldn't find it.

"We need to act, Philip. If we sit on this, we're all in danger," Jack insisted, his eyes scanning Philip's face for signs of agreement.

Stephen nodded in support, "We have contacts that can help us, but it's going to be dangerous. They're watching us, which means you might be under their watch now, too."

Philip furiously poked and prodded and still couldn't find his dad's gun. He felt the house pulsate with a sinister energy, every shadow seeming to hide a threat.

Suddenly, Jack's demeanor shifted. "Are you looking for something, nephew?" The facade of a concerned uncle slipped, and a cold, calculating gaze took its place. Jack was standing over Philip now as he pulled out of his waistband Philip's father's pistol. Without warning, his hand shot out, striking Philip across the face with a force that sent him reeling back in the easy chair. The room spun, Philip's vision blurring as the chair fell backward to the ground, his consciousness slipping away.

Jack towered over him; the last thing Philip saw before darkness took him was his uncle's face kneeling over him, no longer marked by faux concern but a chilling resolve.

Stephen smiled, "your nephew was getting annoying with all of the questions. If he'd have found the gun, we would have had to kill him." Jack shook his head, "I am done with familial concern."

Jack's expression was icy as he looked down at the unconscious Philip. "We've got to move fast now," he said to Stephen, his voice low and urgent. "He knows too much, and if he talks, it could unravel everything."

Stephen nodded, pulling ropes from his bag. Efficiently, they worked together to bind Philip's wrists and ankles tightly. They then stuffed a gag into his mouth, ensuring that any attempt to scream or call for help would be muffled.

"We'll wait for nightfall. It's safer to move him under the cover of darkness," Stephen suggested, glancing out the window where the last rays of the setting sun cast long shadows across the room. His eyes caught the Homeland Continuity Service's SUV, which was keeping a watchful eye on them.

Jack agreed with a curt nod, his eyes scanning the quiet street outside. "We have to deal with them first, and once we get to Shepherdstown, we can secure him at the Consortium Childcare Center. It's the best place to keep him, along with the clones." Jack laughed as he propped Philip's unconscious body up against the wall.

As darkness enveloped the house, Jack and Stephen sat in silence, keeping watch over Philip. The hours ticked by slowly, each minute stretching as they waited for the right moment to act. The house was eerily quiet, the only sounds being the occasional creak of the old wooden structure and the distant hum of traffic.

Finally, as the neighborhood settled into the deep quiet of late night, Jack signaled to Stephen that it was time. They hoisted Philip between them, his limp form a dead weight. Stealthily, they maneuvered him out of the house, careful to avoid any lights or prying eyes from the neighbors. Stephen looked around and didn't see the SUV from earlier but knew they couldn't have left the area altogether. They used the keys, opened the trunk of Philip's car, and shoved his body inside the compartment. Slamming the trunk, they returned to the house to gather other supplies they could use since they would be driving through enemy territory now; they couldn't afford to stop.

Stephen opened all the cupboards and retrieved the few cans of beans and Spam that were left. He packed it all into his bag and filled their canteens with water. Jack locked the house door behind them; he didn't want Agent Bethany Shaw to happen across the mess they made inside. They both got into Philip's blue sedan, and Jack cranked the car.

As they prepared to drive away, the SUV from the Homeland Continuity Service reappeared, blocking their path. Two low-ranking members of the HCS, a young man and a woman, stepped out and approached the car. Their demeanor was tense; suspicion etched across their faces.

"We saw you put something in the trunk. Mind if we take a look?" the young man demanded, his hand resting on the butt of his gun.

Jack and Stephen exchanged a quick glance. "Just some supplies," Jack said, trying to sound casual. "We're heading out to help some folks."

"Open the trunk," the woman insisted, her eyes narrowing.

Jack sighed, pretending to comply. He popped the trunk, but as the agents moved closer to inspect it, Jack and Stephen sprang into action. They drew their zero-energy weapons and fired at the two agents. The darts hit their marks, and the agents crumpled to the ground, their faces contorted in agony as their bodies dematerialized into nothingness.

Stephen quickly scooped up their remaining clothing and piled it in the back of the car. He closed the trunk, and "We need to move now," he hissed.

Jack nodded, his face grim. They got back into the car and sped off into the night, leaving behind the SUV with its doors still open and lights continuing to flash.

The night swallowed them as they headed towards Shepherdstown, the weight of their actions heavy but necessary in their minds. The drive to Shepherdstown was tense, with both men alert for any signs of pursuit or unexpected obstacles. They spoke little, each lost in their thoughts about the implications of their actions. Philip lay in the trunk, still unconscious, as the city lights streaked past the car.

They drove through the late night and into the morning to arrive in Shepherdstown; the sedan turned down a series of winding back roads before pulling up to the back of a large warehouse innocuously named "Consortium Childcare Center." The building was a prison masquerading as a day-care and boarding school, equipped with state-of-the-art security hidden behind cheerful, colorful facades.

They carried Philip inside, bypassing the playful decorations and child-sized furniture of the front rooms to enter a secured area at the back. This part of the building was starkly different, fitted out like a high-security prison, complete with cells and interrogation rooms.

Each of the rooms had kids of different ages pacing around and some staring at the wall.

Jack approached the headmistress, a petite woman with thick-rimmed glasses and short straight hair. Her face was wrinkled, and her eyes stern.

"Did the Chairman order you to bring him here?" She asked firmly as Jack and Stephen looked at each other and shrugged.

"Chairman ordered us back to DC, and this man is my nephew, who now knows too much. His memory needs to be wiped and stored." Jack ordered, as his rank was higher than the headmistress.

"You know the technology is still relatively new and could kill him." She said as she looked at the body of the man between Jack and Stephen.

"I know, but he can be a guinea pig. The tech needs to be rapidly upscaled now that we are making our moves," Jack looked at the woman as she stood there.

The headmistress nodded with an unreadable expression and led the way to a quieter part of the facility. The walls here were flat white, giving the environment a sterile feel compared to the colorful front of the building. She stopped in front of a heavy steel door and entered a code into the keypad beside it. The door clicked open, revealing a room that resembled a laboratory.

Inside, the room was filled with high-tech equipment, monitors displaying complex data, and a single reclining chair that resembled those found in a dentist's office, complete with straps and neurological interface gear. The air was cool, almost cold, adding to the clinical feel of the space.

"Place him in the chair," the headmistress instructed, her tone clinical. Jack and Stephen complied, lifting Philip's still-unconscious form from the floor and securing him into the chair. The straps held him in place, immobilizing him as sensors were attached to his temples and wrists.

Stephen looked uneasy, the reality of what they were about to do setting in. "Are you sure there's no other way? Once we do this, there's no turning back," he muttered, casting a worried glance at Philip's pale face.

Jack's expression was stern, his resolve clear. "It's necessary. He's seen too much. Besides, it's the Chairman's orders to remove anyone that knows too much," he replied his voice void of doubt, "at least my nephew gets to keep his life. I will do that for him. After this, he will become an upstanding citizen of the Consortium."

The headmistress began calibrating the equipment, her fingers moving deftly over the controls. "This procedure will either erase his recent memories or... well, let's hope for the best," she said, not meeting their eyes as she spoke the last part. She then looked up, her gaze stern. "Once I start this, it will take a few hours. You should wait outside; I'll inform you when it's done."

Jack nodded, and he and Stephen exited the room, the door locking behind them with a heavy thud. They found themselves back in the hallway, the sounds of the hidden prison-like facility a muffled hum behind the walls.

Outside, the morning began to dawn, and the sun's rays began trickling over the outside of the building as it hid the dark deeds unfolding within. Jack and Stephen settled into an uneasy silence, each lost in their thoughts about the paths they had chosen. The weight of their decisions and the moral compromises they had made all seemed to converge in the dimly lit corridor of the Consortium Childcare Center.

Back in the lab, the headmistress initiated the memory-recording and wiping process. Philip's body twitched slightly under the restraints as the machine hummed to life, sending electrical impulses through his brain. On the monitors, waves fluctuated wildly, indicating the intense activity happening inside his mind.

As the procedure dragged on, Philip's features relaxed, the initial signs of distress giving way to a peaceful expression. Whether this peace was a good sign or a harbinger of something more final, only time would tell.

Jack paced the length of the hallway, his mind racing with plans and contingencies. The Consortium's grip was tightening, and with every move they made, the stakes grew higher. Stephen leaned against the wall, his face shadowed, the burden of their actions weighing heavily on him.

In the silent hours of the early morning, as the facility remained a bastion of sinister calm, the fate of one man hung in the balance. His future—and perhaps part of the nation's destiny—was being rewritten in the cold, clinical confines of a room disguised as a child's haven.

24

SAMANTHA JOHNSON PAUSED OUTSIDE her father's office, the sudden ring of the telephone cutting through the quiet of the evening. The ringing persisted, urgent and insistent, drawing her in.

She stepped briskly into the office as she walked straight to Jeremiah's desk. Lifting the receiver, she answered with the authority she had inherited from both her military background as a Marine and her political lineage. "Governor Johnson's office, Samantha Johnson speaking."

"Put Jeremiah on the line; it's urgent," the voice was firm and assertive. Samantha knew who it was but decided to ask anyway.

"May I ask who's calling?" she inquired, knowing the question would annoy Althea. But she didn't care — Althea and the political elite in Washington, D.C., had abandoned them when they needed help most and had tried to seize control of the Montana-Idaho Militia, the primary fighting force. Samantha had successfully rallied the Marines to join their side when she served as the unofficial liaison between the Marine Corps and the militia.

"You know who this is, and it is important for me to talk with him—it is urgent, and I may not have another opportunity."

"He's not available at the moment, Althea. Can I assist you?" Samantha's face reflected the irritation of Althea's voice—They had declared independence and wanted no part of her or her government any longer. Jeremiah knew that could mean war. Given the current national turmoil with states declaring independence, the United States was losing more and more power.

"Actually, Samantha, perhaps you can help," the President's voice softened slightly but retained a crisp urgency. "I need to communicate something sensitive, and it can't wait. It's about the Consortium."

The word sent a chill down Samantha's spine. There had been murmurs about a so-called Consortium and how they were manipulating events behind the scenes, including the very conflicts that had driven her from the Marines. Now that the President herself was on the line discussing it only heightened its significance.

"I'm listening, Althea," Samantha replied, her tone firm, reflecting her resolve and readiness to handle critical information.

"I know there's a rumor floating around that I ordered troops to invade your states, and while United States troops are gathering along your border, there is more to the story, and I want Jeremiah to hear it from me." Althea stopped speaking quickly as if trying to be quiet; Samantha thought maybe someone was listening to her.

"I'm going to need more than just assurances, Althea. You're talking about potential military action against people I swore to protect," Samantha stated, her voice steady but her grip on the phone tightening. The thought of U.S. troops positioned so near to her home—ready to potentially march on the soil she now vowed to defend—was more than a political maneuver; it was a personal threat.

"The truth is, Samantha, the situation is complex," President Morris continued, her voice lowering as if the weight of her office and the crisis bore down upon her. "The Consortium is not just a rumor. It's a network of powerful individuals who've been pulling strings at the highest levels of global power since World War 2. They've infiltrated various government sectors, including defense, and I know they're manipulating the troop movements to escalate this crisis." Althea revealed more of the potential puzzle. "We thrived off of division and chaos, and I thought I was doing my duty to protect the United States." Althea finished, her voice trembling as she revealed she had been a part of the very thing she was now warning Samantha about. Samantha's mind raced. The shadows of conspiracy she'd suspected were now taking a more distinct and ominous shape.

"Althea, if what you're saying is true, this changes everything," Samantha responded, her tone shifting from guarded to gravely concerned. "How deep are you in this? And what are you planning to do about it?"

"I've been a part of it more deeply than I ever intended," Althea admitted with a heavy sigh. "But I'm trying to make things right, Samantha. I need Jeremiah's help, and maybe yours too. We need to expose the Consortium to disrupt their plans. If they succeed, it won't just be your states at risk—it'll be global instability unlike anything we've ever seen."

Samantha paced the room, her thoughts swirling with the gravity of Althea's words. This was no longer a simple matter of political disagreement or state rights; it was about unmasking a shadow government that could destabilize the world.

"And Samantha, I am sorry about your brother and his friends Mike and Ray..." Althea paused, her voice shaky more now than before.

"Sorry about my brother and his friends? What are you not telling me?" Samantha's anger flared. The voice on the other end went quiet for several minutes. Althea's voice came back in a whispering tone.

"I ordered their deaths."

"You what?" Samantha barked, her anger raging hot as the revelation hit her.

"I thought what your father did with forming the Montana-Idaho Militia was wrong. I was angry, and I thought that by doing all that I did that... that... I thought I was right." Althea stuttered.

"You killed my brother, and you expect my forgiveness?"

"I have done so many evil things in the name of The Consortium, but I was a pawn on their gameboard the entire time."

Samantha's grip on the receiver tightened, her knuckles whitening with the force of her anger. The air in the room seemed to thicken, charged with the weight of Althea's confession and the heavy burden of betrayal. Samantha's voice was cold, cutting through the tension like a blade. "You were a pawn who made choices, Althea. Choices that killed innocent people, including my brother. You can't hide behind your ignorance or your position."

There was a heavy silence on the line, the kind that felt as if it were filled with the echoes of the past, resounding with the consequences of those deadly decisions. "I'm trying to make amends, Samantha. That's why I'm reaching out. We have a chance to bring down the Consortium, to stop them from causing more destruction,"

Althea's voice was desperate, pleading for under-standing, if not forgiveness.

Samantha's anger simmered a furious energy that kept her voice steady and sharp. "And why should I trust you now, Althea? After everything? How do I know this isn't another one of your games—a way to pull us back in, only to betray us again?"

"I know trust is too much to ask for," Althea conceded, her voice barely above a whisper. "But I have information and evidence that can help you protect your new country and perhaps even help us dismantle the Consortium's network. I'm not asking for forgiveness, Samantha. I'm asking for a chance to set things right."

The words hung between them, a fragile offer of alliance fraught with the shadows of past betrayals. Samantha felt the weight of responsibility settling on her shoulders, the need to protect her people, and the desire to avenge her brother's death pulling her in conflicting directions.

"Send me what you have," Samantha finally said, her tone guarded. "I'll look at it, and I'll decide how we proceed. But Althea, make no mistake—if you're playing games, if you betray us again, I will come for you. And no amount of political power or Consortium backing will save you."

"I understand," Althea replied, a note of somber acceptance in her voice. "You'll have everything in the next hour. Thank you, Samantha."

The line went dead, leaving Samantha alone with her thoughts and a deep-seated unease about the path ahead. She knew she was walking into potentially dangerous territory, engaging with a known adversary who had already caused her family immense pain. But the chance to strike against this new foe, this Consortium, to possibly prevent further chaos and suffering was too important to ignore. The name was new, but she knew that it was the same organization that had been controlling things.

Turning from the desk, Samantha walked to the window, her gaze settling on the quiet streets of Helena beyond the walls of the compound. The night was still, the stars bright against the dark sky, a contrast to the turmoil she felt inside. She made a silent vow to her brother and his fallen friends—she would use Althea's information, but she would never forget the cost of trusting the wrong people.

The urgent ring of the telephone had drawn her into the room, and now, after a shocking conversation with President Althea Morris, she was processing revelations that could reshape their very reality.

As she mulled over the President's words, the door creaked open. Jeremiah Johnson, her father, the Governor, stepped in. His face was drawn, worn by the weight of continuous crisis management, yet alert to the immediate tension in Samantha's posture.

"Sam, what's going on?" Jeremiah's voice was tinged with concern as he closed the door behind him and approached her.

"Dad," Samantha began, turning to face him, her expression grave.

"We need to talk. It's about Althea Morris... and what's really going on behind the scenes."

Deep lines of worry were carved into Jeremiah's forehead as he grappled with the relentless tide of grim news. He had mourned the loss of his son and witnessed the disintegration of the nation his family had served for generations. Now, he faced the heartache of his wife's deteriorating mental state, which had reduced her to a near catatonic state. To compound these personal tragedies, the recent fire that ravaged the East Wing of the Governor's compound in Montana marked yet another loss, gutting a strategic headquarters for the Montana-Idaho Militia during this critical time of war. The accumulated weight of these personal and national losses hung heavily on him, evident in his stooped shoulders and the haunted expression that clouded his eyes.

As his daughter spoke, Jeremiah took in the new information about the Consortium, the murders, the war, and how everything had been planned for some time. He had heard the same rumors as Samantha had about a covert organization pulling the strings behind the scenes but thought much of it was made up.

"What about Althea and this Consortium?" he asked, his voice low, as he moved closer, an instinctive need to be nearer in the face of potential threat.

"She called your office phone," Samantha disclosed, her voice steady despite the rage simmering just below the surface. "Althea confessed to orchestrating the deaths of Mike, Ray, and..." her voice cracked slightly,

"...Jake. She claims she was a pawn in a larger scheme controlled by this so-called Consortium. They're not just influencing politics, Dad. They're orchestrating wars, and now they're aiming to destabilize not just our state but potentially the entire globe."

The room seemed to contract, the air thick with anxiety. Jeremiah paced a few steps, absorbing the shock, then stopped, his own anger and shock mingling with his concern for his daughter. "Samantha, are you sure about this? This is a serious accusation."

"I know, Dad. I didn't want to believe it either. Still, she admitted it," Samantha replied, pulling out her phone to show her father the encrypted files sent over by

Althea, evidence of the Consortium's reach and influence. "She's sending proof. Documents, communications—things she claims will expose the Consortium's network and their plans."

Jeremiah took the phone, scrolling through the preliminary files with a frown that deepened with every swipe. "This... This could change everything," he murmured, handing back the phone. "We need to verify this information. And if it's true, we have to act quickly and carefully. The Consortium, if as powerful as Althea claims, won't take exposure lightly."

"They've already taken too much from us," Samantha said, her jaw set. "It's time we strike back, not just for our family, but for all those threatened by these shadow manipulators."

Jeremiah nodded, a fire kindling in his eyes—a mix of paternal pride and revolutionary zeal. "We'll need to gather our allies, assess our resources, and prepare for what might come next. This isn't just a battle, Samantha; it's a war for our freedom."

"We have the vast majority of the United States' nuclear arsenal, and I just found out that we have taken control of everything in all of the Great Plains Nation. We may not have the manpower, but we certainly have the weapon power." Jeremiah's face creased with even more concern, "if she is responsible for Jake, Mike, and Ray, then she must have played a role in the assassination of Troy Thomason so that she could keep power."

"She didn't say, but I think she may be behind way more than she admitted to."

Charlton Thomason strode into the spacious, wood-paneled office where Ulysses Mars, the former Senator of North Carolina, was absorbed in the morning news. The newspaper rustle ceased as Ulysses looked up, his eyes meeting Charlton's—a sense of solemnity passing between them.

"Charlton, I heard about your father. I'm terribly sorry. His assassination and the massacre of those Congress members... it's a tragedy beyond words," Ulysses began, his voice low, as he set aside the newspaper and gestured for Charlton to sit.

"Thank you, Senator. It's why I'm here. My father believed strongly in unity, and what we we're about to undertake is completely contrary to that unity. But I believe his vision was crucial for what comes next and that he would want me involved. " Charlton replied, settling into the leather chair across from Ulysses, his demeanor composed yet underscored by a palpable urgency.

Ulysses nodded, leaning back in his chair, his hands clasped together. "Indeed, he was a visionary. And it seems his vision is becoming a reality faster than anyone anticipated, just on a much smaller scale. With the formal secession now behind us, we're stepping into uncharted waters."

Charlton leaned forward, his eyes intent as Ulysses continued, "Sam managed to rally the Constitutional Convention successfully. It was unanimous across all the Allied states. We're not just breaking away; we're restructuring. They're even redrawing state boundaries to represent our populations and resources better."

Charlton's expression was one of cautious optimism as he absorbed the weight of Ulysses' words. "Yes, I've been briefed about the proposed changes. We're introducing two new states, aren't we? Jefferson and Everglades, if I'm not mistaken?"

"That's correct," Ulysses confirmed with a nod. "Jefferson will encompass the lower part of South Carolina and the eastern part of Georgia, areas that have long felt underrepresented by their state governments. It's a bold move aimed at realigning governance with the cultural and economic realities of those regions. And the remainder of South Carolina is reunifying with North Carolina and just becoming Carolina."

"That's interesting. I never thought I would see that happen... And the Everglades?" Charlton inquired, interested in how the restructuring would affect the southern part of Florida.

"Everglades will consist of the southern part of Florida, from Orlando and Tampa down through West Palm Beach to Key West," Ulysses explained. "This new state will focus on the unique challenges faced by these areas, including urban sprawl, hurricane response, and environmental conservation of critical areas like the Everglades National Park. It's about giving more tailored, effective governance to regions with distinct needs."

Charlton nodded thoughtfully, considering the implications. "These changes suggest we're not just seceding but actively innovating in how we think about statehood and governance. Jefferson and Everglades seem designed to enhance local autonomy and directly address the specific needs and identities of their populations."

"Exactly," Ulysses said, his expression showing signs of determination and the weight of the task ahead. "By creating states that are more cohesive in their social, economic, and environmental concerns, we're ensuring that governance can be more responsive and responsible. However, this reorganization is not just administrative; it's deeply symbolic. It's a clear declaration that we're building a government that listens to and acts for its people more effectively."

Charlton's face showed anticipation. "This is a significant departure from the centralized oversight that many felt was stifling our regions. It's a step towards a more engaged and participatory form of democracy. But I imagine not everyone is pleased with these changes."

Ulysses' smile thinned, turning more somber. "Indeed, not everyone is. There's substantial resistance from those who view this as a fragmentation rather than a necessary evolution. And we must be prepared for pushback both from within and from the federal government, which sees this move as a direct challenge to its authority."

"Well, it is; we are separating from the United States. For what it's worth, I hope we build a wall to separate us from them." Charlton chuckled under his breath to relieve the tension that had been building.

"I have a feeling there will be consequences for our secession. What is left of the United States is already amassing troops along the border of the Great Plains Nation. The newly formed Texas Republic and the Bluegrass States Republic won't take kindly to it." Ulysses' face turned bleak.

"We shouldn't either," Charlton said firmly.

"We won't."

Althea Morris watched the late afternoon sun cast long shadows across the National Mall; her thoughts clouded with regret and the weight of impending confrontation. She had set in motion events that had fractured the nation, believing herself to be steering the course of history toward a necessary recalibration. Now, the weight of her decisions, marred by manipulation and deceit, lay heavy on her shoulders. The confession she had made to the Johnson family in Montana was a desperate attempt to unburden herself, perhaps even to seek a path to redemption. But deep down, she knew that coming clean might also hasten her end.

The sound of the door creaking open snapped her from her reverie. Hal Bennett, her Vice President, stepped into the Oval Office, closing the door with a soft click that echoed ominously in the spacious room.

"Good evening, Madam President," Hal greeted her calmly, revealing a newfound tension brewing between them. He strolled closer, his footsteps muffled against the plush carpet. Althea turned her chair to face him, her expression composed yet wary.

"The Secret Service alerted me that you made a call to the Johnsons in Montana," Hal said casually, pulling a smartphone from his pocket. He tapped the screen, and a recording of her conversation played aloud, filling the room with her own words about the Consortium's deep-seated influence and manipulations.

"The Consortium is not just a rumor. It's a network of powerful individuals who've been pulling strings at the highest levels of global power since World War 2. They've infiltrated various government sectors, including defense, and I know they're manipulating the troop movements to escalate this crisis," her voice resonated off the walls, now a haunting echo of her faltering resolve.

Hal paused the playback, affixing his sharp eyes on Althea with a scrutinizing gaze. "Come on now, Althea, you honestly didn't think the Chairman would look at this conversation kindly—did you?" His tone was a combination of disappointment and reprimand, as if he were scolding a wayward child rather than confronting a fellow architect of their shared, shadowy agenda.

"Like you understand what the Chairman would look at kindly and what he wouldn't. You forget I selected you, Hal."

"You selected me from a curated list given to you by one of my Board of Leadership members." Hal smiled incredulously as he walked towards the portrait of George Washington.

"Your Board of Leadership?" Althea chuckled at the allusion that Hal was something more than the man she selected as her Vice President.

Hal turned, his smile fading, and looked directly at Althea, his eyes cold and unreadable. "Yes, Althea. My board. Because you see, I am the Chairman." The revelation hung in the air like a thick fog, settling around them with a chill that seemed to seep into the very walls of the Oval Office.

Althea's heart skipped a beat, her mind racing to piece together the fragmented clues she had overlooked. All along, Hal had been orchestrating much of the chaos, not just as her Vice President but as the head of the Consortium. The depth of her misjudgment, her misplaced trust, felt like a physical blow.

Hal continued, his voice smooth as silk but with a sharp edge that cut through the room's heavy silence. "I've always been one step ahead, Althea. Every decision you made was influenced from the shadows by people you never even knew were involved. Now, you've become a liability—a risk to the stability I've worked so hard to ensure under the guise of chaos." Althea stood, her body tensed, as the realization of her precarious position fully dawned on her. "You won't get away with this, Hal. There are others who know, who will fight—"

Hal sighed, almost pityingly, as he produced a small, sleek device from his pocket. "Fight? No, Althea, it ends here. For the greater good and the New Dawn, as we have always said, right?"

Before she could react, Hal raised the device and fired. A quick and precise beam of light struck Althea, and she felt her body seize. An intense cold spread from the point of impact. She collapsed to the floor, her vision blurring, her thoughts scattering like leaves in the wind.

As her consciousness began to fade, the last thing Althea saw was Hal Bennett standing over her. He lifted a featureless mask to his face, the cryptic symbol on its forehead catching the light just right. Hal, the Chairman, gazed down at her—not with malice, but with the detached expression of someone who had just pruned a diseased branch from a tree.

"Goodbye, Althea. History will remember your presidency... differently," he murmured. His voice was calm and final, like the closing of a book. He stepped over her body, moving towards the window. The setting sun framed his silhouette, casting long shadows across the room.

As Hal turned back, the sun glinted off his mask, making the symbol glow ominously. Althea's vision blurred, and she felt herself slipping away. Slowly, her body began to fizzle from existence, leaving only the elegant pantsuit she had worn.

Chuck Gleeson entered the room just as Althea vanished completely. Without hesitation, he bent down and began folding the clothes that now lay lifeless on the floor. Hal watched him for a moment, the mask now fully in place, its expressionless surface reflecting the fading light of the sun.

"My CIA Director, you know the narrative you must weave; see that it is done," the President commanded with a steely gaze. Chuck, feeling a knot of anxiety tighten in his stomach, stood and nodded. He had handed Hal the zero-energy pistol just moments before entering the Oval Office. This pistol was no ordinary weapon; it was a prototype of the latest version of the zero energy weapon, now equipped with a cutting-edge laser instead of the traditional darts. The weight of its implications hung heavily in the room, but Chuck knew there was no turning back now.

Chuck turned to leave the Oval Office, but he was interrupted before leaving, "and Chuck?"

"Y-Yes Chairman."

"Initiate the Veil and begin the re-education program."

"Y-yes, sir, right away, sir."

The door to the Oval Office clicked shut, leaving the room in silence, save for the soft breaths of a new kind of leader, President of the United States Hal Bennett,

Chairman of The Consortium, architect of the New Dawn.

25

THE ONCE TRANQUIL PRE-DAWN silence of the new country of the Great Plains Nation was abruptly shattered as the distant rumble of armored columns and the rhythmic thud of helicopter blades sliced through the crisp morning air. The advancing United States Military, a force that once pledged to protect these lands, now marked the onset of a conflict poised to redefine the boundaries of a country they had sworn to defend.

As the day broke, the horizon filled with the foreboding cloud of dust kicked up by the marching troops, casting a grim shadow over the Montana-Idaho Militia. Positioned behind hastily erected barricades, these men and women—overwhelmed but resolute—gripped their weapons tightly. They were outnumbered and outmatched in firepower, facing an enemy they never desired to combat. The weight of their daunting task was etched on every face, each glance towards the advancing enemy lines thick with dread.

Lieutenant Paul Knox, once a U.S. Army officer and now a key militia strategist, peered through his binoculars at the oncoming military might. His mind buzzed with tactical possibilities, but the reality was harsh; they lacked the heavy artillery and aerial support that their adversaries deployed with veteran efficiency. Early skirmishes had already swayed the battle unfavorably against them.

He reached for his radio to call for reinforcements but was unable to get out because the United States military was using scrambler systems. Paul threw his radio on the ground and stomped on it.

"Alright, everyone, I don't want to lie and say things don't look bleak because they do. I never thought in a million years we would be fighting against our own country or that there would ever be another civil war, but here we are." Paul looked defeated as he tried giving his militia members a pep talk, but he had no illusion that they would probably die today.

All of his members looked terrified because they knew what was coming, but they couldn't surrender.

"These are the bastards that abandoned us when we needed them to help stop the invasion from the Confederation, but here they are mustering up their weapons to kill the countrymen they abandoned all of last year." Paul's voice was desperate, and he knew his voice reeked of that desperation.

"We fight like the Buffalo Patch Patriots we are! I would rather die on my feet than live on my knees!"

Meanwhile, from her command post in Evanston, Wyoming, Samantha Johnson surveyed the unfolding chaos with a critical eye. Clad in battle attire, she directed her thinly spread forces with precision, her voice steady over the radio. "Brace for impact," she instructed sectors two and three, aware that U.S. forces were converging not only from Utah but also from Denver, Omaha, and Fargo—encircling the Great Plains Nation in a tightening noose of military might.

Each report of enemy movement and every burst of gunfire intensified the harsh reality of their plight. Samantha's resolve was fueled by memories of her brother, whose spirit seemed to echo in the tumult, reminding her of the profound personal and collective stakes at play. This was no mere territorial dispute; it was a profound struggle for the identity and soul of their infant nation.

As the sun rose, painting the sky with streaks of orange and red, the serene plains transformed into a fierce battleground. The cacophony of war—cannons roaring and rifles crackling— drowned out the peaceful sounds of nature that once dominated these lands.

The initial military thrust had originated from Salt Lake City, an aggressive display of force that set the tone for the conflict. Armored vehicles thundered across the landscape, and helicopters choreographed a menacing dance overhead, casting fleeting shadows that darted like specters over the terrain.

This full-scale assault was more than a military operation; it was a powerful symbol of the fractured national unity, challenging Samantha and her militia to their limits. As the battle lines closed in, her leadership was crucial, guiding her troops through the uncertainty and danger surrounding them.

In this dire hour, the stakes were clear: they were not only defending their homes and lands but also contesting the very essence of what their nation would stand for in the aftermath of this conflict.

At the same time, in the command centers of the newly formed sovereign entities—the Republic of Texas, the Bluegrass States Republic, and the United Alliance of America—urgent meetings were convened as leaders watched the unfolding battle with growing alarm. The invasion was not just an assault on the Great Plains Nation; it was a direct threat to the stability and sovereignty of their own states, considering the U.S. Military was using their states as staging grounds without permission.

In a bunker beneath the sprawling Appalachian Mountains, General Mason Clay of the Bluegrass States Republic slammed his fist down on the tactical map spread before him. "We cannot let them fall," he barked at his staff, who nodded in solemn agreement. "Prepare our divisions. It's time to show the United States that the bonds of our new alliance are forged in more than just words."

To the south, President Gerald Martinez of the Republic of Texas convened an emergency session with his security council. "If the plains fall, we're next," He stated flatly, his eyes steely with determination. "Deploy the 2nd and 3rd Armored Brigades north. Let's lend our fellow seceding nations a fighting chance."

And in the high-rise offices of the United Alliance of America, Governor Samuel Burris watched the live feeds from the battlefield, his heart heavy with the weight of command. Turning to his advisors, he declared, "Coordinate with our allies. If the Great Plains Nation falls today, the dominoes will continue to topple. We stand together, or we fall divided."

Ulysses Mars stood solemnly at the back of the room, his mind heavy with the irreversible step they were about to take. The room buzzed with the low murmur of tense discussions and political calculations, but to Ulysses, it felt eerily silent—a calm before the inevitable storm. Once American blood was spilled by another American in a war, the secession would irreparably fracture any hopes for a peaceful resolution.

As he turned to leave, reflecting on the gravity of their actions, he nearly collided with Charlton Thomason, who was standing pensively in the doorway. Their eyes met, exchanging a wordless understanding of the somber reality they faced.

Pushing through the door with Charlton close behind, Ulysses stepped into the quieter hallway, the echoes of their steps mingling with the weight of their thoughts.

"My father would have abhorred this conflict," Charlton murmured, keeping his voice low to avoid drawing attention from the nearby politicians exiting other meetings. "And now, Samuel Burris is using this crisis to bolster his image for the upcoming election for the presidency of the United Alliance of America. Ulysses, have you ever considered running for President yourself?"

Ulysses paused, considering the suggestion. He had spent his career in service to his state, navigating the complexities of political life with a deep love for his region and its people. The prospect of leading a new nation was daunting but not unthinkable.

"Charlton, I've always been committed to our cause and the well-being of our people," Ulysses replied thoughtfully. "But the presidency? It's a massive responsibility. Right now, my focus is on ensuring our transition into a new nation is as smooth as possible. Who knows what the future holds? Leadership might call, but it will depend on where I can serve best."

As they walked down the corridor, their steps slow and measured, Charlton nodded, understanding the hesitation but also recognizing the potential in Ulysses' cautious words. "Well, think about it. We need strong, seasoned leaders. With everything that's happening, with the war and the new boundaries... we're on the brink of something new, something that could redefine our lives and the future of this region."

The conversation lingered in the air as they reached the end of the hallway and stepped out into the cool evening. The setting sun cast long shadows, mirroring the long path they were about to embark upon, fraught with challenges and the heavy burden of history in the making.

"War is coming; our former leaders want more blood, and with everything that has happened, we need more adults in the room." Charlton's face betrayed a pensive and uneasy look, "we may need you sooner than later, Ulysses."

President Hal Bennett emerged into the Rose Garden, his steps measured and his demeanor somber. Flanked by members of the D.C. media corps, he approached the microphone, pausing to straighten his crisp blue suit and red tie before addressing the gathered reporters.

"Ladies and gentlemen," he began, his voice steady yet tinged with a hint of sorrow, "it is with a heavy heart that I stand before you today. Early this morning, our beloved President Althea Morris was found in the Oval Office, having succumbed to a heart attack."

He paused, allowing the weight of his words to settle upon the audience. "The stress of recent events—the bombing on election day, the invasion from foreign foes, the assassination of Troy Thomason, the disappearance of Lisa Rice and her family, and now the civil war—has taken a toll on all of us. But no one felt the burden more deeply than President Morris herself."

Hal's expression remained solemn as he continued, "At 3:15 am this morning, I was sworn in as the 48th President of the United States. I assume this role not in a time of peace but as our nation fights to maintain its unity and integrity."

He raised a hand, preempting the flurry of questions that threatened to erupt from the gathered reporters. "I will not be taking any questions today. My purpose here is to inform the American people of this tragic development and to assure them that the government remains steadfast in its commitment to navigating these troubled times."

With a final nod, President Bennett stepped back from the microphone, his message delivered. As President Hal Bennett exited the Rose Garden, the voices of the press erupted in a cacophony of questions and demands for answers. Amidst the chaos, Chuck Gleeson emerged from the sidelines, his presence commanding attention. With a subtle motion of his hand, he signaled for his team to follow, their movements precise and coordinated.

In a swift, almost imperceptible gesture, Chuck flicked a switch on a device concealed in his pocket. Instantly, the live feeds from every camera in the Rose Garden went dark, plunging the area into an eerie silence. The reporters looked around, confusion and concern etched on their faces as they realized their connection to the outside world had been severed.

Before they could fully process the situation, a group of men and women dressed in sleek, black uniforms materialized from the shadows. Their faces were obscured by high-tech masks that glinted in the sunlight. They moved with a fluid, almost supernatural grace, encircling the press corps like a pack of predators.

Chuck Gleeson stepped forward, his voice cutting through the stillness. "Ladies and gentlemen, I understand you have questions, but I'm afraid they will have to remain unanswered today," he said, his tone polite yet laced with an undercurrent of authority.

With a deliberate motion, Chuck pressed another button on his device. A low, pulsing hum filled the air, just beyond the range of human hearing. The reporters' expressions slackened, their eyes glazing over as the sound waves worked their insidious magic.

"You will not question President Hal Bennett," Chuck continued, his words carrying an unnatural weight. "You will only report the pre-approved messages we provide. The only record of this event will be the announcement made by President Bennett himself. When you leave this garden, you will remember nothing else."

As quickly as they had appeared, the enigmatic figures wearing black vanished, slipping through hidden entrances that seemed to melt back into the landscape. Chuck pressed the button once more, and the inaudible sound ceased, leaving only a deafening silence in its wake.

The reporters stirred, their movements sluggish and their faces devoid of expression. One by one, they turned and filed out of the Rose Garden, their steps mechanical and their minds wiped clean of the unsettling events they had just witnessed.

Chuck Gleeson watched them go, a faint smile playing at the corners of his mouth. He knew that the Consortium's grip on the nation was tightening, and with each carefully orchestrated move, they were shaping the narrative to their own ends. The world would see only what they allowed, and the truth would remain buried beneath layers of deception and control.

As the last reporter disappeared from view, Chuck turned and walked back towards the White House, his footsteps echoing off the polished stone. The game was afoot, and he held the strings that would determine the fate of a nation.

United States Army Second Lieutenant Juniper Diaz gripped his Saint Junipero Serra medallion around his neck, the Saint for whom he was named, as he looked onward toward the Montana-Idaho militia gathering in small groups along the border. He closed his eyes, bowed his head, and prayed, "Grant that through his intercession our hearts may be united in You in ever greater love, so that at all times and in all places we may show forth the image of Your Only Begotten Son, our Lord Jesus Christ, who lives and reigns with You in the unity of the Holy Spirit, one God, forever and ever. Amen."

He looked around at his soldiers gathering nearby and began to shout orders, "I know you are tempted to look at these men and women as fellow Americans, but they are not. They have betrayed the sacred trust of the United States Constitution and are, therefore, a foreign enemy. We are under orders to squash this rebellion so that no other state dares to secede again."

Another soldier raised his hand, Private Wayne Jacobs from Pennsylvania, "Sir, are we meant to take no prisoners?"

"We are meant to end this rebellion once and for all, President Hal Bennett orders us as our Commander in Chief. This is not a drill, this is not a war game, this is an actual war." Juniper's face creased with determination and anger.

As the sun began to set over the horizon, casting an eerie orange glow across the battlefield, Juniper Diaz surveyed the terrain before him. The Montana-Idaho militia, a ragtag group of men and women fighting for their newly declared independence, had taken up positions along the border. Their resolve was evident in their stern faces and white-knuckled grips on their weapons.

Juniper's own troops, a mix of seasoned veterans and fresh-faced recruits, stood at the ready, their uniforms crisp and their eyes fixed on the enemy. The tension in the air was palpable, a heavy weight that seemed to press down on them all, a reminder of the urgency of the situation.

As he walked along the front line, Juniper could see the hesitation in some of his soldiers' eyes, the flicker of doubt that came with the prospect of firing upon their fellow countrymen. He knew he had to steel their resolve to remind them of their duty and the consequences of failure.

"Remember," he called out, his voice carrying over the assembled troops, "we are here to preserve the Union, to ensure that no state can simply walk away from the sacred bond that holds us together. These secessionists have turned their backs on the Constitution, on the very principles that define us as Americans. We cannot let this cancer of rebellion spread."

His words seemed to have the desired effect as he saw backs straightened and jaws set with determination. They were ready to fight, to lay down their lives for the cause of the United States of America.

Across the field, the Montana-Idaho militia stood their ground, their faces grim with the knowledge that they were outmatched in both numbers and firepower. Yet, there was a fierce pride in their eyes, a stubborn refusal to back down in the face of overwhelming odds. They believed in their cause and their right to self-determination, and they were prepared to defend it to the last.

As the final rays of sunlight faded from the sky, Juniper knew that the time for talk was over. He had his orders, and he would carry them out to the best of his ability. With a heavy heart, he raised his hand, ready to give the signal that would unleash the dogs of war.

But before he could act, a single shot rang out from the militia's side, a defiant crack that shattered the uneasy silence. The bullet whizzed past Juniper's ear, close enough to feel the heat of its passage. He knew that the die had been cast, and there was no turning back.

"Return fire!" he bellowed, his voice rising above the sudden chaos of shouts and scattered gunfire. "Show them the price of treason!"

As his soldiers began to unleash a hail of bullets upon the militia's positions, Juniper couldn't help but feel a sense of profound sadness, a deep ache for the lives that would be lost and the scars that would be left on the nation's soul. This was not a fight he had ever wanted, but it was one he knew he had to win for the sake of the Union and all that it represented.

With a grim determination, he raised his own rifle and joined the fray, his heart heavy with the knowledge that this was only the beginning of a long and bloody struggle. The Secession War had begun, and its outcome would shape the future of America for generations to come.

As the night descended upon the battlefield, the sound of gunfire and the cries of the wounded filled the air, a haunting symphony of a nation tearing itself apart. At that moment, Juniper Diaz knew that nothing would ever be the same again, that the very fabric of their society had been rent asunder by the forces of division and discord.

But even as the darkness closed in around them, he clung to the hope that someday, somehow, they would find a way to heal the wounds of this conflict, to forge a new path forward as one people, united in their commitment to the ideals that had made America great. It was a slim hope, a flickering candle in the face of a raging storm, but it was all he had to hold on to as the battle raged on into the long, uncertain night.

Final Thoughts

As we close the pages of "Shadow Patriots," I hope you feel as deeply woven into the fabric of this emerging tapestry as I do. Through the birth and turmoil of nations in this story that leads to the world and struggles in "The Lone," we've journeyed together across a landscape both terrifying and thought-provoking. This saga, set against the backdrop of a fracturing nation, serves not only as a narrative but as a mirror reflecting our own world's stark realities and what might yet come to pass.

The themes explored here are heavy and reveal the fragility of our societal bonds. Yet, it is from the heart that I write these words, driven by a profound love for the country I've traversed, witnessing the deepening divides that threaten to rend the fabric of our collective destiny. This love fuels my hope that the divisions—be they racial, political, or otherwise—do not foretell our future.

From the imaginative realms of my teenage years, where Jack Ashby first took form, to the world of The Great Unwinding that we've explored together, my passion for storytelling has only grown. These narratives, though shadowed by dystopia, are crafted with a fervent wish that they remain within the realm of fiction.

As we look toward the horizon, I am eager to unveil new worlds, continuing our exploration of the boundless landscapes of my imagination. I invite you to remain by my side, to find solace, inspiration, and perhaps a cautionary illumination in these tales. Together, let's keep turning the pages, ever hopeful, ever engaged in the unfolding story of our time.

Thank you so much for reading my story and for being invested in my characters and the world I am crafting.

Also by James C Edwards

<u>Non-Fiction/Devotionals:</u>
<u>The Song of You</u>
A 30-Day Devotional
<u>Novels:</u>
<u>The Lone</u>
A gripping tale of survival and resilience in a post-apocalyptic world.
<u>Shadow Patriots</u>
The compelling prequel to "The Lone" explores the origins of its unforgettable characters and events.
<u>Coming Soon:</u>
Audiobooks of both The Lone and Shadow Patriots
Other exciting things in the world of The Great Unwinding

About the author

James Edwards is a prolific writer whose passion for storytelling began in childhood. His journey started with hand-written tales on notebook paper, single-spaced, encompassing everything from steamy romances to intergalactic sci-fi, caped superheroes, and high-stakes political thrillers. One memorable summer, he gathered his first collection of short stories and self-published them using a home printer, binding them in three-ring binders and distributing them as surprise gifts to friends and family. In 2018, James ventured into an unfamiliar genre with his debut book, "The Song of You," a 30-day devotional that delivered inspiration and insight, revealing a surprising facet of his writing talent. During this creative surge, he also developed "The Lone," a gripping story that captivated readers upon its release. Now, he returns to this rich narrative universe with "Shadow Patriots," a prequel that delves deeper into the origins of the characters and events that made "The Lone" a standout. Outside of his writing endeavors, James owns a small printing and marketing business and is the founder of Vanguard Patriot Press, through which he champions new and aspiring authors. He enjoys the tranquil beauty of the Blue Ridge Mountains in North Carolina, where he lives with his lovely wife, Amber. An avid gamer, he continually seeks new and innovative ways to engage with his favorite pastime, always on the lookout for the next big idea.

www.ingramcontent.com/pod-product-compliance
Lightning Source LLC
Chambersburg PA
CBHW022236020726
47496CB00004B/922